Praise for *New York Times*
bestselling author

# FAYE KELLERMAN

and the
## decker/Lazarus novels

"Kellerman does an excellent job. . . . Her novels blend good police procedure with insights into a society cloistered from most of us."
*Los Angeles Times*

"She does for the American cop story what P.D. James has done for the British mystery, lifting it beyond genre."
*Richmond Times-Dispatch*

"Kellerman is a master of mystery."
*St. Louis Post-Dispatch*

"Reading a good thriller is very much like taking a great vacation: half the fun is getting there. Faye Kellerman is one heck of a tour guide."
*Detroit Free Press*

"Kellerman is splendid."
*Milwaukee Journal-Sentinel*

"[Kellerman] takes your breath away."
*Bergen Record*

"No one working in the crime genre is better."
*Baltimore Sun*

## By Faye Kellerman

THE RITUAL BATH • SACRED AND PROFANE
THE QUALITY OF MERCY • MILK AND HONEY
DAY OF ATONEMENT • FALSE PROPHET
GRIEVOUS SIN • SANCTUARY • JUSTICE
PRAYERS FOR THE DEAD • SERPENT'S TOOTH
MOON MUSIC • JUPITER'S BONES
STALKER • THE FORGOTTEN
STONE KISS • STREET DREAMS
STRAIGHT INTO DARKNESS • THE BURNT HOUSE
THE MERCEDES COFFIN • BLINDMAN'S BLUFF
HANGMAN

*And in Hardcover*

GUN GAMES

*Short Stories*

THE GARDEN OF EDEN AND
OTHER CRIMINAL DELIGHTS

*With Jonathan Kellerman*

DOUBLE HOMICIDE
CAPITAL CRIMES

*With Aliza Kellerman*

PRISM

**ATTENTION: ORGANIZATIONS AND CORPORATIONS**
Most Harper paperbacks are available at special quantity discounts
for bulk purchases for sales promotions, premiums, or fund-raising.
For information, please call or write:

Special Markets Department, HarperCollins Publishers,
10 East 53rd Street, New York, New York 10022-5299.
Telephone: (212) 207-7528.     Fax: (212) 207-7222.

# FAYE KELLERMAN

# serpent's tooth

## A DECKER/LAZARUS NOVEL

## HARPER

*An Imprint of* HarperCollins*Publishers*

This is a work of fiction. Names, characters, places, and incidents are products of the author's imagination or are used fictitiously and are not to be construed as real. Any resemblance to actual events, locales, organizations, or persons, living or dead, is entirely coincidental.

**HARPER**

*An Imprint of* HarperCollins*Publishers*
195 Broadway
New York, New York 10007

Copyright © 1997 by Faye Kellerman
Excerpt from *Gun Games* copyright © 2012 by Plotline, Inc.
ISBN 978-0-06-208788-1

All rights reserved. No part of this book may be used or reproduced in any manner whatsoever without written permission, except in the case of brief quotations embodied in critical articles and reviews. For information address Harper paperbacks, an Imprint of HarperCollins Publishers.

First Harper premium printing: April 2012
First Avon Books mass market printing: June 1998
First Avon Books mass market international printing: February 1998
First William Morrow hardcover printing: September 1997

HarperCollins ® and Harper ® are registered trademarks of Harper-Collins Publishers.

Printed in the United States of America

Visit Harper paperbacks on the World Wide Web at
www.harpercollins.com

10   9   8   7   6   5   4   3

If you purchased this book without a cover, you should be aware that this book is stolen property. It was reported as "unsold and destroyed" to the publisher, and neither the author nor the publisher has received any payment for this "stripped book."

*To Jonathan after having reached
the twenty-five-year mark.
There may be silver at your temples,
but there's only gold in your heart.
Thanks a heap, Colonel.*

*Now the serpent was more cunning than any other beast of the field.*

—Genesis 3:1

*Because you did this, you are cursed from among all the animals and beasts of the field.*

—Genesis 3:14

*From this we learn that we do not give one who seduces people [to do evil] the opportunity to justify his actions.*

—Rashi
Sanhedrin 29a

## ❧ 1

*Nobody noticed him.*

Not Wendy Culligan, who was too busy pitching million-dollar condos to a half-dozen Japanese businessmen more interested in her rear than in residences. Still, she patiently went about her spiel, talking about in-house services, drop-dead views, revolving mortgages, and great resale values.

Leaning over the table, showing a touch of cleavage while spearing a jumbo shrimp off the seafood appetizer plate. Along with the prawns were oysters, abalone, gravlax, and raw sea-urchin sashimi, the last item a big hit with the Asians—something about making them potent.

Men—regardless of race, creed, or color—thought only about sex. And here she was, trying to earn an honest buck while they popped squiggly things into their mouths, washing the tidbits down with sake as they licked their lips suggestively.

What's a poor working girl to do?

Inwardly, Wendy acknowledged that Brenda, her boss, had been generous in arranging the dinner at Estelle's. The restaurant was exquisite—all silver and crystal and candlelight. Antique mahogany buffets and chests rested against walls lined with elegant sky-blue Oriental silk screens. Exotic flower arrangements adorned every table—giant lilies, imported orchids, and twotone roses. A hint of perfume, but never overwhelming. The chairs were not only upholstered in silky fabric but *comfortable* as well. Even the bar area was posh—plush stools, smoked mirrors, and rich walnut panels, all tastefully illuminated with Tivoli lights.

She felt as if she were dining in a palace, wondered why the rich ever had any problems. So what if they came with baggage—their scheming mistresses and lovers, their tawdry secrets and perverted kinks, their whining children and mooching relatives. Wendy could have withstood the pain, just so long as those big bucks kept rolling in.

Transfixed by the splendid surroundings, so intent on doing her job—getting a fat and much-needed commission—Wendy didn't blink an eye when the young man with the green sport coat walked through the door, eyeing the room with coldness and calculation.

Neither did Linda or Ray Garrison.

At last, Ray was enjoying a little solitude with his wife of thirty-five years. Recalling the anniversary party that their daughter, Jeanine, had thrown for them even if she had thrown it with *his* money. At least it had gone well. Jeanine was one hell of an organizer. The guests had remarked what a wonderful party it was, what magnificent parents he and Linda must have been to have raised two such devoted children . . . politely including David in the same category as Jeanine. No one had dared to hint at his son's recent jail term.

An elegant affair. But Ray knew it had been just as much for Jeanine as it had been for Linda and him. Lots of her "club" friends—people Ray barely knew—had come along for the ride.

Still, it had been fun. And David had behaved himself. At last, the boy finally seemed to be moving in the right direction, was using his God-given talents. Ray would have disinherited him years ago, but it had been Linda's soft heart that had kept the avenues of communication open.

Linda. Soft, beautiful, generous, and solid, his backbone for three and a half decades. At times, he was aware of the age in her face, the webbing around the corners of her eyes and mouth, the gentle drop of her jaw and cheeks. But Linda's imperfections, completely absent in her youth, only served to increase his desire for her.

He loved her with all his heart. And he knew that she returned the sentiment. At times, their closeness seemed to exclude everyone else, including their children. Maybe that was why David had grown up so resentful. But more than likely, their love for one another had nothing to do with their son's problems. Weak-willed and cursed with talent and charm, Dave had drifted into a Bohemian life at an early age.

But why think about that now? Ray reprimanded himself. Why think about Jeanine—her spending habits, her high-strung hysteria, and her fits of temper when she didn't get what she wanted? Why think about David's repeated stabs at rehab? Concentrate on the moment . . . on your lovely wife.

Ray took his own advice and reserved his remaining attention for Linda. Although his eyes did sweep over the young, grave-faced man in the green jacket, holding a drink, they failed to take him in.

Even if Walter Skinner had noticed the odd man, he wouldn't give the punk the time of day. At this stage in his life, Walter had no patience for youngsters, no patience for anyone. He had worked in Hollywood for over fifty years, had earned himself a fat bank account and a modicum of recognition and respect. He wanted what he wanted when he wanted it with no questions asked. If you didn't like it, you could take a long walk to China.

And what Walter wanted now was the young lady sitting across from him. A lovely lass with big, red hair, and long shapely legs that melded into a firm, round ass that sent his juices flowing.

Not *here*, Walter scolded himself. To calm himself down, he thought about Adelaide.

A good woman, a *tolerant* woman. Once she had been a beautiful woman, a Vegas dancer right after Bugsy had turned the desert sands into dunes of gold. Walter had chased her, pursued her relentlessly. Finally, she gave in. For her, it had paid off. As a minimally talented show girl, Adelaide had been destined for obscurity. Instead, she became a Hollywood wife. He gave her status, money, and a role she could have for life. *If* she was willing to indulge him from time to time. Which she did gracefully.

Good old Addie. As steady as the old gray mare.

Walter looked across the table, through the

diamond-cut stemware. Good grade Waterford. Estelle had done it up nicely. Elegant without being pompous. And *good* food. No wonder the place was always jammed.

He'd had doubts about bringing Big Hair here. She had dolled up for the occasion, and much to Walter's surprise, she had pulled it off without looking cheap.

A gray-haired old lady smiled at him, nodded.

Walter nodded back.

Ah, recognition. It was sweet.

However, it was not quite as sweet as Big Hair's ass. Walter looked deeply into his table companion's baby blues, his eyes shifting downward to her superb surgically designed chest. He felt a tug in his pants and that was wonderful. At seventy-eight, no hardon was ever taken for granted.

Face it, Walter said to himself. At seventy-eight, waking up in the morning was a cause for celebration.

So enamored of his sexual response and his beating heart, Walter didn't think about the serious young man leaning against the bar, his eyes as chilled as the drink he was nursing.

Carol Anger *did* glance at the thin young man in the green coat, thinking he looked familiar. She couldn't quite place him. A face that had changed and had changed again. But she couldn't dwell on it because she was too busy. Gretchen had called in sick and Carol was running double shift.

On her slate was a nice group of tables. Carol especially liked the party of sweet-sixteeners in the corner. Eight giggly girls trying to pretend they were grown-ups, decked out in sophisticated suits and too much makeup.

Like she had been at sixteen—sans the suits and jewelry of course. She had grown up in a home where money had always been tight. But down deep, all sixteen-year-old girls were the same.

Where had the time gone?

At first, right after her divorce, her life had been a blur of tears. Tears of fury at her ex, tears of gratitude at her parents for their love and understanding.

And their *help*.

Mom had come through. Always there when Carol needed her. Saying she'd take care of Billy so Carol could go back to nursing school. Carol had insisted on doing her fair share. Hence the job . . . this job. And it was a doozy.

She had Olaf to thank for that.

She had met him at a bar, had laughed when he had told her his name.

OLAF!

OLAF, THE VIKING MAN!

He had blushed when she laughed. Which of course had made her feel terrible. Olaf had come to America to be a cook. When he told her he worked at Estelle's, she had nearly fainted.

*You're not a* cook, she had chided. *You're a* chef!

Within a month, Olaf had convinced Estelle to give Carol a job interview. A week later, she was dressed in a tux and ready to work.

How she loved Olaf, with his half smile, his stoic manner, and his thick upper lip that was often dotted with sweat from the heat of the kitchen. She had often wondered how she could have been so upset over her failed marriage, since from it came all this good fortune.

So occupied by her fate and work, Carol failed to see the thin young man's mouth turn into a twisted smile, his eyes as blank as snowdrifts.

Ken Wetzel didn't think twice about him. He was too busy slurping up oysters while giving his wife the bad news. He was trying to be as gentle as possible but it wasn't coming out right.

It wasn't that he didn't love Tess. He guessed he still did. She had been there for him, was still a decent wife, a good mother, and a passable lover. Unfortunately, she just didn't fit into his world anymore.

Especially since he had been promoted to *assistant vice president*.

He needed a partner who was more dynamic, not some ordinary woman whose sole occupation was raising children. Granted, the kids were good kids . . . Tess's doing. But that wasn't enough anymore. A woman had to know things—how to dress, how to smile, how to make conversation about the vagaries of the market. A woman like that could help him get *ahead*. Trouble was, Tess was holding him *back*.

A great gal, but a high-school dropout. And with the last kid, she had gotten heavy. Those awful tents she wore. Why did the prints always have to be so garish? Why didn't she realize she would have looked more sophisticated and sleek in a plain black suit?

That was Tess.

Ken sighed inwardly, wishing she'd wipe the tears off her cheeks. Because she was embarrassing him. He closed his eyes for a moment, allowing himself a brief fantasy of Sherrie. Sherrie, with her milky eyes, her sensuous mouth, her wonderful hips, her full breasts, and her MBA from Stanford.

They had met on interoffice E-mail, she being in marketing, he being two floors up in stock research. He joked that it had been love at first byte. The affair was almost immediate, fueled by the thrill of their respective infidelities and what each one could do for the other's career.

Yes, Ken still loved Tess on some level. And yes, Ken still cared for the kids. But life was about reaching one's potential. The marriage just wouldn't work any longer.

Times change, he had told her.

Life changes.

You move on.

With each pronouncement, Tess had shed a new batch of tears.

Still, the drama of the evening did little to quell his appetite. As much as he hated himself, he had to admit that telling Tess it was over was a definite *high*. The exhilaration of liberation.

Flying high with freedom, Ken paid no attention to the thin young man. Not even when the young man's face fell flat, turning his physiognomy into something inanimate, his eyes as murky as pond water.

No one even noticed when he reached into the pocket of his green jacket.

Not until he pulled out a gun and the lead began to fly.

But by then, it was too late.

## ❧2

*A microsecond flash* of yesteryear as images too frighteningly clear burst from the hidden recesses of Decker's brain. A familiar scene with familiar sounds and smells. Charlie's discards. Twisted corpses. Moans of the wounded echoing through a gripping fog of panic. Medics worked frantically, hands and arms bathed in blood and flesh. The metallic odor of spilled blood mixed with the stink of emptied bowels. Surreal. The magnitude of death and destruction. It destroyed faith in a hand clap.

Decker swallowed, trying to lubricate a parched throat. Rationally, he knew Nam was over. So what was this? An instant replay? Except the surroundings were off. Confusion reigned. But only for a moment.

Because there was work to be done.

Instantly, he rolled up his jacket and shirt sleeves, gloved his hands. Saw a woman whose leg had been turned into Swiss cheese by dime-sized bullet holes. Lying in a pool of crimson. Her complexion pasty . . . clammy. Pushing aside debris with his foot, Decker made room for himself . . . knelt at her side.

*Stop the bleeding, treat 'em for shock, get 'em to a chopper.*

9

Scratch the chopper, make it an ambulance.

"You're going to be all right," Decker spoke soothingly as he worked. Perspiration had soaked through his jacket from his armpits. His crotch was as hot and humid as an Orlando summer. Sweat was dripping off his hair, off his face and brow. He turned away from his patient, shook off the water like a drooling mastiff. He said, "Just hang in there."

Lots of bleeding, some of it arterial. Rhythmic squirts of bright red blood. Decker put pressure on the leaking area as the woman screamed, tears rolling down her cheeks.

He bit his upper lip, nibbling on his ginger mustache, trying to keep his own breathing slow and steady. He examined her torn tissue, working through bits of bone. Femoral artery appeared to be intact . . . the other major arteries as well. Arteriole bleeding, probably from one of their branches. She didn't realize it, but she had been a very lucky pup. Much better than her male companion, who'd never again see the light of day.

"I need a blanket, STAT!" Decker shouted.

"We're out!" someone shouted back.

"Then get me a tablecloth, napkins . . . something!" Decker screamed back. "I got shock settling in!"

"You and half the room! Get it yourself!"

"For Chrissakes—"

"Here!" A tiny female paramedic with green eyes threw Decker a tablecloth. She was bent over a bearded man, wrapping a bandage around his neck. Instantly, the starched white linen turned tomato-colored. Her eyes glanced at Decker, at his shoulder holster peeking out from under his jacket. "What ambulance company are *you* from?"

"LAPD. Lieutenant Peter Decker."

The paramedic raised her brows. "Celia Brown. Need anything, just ask."

"Thanks." Spreading out the tablecloth as best he could, Decker raised the woman's good leg, dabbing her forehead and face as she sobbed and spoke. She told him her name was Tess. She had heard popping noises. Then everyone had started screaming, running for cover. Her leg exploded as she dived under her table.

Taking mental notes.

The victim wore a thick gold chain around her neck; her purse was still at her side. A horrific crime but robbery didn't appear to be a motive. Or maybe the gunman just didn't bother with her. She wasn't decked in diamonds and pearls, not like some of the other patrons. She wore a loud print dress that appeared to be a couple of sizes too big for her body. She asked Decker if her leg was still there. She couldn't wiggle her toes. All she felt were throbs of agony.

"Your leg is there." Again Decker checked for bleeding. "You're doing great."

"My husband . . ."

Decker was quiet.

"He's dead?"

Again there was silence.

"I want to know," Tess whispered.

Decker took a deep breath. "The dark-haired man wearing a blue serge suit?"

"Yes."

"I'm sorry, ma'am. He's gone."

Tess said nothing, looked away with tears in her eyes.

"Just keep as still as you can." To the paramedic, Decker said, "Got any spare wound gel, topical, and bandage?"

Celia gave him some equipment. "You need a shot of coagulant?"

"Bleeding's subsided. Besides, I'd prefer if one of you administered the meds."

"Fine." Celia thought a moment, then said, "You're a lieutenant . . . as in a cop?"

"Yes."

"Calling in the big shots for this one."

Muted by the enormity of destruction, Decker couldn't make chitchat.

Celia said, "They must be training you guys pretty well in ER services."

"I was a medic in the army."

"Ah, now it makes sense. Vietnam?"

"Yes."

"Betcha had lots of experience."

*Too much*, Decker thought. He applied the salves, unfurled a roll of gauze. "She's going to need a neck brace and a hip and leg splint. Can you finish her up for me when you're done?"

"No problem. Thanks for helping. We need it."

They both worked quickly and quietly. When she was done with her man and his bloodied neck, she yelled out. "Gurney and transport."

Within seconds, she ungloved and regloved. Walked on her knees over to Decker's patient. "Unbelievable."

"Truly."

"I'll finish her up now."

"Thanks. Her name is Tess. She's doing great."

"Hey, Tess," the paramedic said. "We're taking good care of you."

Decker stood. A dozen doctors charged through the door, scattering themselves about where needed.

Trampling on evidence.

As if that were important at the moment. But down the line it would make his job harder. As yet, no one was in charge. Since there seemed to be enough medical staff, he figured he might as well take control. He called over some officers, flashed his badge.

"We need to secure the area. I want a fifty-yard radius around the place, two officers stationed at every entrance. No one will be allowed *in*, no one will be allowed *out* unless it's medical personnel or Homicide detectives. And I mean *no one*. Not even survivors of this mayhem may leave until it's cleared with me. As hard as it will be, don't let in any family members. Be polite and sympathetic, but firm. Tell them I'll come out, speak to them, tell them what's going on. I'll inform them of . . . of their loved ones' conditions just as soon as we make identifications. Certainly no one from the press corps will be permitted on the premises. If they start asking questions— which they will—tell them someone from the department will hold a conference later. Reporters who break the rules get arrested. Go."

From the middle of the restaurant, Decker surveyed the room—the disheveled tables, the knocked-over chairs, the pocked walls, and shattered window glass. Graceful wallpaper had been turned into

Rorschachs of blood and food, gleaming parquet-wood floors were now deadly seas of spilled fluids, broken crystal, and pottery shards. His eyes scanned across the bar, the kitchen doors, the hallway leading to the rest rooms, the windows, and the front entrance. He took out a notebook, began dividing the area into grids. He heard someone call his name—or rather, his rank. He turned around, waved Oliver over.

"I think I'm going to throw up," the detective said.

Decker regarded him. Scott Oliver's naturally dark complexion had paled even through his six o'clock shadow; his normally wiseass eyes were filled with dread.

"We've got to ID the dead." Decker ran a hand through sweat-soaked, pumpkin-colored hair. "Let's start a purse and pocket search." He showed Oliver his sketch. "I'll take the left side, you do the right. When the rest of the team comes in, we'll divide up the room accordingly."

"There's Marge." Oliver beckoned her near with frantic hand gestures. She arrived ashen and shaking, her shoulders hunched, taking a good inch off her five-foot-eight frame.

"This is horrible." She touched her mouth with trembling fingers, then pushed thin blond hair off her face. "What happened? Someone just started shooting?"

Oliver shrugged ignorance. "We're doing a pocket and purse search for ID of the dead. Loo, what about interviewing the survivors?"

Decker said, "Scott, you do the search. Marge,

you start interviewing on Scott's side—Bert, over here!"

Martinez pivoted, jogged over to his team. "Mary Mother of God, I think I'm gonna be sick."

"Take a deep breath," Decker said. "Bathrooms are in the back."

Martinez covered his face with his hands, inhaled, then let it out slowly. "It's just the putrid smell. Actually, it's . . . everything. God, I'm . . ."

No one spoke.

Then Decker said, "Scott and Marge are working the right side. You work with me on the left."

"Doing what?" Martinez picked at the hairs of his thick black mustache.

"Interviewing the survivors or IDing the dead. Take your pick."

"I'll do the survivors," Martinez said. "Tom's on his way. You heard from Farrell?"

"Got hold of his wife. He's coming down."

"Think that's a good idea, Loo? Man's got a heart condition."

"Gaynor's survived close to thirty years on the force, he'll survive this. Besides, he's a wonder at detail work . . . which is what we're going to need . . . lots of detail work."

"And the captain?"

"He was at a meeting in Van Nuys when this went down. Should be here momentarily."

Decker started in the far left corner of the room, at a large round table for twelve. Two Asian men lay crumpled and unattended on the floor, spangled with bits of china and slivers of crystal. Loose flowers had fallen upon their torsos as if marking the grave site.

Decker did a once-over of the area. About fifty feet away sat a huddle of business-suited Asian males. Nearby were two Caucasians—one female and one male wrapped in blankets and bandages. He nodded to the woman, she nodded back. Her hands and face appeared cat-scratched, probably scored by flying glass. Decker shook off anxiety, gloved, and carefully kneeled down. He checked the bodies' pulses.

Nothing.

He went through one of the men's pants pockets. A portly man shot several times in the face and chest. He pulled out a wallet. Carefully, he wrote down the deceased's vitals from his driver's license.

Hidai Takamine from Encino. Black hair, brown eyes, married, and forty-six years old.

Decker winced. His own age.

He glanced up. Martinez hadn't moved, was looking down, staring at the bodies with vacant eyes.

Gently, Decker prodded him. "Get to work, Bert."

Martinez blinked rapidly. He said, "You in Nam, Loo?"

"Yep."

"So was I. Sixty-eight to seventy."

Decker said, "Sixty-nine to seventy-one."

Silence.

Martinez took a swipe at his eyes, then got to work.

By the time Strapp showed up, Decker had finished identifying the bodies on his side of the restaurant. The captain had given up the pretense of maintaining a calm demeanor. His thin features were screwed up in anger, his complexion wan. Decker brought him up to date as Strapp tapped his toes, his right hand balled into a fist that continuously pounded his left palm.

"Seven dead on my side." Decker rolled his massive shoulders, stretched his oversized legs as his kneecaps made popping sounds. The bending was doing wonders for his floating patellas. "I've identified the victims from driver's licenses. I'll go out and inform the next of kin just as soon as I get a body count and names from the other side."

He looked around, saw that Tom Webster and Farrell Gaynor had arrived. Tom was interviewing survivors along with Bert. Farrell was going through the pockets of the corpses on the right side as Marge and Scott attempted to calm the distraught.

Strapp shook his head, mumbled something.

"Sir?" Decker asked.

"Nothing," Strapp said. "Just cursing to myself. At last count, there's something like twenty-eight over at Valley Memorial's ER. This is just . . . I've got a slew of shrinks outside for support groups . . . some ER docs as well . . . in case someone has a heart attack or faints when the news hits."

"Shall I do it now, Captain?"

Strapp was still hitting his palm with his fist. "We'll do the dirty work together."

"What about the press?"

"Okay, okay." Strapp started bouncing on his toes. "You handle the press, I stay with the family members. Keep the vultures behind the ropes. No announcements until I've finished dealing with the next of kin."

Decker said, "Here's a partial list of the dead. I'll bring you the completed list as soon as I can."

Both of them stalled for a moment; then they went their separate ways.

## ❦ 3

*Though bandaged tightly,* the arm was still leaking blood. But the waitress refused to budge, watching over her brood of eight teenage girls with hawkish eyes. Her face was damp with blood, dirt, sweat, and fury. "I am not leaving them until they're safe and sound with their parents."

Marge said, "That may take a while, Ms. Anger. You really need to take care of that arm."

The man sitting with them was the kitchen's assistant chef—Olaf Anderson. He was pale, but his eyes were steady and his manner stoic. "You don't do any good if you make yourself sick, Carol."

"I am *fine*, Olaf!"

One of the girls—dressed up in a pink mock-Chanel suit—spoke up. She had long permed hair and red-rimmed blue eyes. Her mascara had streaked down her cheeks. "We'll be okay, ma'am. You should get fixed up."

Immediately, the girl collapsed into tears.

The waitress hugged her with her good arm, looked up at Marge. "When can they leave? It's inhuman to keep them here. Right now, everyone's too hysterical to help you out."

"It's true," said the Chanel girl. "No one was paying attention, we were just like . . . ducking, you know. And screaming. Everyone was screaming."

"And praying," added another.

"You're . . ." Marge looked at the pink-suited girl, then down at the list. "Amy Silver?"

The girl nodded.

"You just ducked under the table when the shooting started."

Again, she nodded. "And screamed. I must have screamed a lot. My throat hurts."

"Everything hurts," added another teen.

This one wore a navy suit. Marge consulted her list. Navy suit was named Courtney. "Do you need medical attention, honey?"

Courtney shook her head, her eyes filling with tears. "We just heard like these pops. Then everybody like started to scream. Then we like ducked under the table and like hugged each other. And cried . . . but like quietly. We were real scared."

"Too scared to look at anything," Amy said. "Except that awful green jacket . . . moving like a blip on a radar."

"I didn't see a *thing*," Courtney said. "I had like my eyes squeezed shut and was praying real hard— Please, please, just let this be over." Her eyes overflowed with water. "I'd like to call my mom if I could."

"When can we see our parents?" Amy asked.

"Soon—"

"*How* soon?" Carol demanded. "At least let her *call* her mother?"

"I'm sure she's outside."

"So tell her that her daughter's okay, for godsakes! And when can I call *my* mother? She must be worried sick about me. She's not in the best of health."

"Please, Carol," Olaf said. "The woman is just trying to do her job—"

"I know that, Olaf. We are all trying to do our *job*!"

"You must have patience—"

"I've been plenty patient," Carol shot back. "Now I want some action!"

Marge said, "Let me consult with my boss. You all stay put—"

"Well, we can't exactly go anywhere with the Nazis blocking the doors."

Marge kept her expression neutral. "I'm so, so sorry. Believe me, the last thing I want to do is cause anyone additional pain. I'll be right back."

Carol's face was still irate, but she held her tongue.

Marge tried out a smile, but Carol responded by rolling her eyes. Before Marge made it to the door, Oliver flagged her down. "You're going to see Decker?"

"Yeah, we've got to start letting some of the people out of here. It's not fair—"

"I'll go with you," Oliver said.

They both stepped into the cool night air, shielding their eyes from the blinding glare of the headlights. Marge quickly counted fifteen vehicles—police cars, press vans, ambulances, and several meat wagons. Her eyes adjusted to the shadows as she made out a group of people inside the tape barrier, off to the left. They'd been sidelined. She could hear their anger stabbing through the mist.

The family members.

The gawkers, along with the press, had been penned outside the yellow tape perimeter, at least fifty yards away.

Marge spotted Decker. His complexion had turned pasty, his big hands had been tightened into white-knuckled fists. She shouted his name. He stopped walking, turned, and came toward them.

Decker said, "You have the finalized list of the dead?"

Oliver showed him the ominous white sheet. "Give it to the captain?"

"Please. I've already delivered my allotment of bad news."

Marge said, "I've got a group of teenage girls—"

Decker said, "Go tell their parents. See some tears of joy instead of tears of agony."

Marge felt her throat tighten. "You all right? What a stupid question."

"I'm lousy," Decker said. "Not a fraction as shitty as the group I just left."

He took a deep breath, let it out slowly, and looked upward. A starless foggy night, a crescent of moon floating in an endless gray sea. "I've got to deal with the press." He turned to his detectives. "Anyone tell you anything useful?"

Oliver said. "Everyone ducked as soon as the shooting and screaming started."

Marge added, "Lots of screaming, lots of praying."

"Bullets flying around the room from all directions."

"From *all* directions?" Decker asked.

"I think they were using hyperbole," Marge said.

"Most of them were too busy ducking," Oliver said.

"Shooter say anything?"

Marge shook her head. "People I spoke to said someone just opened fire. No warning, no nothing."

"Ditto."

"So that seems to eliminate robbery as a motive." Decker rubbed his eyes, told them to go and bring some good cheer.

As he watched them approach the anxious relatives, he tried to collect his thoughts . . . rid himself of the shrieking and sobbing he had just heard from the unlucky family members. Slowly, he let his fingers uncurl, realized his hands were shaking. He wiped wet palms on his pants, tucked them into his pockets.

He needed something.

He needed a smoke.

As he neared the press corps, he bummed a pack of cigarettes and some matches off one of the uniformed cops. He tried to steady his hands as he lit up, sucking hot, dry smog into his lungs.

It felt acrid, but it did the trick. As nicotine coursed through his body, Decker felt his hands settle down, his brain beginning to clear.

He polished off the cigarette in four inhalations, immediately went for number two. Only after he had smoked it down to the butt was he ready to face the cameras. He ducked under the crime tape ribbon, was charged upon by a cavalry of multimedia representatives. He held up his palms, keeping them at arm's length, then shouted as best he could. His voice traveled well in the night air. "I'm only going to do this once, so let's give everyone a fair shot. Anyone out there need a little extra time to set up?"

"Five minutes to set up my camera?" a male voice yelled out.

"Make it ten," replied a female.

Decker said, "Ten minutes. I'll read from a prepared statement. Please, please, be respectful, ladies and gentlemen. I will take questions afterward for about fifteen, twenty minutes. Then I'm going to have to get back to work."

With his announcement, Decker turned inward, lit up a third cigarette, and spoke to no one, ignoring the questions that were thrown at him. He smoked two more cigarettes until the requisite time had passed. After checking his watch, he threw down his fifth butt of the evening, crushed it harder than necessary with his heel. He smoothed his hair and spoke to a wire wheel of microphones. Flashbulbs and video lights attacked his eyes.

"Our first concerns are with the people who need immediate medical attention. All the hospitals and medical institutions in the area have been notified and are giving those inside the benefit of their expertise as well as their staff, facilities, and supplies. We've received an abundance of community help from local physicians. The help is needed and appreciated. To everyone out there viewing this broadcast, please, *please:* If you are not involved in the primary medical care of those injured, stay away from the area so that doctors, nurses, medics, ambulances, and police personnel can move in and out of the area freely."

The questions started.

What happened?

How many killed?

How many wounded?

Do they have a suspect?

Do they have a reason for the shooting?

What's it like in there?

Decker turned to the last questioner. A Latina. Sylvia Lopez from the local news station. One of the few broadcasters who gave LAPD a fair shake during its bad times. He took her question.

"What's it like in there?" Abruptly, he broke into a cold sweat, shuddered involuntarily. "It's your worst nightmare."

He wiped his face, was about to field another series of questions, but over an ocean of scalps, he saw Martinez waving at him. One of the many benefits of being six four.

"I've got to go," Decker said. "Excuse me."

He extricated himself from the lights, cameras, and actions, ducking under the yellow tape and meeting Martinez halfway across the parking lot. Decker threw his arm around Bert's wide shoulders. "What?"

"There are a lot of people unaccounted for, Loo." Martinez pushed strands of black, wet hair from his forehead. His face had been bathed in sticky sweat. "We're directing the families to Valley Memorial, but some of the wounded may have gone to Northridge Pres. We're trying to get names, but everything's such a mess—"

"One step at a time."

"Speaking of which, we may have found the perp. He could have been one of the victims, but it looks like a suicide. Close-range single shot to the head around the temple region. You can see the powder burns—"

"Got a weapon?"

"Smith and Wesson double-action, nine-millimeter automatic—"

"Jesus!"

"Yeah, lots of spraying ability. Pistol's about five feet away from the body. Forensics is waiting for you or Captain Strapp before they move in. Farrell's guarding the corpse. No ID on the body, but we got a name from a couple of Estelle's employees: Harlan Manz."

"Disgruntled postal worker?"

"Disgruntled bartender."

# ❧ 4

"*Harlan worked here* for around three, four months—"

"Closer to six months—"

"Yeah, well, maybe it was closer to six months." Marissa, the waitress, sneaked a sideways glance at Benedict, the waiter. "God, I can't believe it." Sitting on a barstool, she shivered under her blanket, blond hair falling over her shoulders. "I knew he was angry when he left, but who would have expected . . ."

Decker stood between the two food servers, his back against the smooth oak bar top. Ten minutes earlier, he had gone through Harlan's empty pockets, observed the man's twisted body and blood-soaked head. A close-range shot and a clean one. A 9mm automatic lay a few feet away.

As a corpse, Harlan evoked pity rather than fury. Once he had been a good-looking man. Dark, brooding features now covered with sticky serum. He had died wearing dark slacks, a white shirt, and a green jacket that was splattered with blood, turning him Christmas-colored. The whole evening defied logic.

He returned his attention to the witnesses. "Was Harlan fired from his job?"

"Rather unceremoniously." Benedict shifted his weight on the stool, scratched a nest of black curls. He was sipping hot water, shaking as he talked.

"What happened?"

"Some asshole at the bar got plastered, started giving Harlan a real hard time. He just blew it, told the guy to get the hell out."

"A big no-no," Marissa interjected. "You have trouble with a patron, you're supposed to report it to the manager and let her deal with it."

"Any idea why Harlan decided to handle the matter?"

"He probably just had it up to here with rich dicks." Benedict looked upward. "You get tired of being pushed around."

Marissa said, "Robin must have heard all the commotion. She came charging in . . . it was real intense."

"Is Robin the restaurant's manager?"

"Yeah," Benedict said. "She just . . . started in on Harlan, told him to pack his bags and leave. That was that."

Decker was skeptical. "Harlan left without a fight?"

"Nothing physical," Marissa said. "But Harlan and Robin exchanged a few choice words. He was really mad. But she didn't have to call the cops or anything like that."

"Was this the only time either of you had ever seen Harlan explode?"

"Harlan was impulsive," Marissa said. "Did what suited him."

The servers exchanged brief glances. Decker's eyes darted between Marissa and Benedict. "What's going on?"

Marissa looked down. "I went out with him a couple of times. Nothing big. Just a drink after work."

Silence.

Marissa's eyes watered. "I had no idea he was . . ."

"Of course not," Decker soothed. "Tell me about him, Marissa."

"Nothing to tell. I thought he was kind of cute."

Decker looked at Harlan's corpse, now being worked on by Forensics. It lay some ten feet from the entrance to the bar, resting faceup, eyes open, mouth agape, arms splayed outward, legs bent at the knees. The complexion had taken on a grayish hue, but once it had probably been mocha-colored. Skin that showed wear and tear. Not craggy, but wrinkles about the eyes and mouth. Dark eyes, black hair, a broad nose and strong chin. Latino mixed with a hint of Native American. Looked to be around six feet. Well-proportioned.

"He seems like he could have been a very sexy guy." He homed in on Marissa's red cheeks. "Maybe we should talk in private?"

Marissa averted her gaze. "It was nothing serious. Does it really matter?"

"I was just wondering if maybe you were the intended target?"

The girl turned pale.

"No way," Benedict said. "If he was after anyone here, it would have been Robin." His voice dropped to a shadow. "And she's dead, isn't she?"

Decker nodded. The young man just shook his head. Marissa had tears in her eyes.

"We were never serious, Lieutenant. Honest. He was just studdin' around. Harlan did a lot of that."

"A lot of what?"

"Messin' around. I wasn't even his *real* girlfriend."

Decker sat up. "Who was his *real* girlfriend?"

"Rhonda Klegg," Benedict said. "Used to come in here sometimes. Harlan would comp her drinks. Tequila. She could down shooters as fast as any guy I know."

"Was she an alcoholic?"

Again they exchanged glances. Benedict said, "Well, she could get a little intense. But she kept it under control. I never saw them going at it in public."

"Going at it?" Decker asked.

Marissa said, "Harlan would come in with a black eye every once in a while. I asked him about it, he laughed it off." She studied her hands. "God only knows what she looked like."

Decker said, "Did you ever see them fighting?"

"Not personally, no."

"Is she also a wait . . . an actress?"

Benedict said, "Artist. She actually makes money in her chosen field. Got a great gig going. Paints pictures on the walls of rich people's houses."

"Murals?" Decker asked.

"No," Marissa said. "She'll paint a make-believe garden scene on a wall. There's a word for it."

*"Trompe l'oeil,"* Decker said.

"That's it," Marissa said. "Her apartment is full of her stuff. It's real weird. She's got the statue of David on the wall of her john."

"You've been to her apartment?" Decker said. "With Harlan?"

Marissa turned bright red. "Well . . . just once."

"Did she and Harlan live together?"

"No, Harlan has . . . had his own place. But he liked being bad . . . God, I feel like an *idiot*." Marissa rubbed her face. "It seemed so harmless at the time."

Rule number one. Fooling around is *never* harmless. Decker asked, "Did Harlan have a key to her place?"

Marissa nodded.

Decker became aware of his heartbeat. "Where does Rhonda live, Marissa?"

"The apartment was called the Caribbean. Third floor. It's near Rinaldi. I could get you the address."

"I'll get it." Decker looked at Benedict. "Anything else you want to add . . . something that might give us a clue to what went on?"

"Sorry, but I didn't see a thing," Benedict said. "When the shooting started, I ran for cover."

"Where?"

"Made a beeline for the coat closet. I hid there the entire time, too scared to even breathe."

"I couldn't tell you anything, either," Marissa added. "Everyone just started screaming. I dropped under a table."

"Where were you?"

"Carol Anger and I were working the left rear portion of the room. I had the odd tables, she had the even."

"Do you recall where the shooting originated?"

"God, no. It seemed like bullets were flying from all directions. I was too petrified to look up."

Decker looked over his notes, showed them a page. "These are your current names, addresses, and phone numbers?"

Both servers nodded.

"Okay, you can leave." He handed them each a business card. "If you think of something important about what happened here . . . or anything important about Harlan Manz, give me a call."

"Why bother with Harlan?" Benedict said. "He's dead."

"Yes, he is," Decker said. "But by studying men like him . . . just maybe we can avert . . . another tragedy. Workplace violence is on the upswing. Least we can do is publicize warning signs."

Marissa said, "So where do you go from here?"

Decker said, "Right now, I'm going to call Rhonda Klegg. If I have any luck at all, she'll be alive and pick up the phone."

"Oh my God!" Marissa said. "You think that maybe Harlan . . . before this . . ."

No one spoke for a moment.

Marissa said, "If she's alive . . . are you going to tell her . . . you know . . . about Harlan and I?"

*Harlan and me*, Decker thought. He regarded the waitress, looked at her straggly hair falling over a war-ravaged face. "I don't think it will come up."

Tears streaming down her cheeks, Marissa thanked him profusely. Decker patted her shoulder, then left to search out a private phone.

There were two offices upstairs, each fitted with phones attached to answering machines that winked red in the dark. Decker flipped on the light switch in the larger of the two rooms. This one was Estelle Bernstein's personal salon, done in wood paneling with plush hunter-green carpets. Expensively furnished— antiques or good replicas. The abstract artwork wasn't his style, but it didn't look cheap. Decker closed the office door from the outside, chose to use the phone in manager Robin Patterson's hole in the wall.

Small. Utilitarian. A metal desk with a secretary's chair parked inside the kneehole. A scarred leather couch. The back wall was lined with file cabinets. A swinging door was tucked into one of the corners. Decker pushed it open. An old white toilet, a scratched sink, and a fan that made a racket when the light was turned on. Robin had tried to dress it up by adding a mirror to the wall and a crocheted toilet-paper cover. On top of the john's tank was a bowl of potpourri. Staring at the dried leaves, flowers, and spices, Decker felt a wash of sadness.

He called the station house, got the number he wanted. Within moments, Rhonda Klegg's phone was ringing. Her machine picked up. Decker waited until the beep.

"This is Detective Lieutenant Peter Decker of the Los Angeles Police Department. I need to talk to Rhonda Klegg. I don't know if you're home or not, Rhonda, but if you are, please pick up the phone. If you don't do that, I'm going to come over and have your apartment opened up. I have concerns for your safety. So if you don't want—"

"I'm fine! Go away!"

The phone slammed down.

Obviously, she had seen the news. Decker called back. This time she picked up.

"Look . . ." Her voice was slightly slurred. "I meant what I said. I don't wanna talk to the police or anybody else."

Decker said, "I'm at Estelle's. Been here since eight-thirty. Thirteen people are dead, Rhonda. At least thirty-one are wounded—"

"It's not my *fault*!"

She erupted into sobs. Decker waited until he could be heard. Calmly, he said, "Of course it's not your fault. You are completely blameless—"

"Then *why* are you calling me?"

"I wanted to make sure you were okay."

"I'm okay. Just . . . leave me alone."

"Be nice if I could talk to you, Rhonda."

"Do I *gotta* talk to you?"

"No."

Silence.

Her voice got very heavy. "What time is it?"

Decker checked his watch. "One-thirty."

A heavy sigh. "Can this wait till morning?"

"Yes, it can wait. Is anyone staying with you, Rhonda?"

"No."

"Can I call someone for you?"

She began to sob. "No. No one. Just . . . let me sleep."

"Did you take anything to help you sleep?"

"Coupla Valiums."

"And that's it?"

"Yeah, course that's it. Whaddaya think? What did you say your name was?"

"Lieutenant Decker. LAPD. Devonshire Substation."

"LAPD?"

"LAPD."

"If you're a reporter, I'm gonna sue you."

"I'm not a reporter."

"I'm not talkin' to reporters."

"A very good idea. Can I drop by your apartment around . . ." Decker checked his watch again. Yes, it was still one-thirty in the morning. There were still witnesses to interview, bodies to transport to the morgue, and he hadn't even touched his paperwork. Definitely an all-nighter. "How about eight in the morning?"

"Fine." She paused. "If you're a reporter—"

"Peter Decker, detective lieutenant one. LAPD, Devonshire Substation." He gave her his badge number. "Give them a call."

"I will, ya know."

"You should. So I'll see you at eight, Rhonda?"

"Fine. Good-bye."

Once again the phone slammed down.

At least she hadn't added "Good riddance."

# ❧ 5

**Decker expected to** talk to the machine. Instead, Rina picked up after a half ring. He said, "You should be asleep."

"I was worried about you. I'm glad you called."

"Nothing to worry about. I'm fine. I'm just not going to make it home tonight. You probably figured as much."

"Can I do anything for you?"

"Kiss my kids. Say a prayer. I don't know."

He sounded drained . . . lifeless. She said, "I love you, Peter."

"Love you, too."

"Don't hang up."

No one spoke.

Rina said, "I guess you have to get back to work."

Decker could picture his wife fidgeting with her hair, wrapping a long, black strand around her index finger or nibbling on the ends with her luscious mouth . . . her long pink tongue. Gave him a nice buzz between his legs. Obscene to think about sex after witnessing such atrocity. But he wasn't shocked by his response. After clearing the trail of Charlie's carnage . . . after doing the body count . . . Decker had often made a trip to the whorehouses the first item on his agenda. An old man housed in a nineteen-year-old body. Sex had been the thing that had made him feel alive.

He said, "I have a couple of minutes. Tell me about my kids."

"They send their love."

"Did they see the broadcast?"

"The boys did, sure."

"Are they upset?"

"Honestly, yes, they were upset. You looked so . . . pained. Are you sure I can't do anything for you, Peter?"

"Feeling helpless?"

"Exactly."

"Join the crowd. No, I'll be all right. The shock's starting to wear off . . . that old wartime numbness—"

"Oh, my God! This must evoke such terrible memories for you."

Decker waited a beat. "I used to get nightmares, Rina. Didn't remember too much in the morning, but Jan said they were pretty bad. She never admitted it, but I think I scared her. Maybe we should use separate bedrooms for a couple of weeks—"

"I wouldn't hear of it." Rina paused. "I love you. Just . . . know that."

"I know you want me to be okay. Honestly, I am okay. It just has to run its course. You want to help me, just take care of the kids and yourself. Did Sammy pass his driver's test, by the way?"

"He is now officially licensed for solo expeditions."

*Something else to worry about*, Decker thought. "Tell him congratulations. I'm really proud of him."

"He wants to take the Porsche out for a spin."

"Uh, that will have to wait."

"He thought that might be the case."

"Your voice is wonderful. I'd love talking, but you need your sleep. And I still have a mound of paperwork facing me."

"You're not going to sleep at all?"

"Oh, I'll probably catch a few fitful hours at the station house. I promise I'll be home tonight. Did I tell you I love you?"

"Never tire of hearing it," Rina answered. She kissed the receiver. "Can I call you up in an hour or so?"

"I may not be available. I'm going out for a little bit."

"Catch some air?"

"I wish." Decker let out a tired laugh. "I'm planning to break into the apartment of a mass murderer. Not part of the job description when I joined the force. But sometimes you've just got to wing it."

Using a Thomas map and dimly lit street signs, Decker managed to find Harlan Manz's apartment. It was located on a deserted side road, shaded with oversized eucalyptus that loomed spectral in the gauzy night. No sidewalks. Pedestrians trod upon a dirt path that hugged the street. The block owned about a half dozen old multiplexed residences, all of them two-story stucco squares with small balconies. An occasional weed-choked vacant lot was interspersed between the buildings. Probably the land had once held structures that didn't make it through the '94 quake.

The former bartender had lived on a top floor, access to his unit provided by a rusted, wrought-iron outdoor staircase. The night was as still as stone. Not a soul in sight and that was good. Decker gloved, took out a penlight, and examined the door lock—a snap. Keeping his picks in his pocket, he removed a credit card from his wallet, snapped the latch bolt, and turned the knob. Closed the door and flipped the light switch.

He was standing in the living room. A beige couch, a couple of chairs, and a coffee table that held a remote control, a mug with a brown-stained bottom, and yesterday's local newspaper. A TV rested against the wall opposite the couch, a twenty-six-inch Sony sitting inside a particle-board bookcase. A half dozen paperbacks rested on the shelves alongside numerous videotapes. Most of them seemed to be action/adventure films but there were the requisite adult films as well. Harlan liked blondes. A stereo/cassette/CD player complete with speakers. Decker flipped through a few CDs; Harlan's taste leaned toward thrash bands and rap.

Decker's eyes scanned the walls. A few framed movie posters hung from single nailheads on white walls. Cable TV films that Decker had never seen, had never heard of. The carpet was brown and worn—a few scattered crumbs, but relatively clean.

The kitchenette was an outpouching off the living room. The compact fridge contained a quart of juice, a quart of milk, three six-packs, and a tub of margarine. Decker opened the fruit bin—two apples dotted with soft spots, and an orange. Cabinets stocked with salsa, chips, a half loaf of moldless bread, a yellow plastic bottle of French's mustard, Heinz's ketchup, a box of raisin bran, mismatched dishes and cookware, and a dead fly. Built-ins included a two-burner cook-top and a microwave-oven combo. No dishwasher, but the sink was cleared of plates and cutlery.

Completely unremarkable.

The bedroom was the same story. Queen-sized bed topped with an older but clean spread. One night-stand containing packets of gum, a bottle of aspirin, and a pack of cigarettes. A small desk was tucked into the corner.

Decker rummaged through its contents. Piquing his interest were several black-and-white head shots. Eight-by-tens of Harlan peering into the camera lens with intense eyes, his full lips slightly agape, and a well-trimmed—ergo calculated—five o'clock shadow. He'd been posed to make the most of his exotic sen-suality. Dark and brooding. Heathcliffian.

Portfolio pictures. Like everyone in Hollywood, Manz had been touched by the industry, had taken a shot at the tarnished screen.

The closet was another insight into Harlan's per-sonality. Lots of clothes. Not expensive threads but the duds had a flair. Well-designed knockoffs. Decker counted seven pairs of shoes, including an expensive pair of Nikes.

The bathroom was a tiny thing which squeezed in a tub with a shower curtain, a toilet, and a sink with a medicine cabinet. The shelves were chock-full of an-algesics, nasal sprays, and decongestant capsules. Harlan also stocked disposable razors, several sticks of antiperspirant, and a sandwich bag dusted with white powder.

Decker dipped his pinkie into the bag and touched it to the tip of his tongue.

The real stuff.

He'd bag the rest and submit it for evidence.

Evidence of *what*, he wasn't sure. But he wasn't about to leave cocaine sitting around.

Cologne and aftershave sat on the rim of the tub. Cheap stuff. Decker organized his thoughts as he walked back into the living room. This time he examined the movie posters with a keen eye. As plain as daylight, Harlan's name had been listed in the cast.

The man had met with some limited success. Of course, that meant nothing.

Decker sat on the couch, rubbed his tired eyes, a puzzling picture emerging in his sleep-deprived brain.

Movie posters on the wall.

Portfolio pictures in the desk.

Stylish clothes and lots of shoes.

Bottles of cologne.

Someone who took pride in his appearance.

Someone with an *ego*.

Yet the place was completely devoid of personal effects. No scrapbooks, no picture albums, no reminder notes or scratch pads, no would-be scripts, no appointment book for the *big* auditions, no Filofax, no little black book of phone numbers, no desk calendar . . . no calendar, *period*.

There was beer in the fridge, cigarettes in the drawer, cocaine in the medicine cabinet. Which told Decker that the guy was a user. Then there was the coffee table on which lay a dirty coffee mug, yesterday's newspaper, and the remote control. Forming an image of a lived-in room . . . un-tampered with . . . untouched.

But something was off.

As if someone had carefully emptied the place of Harlan's true personality, leaving just enough items to form a sketchy impression—like his taste in drugs. The home of a disturbed man, a vicious mass murderer. Yet Decker didn't find a single threatening note, any written psychotic ramblings, nothing that even hinted of a desperate man driven to murder and suicide.

Decker exhaled, his brain buzzing.

Not all psychos leave behind their history—a blow-by-blow schemata, explaining what had led them to their atrocities. Some just explode, spontaneously combust, letting their bloody legacies talk for themselves.

Maybe Harlan had been one of those.

Maybe he woke up one morning . . . and simply popped.

## 6

**The girl reeked** of mint—hiding her booze breath with Scope or Certs—leaving Decker to wonder if the orange juice glass Rhonda Klegg held in a white-knuckled grip had been laced with vodka. He presented his badge. She examined it carefully, then allowed him inside. The place pulsated with color, throwing Decker's equilibrium off balance. The slamming door brought him back into focus.

"Sorry about being so paranoid," Rhonda stated. "Thought you might be the press."

Decker blinked. "Have people been bothering you?"

"Not since I took my phone off the hook."

She offered him coffee; Decker nodded yes. Cream and sugar? Straight black was fine.

With trembling hands, Rhonda sipped her orange juice, stared at him. He stared back at a ravaged, ashen face, lifeless blue eyes and thin pale lips. She probably hadn't gotten much sleep. She looked to be in her mid-twenties. Her hair had been bleached candy-apple red and was tied back into a ponytail. She had a nose-pierce, the helices of her outer ears completely covered with tiny hoops and studs. Lots

43

of chains dangled from the many holes in her earlobes. She was garbed in jeans and a white T-shirt, wore a denim work shirt as a jacket. Her feet were stuffed in lace-up ankle boots.

She finished her juice and said, "I really don't have anything to say." She held aloft her empty glass. "Get you one of these along with your Colombian?"

"No, thank you. Just a cup of coffee would be fine."

"Mind if I take another?"

"Of course not."

"S'cuse."

She disappeared behind a swinging door painted to simulate a wooden lattice intertwined with blooming pink rose vines. Indeed, Rhonda had used her entire apartment as her canvas, living art done up in the style of classical Mediterranean gardens. Painted boxwood hedges replaced baseboard molding. Behind the hedges—on the wall itself—were trellises of ivy and flowering vines, citrus orchards, classical marble statuary, and fountains—all of it serving as a foreground for distant, rolling green hills. Her perspective was outstanding. Decker felt dizzy from the three-dimensional effect. The molding and ceiling had been bathed in light blue hues, tufted with clouds, and populated with gliding blackbirds and a circling hawk.

So distracting was the scene, Decker hadn't noticed the furniture. But it was there and it made a statement. An old carved English park bench sided by two upside-down garbage cans doubling as end tables. The room also had an Adirondack lounge upon which rested a duffel bag, and two bentwood rockers. Old-fashioned streetlamps had been placed in the corners, and the hardwood floor had become a windblown field of grass—green swaying blades laced with yellow dandelions and clumps of white clover.

Rhonda returned with Decker's coffee, more orange juice for herself.

Decker thanked her. "Interesting place you've got here. You're very talented."

She sipped her juice. "Ain't gonna make *Architectural Digest*, but it suits me." Her eyes hardened. "Although this town is sure filled with star-fuckers. Think the ex-girlfriend of a homicidal maniac counts?"

Decker was quiet.

"Hollyweird. A penchant for the bizarre. Sure I can't get you some OJ as in orange juice?"

"I'm fine, Rhonda." Decker's eyes fell on the duffel bag. "Impromptu vacation?"

"I'm getting outta here. At least until this thing blows over. Who the hell wants this kind of notoriety?"

A savvy point. Decker placed his mug on an upside-down trash container. "Is that okay?"

Rhonda laughed. "It's a garbage can. I'm not exactly worried about coffee rings." She looked him up and down. "You're cute. Wanna fuck?"

"No, thank you."

"I look like shit, huh?"

"You look fine, Rhonda." Decker took out his notepad. "You know, the sooner we get started, the sooner I'm out of your hair."

"You're gonna ask me questions about Harlan?"

"Yep."

"Why do you care? He's dead." Her eyes watered. "They're all dead. I thought the only things that the pigs cared about were looking good on the witness stand and beating up minorities. You're real big. I bet you've punched around more than your fair share of niggers."

Decker said, "Me? I shuffle paper."

"Bullshit," Rhonda shot out. "You look defensive, cop. Betcha I hit a nerve. See, we all have pasts. So don't you go judging me like I'm some freak because I hooked up with a nutcase."

"I don't think you're a freak, Rhonda. Right now, I see you as a very vulnerable woman."

"Where'd they teach you that? Cop Psych 101? You should stick to pounding the shit outta motorists."

Decker was quiet.

She gave him a long hard stare. "You were there last night, weren't you? At Estelle's?"

"I was there the entire night."

"I saw you on TV. You're the one who said it looked like your worst nightmare."

"Glad to be remembered as a sound bite."

"You're also in today's paper—picture, quote, and all." She glared at him. "You had tears in your eyes."

"Did I?"

"Yeah, you did. Did they also teach you how to cry in Cop Psych 101? Or was it Cop Compassion 101?"

Decker offered a sad smile. "Wish I conformed to your hard-ass image. I'd sleep better at night."

Again, her eyes moistened. She rubbed her cheeks, wiped away tears. "I'm real attracted to you. Sure you don't want to fuck? Might put me in a gabby mood."

"I'm going to have to pass."

"You're married?"

"Yes."

"I don't care."

"But I do. Can we get started?"

"Why do you need to ask any questions if the case is solved?"

"Because there are still lots of unanswered questions—"

"Like *why* he did it?" She gulped her juice. "Hell if I know." She cocked her hip. "I knew I had bad taste in men. But this . . ."

"You called yourself an ex-girlfriend."

"This is true."

"When did you two break up?"

"You mean, when did I kick him out? 'Bout four months ago."

"Why?"

*"Why?"* Rhonda let out a bitter laugh. "'Cause I got sick of his running around. More than that, I just got sick of Harlan Manz. The man with the plans that never panned out."

"He was an actor?"

"He was a jerk."

Decker waited.

Rhonda sighed. "Harlan was a professional *wannabe.* Wannabe actor, wannabe model, wannabe tennis pro, wannabe stud, wannabe this, wannabe that. What he was . . . was a nothing."

Decker said, "In his apartment, I saw film posters with his name on them."

"Yeah, he was a card-carrying member of SAG. Showed it to you at every opportunity. Those films were shelved, never even made it to *video* . . . what is your rank again?"

"Lieutenant."

"A big shot."

"A legend in my own mind."

Rhonda smiled briefly. "Harlan was . . ." She sighed. "He was a slacker . . . a loser with a good backhand. And that's about it, bub."

"A wannabe tennis pro." Decker waited a beat. "So he had tennis ambitions?"

"Maybe. Guy had some talent but not good enough to be pro. He used to teach tennis at a country club—"

"*What?*"

"No joke. The big one about two miles up the road."

"Greenvale?"

"That's the one. Greenvale Country Club."

"This wasn't one of Harlan's delusions? You know this for a *fact*?"

"Check it out yourself." She grinned. "Bet they'll welcome your inquiries with open arms."

Decker wrote furiously. "How long did he teach at Greenvale?"

"Off and on for about three years."

"Off and on?"

"Yeah, Harlan couldn't hold anything steady. Greenvale took him in for summer work. He taught tennis in the day, tended bar at night. Harlan could maintain in short spurts. I mean the guy was good-looking, had a certain amount of charm. And he was well endowed. Used it, too. He made more than a few lonely women very happy."

"Married women?"

"I said *lonely* women. 'Course they were married."

"Lucky he didn't wind up with a gun to his head."

"Nah, he wouldn't do anything dangerous. Greenvale has lots of married women whose husbands are fuckin' sweet young things. I know because I've *been* there. Not the old, lonely, married woman, but the sweet young thing. Lots of rich geezers in this city. Am I shocking you?"

"Not at all."

"Yeah, you look pretty worldly. You mess around on your wife?"

"No. So Harlan taught tennis to lonely women?"

"No, he taught tennis to anyone who was assigned to him. Women, girls, men, boys." Rhonda paused. "Occasionally, he'd give a lesson to some hot shit producer or director. Harlan was big on name-dropping. He'd brag to me that *this time*, he really made an impression. Jerk ... he just didn't *get* it. What that poor schmuck wouldn't have given for the life of a big shot ... partying ... tennis ... doing beautiful, rich women ..."

She stared at her empty glass.

"Will you excuse me?"

She left, then came back with a fresh glass. The liquid looked pale, lots of vodka, not too much juice. This time, she nursed her drink.

"I tried to tell him that just because you teach some jack how to ace a serve doesn't mean he's going to star you in his next movie. But Harlan ..."

"But he must have been a good tennis player to teach."

"Good enough to teach those yahoos."

"Good enough to make the circuit?"

"He told me he was actually seeded in the top two hundred or something like that. Maybe it was true. But probably not. Harlan lived in fantasies."

"But he was a member of SAG."

"Sure, he got a few parts . . . just enough to feed his delusional brain. Lieutenant, Harlan was a hanger-on. A walking-around guy."

"Pardon?"

"A walking-around guy. There's lots of egomaniacal people out there. No offense to Barbra, but people who need people are *not* the luckiest people. In fact, they're cursed. They need people to create their identity, to feel important, to look busy, and to be wanted. And they're rich enough to buy these little trained spider monkeys like Kato and his ilk to walk around with. So the hot dogs never look unattended. *That's* what Harlan was. He was a walking-around guy."

Tears ran down her cheek. She turned her head, fiercely swiped her eyes.

"I still have feelings for him. That shock you?"

"Not at all." Decker waited a beat. "Can we talk a minute about Harlan's termination at Estelle's?"

"Nothing to say. He broke their cardinal rule. Customer is always right."

"But he was upset—"

"Of course he was upset. He was furious. Some drunken A-hole gets abusive and Harlan's canned. I was so angry, I almost came down and made a scene."

She seemed to wilt.

"Then . . . I don't know. I guess I thought it was par for the course. Harlan getting axed."

"Did Harlan continue to talk about it?"

"At first, he talked about getting even. I thought it was just talk . . . venting." With watery eyes, she looked at Decker, pointedly. "God, I need to fuck."

"Why'd you kick him out of your life, Rhonda?"

She sighed. "I found someone else. Also a loser, but at least he's *gainfully* employed. A porno actor. Ernie Beldheim aka King Whopper. Can you believe that name?"

"It shows a certain amount of creativity. How did Harlan take the breakup?"

Rhonda sat on a bentwood rocker, legs pushing against the floor, her body moving back and forth. She gazed upward, eyes on her sky ceiling. "I wasn't real tactful. I told him I was dumping him because he wasn't big enough."

Tears streamed down her face.

"I wanted to *hurt* him. Because he'd been messing around on me for so damn long. If I had known he was so unstable, I wouldn't have . . ."

"You couldn't have known, Rhonda."

She looked down into her orange juice glass as if reading tea leaves. "After we broke up, he did things. Weird things. I guess I knew he was flipping out. But I didn't know it would lead to this."

"Of course not. What did he do?"

Rhonda returned her eyes to Decker. "Tried to scare me. Made calls in the middle of the night, ranted on about how he was going to get me. But I never took him seriously." She looked up. "Thinking it over, I have a feeling I was one of the lucky ones."

*True enough.* Decker pointed to her duffel bag. "Where are you planning to go?"

Rhonda stopped rocking, blew out air. "I got an offer to do a gig in Hawaii. Some honcho wants me to paint *Playboy* playmates on his walls. No accounting for tastes."

"Vacation might do you good."

"Hope so."

Decker said, "Do you have some old pictures of him?"

"Maybe one or two. Why?"

"I didn't find any recent pictures of Harlan in his apartment."

Rhonda was taken aback. "That's odd. I know he has a portfolio—"

"No, I found that. I'm talking about things like photo albums."

She shrugged. "Weird. Because we took quite a few . . ." She smiled. "Quite a few *compromising* ones. After we broke up, he told me he was going to send them to my mother. I told him to go ahead . . . ain't nothing she's never seen before."

"Did he?"

"If he did, Mom never said a word."

Decker said, "Rhonda, if Harlan was a member of SAG, he must have had an agent."

"He had a couple light-years ago. Fired them all."

Decker's beeper went off. Rhonda stood up from the rocker. "Phone's on the wall."

Decker's eyes scanned the mural, rested on a painted phone kiosk. Mounted on the wall, inside the painted booth, was a real, three-dimensional pay phone. "Do I need money to make the call?"

"Credit card's fine."

Decker said, "I'm slow on the uptake, didn't get much sleep. I can't tell if you're putting me on."

Rhonda smiled tightly. "It was a joke."

"Sorry to be so dense."

"Mr. Dumb Lug." Rhonda rolled her eyes. "About as slow as a roadrunner. Sly, too. So why do I find myself trusting you? Is that how you extract confessions? You get people to trust you, then you slam them?"

"I don't slam anyone, least of all someone like you." Decker looked at the pager's number. Strapp's office.

Rhonda said, "I'll be back in a minute. Help yourself to the phone."

"Thanks." Decker punched in numbers; the captain picked up on the fifth ring.

"Get over to the station house. Community is planning a major memorial for Estelle's victims this afternoon. You're expected to be there. Show some community support and help me field the press."

"I'll be at my office in ten minutes."

Strapp said, "Good quote yesterday, Decker. About the scene being your worst nightmare. If you can think up a few more like that . . . something that shows compassion . . . that would be good for us . . . for LAPD."

Decker was silent.

Strapp said, "Look, I know it sounds politico, but tough. This is our chance to make a *good* impression. Our asses have been fried in print for so long, it would be real nice if we could be represented as the public servants we really are."

"I understand, sir."

"Good, then. Get down here. We'll strategize together."

## ❧ 7

*After a full* day of hospital visits, bereavement calls, and heart-wrenching services for the dead, Decker made it back to the station house, his energy depleted, his brain crashing against his skull like a tidal wave. Advil wouldn't cut it. Dry-mouthed, he swallowed a couple of Darvocets, but knew even that wouldn't be enough. Rooting in his shirt pocket, he pulled out a pack of cigarettes. Lit up a smoke and rubbed his aching temples. Marge came in a few moments later, holding a half-dozen manila envelopes which she used to fan away smoke.

"You must feel like shit warmed over."

Decker stubbed out the cigarette. "Trying to compose myself before I go home. I don't want Rina to see me like this. How'd the interviews go? Learn anything?"

"Depressingly unremarkable. Can I sit?"

"Of course." Decker pointed to a chair, eyed his smoke.

"Go ahead, Pete. I remember well your smoking days."

"Just a temporary lapse." Again, Decker lit up. "Tell me about the interviews."

"Nothing to tell. Bullets started flying, people started screaming, running for cover. Truly terrifying." Marge paused, collected her thoughts. "From what I could gather, it seems that Harlan wasn't deliberate in his shooting. Didn't shoot at any one person specifically, or even aim at people for that matter. He just opened fire. A lot of it. The boys and I have been comparing notes. They agree with that assessment."

Marge paused.

"Since this kind of thing is rare, I don't really know what's considered the typical behavior for mass murderers."

"Off the top of my head, the compatibles that come to mind are Tasmania, the Long Island Railroad, the San Ysidro McDonald's, and Dunblane—"

"The elementary school in Scotland." Marge paled. "God, what a world!"

Decker inhaled his smoke, tried to keep his mind focused. "I remember that in Tasmania and in San Ysidro, the murderer aimed at people. Picked them off like prey. But you're saying that *wasn't* what happened. Harlan just sprayed the place."

"Appears that way. We've been working a time frame . . . how many minutes did the actual shooting last? Time elongates during these catastrophic events. What seems like hours could have been minutes. At the moment, we're guesstimating."

She held up the manila envelopes.

"I picked these up for you. Just came in from the Coroner's Office. Probably some prelim autopsy reports. Want me to go over them? You look tired."

Decker sat back in his chair, closed his eyes,

breathed in wisps of nicotined air. "Who's still out there?"

"All of us—Scott, Tom, Bert. We're still writing up reports. Oh, Gaynor left about an hour ago. He said you told him to work on the case at home."

"I've got him doing some computer work. His home equipment is better technologically than what we've got here." Decker stubbed it out. "Give me the reports. Call the others in."

"Right away." Marge handed him the envelopes and left.

Decker broke open a seal, pulled out some slice-and-dice autopsy photos. Hitting him like a mace in the gut. He sifted through them with deliberation . . . concentration. Marge soon returned with the others. They pulled up chairs, sat in front of Decker's desk, all of them uncharacteristically quiet.

Decker said, "I've got some prelim autopsy reports. Finals won't be ready for days, so we'll go over these—"

Oliver interrupted, "Like they're going to tell us something we don't know?"

"Never know." Decker placed the photos back in the envelope. "We've got to re-create the shooting. Where Harlan first stood when he opened fire, who appeared to be his first victim, who was his next, and so on and so forth."

"How do we do that?" Martinez asked.

"We'll start with the floor plan. Draw each table and who sat where, using the reservations book. Who checked the book into evidence?"

"Yo." Marge held up her hand.

Decker said, "Okay. We draw each table and label

them. Next comes the brain work and the tedium. For this part, we'll need basic geometry and gunshot angles. Since we couldn't rod the victims, we'll have to rely on Forensics."

Decker leaned forward.

"Harlan was found dead at the bar. Don't know if he started his shooting at the bar, but assume that he did. The bar area is off the entrance, correct?"

Nods all around.

"So assume he entered there and just started shooting. Here's what we're going to do. We ask ourselves . . . *if* Harlan started shooting from the bar area and was facing left, where would the first bullets have landed? Say they would have landed on table three. We look in the reservations book, find out who was at table three, and determine the nature of their wounds, if any. If it seems consistent with Harlan's position, we go on to our next assumption. If it's not consistent, we change our first assumption—"

"I'm lost," Martinez said.

Decker said, "We're trying to trace bullet paths using geometry. Go down the friggin' list. If Harlan shot from the bar, where would his first bullets have landed? If that matches, we move on.

"If Harlan had turned to the left and shot, who would have been his next hit?

"If Harlan had turned to the right and shot, who would have been his next hit?

"If Harlan had taken a couple of steps forward, who would have been his next hit?

"If Harlan had taken a couple of steps forward and *then* turned to the right, who would have been his next hit?

"If Harlan had taken a couple of steps forward and then turned to the *left*, who would have been his next—"

"This could take months!" Oliver blurted out.

"Yes, it probably will take months," Decker said.

"Loo, pardon mah ignorance," Webster drawled, "but just what do you reckon to accomplish?"

"Let's talk politics for a moment. There are bound to be lawsuits—against Estelle's, maybe even against the city. Our police reports are going to be scrutinized with a microscope. And we're going to be judged, folks. Every single one of us. You, me, and this entire beleaguered department."

Decker rubbed his temples.

"I want every single bullet accounted for. Make sure that all the slugs came from Harlan's gun and not some other outside source that we overlooked because we were too lazy—"

"Outside source?" Marge grimaced. "You think there was more than one shooter?"

"Who knows? Last count we've got thirteen dead, thirty-two wounded. Lots of damage for one guy, Margie."

Martinez said, "Harlan was packing a nine-millimeter automatic double action, Loo. Fourteen rounds per magazine—"

"How many rounds did he fire, Bert?"

Martinez was quiet. "Don't know."

"Anyone?"

No one spoke.

Decker said, "Thirteen dead people, thirty-two wounded, and we can't answer a simple question like how many rounds the fucker fired."

Oliver said, "So we'll do a bullet count."

"We'll do a lot more than a bullet count. I want this crime scene *nailed*. Every step and every shot that Harlan took must be checkbook-balanced."

Decker leaned back in his chair.

"We'll start tomorrow with the bullet count. Dunn and Oliver, you two take the corpses in the morgue as well as the shells and bullets left behind at Estelle's. Check the walls, check the furniture, check the potted plants, turn the place upside down if you have to. I want every bullet, every shell, every empty magazine cited and bagged."

"Talk about tedium," Oliver muttered.

Decker looked at his detective—worn, disheveled, spent. "I don't envy your assignment, Scott. The place gives me the creeps. But someone has to do it."

Oliver ran his hands through his oily black hair. "I'm not complaining, Loo. I'm just tired."

"I know." Decker looked at Webster and Martinez. "You two go over to the hospitals, talk to the victims' doctors. Have them help you get a bullet count from their patients' medical charts or surgery dictation or even from the X rays. And if any of the victims feels like talking, you can start conducting interviews. Once we get the bullets accounted for, we'll start analyzing the angles—"

"Y'ever think of using a computer, Loo?" Webster asked.

"Forensic reenactment." Decker said. "Farrell's working on a program for this as we speak. It's a very useful tool, but first we've got to have data to plug into the computer. Then it'll probably take months before he comes up with something. But that's all

right. We have time. If we're meticulous in our cal-
culations, maybe the computer will spit us back a
step-by-step simulation of Harlan's movements at
Estelle's."

Webster said, "Welcome to Cybermurder."

"Except the victims were flesh and blood." Decker
stood. "We start tomorrow. For now, *all* of you. Go
home."

As Decker pulled into the driveway of the ranch, he
noticed the living-room light shining through the
bay window. Immediately, his heart took off. Not
that it was late—quarter after ten. Still, when Rina
waited up for him, she always kept vigil in the kitchen
or their bedroom.

He shut off the Volare's motor, jogged to the front
door, and opened it. His wife was asleep on the
living-room couch. On the floor was his dog, Ginger,
nestled among piles of loose papers. Next to the
sheets were a calculator, pens, pencils, and a couple of
ledgers.

Instant relief. Everything was all right.

Then came the curiosity. What was Rina working
on? He considered rifling through the pages, but
discarded the thought. All in due time. For now, let
her sleep.

He regarded the room. In dim light, it seemed
worn, his furniture over a decade old, purchased during his divorced days. The buckskin couch had been
rubbed shiny in spots, the coffee table was scratched,
the two wing chairs had faded. Keeping guard at the
bay window was Rina's pine rocker purchased after
Hannah was born—the only new thing standing.

Yet Rina never said a word about replacing his shopworn pieces. Guess she was waiting for him to relinquish the last vestiges of his bachelor years. Not that his wife hadn't added her own feminine touches. The silk-screened floral couch pillows, two hand-crocheted throw blankets, fresh flowers, and lots of framed family photos. Observing her sleeping form . . . he really needed to do better for her.

She stirred. Even without makeup, her face was striking, though her creamy skin was a shade paler than usual. Her lips—lush and red and always alluring. Eyes moving behind translucent lids. She was dressed in a black angora sweater and black knit skirt. Her outfit matched her raven hair, which fell over her shoulders like a sable shawl.

He shut off the light, put Ginger outside, debated checking the horses' stables but nixed the idea. Too damn tired.

He headed into the bedroom, stripped in seconds, then beelined into the shower. Turning the water up to full pressure, he stood under the faucet, allowing the blast to run over his stubbled face while razor-hot needles rained down on his aching back, cooking his freckled skin bright red. He continued his baptism by fire until the water grew cold. By the time he was done, Rina had tucked herself into bed. She was half awake, her lids still hooded. But she spoke. "S'right?"

"I'm just fine." Decker toweled himself off as he spoke. "Go back to sleep."

"Boys send their regards."

"Regards back." He ran his hands several times through red shocks of wet hair, then went over and kissed his wife. A short one, then a long one. She purred. "That was wonderful."

He slipped under the sheets. "That's because you're half asleep."

She opened her eyes fully. "How are you holding up?"

"Been better, but I'll survive." Immediately, he switched the topic. "What were you doing out there in the living room with all those loose papers? Building a nest?"

Rina thought a moment. "Oh. That. Rav Schulman called—"

"Why? What's wrong?"

"Nothing. He had some bookkeeping questions. They turned out to be a bit complicated, so I stopped by the yeshiva and picked up some of the ledgers."

"The yeshiva doesn't have a bookkeeper?"

"Peter, I didn't question him. He asked me to do him a favor, I said yes."

"You have that much spare time, go ahead."

Rina was quiet. Decker forced himself not to push it. But he knew there was more. Lately Rina had been using the learned Rabbi for therapy . . . just as Decker had done many times in the past. His wife had been very depressed since an old friend of hers— and her late husband's—had died. Abram Sparks had also been a friend of Rabbi Schulman. Decker was sure that Bram's name had come up in the course of their conversations. Holding that thought, Decker rolled over, buried his head in the pillow.

Rina turned off the light. "Your father called today."

Decker pivoted to face her. "And?"

"The shooting must have made the news over there. He was concerned about you."

"What'd you tell him?"

"I lied. I said you were fine."

"That's not lying, I am fine."

Rina didn't answer.

Decker hesitated. "Did he mention my mother at all?"

"No . . . why?"

"No particular reason. Let's go to sleep."

Rina knew he was fibbing, that tight catch in his throat. He was worried about his mother, leaving Rina to wonder if her mother-in-law was ill. Eyes closed, Rina waited and waited, then gave up. She was just about asleep when he finally decided to talk.

"She called me about two weeks ago. She'd been cleaning out the garage . . . had some of my childhood junk and wanted to know what to do with it. I told her to send it here . . . or throw it away . . . whichever was easier. Then . . ."

He paused.

"Then I asked her why . . . at this moment in time . . . was she cleaning out the garage . . . which has been a storage house of our family junk for God only knows how many years. She just said, 'If not now, when?'"

Rina touched his arm. "Did you ask her if something was wrong?"

"Yes, of course. As I expected, she denied any problems."

"Did you press her?"

"I can't press my mother, Rina. This is as big a hint as I'm going to get."

He waited a beat.

"I can't approach my father. Because she could be keeping something from him, too. I did call Randy. He doesn't seem to know anything, so I guess they've kept him in the dark."

"Or maybe nothing's wrong."

"Maybe. Either that or my brother hasn't picked up on Mom's nuances. He's not a font of sensitivity."

"Peter, why didn't you tell me this earlier?"

"I don't know. You have your own parents to deal with . . . your own problems as well."

Rina was silent, guilt coursing through her body. "I know I've been very upset since—"

"It's not important."

Again neither spoke.

"Do you want to go out for a visit, Peter?"

"She wouldn't like that . . . me, just popping in. She needs her privacy, I've got to respect it."

"Darling, can you try talking to her? Hiding behind a wall of stoicism isn't good for either of you."

"Rina, I respect your culture. You respect mine."

She counted to ten, told herself to breathe calmly. "How about if I called her up—"

"No—"

"Can you let me finish?"

Decker waited a moment. "Sorry. Go on."

"I'd like to invite them out here for Thanksgiving."

"A nice thought, honey, but I'm afraid it would rob her of her dignity. You *know* what Thanksgiving means to her."

"Yes, I do. But hear me out, okay?"

"Sure."

"Peter, *I* don't like making Thanksgiving. It's no

charge for me to make yet another big feast, a month after our major holidays are over. And yes, I *do* know what that holiday means to her. Peter, we've gone down to Gainesville twice for Thanksgiving. It's lovely, but it isn't the kind of holiday she wants. It hurts her tremendously that we can't eat her beautifully cooked food in *her* house on her *special* china."

"Why? She says things to you?"

"No, of course not. But that doesn't mean I don't notice her wincing when we sit there at her table with fruit and raw vegetables on our paper plates."

Decker was quiet.

Rina said, "I can't change the fact that we're observant, kosher Jews and they're Baptist. That's just life. I can't take over her kitchen. But she can take over mine. Let me invite her out here to make *her* Thanksgiving with my pots and pans. Cook everything in *my* house in *my* kosher kitchen—"

"Rina—"

"I'll buy the meat and all the trimmings, but she can have free rein. I'll even go shopping with her to pick out a set of china of her choice. I have so many sets of dishes, one more won't hurt. She can cook to her heart's content. Do all her favorite recipes including her pumpkin pie. Only accommodations she'll have to *kashrut* is using nondairy margarine and Mocha Mix instead of butter and milk. And, of course, no honey-glazed ham."

"She won't do it."

"She doesn't even like ham—"

"It's not the *ham*, Rina, it's the whole thing. She'll feel displaced."

"At least let me try. I think she'll come out. I think

she'd love to cook up a storm, actually have us *eat* her meals. And then there're the grandchildren—Cindy as well as our Hannalah—"

"That means Randy's left alone."

"So I'll invite Randy and the kids and wife number . . ."

"It's still three."

"Your nieces and nephews will love it here. Disneyland—"

"They've got Disney World, Epcot Center, and Universal Studios. Theme parks are no big deal to them."

"Yes, but we've got Las Vegas—"

"Oh, my sister-in-law will love that."

Rina sighed. "Just *think* about it, okay?"

Decker was quiet. "You'd put up my brother's family?"

"Absolutely. I find Randy . . . interesting—"

"I love my brother."

"I know that." Rina smiled. Even though Randy worked two jobs—he was a vice cop and moonlighted as a security guard—he was always flat broke. Peter had been sending him cash for years.

Silence. Then Decker said, "I'll call Mom tomorrow."

Rina said, "*I'll* call her tomorrow. She'll say no to you, but yes to me."

Decker knew that was all too true. He turned toward his wife, draped an arm around her shoulders, and drew her to his chest. He kissed her mouth, licked her lips. "I love you."

"I love you, too." She kissed him again. "Want to make more out of this?"

"Wish I could." He laughed. "I'm afraid I'd be arrested on charges of Assault with a Dead Weapon—"

Rina laughed, slapped his shoulder. She kissed him gently, licked his mustache. Her hands snaked around his body, stroked his long muscular back with tender fingertips.

He let out a soft rumble. "Feels good."

"I think I detect signs of life—"

"That's not life, that's just a reflex."

"Whatever it is, it's good enough for me."

# 8

*Waking up before* the sun, Decker showered, shaved, and said his morning prayers alfresco, bathed in the golden light of dawn. Afterward, he let the dog out, pitched fresh hay to his stable of four horses, changed the animals' water, went through yesterday's mail, and had coffee brewing by the time Rina roused the crew for school.

Although anxious to get his professional life going, Decker forced himself to make a little time for breakfast and family affairs. The day's topics included his stepson's driver's license, buying a newer car for Rina, and giving Sam his own set of wheels in the form of Rina's old Volvo. Decker promised they'd hit the car lots on Sunday. And if Rina had the inclination, maybe they'd look at new living-room furniture as well. His wife was surprised, delighted. Immediately bright with ideas. Decker felt good. It had been a long time since he'd seen Rina's smile.

After the boys left for school on the bus, Decker played zoo with Hannah, her stuffed animals being nefarious creatures of prey, and Ginger, the Irish setter, doubling as Simba the Lion. Then Decker carted his daughter off to school. Hannah threw her pipe

68

stem arms around his neck, kissed him on the cheek with soft little lips. Decker felt an overwhelming desire to cling to her, to lug her into work in a papoose. Instead, he lowered her to the ground and watched her scamper off. The experts talk about separation anxiety. Were they referring to the child or the parent? Cloaked in wistfulness, Decker left the neon-painted schoolhouse, arriving at the station by half past eight.

All business, he made phone calls, signed papers, went over reports, checked in with his detectives, then buried himself in pathology reports and bullet trajectories for the next four hours. Head buzzing, he finally broke for lunch at one-thirty. At his desk, he opened his brown bag—two chicken sandwiches, two pieces of fruit, two bottles of Martinelli's sparkling apple juice, and a half dozen cookies. Food that could be easily eaten in a car.

He took his lunch and his briefcase and headed for the Volare. Within minutes, he was on the road, felt his shoulders relax, his face go slack with freedom.

Devonshire division patrolled a varied geographical area—some residential, some small business, some factories, and lots of rolling foothills and fallow acreage waiting for a land boom that was always "just around the corner." Developers ran scared out here and not without reason. The district had been the center of two major earthquakes, was Saharan hot in the summer, and was situated far from city action. Still, it was God's green acres in the late autumn—glorious blue skies with long stretches of wildflower fields and oak-dotted hills ribboned with miles of hiking and horse trails. Giant sycamores and menthol-laden eucalyptus swayed in the winds.

The division also contained several million-dollar housing developments—big mama, multiroomed mansions floating in seas of green lawn. The gated communities ran complete with pools, spas, tennis courts, recreation rooms, and banquet facilities. When Greenvale Country Club opened its doors fifteen years ago, Decker wondered why the rich would join a club, paying hefty premiums for amenities available on their own premises.

Yet Greenvale had made itself a known quantity. Though it wasn't as prestigious as some of the older, established L.A. clubs, it had its own cachet, boasting an elitist membership and hosting its fair share of society weddings and black-tie-only charity events. It seemed that human beings had an infinite capacity to rate—to separate and segregate into in-or-out crowds.

The club sat on twenty-five acres, the buildings obscured by umbrellas of specimen trees. As the Volare chugged up the long, shaded drive, Decker noticed several gardeners tending the lawns and numerous flower beds. Going into the fall, they were planting jewel-colored pansies. Within moments, the buildings came into view, Tudor in style, but with L.A. modifications: thin brick facing over stucco because solid brick crumbled in earthquakes. There were several structures loosely connected to one another, probably built at different times. Lots of stained glass, lots of crossbeams and peaked roofs. A theme park re-creation of the Tower of London.

By the time Decker reached the gatehouse, he had finished his lunch. Displaying his badge, he told uniformed guards that he was there to speak to the manager. And no, he did not have an appointment. His sudden appearance was disruptive to their sleepy flow. The guards conferred, scratched their heads, made phone calls, until one of them decided to lift the booth's restraining arm, told Decker to handle it at the front desk.

Instead of parking in the ample lot, Decker used the circular entrance driveway and instructed the valets to keep the car in front. With reticence, a red-coated attendant settled the ten-year-old algae-green Volare between a sleek black Jag and a dowager brown Mercedes.

Through the double doors and into a two-story white-marble-floor rotunda. The walls were wainscoted—walnut panels on the bottom, cream-colored paint on top. A circular band of white rococo molding marked the division between the walls and the ceiling. A giant canopy of crystal lights dangled from an ornate plaster medallion. The rest of the dome was painted with angels and cherubs floating on cotton clouds in a turquoise sky. A winding staircase carpeted with plush peach pile led to a second-floor landing. In front was a short hallway that bled into a paneled library/reading room. Decker strolled to the front desk which was tucked away on the right-hand side. A bespectacled thirtysomething blonde sat behind a glass window; she slid it open and smiled.

"Can I help you?"

"Probably." Decker held up his badge. "Lieutenant Peter Decker, LAPD. Who's in charge at the moment?"

The blonde's smile faded, wary brown eyes looking him over. "Let me make a phone call, sir."

With that, the woman shut the glass window and dialed. Her face was expressive—the wrinkled brow, the down-turned lips. It was clear she was getting bawled out by the person on the other end of the line. She hung up, reopened the window.

"Can I take your name and number and have someone call you back this afternoon?"

Decker smiled. "Why don't you get back on the phone and tell your boss that I'm getting pushy."

She closed the window a second time. Reopened it, told him that someone would be coming and he should take a seat. Decker glanced at the satin-covered French-style benches. Looked way too small and very uncomfortable. He elected to stand.

Within minutes, a man jogged through the hallway. Short, stocky, a head of curls and a shadowed face even though he'd recently shaved. He was built like a tank—barrel chest, thick legs creasing his gray slacks, muscle-packed forearms. The sleeves of his white shirt were rolled to his elbows. He stuck out a meaty hand but kept walking.

"Barry Fine. Follow me."

Fine never broke step. Decker kept pace with him through the hallway, into the club's library/reading room—as big as an arena. More leather here than at a rodeo. Hard to notice any people in the soft lighting. Perhaps it was because they were hidden in the corners or behind the backs of wing chairs. But Decker could ascertain signs of life—the clearing of a throat, the rustle of a newspaper, a hushed conversation between a man and his cellular phone. A uniformed waiter traversed the furniture maze, a tray of drinks balanced on the palm of his hand.

"This way," Fine said.

Steering him away from the room. The message being: no fraternizing with the elite.

Fine unlocked a piece of paneling which turned out to be a door. He held it open for Decker, who crossed the threshold.

The business offices. No luxury here. Just working space and cramped at that. As Decker's eyes adjusted to the glare of bright, fluorescent lighting, he noticed stark-white walls, linoleum flooring. A phone was ringing, lots of clicking computer keys. Fine led Decker into his cubicle, shut the glass door. He sat back in his desk chair, thick sausage fingers folded together, resting in his lap.

"Mind if I have a look at your identification?"

Decker showed him his badge, flipped the cover back, and pocketed the billfold after Fine had nodded.

"Please." Fine pointed to a folding chair and Decker sat. "Must be important to send out a lieutenant."

"Thanks for seeing me. I have a few questions. Thought that you might be able to help me."

"Questions about . . ."

"Harlan Manz."

Fine's face remained stoic. "The monster who shot up Estelle's."

Decker said, "I understand he worked here for a while."

Fine said, "You've been misinformed."

Decker rolled his tongue in his mouth. "How long have you worked here, Mr. Fine?"

"Seven years."

"And you're saying that Harlan Manz never worked here?"

"To the best of my recollection, that is correct."

"To the best of your recollection?" Decker waited a beat. "Sir, this isn't a grand jury."

Fine didn't flinch. "I always try to be as specific as possible."

"Perhaps you knew him under a different name—"

"Don't think so." Fine stood. "I'll walk you out."

Decker remained seated. "Mr. Fine, are you honestly telling me that Harlan Manz never worked in this country club?"

"Never heard of the man until he hit the news," Fine said. "Not that I'm about to do it, but if push came to shove, I'd open my books and show you. Never had a Harlan Manz on the payroll."

"Ah . . ." Decker licked his lips. "You paid him in cash."

Fine's smile turned hard. "Lieutenant, I don't have to talk to you. You get pushy, I call the owners. The owners get upset and they call their lawyers. The lawyers get upset, they call your captain. Gets you a black mark on your record."

Decker stared him down. "Are you threatening me, sir?"

The tip of Fine's nose turned red. He stammered, "No, I'm just pointing out a logical chain of events."

Decker lied straight-faced. "Harlan Manz had listed income from Greenvale Country Club on his 1040 federal tax forms—"

"You're bluffing," Fine busted in.

"As well as state—"

"What is this? A shakedown?"

"No, Mr. Fine, this is a simple fact-finding mission. Quiet, discreet, friendly. Be a shame if damaging information was leaked to the press, that an insane mass murderer once worked here as staff."

Fine raised his voice. "He was never on staff!"

"You explain that distinction to the press."

"Now who's threatening whom?"

"I'm not threatening you, I'm *telling* you. Press wants information about Harlan, I'm more than happy to oblige. You want to sue me for false allegations, go right ahead. Only in court, you can't bluff. Because if you do, that's perjury."

Fine started to protest, but turned quiet. He buried his head in his hands. "The stupid *idiot*! I told him it was strictly off the record. He promised me . . ." He looked up at Decker. "I can't read your face. Ever play poker?"

Decker took out a notebook and pen. "Tell me about Harlan."

Fine let out a gush of air. "Worked here about two years ago. Used the name Hart Mansfield . . . supposedly his *stage* name, though I've never seen him on any sort of a screen. A summer fill-in. All cash. Nothing on the books. That's it."

"What were his assignments?"

"Not much. Which was why he wasn't on staff. He taught tennis when we were short-staffed. In the summertime, our regular instructors go on vacation."

"I was told he tended bar as well."

"He was an extra pair of hands when we had a big event."

"And you paid him in cash for bartending as well?"

"Yep." Fine bit his lip, ran a hand through his curly hair. "Not that I was doing funny business with the books. The cash-out was listed under miscellaneous expenses. I just never bothered to put him on the payroll."

"Owners know he worked here?"

Fine rubbed his face. "Hasn't come up . . . yet."

"You haven't received phone calls from some of the membership?"

"Sure I got a few phone calls. People asking 'Was that asshole at Estelle's the guy who used to work here?' kind of thing. Names were different. I told them no."

"You lied?"

"If it should come back to haunt me, I simply made a mistake because the names were different."

Fine grimaced.

"You want to know something, Lieutenant? The people who called me . . . far from being squeamish . . . they hung up from the conversation *disappointed*. It was an exciting notion to them . . . a safe brush with the dark side. Personally, I think it's sick. But then again, I just cater to the rich. I don't really understand them."

"They accepted your denials?"

"I tell them it's not the same guy, they don't have the conviction of character to debate me."

"And the owners don't know about Harlan working here?"

"No. Owners know a great deal about the membership, but not too much about staff. They don't want to be bothered with business details. That's what they pay me for. And like I said before, I've accounted for Harlan's expenses. Just not on the payroll—"

"Avoiding taxes and Social Security—"

"Hired him as freelance. Club's only responsible

for the taxes and Social Security of its full-time employees. And Harlan never worked enough hours to warrant putting him on the payroll. Our books are clean. You find cause to subpoena our books, you won't find a hint of an irregularity."

"Owners won't be happy if Harlan's alias is publicized."

"No, they won't be. I'll probably be blamed. And I'll probably lose my job."

"That's not my goal, sir."

"But it still may be an end result." Fine blew out air. "Hell with it. What else do you want to know, Lieutenant?"

"Harlan taught tennis?"

"Yes."

"Groups? Individuals?"

"Mostly private lessons."

"How was Harlan with his tennis students?"

"Never had a complaint. If I had, Harlan would have been out on his ass." Fine smiled, but it lacked warmth. "I wish someone had complained. It would play a lot better with the bosses if I had *fired* the guy."

"Why didn't you hire him on as a regular?"

"'Cause he was a jerk. Sure, he was okay for an occasional lesson, but that's about all. All these wannabes." He shook his head. "If I hired tennis instructors and bartenders on the basis of stability, I wouldn't have much of a roster. Harlan was also chronically late and drank a lot. *But . . .*"

The manager paused, held a finger in the air.

"He usually showed up when called. And that's about as much as you can hope for in a temp. You have no idea how flaky a summer staff can be."

"I've heard that Harlan had some potential as a tennis player."

"Actually, he wasn't bad. Wasn't pro quality, of course, but he had some power serves. Good speed. A natural athlete. But that isn't enough. You want to make it big, you've got to work . . . train. We've got a couple of members on the circuits. They train here every single day, usually start at something like six in the morning. They're talented, but even more, they're dedicated. Harlan? Sure, he had *some* talent, but he lacked drive. Takes a heap of both to make it in the pros."

"Did Harlan have any regular students when he worked here?"

"Strictly fill-in. His schedule changed daily depending on who was on vacation or who called in sick."

"Did he ever get chummy with any of his students?"

"If he did, I never heard about it."

But Decker wasn't so sure that Fine was being up front. "If you didn't get complaints about him, did you ever get *compliments* about him?"

A fire lit in Fine's eye, smoldered quickly. "No."

"None of your ladies ever say to you what a fine teacher he was?"

"Are you implying something?"

"Asking a question, sir."

Fine said, "It was a long time ago, Lieutenant. I don't remember so well."

"I don't suppose you'd be willing to give me names?"

"You're right about that. Anything else?"

"Just one more question. Were any of the people tragically murdered at Estelle's also members of the club?"

Fine turned red. "You know I'm not going to answer that. I think I've been very patient."

Decker smiled. "You've been helpful. Thank you."

Fine said, "Explain something to me, Lieutenant."

"If I can, sure."

"What do you possibly . . . *hope* to accomplish by digging up Harlan aka Hart's past? He's dead. I thought analyzing nutcases was the bailiwick of shrinks, not cops."

Man had a point. Decker's job was cleaning up the crime scene, not doing psychiatric Monday morning quarterbacking. Truth be told, he wasn't sure why he was there . . . trying to make sense out of the incomprehensible.

Decker said, "This was a horrible event. A very big case with lots of publicity, lots of questions and finger-pointing. LAPD has a vested interest in tying up loose ends."

Fine was incredulous. "That's it? You take time away from my business to grill me . . . just to tie up loose ends?"

"Yes, sir, that's exactly right. I'm tying up loose ends. You know *why*, Mr. Fine? Because you leave a loose end hanging around, the sucker has an annoying tendency to unravel."

# 9

*Marge knocked on* Decker's doorjamb, walked through the open door to his office. "A one eighty-seven came in while you were gone—a domestic turned nasty. Wife took the bullet between her eyes. I was in court, so Oliver and Martinez caught the call. If you want, I can go join them."

Decker frowned, took off his reading glasses. "Why didn't someone page me?"

"We did," Marge said. "You didn't answer."

"What?" Decker checked his pager. "What the . . ." He stared at the blank window, flicked his middle finger against the instrument. When nothing happened, he tossed it on his desk. "Remind me to pick up a new one from Bessie. Tell me the details."

"Husband and wife were slugging down shooters when the altercation broke out. A neighbor heard them arguing, didn't think too much of it."

"Frequent occurrence."

"Yeah, except *this* time the husband . . . his name is Meryl Tobias . . . went psycho. Showed up at the neighbor's door—gun in his hand—bawling like a baby. He didn't mean it, he didn't mean it. The neighbor called nine one one. The rest is . . ." She threw up her hands. "His blood alcohol was over point-two-o. Hers wasn't much lower. What a waste!"

Decker glanced at the clock. "It's almost four. We've all been working overtime. Pack it in, Detective."

Marge sat down, dropped her head in her hands. "Honestly, Pete, I'm all right. Just give me an assignment that doesn't involve counting bullets."

Decker smiled. "How's it coming?"

"I wouldn't have made a good accountant."

"Why?" Decker's interest suddenly perked up. "You've got discrepancies?"

"I don't know yet." Marge lifted her head. "Because we're not through. So far we've recovered an awful lot of shells for one shooter . . . even if the shooter was using a double automatic."

"Interesting." Decker started making notes. "Tell me."

Marge was thoughtful. "We picked up lots of strays, Pete. In the walls, in the floor, in the furniture. Which puzzled Scott. He mentioned the same point that you did yesterday. That mass murderers often hunt their victims. Part of the thrill."

"But that wasn't what happened," Decker said.

"No, not according to witnesses. The killer just sprayed the place."

No one spoke. Then Marge said, "You know, it's a miracle that more people didn't die."

"How many bullets did you recover?"

"So far enough to account for around . . . ten, maybe twelve magazines. We've found eight empty cartridges."

"About a hundred and fifty rounds upward. And

Harlan's shooting time was what . . . three to six minutes?"

"It's possible to peel off twelve rounds in a double automatic in six minutes if you're not aiming at anything. But you'd have to work quickly. Go in and blast the place and hope the sucker doesn't jam."

Marge studied Decker, reading his face not as her boss but as her ex-partner.

"You've got something on your mind, big guy?"

"Just speculation." Decker began to doodle. "Doesn't amount to much." Marge pushed hair out of her eyes, stared at him with purpose. "Out with it."

"I've been going over some of the prelim autopsy reports on the victims." Decker paused. "I'm . . . disconcerted by them."

"What in particular?"

"The bullet trajectories. People at the same table being hit with shots at different angles."

"They were probably facing in different directions."

"I took that into consideration. Still, there are things that don't make sense." Decker spread out several police photographs. "For instance, look at this couple. Victims numbers nine and ten—Linda and Ray Garrison."

Marge's eyes swept over the snapshots. She winced.

"The couple was seated . . . here." Decker showed Marge a floor plan of Estelle's. "Right here. At table number fifteen. I figure they must have been among the first to be hit because they died in their seats. Didn't even have enough time to duck under the table."

Marge studied the prints. "They weren't really close to the entrance to the restaurant."

"About a hundred feet away. If the shooting took place as soon as Harlan entered the place, they should have realized what was going on . . . had enough time to duck or run for cover."

"Which may mean that the shooting broke out closer to them."

"Or possibly they both just froze," Decker added. "Anyway, look at the photograph. They died in their chairs, sitting opposite each other, slumped over the table. Both of them . . . riddled with holes. On the surface, no difference. Except Forensics tells us an alternate story. The bullets entered Linda Garrison's back and exited through her chest. Mr. Garrison was *also* shot from back to front."

Decker paused.

"Think about it, Margie. If Harlan was shooting from one position—say he stood in back of Mr. Garrison—the bullets would have entered Garrison's back and exited Garrison's chest. Agreed?"

"Yes. Go on."

"Those same bullets . . . flying in the *same* direction . . . should have entered Mrs. Garrison through her chest and exited her back. Instead, it's just the opposite. What'd Harlan do? Shoot in one position, then move to the opposite side and shoot in the other?"

Marge was silent. "Weird."

"Perhaps a bit suspicious," Decker said.

"Maybe Harlan immediately picked off one of them, walked around and shot a little bit more, then changed his direction and picked the other one off."

"But that contradicts what you just reported . . . that the shooter wasn't picking people off." Decker sat back in his chair. "Taken out of the context of Estelle's . . . even forgetting about all the eyewitness accounts . . . just looking at the forensics . . . it looks deliberate. It warrants further investigation."

"I concur."

"So this is what I want you to do. I want you to go over the list of the victims and find out if any of them belonged to Greenvale Country Club."

Marge stared at him. "Now there's a non sequitur. Why?"

"Because Harlan once worked there."

"So?"

"Well, it's like this. I see lots of stray bullets and unexplained bullet trajectories. Suggestive of maybe more than one shooter—"

"Possibly."

"Possibly. I told you this is speculation."

"Go on," Marge urged.

"I'm just wondering if this isn't a botched hit masked as a mass murder. Looking at the case from that perspective, I'd like to see if maybe we can find a connection between Harlan and a specific victim."

"Harlan Manz committed suicide, Pete. Most hit men don't whack themselves."

"Maybe he didn't whack himself. If it was a botched hit, maybe the second shooter whacked him by accident—"

Marge made a face.

"I know I'm stretching. Ballistics confirms that the bullet in Harlan's head matches the gun." Decker paused. "I'm trying to make sense out of it . . . looking for a catalyst that drove him over the edge. Even if I'm completely off base, it wouldn't hurt us or LAPD to be thorough. Get all the possible connections so we don't get caught with our pants down."

Marge nodded. "No big deal to cross-check the victims against Greenvale's membership list. How do I get hold of the names?"

"Uh . . . that might be a bit of a problem."

Marge stared at him. "You've asked them for a list?"

"Yes."

"And they've refused."

"That sums it up."

"So now what?"

"Harlan's employment at the club was kept secret . . . off the record. Now you could go down and be intimidating . . . threaten you'll leak the information to the press unless they help you out. Or you could be quiet and discreet. There are thirteen victims. You could try to contact their surviving relatives and friends. Casually ask them if the victims belonged to Greenvale."

"And if they did?"

Decker twirled his thumbs. "Ask them if the victims took tennis lessons at the club. If they did, maybe they've met an instructor named Hart Mansfield, known to us as Harlan Manz."

Decker recapped his conversation with Barry Fine. "Or maybe they might have met Harlan/Hart at a party."

"And?"

"I don't know, Marge," Decker said. "Just go out and seek and maybe we'll find something. Or if you're tired, you can call it a day. All of this can wait."

"No, it's all right." She smiled bitterly. "Lucky for you, I canceled my heavy date."

Decker looked at her. "You need some time off, hon?"

Her smiled turned warm. "You care. That's so sweet."

Decker laughed softly. "Why don't you and Scott come over on Sunday for a barbecue."

"Why do you always invite me *and* Scott?"

"Margie, I invite you, he finds out, calls you up. Then you wind up inviting him along out of pity. I'm just saving you the agenting."

He was right. Marge said, "Sure, I'll come. I'm tired and lonely and ain't about to play hard to get. Your family's the only thing that gives me a sense of normalcy. It's really pathetic."

"Honey, my family's the only thing that gives *me* a sense of normalcy."

"Then we're both pathetic."

"I call it dedicated." Decker grinned. "But I'm big on euphemisms."

Pulling the Volare into the driveway, shutting off the motor, Decker sat for a few moments, enjoying the dark and the silence. It was restful. It was peaceful. For a few blissful seconds, he was utterly alone and without obligation and it felt wonderful. He took a deep breath, let his body go slack, allowed his eyes to adjust to the shadows and starlight. He might have sat even longer except he suddenly realized there was a red Camaro parked curbside.

Cindy's car.

His heart started to flutter. His daughter was supposed to be in school three thousand miles away. What did this mean? After he had asked the question, he wasn't sure if he wanted to hear the answer.

He bolted out of the Volare, unlocked his front door. She stood when he crossed the threshold, gave him a timid wave and a "Hi, Daddy."

A beautiful girl in a big, strong way. She was around five ten, built with muscle and bone. Her face was sculpted with high cheekbones; her complexion was overrun with freckles but as smooth as marble. Wide-set, deep-brown eyes, long, flaming red hair, a white, wide smile. She photographed well, had done some small-time modeling to make some pocket change a few years back. But it wasn't for her. Her career goals focused on jobs involving her mind equally with her heart. Cynthia was a girl of extreme generosity and blessed intellect.

She was dressed in jeans and a white T-shirt, some kind of army boot as shoes. She looked troubled. No doubt why she was here instead of in New York.

"My goodness!" Decker gave his daughter a bear hug. "To what do I owe the pleasure? Aren't you supposed to be in school?"

"Something like that."

Before he could question her, Rina came into the room, smiled, and said, "She just showed up on the doorstep. I let her in. I take it that's okay with you."

"More than okay."

"Are you hungry?"

"Starved."

"Go wash up and sit down."

"Baby asleep?"

"For about an hour, *Baruch Hashem*. She is getting

so feisty. But sharp as a whip. Takes after her daddy . . . and her sister."

"In the feistiness or sharpness?"

"Both."

Cindy laughed.

Decker said, "Maybe I'll say hi to the boys first."

"They're not home. Sammy and Jake went with some friends for pizza."

Perversely, Decker felt relieved. One less human element to deal with. Then he felt guilty. They were his sons, for godsakes. But then again, they were doing what they wanted to do. Why should he feel negligent if they were out having a good time? He realized that within the span of a few moments, his emotions had gone the gamut. Which meant he was unstable. Not the best time to deal with his daughter, who obviously had a thing or two on her mind.

After he had washed, Cindy led him to the table. "Sit. Rina made a delicious stew. One of those dishes that gets better the longer you cook it."

"With my hours, she cooks a lot of those," Decker said wryly. "Are you going to join me? Tell me what's going on?"

"It can wait until after dinner."

"That bad?"

"It isn't bad at all."

Rina came back in, set up dinner for her husband. "I told them to be home by eleven. Do you think I gave them too much freedom?"

"No, not at all."

"It's just that Sammy's so excited."

"It's a big event in a boy's life."

"A girl's too," Cindy said. "I remember when I got

my license. The feeling of freedom . . . it was . . . exhilarating."

"Never knew you felt that oppressed." Decker smiled.

"It wasn't that—"

"Cindy, he's teasing you," Rina broke in. "It doesn't deserve an answer." She gently slugged her husband's good shoulder. "I know you're tired and cranky, but be nice."

"I am cranky." Decker ate a few heaping tablespoons. "This is wonderful. Did you eat, Cin?"

Cindy nodded, smiled. But she seemed anxious. Decker felt a protest in his stomach. He wasn't sure if it was his daughter's nervousness or hunger pangs. After two bowls of stew, two helpings of salad, and a couple of cups of decaf, he felt ready to take on his daughter.

Take on.

As if there were an impending battle.

Rina excused herself, went into the kitchen to clean up. Cindy suggested they talk in the living room. Decker took a seat on the suede couch, patted the space next to him. Cindy sat, but her spine was ramrod straight. She was all tics and fidgets. Finally, she said, "I quit the program."

Decker absorbed her words. "You quit the program. Meaning you're no longer in school."

"Yes. I have my master's, I'm tired of all the bullsh . . . of all the academic hurdles. I don't need a Ph.D. It does me no good other than to teach the same material to other Ph.D. candidates."

Decker rolled his tongue inside his cheek. "After six years of tuition and room and board, when you're finally self-supporting with scholarships and fellow-ships, you now decide to *quit*?"

Cindy glared at him. "You *are* kidding, aren't you?"

"Of course I'm kidding." *Sort of.* Decker leaned back. "So . . ."

"So . . ."

Decker said, "I guess I should be a parent. Maybe ask about your plans. Like . . . do you have any?"

"I think I need to get a job."

"Good start." Decker bit his mustache. "Want me to ask around the department . . . see if I can get you on as a part-time consultant?"

"Won't be necessary."

"You've found a job."

"Yes, I have." She closed her eyes, then opened them. "Daddy, I joined the Police Academy. Actually, I signed up a while ago. But you know how it works. There's the exam, then the personal checks, then I had to wait until they started hiring again. Anyway, it's a done deal. I'm starting in three months, right after the first."

Decker stared at his daughter. "This is a joke, right?"

"No joke." She opened her purse, pulled out a few sheets of paper. "Here's a copy of their letter of ac-ceptance. Here's my letter of commitment—"

"So you haven't mailed anything in."

"Yes, I have. See, these are just copies. The origi-nals are at home or with the Academy." She held the paper up for her father to see. "See, right here—"

Angrily, Decker batted them away. He stood up and began to pace. "Cynthia, what on earth could have possibly possessed you—"

"Dad, before our emotions get the better of us, can we be reasonable?"

"No, we *can't* be reasonable! Because you did something *unreasonable*. How could you act so . . . so damn impulsively?"

"It wasn't an impulsive decision. I told you I signed up a while ago."

"So you've thought about this? For a long time?"

"Yes."

"And it never even *dawned* on you to talk this over with me?"

"Of course it *dawned* on me, Daddy. I thought about telling you for quite some time. But I knew you couldn't possibly be objective—"

"Cindy, that's a truckload of bull."

"Can we keep this civil?"

"Are you trying to get even with me for not being around when you were growing up?"

"What are you talking about?"

"You're obviously trying to rile me—"

"Dad, believe it or not, I really want to be a cop, actually a detective." She smiled sweetly. "Just like you."

"Oh, cut the *crap!*"

"Peter!" Rina said.

Decker whirled around, focused on his wife. "Rina, this isn't your affair. Would you kindly leave, please?"

"Last I checked this was my house, too."

"I'm not telling you to leave the house, just the room."

"She can stay," Cindy said. "I don't mind."

"You stay out of this!" Decker directed a pointed index finger at his daughter. "This is between me and my wife."

"No, Daddy, it's between you and me and you're taking it out on her."

"You've got a lot of nerve, talking to me like that—"

"I'll leave," Rina said.

"Good idea," Decker said.

Rina went into the bedroom without slamming the door. Which surprised Cindy. If that had been her, she would have made her displeasure known very loudly. Dad was talking, more like ranting . . . as *usual*.

". . . even *bother* to come and talk to me about it?"

"I knew what you'd say," Cindy retorted.

"So you're a mind reader."

"No, just a dad reader. And I'm right. You're not objective."

"It's not a matter of objectivity," Decker shot back. "Not only would I discourage you from joining, I'd discourage *anyone* from joining."

"Good thing you don't write ad copy for LAPD."

Decker honed in on her. "Cindy, there are *some* cop types. And even most of them don't make good officers. But if you're of a certain ilk and *if* you have a little bit of brainpower and *if* you have untold patience and *if* you can keep your mouth shut and *if* you have a good intuition and *if* you think before you react, then maybe you'll make a good cop. And yes, political correctness notwithstanding, it helps to be big and strong. Which you are not!"

"I'm not a ninety-pound weakling—"

"Any man your size with normal musculature could take you down in a minute."

"So that's where my superior brain will come in."

"You do have a superior brain. You just aren't

choosing to use it. Cynthia, you don't have patience, you don't like orders, you're not detail-oriented, you're way *too* emotional, and you're impulsive . . . like just . . . dropping out of school—"

"I thought about it for a long time—"

"Then you didn't think it through. And I don't care *how* much you work out, you're no match for most men. Someone my size could squeeze you like a tomato."

"We're going around in circles, Daddy."

"You've neither the temperament nor the inclination. You'd make a lousy cop and a lousy cop is a dead cop—"

"Gee, Dad, thanks for the encouragement—"

"Better for you to be furious than for me to accept a flag at your funeral." He turned to her, his eyes burning with anger. "Do yourself a favor. Find a better way to get even with me."

"So you think I'm doing this from some sort of Freudian revenge motive?"

"Frankly, I don't know why you're doing this. This isn't the first time in your life that you've done something outrageous. But it *is* the most dangerous stunt you've ever pulled."

Cindy's eyes filled with water. "You're not being reasonable *or* fair."

"And you, Cynthia Rachel, are *crying*. You think I'm talking tough, just wait. You think your drill sergeant's going to be impressed with your tears? Or worse, how 'bout your perp. 'Better stop shitting around or I'll charge you with ten to fifteen for felonious tear-jerking.'"

Angrily, Cindy dried her eyes. "Touché."

Decker suddenly stopped pacing. He closed his eyes, tried to vent some of the rage. This was his daughter he was talking to. Gently, he put his hands on Cindy's shoulders. Angrily, she wiggled out of his touch. What did he expect?

"Cindy, I'm not trying to win points. But I am being brutally honest. This is one area I know."

Her voice was a whisper. "And I respect that. But with all due respect to your knowledge, I'm twenty-four. I'll make my own decisions. And suffer the consequences if they're bad ones. Dad, I think we've both said enough—"

"No, we haven't said *nearly* enough—"

"Telephone, Peter," Rina said.

Decker whipped his head around, asked her a testy "*Who* is it!"

"Marge."

Decker barked. "Is it an emergency?"

"I don't know," Rina answered quietly. "Would you like me to ask her?"

Decker made fists with his hands, released his fingers. "You stay here, young lady. I'm not through yet."

Decker charged into the bedroom and slammed the door, which made Cindy startle.

As soon as he was gone, she leaped from her chair and started to pace.

"What a supreme jerk! No wonder Mom had an affair." Then Cindy gasped, suddenly remembering that Rina was in the room. She felt herself go hot and cold at the same time. Sheepishly, she looked at her stepmother's face. "Oh, my God! Did you . . . did he . . . did . . ."

"It's all right, Cindy. I knew."

Cindy covered her mouth. "Oh, my God! I can't believe I said that! God, I'm such a *moron*!"

"You're riled. Would you like some coffee? Maybe tea?"

"How about a half dozen Advils."

"How about one?"

"He's right, you know!" Cindy flopped into one of the buckskin chairs and dried her eyes. "I've got an incredibly big mouth. Things just . . . slip out!"

Rina said nothing.

Cindy looked at Rina. "So he told you?"

Rina nodded.

"He must feel real close to you."

Rina stifled a smile. "Guess so."

"It's not as idiotic as it sounds. Dad never ever talked about it. And it didn't come up in any of the divorce proceedings. Even during their worst arguments, Dad never brought it up or threw it in Mom's face. There were times I actually wondered if he even knew. But then I figured how could he *not* know. Mom wasn't exactly subtle . . . all those hang-ups every time I picked up the phone."

Rina nodded.

"It wasn't all Mom's fault, you know. He was never home. Even when he was home, he wasn't home. He was a decent father. Did the right things. Showed up at all the school events and conferences. But there was this distance. He was dreadfully unhappy. So was Mom. They had to get married, you know. Because of me."

"They both love you very much."

"I know that. They dragged it out as long as they

could. Though I never asked them to do that. They're so different. You know how they met?"

Rina nodded. "Your dad arrested your mother."

"Some stupid antiwar rally. The pregnancy meant Mom had to drop out of college. At twenty, she was stuck at home with a whining baby and no help at all, while all her friends were out partying. I don't know why she didn't get an abortion."

The room was quiet.

"Actually, I do know why. Dad wouldn't have let her. Anyway, I know she was very resentful. To this day, she still talks about her lost youth."

"Your mom and Alan have made a nice life for themselves. I think you're feeling worse about it than either of your parents."

"I suppose." She sighed. "Dad seems happy now . . . happi*er.*"

Rina smiled. "Yes, your father isn't exactly a jolly fellow."

Cindy smiled.

"You comported yourself very well," Rina said.

"Yeah, felons should be a snap in comparison." She paused. "You heard us then? We were screaming that loud?"

"It's a small house."

"God, I have a headache."

"I'll get you the Advil."

"Thanks."

Rina left, came back a few moments later. "Did you tell your mother yet?"

"No. Believe it or not, Dad's the lesser of the two evils. Mom will not only go hysterical—just like

Dad—but she'll start blaming Dad. I hate it when she does that. Those two are incredible. They really hate each other."

"I'm sure they don't."

"Oh, I'm sure they do."

Rina said, "What made you decide to join the Academy?"

"Oh, my goodness, someone really wants to hear *my* side of the equation."

Rina nodded encouragement.

Cindy cleared her throat. "I thought I wanted to study criminal behavior. I found that what I really wanted to do was solve crimes. Analyzing the deviant mind is useful, but it's too academic. It doesn't make neighborhoods safer places to live. It doesn't give victims a sense of justice. It doesn't do anything to enhance the quality of life. Criminal Sciences is about publishing papers, not about community service. And that's what I want to do. Use the knowledge I've learned and *apply* it. To *help* people. Pretty corny. But as I speak, it is the truth."

"I think that's wonderful."

"In theory, yes. Unfortunately, Dad has a point. I am impulsive, I am emotional, and I don't take orders well."

She leaned forward.

"But I'm also *very* adaptable. Had to be to get along with my parents. I can learn, Rina. Because I really want to do this. I'll make it. I'd like his help and blessing. But if not, I'll make it anyway. If he can't deal with it, too bad."

She sat back.

"I love my father, but there are times he is just impossible. So domineering! So *bossy*! How do you deal with him?"

"He's a good man."

"I didn't say he wasn't. I just said he was a control freak. You know, I'm not excusing Mom. But my dad is just . . . such an imposing man. I guess she felt just so . . . swallowed up. I don't know how you put up with him."

Rina shrugged. "I'm not much of a fighter."

"I wish I were like that. I just refuse to be stepped on."

"I didn't say I get stepped on."

Cindy blushed. "I'm sorry. I didn't mean . . . God, I've got a big mouth. I guess I'm more like Mom than I'd like to believe."

"I do express myself, Cindy. I'll stick up for what's important. Which I've learned isn't too much. This baby boomer generation on down . . . all of us . . . we've become so . . . confrontive. Stand up for yourself! Speak your mind! Tell it like it is! All this righteous anger . . . I find it very loud."

"Better that than being walked on."

"No one wants to be a *shmatta* . . . a dishrag. But sometimes it's a good idea to keep your mouth shut. Think if it's worth the effort. And yes, I freely admit to being occasionally two-faced. There have been times when I had agreed with your dad to do things his way, then turned around and did it the way *I* wanted. Most of the time, he forgot what he had been so insistent on. And the couple of times he was cogent enough to call me on it, I played *dumb*. I'm sure some psychologist would call me sneaky or tell me I have low self-esteem. Or tell me I was paralyzed by my domineering mother and an unapproachable father or something or other. *I* call it being practical. Because in the end, I get what I want and he saves face."

"I don't think Gloria Steinem would approve of your methods."

"Oh, forget about Gloria Steinem! She never nursed a husband through cancer, only to watch him die. She never labored in childbirth. She was never a widow with two small children. She's never been married to a police lieutenant. She never had a hysterectomy at thirty. And she's *not* an Orthodox Jew. So she has no concept of *shalom bais*—peace in the house. Which, in my humble opinion, is to her detriment!"

Cindy looked at her. "You're tough."

"Tough enough to handle your dad." Rina sat down next to Cindy. "And so are you." She gave her a kiss on the cheek. "You'll work this out. You'll be okay."

"If I ever learn to keep my mouth shut."

"Cindy, youth is impulsive, thank God. Like you said, it was the reason you were conceived. It's what made me run off and get married at seventeen, then go have a baby a year later, then have yet another before my first son was out of diapers. It's what made me enter into a heartbreaking relationship after my husband died, knowing it was doomed from the start. And it's what made me ignore raised eyebrows in my community when I started dating your father. Within days of meeting him, I was head over heels in love. Impulsive yes. But it worked out."

Cindy said. "Yes, I *am* impulsive. But this wasn't an *impulsive* decision. It's really what I want."

"How could you know?" Decker retorted. "You haven't the slightest notion what it is to be a cop."

Both women turned around as if he had intruded in their conversation. Fine with him! Let Rina handle it! Tempted to escape and go burn the Porsche out at 120. Instead, he sat back down on the couch, rubbed his temples.

"How about this? We talk this over calmly. I tell you what being a cop is all about. You ask me questions. If you're still gung-ho . . . after I get done with you . . . then you can go ahead and join."

"What happened to *you* in ten minutes?" Cindy asked.

Rina said, "He overheard me talking about how much I loved him and it made him feel guilty for his outbursts."

Decker grumped, "Got it all figured out."

"True or false."

Decker ignored her, turned to Cindy. "Well?"

Cindy said, "Daddy, nothing would give me greater pleasure than to talk to you about my decision. I'd love to hear about your experiences and your insights. But I'm in the Academy regardless."

"That's being very pigheaded."

Rina interjected, "Peter—"

"She's acting like a mule."

"There's no reason to name-call—"

"Why is she afraid of hearing the truth?" Decker said.

Cindy said, "Listen, guys, I'm really tired. I want to go home."

"You tell your mom about this?"

Cindy sighed.

"You haven't *told* her?" Decker began to pace. "Great. I don't have enough garbage in my life dealing with friggin' mass murderers—"

"Dad, I'm really sorry about that. It must be terrible. And I certainly don't mean to add to your stress—"

"But you'll do it anyway."

No one spoke. Cindy sighed. "I'm going. We'll talk later. When everyone's calmer." She smiled at her father. "Good night."

Abruptly, Decker stopped walking, plunked himself down in a chair, and stared out the window, his eyes a thousand miles away.

"She said good night, Peter."

"Good night, good night," he muttered.

"Give her a hug, for godsakes."

Cindy waited a beat. When Decker didn't move, Rina said, "Peter, did you hear—"

"Yes, I heard you."

Cindy felt her eyes start to moisten, but quickly she held back the tears. "That's okay, Rina. Everyone needs their space. Even parents."

Again, she waited a moment. When Decker didn't move, she bade Rina good night and left quietly. Soon the car's engine faded to nothingness. Rina broke the silence.

"You should have given her a hug, Peter," Rina rebuked him. "Your intransigence was nasty. God forbid, suppose she has an accident or something. How would you feel?"

"Horrible. I'd never forgive myself."

"So how could you let her leave like that!"

He turned to her, his own eyes moist. "Because . . . I was afraid if I hugged her, I would have never let her go."

# ❧ 10

*The temperature in* the office was arctic. Why did the city feel it necessary to keep the station house in a deep freeze? Or maybe it was just Decker's mood. Because things weren't going well. He sat at his desk, looking out at a wall of eyes. His Homicide team arcing around him. Protective. Like a moat. His brain pounded. With any luck, ibuprofen would work its magic. He nodded for Oliver to begin.

Scott scanned his notes, hand raking through his black hair. "Loo, we've gone through Estelle's room to room, wall to wall, floor to floor, ceiling to ceiling. Neither Dunn nor I could find enough empty magazines at the scene to account for all the bullets and casings."

Decker's eyes glanced at the newspaper on his desk. A couple of days had passed, but Estelle's was still front-page news. He spoke quietly. "Would it help if you looked again?"

"We were very thorough." Marge smoothed out the leg of her beige pants. She wore lightweight fabrics today—white cotton shirt, viscose pants. But if the weather continued its cooling trend, it would be time for the wools. "I'll show you our grid maps if you want. Right now it doesn't look like much . . . a mass of dots."

"We marked every place where we extracted a bullet or found an empty casing," Oliver explained.

Bert Martinez twirled the ends of his bushy mustache, his stocky frame bowing the seat of the folding chair. "Whole damn case is starting to smell fishy. Anyone show the Loo Harlan's autopsy report?"

Decker sat up. "When did that come in?"

"You were in a meeting with the mayor, city council, and Strapp," Marge said. "We tried paging you . . ."

Decker grimaced. He'd forgotten to pick up a new pager.

"How'd that go?" Oliver was concerned. "Are our asses on the line?"

"Why should our asses be on the line?" Martinez asked. "We've got the perp . . . of sorts."

"Lawsuits, right?" Oliver said. "Police should have showed up sooner, right? If they had, more lives would have been saved, right? What was time of arrival on that one? Something like two minutes?"

"First cruiser arrived in two-twenty-eight," Webster said.

Oliver said. "Am I right, Deck?"

"Close."

"No matter what happens, we'll get blamed. Earthquake could drop the city into the center of the earth, it would be our fault."

"For the time being, the Detective division isn't a point of concern." Decker paused. "But if this turns out to be . . . how should I say this? If this is something more than a straightforward mass murder, the focus will shift to us. Who has that autopsy report?"

"That would be me." Webster handed the folder to Decker, his blue eyes focused, alert. Today, Tom was dressed in a black suit, sunglasses dangling from his jacket pocket. Looked more FBI than LAPD with his permapressed Anglo good looks. Suave manner. But Decker didn't hold it against him. Webster was a damn good cop.

Decker thumbed through the pages, eyes working like strobes. "What should I be looking for?"

Webster drawled, "The bullet that killed Harlan Manz. It was fired at a range consistent with a distance of around two to two and a half feet—"

"*What!*" Decker raced through the report. "Where?"

"Page eleven or twelve. I marked it with a pencil."

Decker fast-forwarded to the paragraph. Read it once, then read it again. He sat back in his chair, ran a hand down his face.

Martinez said, "I called up the morgue . . . asked if they were sure about that distance."

"And?"

"They were sure. Said that if the gun had been fired at a closer range, more damage would have been done to the brain."

Webster said, "Bigger entry and exit holes, more tearing and ripping, more extensive powder burns on the hands and temple."

"So when Harlan fired, he looked something like this?" Oliver made a gun with his fingers, extended his arm from his shoulder, then flexed his wrist so that his fingers were pointing back to his temple. "What's this, guys? About three feet?"

"Anyone have a measuring tape?" Marge asked.

Decker pulled one from his desk, gave it to Marge.

Marge measured. "Thirty-seven inches. Bend your elbow a little bit, Scotty."

Oliver complied, his elbow making a hundred-and-fifty-degree angle. "Now I'm pointing over my head."

"So lower your arm." Martinez got up, positioned Oliver as if he were a Gumby. "There. About like this. That looks like two and a half feet."

Marge measured. "Thirty-one inches to be exact."

Webster said, "Now point to your head."

Oliver did so, maintained the pose. They stared at him.

Marge said, "Might be me, but I think he looks awkward."

Martinez said, "He looks ridiculous. You want to pop yourself, you put the gun to your temple. You don't hold it two feet away."

Marge said, "You know, I could understand someone holding the gun away from his head if he had doubts or wasn't used to a firearm. Almost like an avoidance thing."

"Maybe at a little distance," Martinez said. "But not in the position Scotty's in. Unless you like contorting."

"Maybe he had short arms," Marge suggested.

"Not that short," Martinez answered.

"Could it have been a misfire?" Oliver asked.

Martinez made a face. "You mean he was aiming for someone and caught himself in the *head*?"

"No. I mean the gun just accidentally went off."

"Catching him square in the temple?" Marge was dubious.

"Excuses, excuses." Webster shook his head. "Why aren't we saying what we're all thinkin'?"

"Two shooters," Oliver said.

"Just what you said yesterday, Loo," Marge said.

Oliver said, "You did?"

Decker replied, "I was looking over some of the victims' autopsy reports. Some of the bullet trajectories were inconsistent with a one-killer theory."

"And you didn't like the number of bullets we recovered."

"A lot for one shooter," Webster said. "Even for someone using a double automatic. What did we recover? Something like two hundred bullets?"

Martinez said, "Two killers means Estelle's was planned."

Oliver said, "What do you mean by planned, Bert?"

"Harlan went into Estelle's with the intention of killing someone specific. He and his cohort masked it by popping others. Like putting a bomb in an airplane to collect insurance."

"A hit gone bad," Marge said. "If so, next step is to figure out who the intended target was."

Webster said, "So y'all take a look at the victims."

Decker said, "We need to look at the victims who might have crossed paths with Harlan in other capacities."

Marge reached into her oversized purse and pulled out a sheet of paper. "Which brings us up to date with my current assignment. Discovering which victims—if any—belonged to Greenvale Country Club."

"What's this?" Webster asked.

Decker filled them in on Harlan's job at the country

club, on his conversation with Barry Fine, and on yesterday's brainstorming with Marge. "Harlan Manz worked at Greenvale about two years ago. You know how snobs can be. Treating the hired help as nonentities. I was trying to determine if Harlan had a long-standing grudge against one of the restaurant's victims."

Oliver said, "Deck, if a grudge from Greenvale was the motive behind Estelle's shooting, why didn't Harlan shoot up the club?"

"Maybe security was too tight. Look, I don't know any more than you do. But something's hinky here."

Oliver asked, "So you're thinking that one of Estelle's victims offended Harlan at the club *and* at the restaurant. And that's why he went batshit?"

Decker said, "Just trying to find a connection."

Marge asked, "Maybe you'd like to hear if there *are* any connections?"

Decker laughed. "We're going on with these flights of fancy and we don't even have facts. What do you have?"

Marge settled herself. "Okay. Table number twenty-two: People there were from Ashman/Reynard. A Realtor named Wendy Culligan was pitching to a bunch of Japanese businessmen. Some of the businessmen were murdered, but she survived . . . which made my job of asking questions a lot easier. The firm is a corporate member of Greenvale. Has been for the fifteen years since the club opened."

"Is she a member?" Oliver asked.

"Through her business. Wendy's been at the club maybe six times . . . goes there for power lunches.

Theoretically, she could have crossed paths with Harlan."

Oliver said, "But she's still alive, Margie. She obviously wasn't the target of a hit."

Webster said, "Or maybe Harlan missed."

"So what does Greenvale have to do with a bunch of Japanese businessmen who probably never set foot inside its doors?" Martinez asked.

Marge shrugged. "Well, they were making deals with Ashman/Reynard, Bert. Maybe Harlan was resentful of some of the realtors. So maybe he was trying to screw up the agency or block the deal."

Decker wrote as he spoke. "What else do we have?"

Marge said, "Then we have Walter Skinner, the actor. He was also a member of Greenvale."

Martinez said, "Now that was a real shame. I used to love him in *High Mountain*. Anybody remember that show?"

"Yo," Oliver said. "Saturday morning, ten o'clock."

"You coulda set your watch by me, I was that loyal a viewer," Martinez said. "Remember the stampedes? Each episode had at least one stampede. All that sand and dirt and stomping hooves. Scared the shit outta me when I was a little boy."

"Y'all see *The Lion King*?" Webster asked. "Took my son to see it. They had a cartoon stampede. Scared the shit outta him. Had nightmares for weeks."

Oliver said, "Yeah, *High Mountain* always had a stampede or a twister. Couple times it was both."

"Yeah, I remember that show!" Martinez said.

"The one where the wagon train stopped in Laredo, Texas," Decker added.

"That's the one!" Oliver said, bringing his hands to a clap. "God, that brings back memories. Man, wind was whooshing all over the place. And there was Walter—aka Cattle Foreman Kirk Brown—riding high in the saddle, barking orders, doing a jig with his horse, trying to bring in all those raging dogies while a tornado was blowing everything to shit."

Marge said, "Maybe we could get back to the business at hand?"

The men stared miserably at her. Decker held back a smile. "So Walter was also a member of Greenvale?"

"Yes. A founding member," Marge said. "Both he and his companion were murdered in their seats." She looked at Decker. "Their table was right next to the Garrisons'."

"Ah, interesting." Decker took notes. "I haven't gone over their entrance and exit wounds. Be interesting to see if it matches the patterns of the Garrisons."

"Skinner and his companion . . ." Webster paused. "As opposed to a wife. By any chance, is there a wife?"

Marge said. "Yes, there is. Adelaide Skinner. I haven't talked to her yet."

The room went quiet.

Oliver grinned. "So the old goat was stepping out on her."

"It doesn't mean he deserved to die," Marge said.

"Certainly *I* don't think so. But his wife may have had other ideas."

"So she hired someone to whack him by shooting up a restaurant?" Webster made a face. "How old is she anyway?"

"Seventy-seven," Marge answered.

"Y'all picture a little seventy-seven-year-old lady telling someone to massacre thirteen innocent people just to get to her old man?"

"Maybe she hired out without knowing what the killers were going to do," Oliver said.

Martinez said, "So they decided to execute the hit by attacking an entire restaurant? Pretty clumsy."

"Worked in the past for the Mafia," Oliver said.

Martinez added, "Then, for a topper, one of them decides to whack the other?"

"More money for himself," Oliver said. "Plus someone to pin the blame on."

Webster said, "Is Walter's wife a member of Greenvale?"

"Yes, of course," Marge said.

"Let's slow it down," Decker said. "We're getting wild with our speculations. Any other connection, Marge?"

"Linda and Ray Garrison. From the people I've talked to, it's clear that the couple was worth beaucoup bucks."

"So who inherits the estate?"

"Don't know for sure, but they have two adult children, a son and a daughter. David Garrison is twenty-six. And guess what? He has a record. Drug arrests. First time was probation. Second time, he served two years. He's now out on parole. I've got a call in to his officer."

"Good going, Dunn," Webster said.

"Daughter Jeanine is completely different. Twenty-eight. A patron of the arts and theater and ballet. Very big in society events . . . raising money for charities. Now get this, guys! She specifically raises charity money with *tennis* matches."

Oliver said, "Didn't you say that Harlan taught tennis at Greenvale?"

"Yes, I did." Decker's intercom rang. He excused himself, took the call. A rape. Everyone from Sex Crimes was busy in the field. Did he want to send down someone from CAPs? Decker turned to Marge. The woman had been a top-notch Sex Crimes detective for six years. He had almost felt guilty when he pulled her away from the detail to follow him into Homicide. After the call was completed, he looked at Marge. "I need someone with experience, Detective Dunn."

Marge checked her watch. "Sure, I can catch it."

"Thanks."

"Are we done here?"

"For the most part," Decker answered. "Just let me get a couple of assignments out. Bert, you remember Walter Skinner as Walter Skinner the actor. Why don't you go out to his house and feel out the wife?"

"Feel her up?" Oliver said. "Feel *who* up?"

"*Out*," Decker said. "Feel her *out*. What are you doing now, Scotty?"

"I got a court case in a half hour. Meryl Tobias."

Martinez groaned. "Mr. 'I'm sorry, I'm sorry.' What a stupid shit!"

"At least he was sorry," Marge said.

"Don't help Mrs. Tobias."

Decker said, "What's the DA going for?"

"Man one."

"Cut-and-dried case?"

"Should be."

"So when you're finished, go over to Ashman/ Reynard. Find out what business they were conducting at Estelle's. While you're there, check out the other agents, see if any of them had had prior contact with Harlan." He turned to Webster. "You're the youngest of the bunch, Tommy. You take on David Garrison."

Oliver grinned. "Two young, good-looking white boys mentally duking it out."

Marge said, "How do you know David Garrison's good-looking?"

"I don't know that he is," Oliver said. "He just *sounds* good-looking. Aristocratic. Like he should have a 'the third' after his name."

Webster said, "What about Jeanine Garrison, Loo?"

"You want to take her, Marge?"

"You mean after I catch the rape call?"

"That's right. I'm going senile." Decker glanced at the clock. "No, catch the call, then meet up with Scotty at Ashman/Reynard. I've got an open lunch hour. I'll take Jeanine myself."

# ✤ 11

*The house was* small, disappointingly so. Martinez hadn't been expecting anything ritzy, but at least "Cattle Foreman Kirk Brown" should have been living in something *western*. A ranch house set on acres replete with tumbleweeds and cacti. Maybe a couple of horse stables. Instead, Walter Skinner, the man, had lived out his last years in a three-bedroom one-story bungalow in an anonymous residential block in the heart of the Valley. A simple house plopped onto a patch of recently fertilized lawn. A lifetime of nostalgia washed away by the stench of manure.

Badge in hand, Martinez trod up a red-painted cement walkway, hopped the two steps up to the porch. Knocked on the door, and when no one answered, he knocked again. This time he heard someone telling him just a minute. An elderly voice—not feeble, just old. A minute later, she opened the door a crack. Just enough room for Martinez to show her his ID. Then the door opened all the way.

She must have been under five feet, hunched over, hands resting on a cane. Her face was as round as the moon, lined but not overly wrinkled. Her cheeks had a dash of blush, her lips were painted pink. Her eyes were clear blue; her hair, thick and silver, was tied neatly into a bun. She wore a red turtleneck top over black pants, mules on her feet. Her hands were spotted, the fingers bony and bent. Though she had lived almost eight decades, she still struck a nice pose—all seventy-seven years and about eighty pounds of her.

One palm remained on the knob of her cane, the other extended itself to Martinez. "Adelaide Skinner. Pleased to meet you, Detective."

Martinez took the birdlike hand. "Likewise. Thank you for letting me in."

"I was afraid you'd arrest me if I didn't." A brief smile. "Come in, come in before you catch a chill."

Martinez stepped inside. Adelaide closed the door. "Is this a condolence call from the police? Someone named Strapp already did that."

"My captain."

"A nice man. Sharp. A good politician."

Martinez went inside the house. "Actually, I came to talk to you, Mrs. Skinner."

"Me?"

"If you wouldn't mind."

"No, I don't mind."

She stood for a moment, caught her breath. "Fine. We'll talk. First let me give you a tour. Which shouldn't take very long. Because it's a small house. My idea, not his. If it had been up to Walter, we would have been living on a grand-scale *Ponderosa*."

Martinez smiled to himself. Her admission made him feel better.

"Not that Walter was the ranch type." She walked in tiny steps, directing him toward the left. "But when you're Kirk Brown you have an image to keep up."

She stopped, regarded Martinez.

"Or maybe you're too young to remember—"

"Oh no, ma'am. I grew up on *High Mountain*."

She smiled. "Anyway, this . . . was Walter's living room. It shows his personality, I think."

Martinez looked around, his heart beating like a little boy's. The personification of his western hero, the room's couches and chairs all done in brown suede and horn. The tables were fashioned from old driftwood. A handmade Navajo rug sat on a floor of knotty pine. A tremendous stone fireplace. And the walls. Loaded with pictures of Skinner as Cattle Foreman Kirk Brown, dressed in western gear, posing with past cowboy luminaries. The daytime ropers— Hopalong Cassidy, Roy Rogers, the Lone Ranger, Wild Bill Hickock, and Sky King. Then there were pictures of Skinner and the *nighttime* biggies, on the set of *Wagon Train*, *Death Valley Days*, and *Paladin*. Kirk with Bat Masterson and Sugarfoot and Mr. Favor. And *Gunsmoke*. Lots of pictures of Skinner on *that* set. With Matt Dillon and Chester and with the beautiful and alluring Miss Kitty. As a boy, Martinez dreamed of Kitty's boobs, dreamed about them for many years. Then the series got old and so did Amanda Blake. . . .

The snapshots weren't the only things on the walls. Sharing the space was a display of stuffed and mounted sports fish—a huge mother salmon, barracudas baring teeth, swordfish and marlins flashing weapons on their snouts. The bookshelves had been turned into showcases for more snapshots, also for

Skinner's fishing awards and trophies. Adelaide saw Martinez eyeing the shiny gold cups. She picked one up, hefted it in her hand.

"Yeah, Walt was quite the Ishmael in his prime. When he got too old to fish for barracudas, he started netting in the Barbies."

She raised a gray eyebrow.

"Which are practically the same thing as barracudas. I'm sure if it was up to Walt, he would have gladly pegged some of his tarts to the wall. 'Cause that's what he was doing. Sports fishing of a different type. Much cheaper, I'll say that much."

"Cheaper?" Martinez asked.

"I see you never chartered a fishing boat."

"No, ma'am."

"Money for the boat, money for the captain, money for the trip, money for the supplies, money for this, money for that. The tarts are bargain-basement prices in comparison."

A deep sigh.

"You had enough, Detective? I know I have."

"Anything you want, ma'am."

"I'll show you the back bedrooms if you want. But it's a bit of a walk for me and there isn't much to see."

"You don't have to bother—"

"Just my bedroom, Walter's bedroom, a spare room for our daughter and son-in-law or whichever grandchild happens to be in town. There're three of them." Her face lit up. "And of course, the newest. The first great-grandchild. A girl. Ashley."

"That's wonderful."

"Oh, she is such a love." Her face turned wistful, a tear rolled down her cheek. "Walter adored her. He was a doting grandfather. A good father, too. And a decent husband. I think . . ."

She looked up at the ceiling.

"I think he just didn't want to be an old man. Come, I'll show you my living room."

They did an about-face, headed to the right. Once the space might have been used as a dining room. Now it functioned as separate entertaining quarters. *Her* quarters. Chintz wallpaper decorated with old-fashioned oil landscapes. Velvet couches with lace throws and satin pillows. Overstuffed chairs. Little tea tables covered with doilies. Pleated lampshades rimmed with fringes, silver picture frames, knickknacks and bowls of potpourri permeated with cinnamon. Probably drowned out the stink of the fertilizer.

"Mind if we talk in here?" Adelaide lowered herself into a chair. "I'd prefer it."

"Not at all." Martinez paused, wondering where to sit.

"Just sit on the couch." Adelaide pointed a twig-like finger in its direction. "It's quite sturdy. Actually it's lasted through twenty years of grandchildren jumping on it, so let's amend that to *very* sturdy."

Martinez sank into down cushions. Had to right himself quickly to sit up. "Real soft."

"No support whatsoever. What the kids didn't accomplish, gravity finished off. How rude of me. Can I get you some tea?"

She took a bell from one of the doilied tables, rang it hard and furiously. A minute later, a thin young woman came into the room. She was wearing a white uniform and a nurse's cap. Probably an LVN. "Yes, Mrs. Skinner?"

"Two teas, Nicky. And bring in the cookies, too. The good ones. The butter cookies."

Nicky turned, disappeared.

Adelaide grinned. "Isn't this fun? Just like *Arsenic and Old Lace*."

Martinez smiled nervously. "Not *too* much like it, I hope."

Adelaide was puzzled, then she laughed. "No, no, no. That would be carrying things a little too far."

The room fell silent.

Martinez said, "Truly, I am sorry for your loss."

"So am I." Again, her eyes moistened. "I loved Walter. My bitterness is a hollow shell. If I remember the bad times, maybe I won't miss the good so much." Her lip trembled. "Faults and all, I did love him."

Martinez cleared his throat. "The monster who did this to your husband . . . to all the victims—"

"Harlan Manz." Adelaide's face went hard. "Who is this . . . this . . ."

"That's what we're trying to figure out." Martinez took out a photograph. "I know this might be hard for you. But can you look at a snapshot of him for me?"

"Why?"

"I'd like you to tell me if he looks familiar."

Martinez held out the picture. Slowly, she secured it, brought it into her line of vision.

"Should he look familiar to me?" She looked up, saw her nurse carrying a tray of goodies. "Ah, Nicky's back. What kind of tea did we make, love?"

"Chamomile. It's still brewing in the pot. And it's very *hot*. Don't burn your lip like you did last time."

"Scold, scold, scold." She frowned. "Where are the butter cookies?"

"They're not on your diet. I brought tea biscuits—"

"Oh, bosh!" She picked up a hard biscuit, nibbled it. "These taste like cardboard. I can't serve these."

"I'm not hungry anyway," Martinez said. "Tea's just fine."

"It's hot," Nicky reiterated as she poured. "She likes it very hot."

"Only way to drink tea," Adelaide insisted.

Martinez cooled his heels as he drank hot tea. They made genteel chitchat—about the tea, about the biscuits, about butter cookies, and the weather. Then he reopened the conversation. "So, what do you think of the snapshot? Could you have seen Harlan Manz before?"

Adelaide picked up the photograph again. "He might look *slightly* familiar. Now I know I'm old. But I'm not brain-dead yet. I don't think I ever met anyone named Harlan Manz."

"How about Hart Mansfield?"

The old woman furrowed her brow. "Now, why does *that* name sound familiar?"

"He taught tennis at Greenvale Country Club."

A slow smile formed on her lips. "Detective, do I look like a tennis player?"

Martinez felt his face go hot. "He also tended bar there. For parties and charity occasions."

Adelaide continued to think, then she turned pale. "Yes . . . yes, he did. Oh my! Oh my, oh my—"

"What, Mrs. Skinner?"

She brought her hand to her chest. "Oh my goodness!"

Martinez stood up. "Are you okay, ma'am?"

"Oh yes . . . I'm okay . . . this is the bartender Walter had words with at the Hausner party."

Martinez felt his heart hammer. He picked up his notebook, scribbled furiously. "Words? What kind of words?"

"Nothing earth-shattering. Just that I remember him . . . because I talked to him . . . for a minute or so after Walter lost his temper."

"What happened?"

"Oh, the usual. The line at the bar was moving too slowly. Walter was in a bad mood and made a fuss. Something like 'Stop making time with the girls and gimme my Scotch!'"

She looked down.

"Walter called the boy a nitwit. He was half drunk and half joking. But he said it in a loud voice, and I think it embarrassed the poor child—"

She stopped herself, her face angry, her hands shaking, her eyes far away.

"Anyway, I told this . . . this whoever he is . . . that Walter was just a little grumpy. He seemed to take my explanation with equanimity and went about his business. I went about mine."

She focused her attention back to Martinez. "You couldn't possibly think that . . . he *remembered*!"

Martinez played with his mustache. "It doesn't seem real important. Did they ever have any other dealings with each other?"

"Not that I know of." She thought a moment. "But I do know that . . ." She closed her eyes, then opened them. "That Walter went to the club with other women at times."

"I see."

"So it's possible that Walter could have had other runins with this . . . this . . . this . . ."

"Did Walter ever mention Harlan/Hart again to you?"

"No, he didn't. Still, it's eerie. A random crime that cuts off Walter's life. And here I live, having met my husband's murderer face-to-face."

Martinez nodded.

Adelaide said, "You don't think it's random, do you?"

"We're investigating all aspects of the case—"

"A two-year-old insult? It doesn't seem like a decent reason for murder!"

"No, it doesn't."

"Still . . ." She picked up her teacup, sipped quietly. "You never know what motivates people to do such vile deeds."

"You're saying that this whole bloody mess was a conspiracy?"

Marge looked out the window. She was on the tenth floor of a fifteen-story building, had a view of other tall buildings and a peek at the distant mountains. Ashman/Reynard was located in an industrial park in Woodland Hills, one of the older parks in the Valley, old in these parts defined as built twenty years ago. Her eyes returned to Brenda Miller, executive veep. She was dressed in a red power suit, wore black stockings and pumps that could have been lethal weapons. A petite woman in her thirties with short dark hair, active brown eyes, and good skin.

Oliver said, "No, we're not saying that. We were just wondering if you or anyone else at Ashman/Reynard had ever had dealings with Harlan Manz prior to this incident?"

"Dealings where? At Estelle's?"

"Anywhere," Marge said.

"What kind of dealings? Or are you really asking me if I remember Harlan? The answer is yes, I remember him. Cocky kid. He worked the bar there."

"At Estelle's?" Oliver said, writing as he spoke.

"Yeah, at Estelle's." Brenda frowned, rested her elbows on her desk. "Isn't that what we're talking about?"

"He also tended bar for Greenvale Country Club. Your company's a corporate member at Greenvale," Marge said.

"I know that." Brenda was irritated.

"Do you remember Harlan Manz from Greenvale?" Marge asked. "He might have been using the name Hart Mansfield."

Brenda took a breath, then let it out slowly. "I knew him . . . took a couple of tennis lessons from him."

Marge tried to hide her surprise. This might prove to be more productive than she had originally thought. She slowed it down. "Tell me about Harlan."

"What's to tell?" She laughed but it lacked mirth. "Good ole Hart. Mr. Charmer. He was there for maybe . . . one summer. Then, poof, he was gone. Like most of Greenvale's employees. All of them . . . pretty people without brains."

She became quiet.

"About . . . oh, I don't know . . . a year later, I took some clients out to Estelle's. And there was Harlan tending bar. I gave him a hug." She shuddered involuntarily. "Gives me the creeps thinking about it. Anyway, I saw him at Estelle's maybe half a dozen times. Then he was gone. You know these hangers-on. They're always moving . . . moving."

"Ever have any words with him?" Oliver asked.

Brenda thought a moment. "Not that I can remember."

"So you don't recall ever offending him?"

"I offend lots of people. Him, specifically?" She shrugged.

"Did he ever ask you for a handout?" Oliver said. "Could be you refused?"

She hesitated. "You know, I do remember him talking about needing temporary work . . . until he got his *big* break." She smiled sarcastically. "I told him to come by the office. We can always use temp workers. He never took me up on it. I knew he wouldn't. Must have made that offer to twenty people and not one of them has ever been sincere."

Brenda got up, walked over to the window, her gaze focused outward.

"All of them. Male and female bimbos. Always with the big break just around the corner. Meanwhile, they ain't getting any smarter. But they are getting older. New studs and starlets come in. See it all the time. Competition's fierce out there."

The room was quiet.

Marge said, "So you took tennis lessons from him."

"A couple of times. Hart was strictly fill-in.

Good player, though. Strong legs. Who would have thought . . ."

Marge said, "Did he ever try to pick you up?"

"Me?" She shook her head. "No. As I recall, he went in for the older set—fifty-plus with big bucks. And he also went for the cuties. I don't fit into either category. Besides, I'm way too threatening for him. Too independent and successful."

Marge said, "Did he ever try to pick up Wendy Culligan?"

"I don't know. Ask Wendy."

"I did," Marge said. "She said no. But I don't know if I believe her. I didn't press her because she's still in bad shape. No sense adding insult to injury. But I'm asking you, Ms. Miller. Did Harlan ever try to pick up Wendy Culligan?"

Oliver looked at Dunn questioningly. First he had heard about a connection between Wendy and Harlan. When Marge gave him a quick wink, he realized she was winging it.

Brenda appeared uncomfortable. "If Wendy said no, it's no."

Marge hesitated. "Are *you* being straight with me, Ms. Miller?"

Brenda turned to Marge, her face tense and hard. "Listen, Detective. The poor kid has gone through major trauma . . . lost four pounds in three days. She doesn't eat, can't sleep or work. I've begged her to see a specialist. The company would pay for it. Wendy's a real asset here, one of our top sellers. But she refuses. Right now, the woman can barely function. Let's not make things worse for her."

"That's why I'm asking you these questions and not her."

Oliver said, "If there's a connection, it's going to come out. Why don't you tell us the story before some other jerk gets wind of it and leaks it to the tabloids for money—"

"What?" Brenda spat out. "*Who'd* do that?"

"I'm just talking theoretically—"

"Are you talking about yourself?" Miller's eyes were fire. "You got ambitions, Detective?"

"If I did, think I'd be talking to you about them?" Oliver laughed. "Believe it or not, Ms. Miller, I have integrity." Under his breath, he added, "It's about all I *do* have."

Brenda softened, looked at Marge. "Is he married?"

"Divorced."

"Is he seeing anyone?"

"Not that I know."

Oliver said, "I'm in the room, ladies. You can talk to me directly."

Brenda waved him off. "I never ask the men these questions. They always lie." She looked at Oliver. "You promise me dinner, you might break through my ball-breaking exterior."

Oliver broke into a big grin. "I'd be happy to buy you dinner, Ms. Miller. But it won't be at Estelle's."

Brenda said, "How about Crab and Barrel?"

"A little rich for my wallet . . ." Oliver looked dubious. "Maybe you could make it work."

Brenda said, "When?"

"Pick a night."

"Friday?"

"You're on."

Marge said, "Tell us about Wendy Culligan and Harlan Manz."

Brenda turned serious. "They went out for drinks a couple of times. Nothing serious because he had a girlfriend, she had a boyfriend. I told her she was crazy. Yeah, Harlan was good-looking, better-looking than her boyfriend, that was for sure. But Ken—that's her boyfriend—he's got a job, he's got his own car, he's got his own condo . . . he's got a *future*. Harlan was a *loser*. I guess Wendy caught on because they stopped seeing each other . . . remained on good terms according to her—"

"She spoke to you about this?" Marge said.

"Yes. When I came to visit her, she immediately pulled me aside and begged me not to tell anyone. First off, she didn't want her boyfriend finding out. Second, she didn't want to be associated with him. Can you blame her?"

"No," Marge said. "But she should have been truthful with the police—"

"Are you going to call her up?" Brenda was nervous. "Ask her about it?"

"Yes," Marge said. "But I don't have to say it came from you."

"I'd appreciate it." Brenda sighed. "I didn't tell you to be a fink. I told you because I didn't want anyone else to make more of it than it was."

"You have anyone specifically in mind?" Marge asked.

"No, and that's the God's honest truth. But you know people talk. After something like Estelle's, they feel nervous . . . helpless. Sometimes they make up stuff. Poor Wendy doesn't need shit like this after what she's been through."

"You did the right thing," Oliver said soothingly.

"Honestly, Detective. Wendy's a straight arrow. She says it was only a couple of times, it was only a couple of times. If she says it was no big deal, it was no big deal."

"Maybe to her it was no big deal," Marge said. "But to Harlan it could have been a very big deal!"

Oliver dropped a fistful of pumpkin seeds into his mouth, smirked. He was very proud of himself. Marge rolled her eyes, opened the passenger door to the unmarked. Oliver slid in, leaned over and opened the driver's door from the inside. When she got in, he made a point of going through his wallet.

"Well, I got three dollars to my name. Maybe it'll buy Brenda a glass of house wine."

"I know what I make, I know what you make." Marge started the engine. "I'm not falling for that, Scotty."

Oliver laughed, offered Marge pumpkin seeds. Marge shook her head no and backed the car out of the parking lot. She headed for the 405 Freeway, turned into the north on-ramp, revving up the motor until they were flying. She said, "We might be onto something. Harlan knew Wendy. *More* than knew her. They dated."

"But Wendy isn't dead, Marge."

"So Harlan aimed at her, but missed."

"Meanwhile, he caught thirteen other people in the process, including two men at her own table?" Oliver was skeptical.

"Maybe he was showing off for her. 'Look what you drove me to.'"

"Why would there be two shooters at the scene if Harlan just wanted to show off to Wendy? He could have done that without help."

"We don't know that there were definitely two shooters."

"But we're leaning in that direction."

"Frankly, I don't know what we're leaning toward. Because we don't know what we're looking for."

Oliver was quiet. Then he said, "Before we came here, I talked to Bert about Walter Skinner's widow. She's fond of *Arsenic and Old Lace*."

"The movie?"

"Yeah, the movie."

"I can see why she'd like it. Central characters are two old ladies."

"Two old ladies who *kill* people."

"People at Estelle's were shot, Scott. Not poisoned."

"Still, it gets you thinking. Her old man was stepping out on her."

"Did Bert say she acted psycho about that point?"

"No, he didn't. He said she seemed to bounce back and forth between being pissed at Walter for messing around and feeling truly sad about his death."

"Sounds normal to me," Marge said. "Only thing about the case that does sound normal."

"Yeah, it's getting complicated." Oliver ate more pumpkin seeds. "You hungry, Marge? These morsels ain't cutting the pangs."

"I could use a bite."

"How about Oscar's Deli?"

"Where is that? Woodley and Ventura?"

"A block west." Oliver ate the last batch of pumpkin seeds. "You can pay. I have to save up my dimes for Crab and Barrel."

# ❧12

*Jeanine Garrison was* a hard person to reach. Decker was put on hold, talked to a series of secretaries and assistants, all of it puzzling to him because he was not sure exactly what Jeanine did that required a staff. Marge had mentioned something about her being a patron of the arts and being involved in charity work. But how she earned her keep was anyone's guess. When she finally did come on the phone, she sounded polite enough. They made an appointment to meet at her office, which was one of those retro-Victorian numbers with stained-glass and mullioned windows. Like Greenvale. Decker wondered if the same architect had designed them both.

Her office was the penthouse suite. The waiting room was small but posh, paneled in high-polished walnut; a burnished chesterfield, flanked by two tray tables, rested against the wall. One table held fresh-cut flowers; the other was topped with local weekly newspapers featuring Valley notables on the front pages, and several issues of *Architectural Digest*. A fortysomething secretary told Decker to have a seat, that Jeanine would be right there. "Right there" turned out to be a half hour later. But if Decker had been a single guy, he would have felt it was worth the wait.

Because the woman was very, very nice.

A lovely face with an excellent figure. Shoulder-length blond hair that shimmered and swayed as she walked. Wide-set aqua eyes—an unnatural shade, probably enhanced by contact lenses. An oval face, high-set cheekbones, and lips coated with something that made them look wet and sexy. Statuesque—around five eight with shapely legs. She might be—or have been—a dancer. Tapered ankles and slender feet. Pale, flawless skin, pale hands. She was dressed modestly in a black double-breasted skirt suit, a bright, almost garish, Versace scarf draped around her neck.

Her eyes hooked into his, hands delicately wrapping around his fingers. She sighed heavily. "Would you think I was too terrible if I asked you to come back in an hour?"

Decker broke physical contact. "Not at all. Something come up?"

"Something *always* comes up, doesn't it?" She looked away, her face troubled ever so slightly. "You're a love. I'll see you in an hour then."

*A love?* Decker thought.

"Certainly," Decker said.

Without another word, she turned and walked away . . . very slowly . . . hips sashaying with a beat.

Decker went back to the car, aware that he had become hot . . . confused.

*Who* was *that woman?*

*What did that matter?*

An hour to kill. Might as well go back to work.

\* \* \*

Easier to sustain bodily injuries than to deal with ex-wives. Having done both, Decker knew this to be true.

Five messages from Jan.

He made himself comfortable at his desk, stared at the phone. Grimacing, he punched in the numbers, wincing at each ring. When he heard his daughter's voice, he breathed instant relief. She was cool to him. As to be expected. But he didn't care. Too steeped in gratitude.

"I was actually returning your mother's calls."

"She's not home."

"Tell her I called. Tell her I'm swamped and I'll try to get back to her tomorrow. So she can stop calling the station house—"

"How many times did she call?"

"Five."

"I'll speak to her—"

"Don't get in the middle, Cynthia. You don't need any more grief."

A pause over the line. "I started the whole thing."

"I appreciate your help, but please don't take sides. It will make both our lives more difficult." Decker turned quiet. "Are you mad at me?"

"I love you very much, Dad."

Her voice remained chilly, but on the verge of a thaw. He said, "Cin, I want to apologize. You were very civil last night. I wasn't."

"You were angry."

"Yes."

"And hurt that I didn't talk it over with you first."

"A bit."

"Frustrated?"

"Definitely. I haven't changed my mind. I'm still against your decision. But you *are* twenty-four. If I can't talk you out of it, maybe we could have lunch next week. Perhaps you wouldn't mind a few pointers from a veteran. Tell me again when you're scheduled to start?"

"Right after the first of the year."

"Too bad baseball season is over," Decker said. "You're a stone's throw away from the Dodgers box office."

Cindy laughed over the line. "Daddy, I have a request."

"Shoot."

"I'd love to hear what you have to say. I respect you not only as a father but very much as a cop. But don't run interference for me, all right? Don't call up the Academy. Don't talk to my supervisors or my sergeants or my teachers or whomever and ask about me. I really thought hard about using Mom's maiden name because I didn't want people to know we're related. I'll have enough problems as it is. Everyone comparing me to you—"

"Whoa, this sounds serious."

"You're patronizing me. That's all right. Patronize all you want. Just as long as you actually *honor* my request. Then we'll both be fine."

Decker paused, realizing his little girl was in fact a young woman who needed and deserved independence and respect. The transition was excruciating.

"I'll do my best, Cynthia."

There was silence over the phone. Even with all the pain, it was still infinitely better than talking to Jan.

She said, "So we're squared away on this?"

"I wouldn't say squared away. I'm not actively fighting you anymore."

"I'll call you later, Daddy. Take care of yourself."

"I love you, princess."

"Love you, too. Bye."

Abruptly, she hung up the phone. For a moment, Decker sat, receiver in hand, dial tone humming in his ear. Finally, he disconnected and turned on his computer and modem, hooking into the L.A. public libraries' data banks. One of the splurges from last year's tight budget. It had saved the squad room infinite hours of tedium. After logging in, presenting the passwords, he was offered a menu. A few minutes of searching and he found what he was looking for—back issues of the local West Valley throwaways.

Punching up the name Jeanine Garrison. Searching for the information. Most of the data came from society columns and articles relating to charity events. Some of the older issues—ten years prior—showed pictures of the slain parents, Ray and Linda Garrison. A handsome couple. Linda had been blond and beautiful. Kindly eyes. A warm mouth. Young-looking. From the pictures, Decker could hardly believe she had been forty-three at that time. Looked more like twenty-three. Ray had shown his age even then. Salt-and-pepper hair, craggy complexion. Ruggedly handsome. Type of father a girl would have adored.

Decker continued to scan the columns.

Jeanine was first mentioned on her own at her "coming out" party. A debutante ball. Decker could hardly believe they still did things like that, especially in Los Angeles. But there she was in her full glory. A stunning eighteen-year-old in a gown that was anything but virginal. A long, form-fitting job with a seductive center slit to mid-thigh and a plunging neckline. It plunged into plenty of womanly pulchritude.

Decker took off his glasses, rubbed his eyes. For some reason, he found reading a monitor more taxing than a newspaper. Maybe it was the stiff position. He put on his glasses, continued to glean through the electronic print. Jeanine and her parents hosting a charity fete for Children's Services. Jeanine and her father organizing a dinner for a local old-age home.

Increasingly, the articles had more of Jeanine and less of her parents. Jeanine and her charity parties. Lots of them and all for good community causes. Celebrity-studded. Not A-list people, mostly retired character actors—has-beens hoping for a resurrection. But they had turned out. Not only stars, but Strapp and the mayor. Jeanine sandwiched between the two, giving the photographer a mouth full of ivories.

Again, Decker rubbed his eyes, checked his watch.

A full hour had passed. Now he was late for the appointment.

What the hey. He'd just tell her that something came up.

Because something always does come up.

David Garrison opened the door wearing a bathrobe, pajama bottoms, and slippers, leaving Webster to wonder if this was his normal dress or if he had actually woken the man up at three in the afternoon.

The detective presented his badge, and a pair of anxious hazel eyes scanned the ID as well as the cop. Red-rimmed eyes. Garrison was pale and thin and sported a day's growth of beard. His head held a blond thicket of unkempt oily tresses and dark shadows sat under sunken orbs. Musta been one hell of a party last night.

"May I come in?" Webster asked. "Unless you'd prefer to talk out here."

The door opened and Webster went inside. Garrison had yet to speak.

An incredible view. Two walls of glass framing canyons as well as the Valley skyline. The place had been done up as sleek as a leopard, everything cold and unyielding and achromatic. A scheme of gray, white, and black. Marble floors. Stark white walls holding abstract art. Black leather sofas devoid of adornment. Glass tables. A stereo system resting in ebony bookshelves. Metal blinds instead of wooden shutters or cloth curtains. The only hint of color came from the outdoor vistas.

"Did I wake you, sir?" Webster asked, politely.

Garrison shook his head. "Wish it were so. And call me Dave. Sir is . . . was . . . exclusively reserved for my father."

"All right." Webster strolled over to the stereo, regarded the CDs. Classical works. Good pieces and good recording editions. His eyes swept over the titles. "This is interesting."

"My little hobby." Garrison's voice was bored.

Webster said, "I specifically meant this '62 Bernstein release of Sibelius's *The Oceanides*. I have the vinyl. When did they master it for CD?"

A pause. Garrison said, "It's a new edition."

"Obviously." Webster smiled. "Been doing a lot of overtime. I know where I'm going as soon as my working hours are up. Can I take a seat?"

Garrison pointed to the couch. "Get you something to drink?"

"No, thank you."

"Mind if I take something?"

Webster said, "It's your house, Mr. Garrison. You're doin' me the favor."

"Well put." Garrison walked over to a mirrored wet bar. He took out a cut-crystal tumbler. "Would you like to hear the CD?"

"You put it on, reckon I won't object."

"So I reckon I'll put it on." He poured himself a double shot of Johnnie Walker Blue straight up. "You work that Southern Boy shit very effectively. It must bring you an ample supply of pussy."

Webster grinned. "Ah suppose it did when ah was single."

The young man took a swig, then removed the cassette from the disc player and slipped in the Sibelius CD. "And now you're a faithful married man as well as a hardworking, dedicated cop."

"Correct."

Garrison turned on the receiver. Instantly, the room filled with pastoral beauty. What Webster wanted to do was close his eyes and be swept away. Instead, he took out his notepad, waited for Garrison to finish his booze and sit down. After polishing off the Scotch, the young man refilled his glass and sat in a slouch leather chair. His bathrobe had fallen open, revealing a thin upper torso tufted with fine chest hair. He sat with his legs spread apart, revealing the partially opened fly of his pajama bottoms.

The man weren't wearin' underpants.

Webster said, "I'm sorry for your loss, Mr. Garrison."

David looked directly at him. "Don't feel too bad on my account."

Webster digested his response. "Mind if I ask you a couple of questions?"

"Phrasing it as if I have a choice." He smiled. "Do I?"

"Just a couple of questions, sir."

"Whatever is your wish, *suh*."

Webster smiled. "You're a toughie."

"Ply me with enough alcohol and I'm putty." Garrison winked, laughed. "Going through a little panic, suh? Don't worry. You're not my type." He leaned in close. "I've done lots of experimenting, but alas, I am a dull, dull boy. Much to my Bohemian nature's dismay, I really do prefer girls. Pity. Except for this one minor flaw, I might have made a most excellent queer."

He finished off his booze, got up, and poured himself another shot. "In reality, I'm just a boring, bisexual drunkard."

"Do you work?" Webster asked.

Garrison swallowed liquor. "Set design. I just finished *Tosca* at the Dorothy Chandler. Berticelli's conducting if you're interested."

"I don't know the man."

"A . . . limited man with a limited vision. I created a magnificent set—larger than life, full of pomp and special effects. Extremely garish and very Disney. Tailor-made for the vapid L.A. audience."

Another gulp.

"I also work for the movies. But less so each year since many of the sets are now done with computer graphics. Not to fret, though. I've just landed a very lucrative contract with a movie F/X computer company."

He gave Webster a loopy smile.

"Garrison is my name, graphics is my game."

"You do well for yourself, sir?"

"I do *exceedingly* well since my parents died."

A hesitation. Then Webster asked, "How much are you worth now?"

"Nosy little critter, aren't you?" Garrison allowed himself another finger's worth of booze. "I'm not worth nearly as much as my sister. But at least I wasn't disinherited. That came as a shock to me. I thought Dad had given me the boot. Mom must have talked him into something right before they . . ."

He looked down at his drink.

"I really don't know the exact amount. Something in the low seven-figure range, I suspect. Jeanine has all the details. She is to dole out my money to me at certain intervals marked by the passage of time. She's my . . . *trustee*. Which I suppose designates me as the *trustor*. Which would be comical if it wasn't so ludicrous."

"You don't trust your sister?"

"In a word, no." Garrison held a finger in the air. "But even if Jeanine embezzles everything, well then, I suppose I'm no worse off than I was two years ago. When I was in jail and disinherited. Ah! Here it is! My favorite passage of the work! Those harmonies!"

Webster listened to the music for a moment, trying desperately not to be distracted with the siren's call. "Lovely."

"It's sublime, Detective."

"Yes, it is."

"But you have work to do."

"Yes, I do." Sourly, Webster returned to his case notes. "Why did you think your father disinherited you?"

"My cocaine use. He really didn't like drugs." He held up his glass. "This doesn't count, of course."

Garrison sipped Scotch.

"He must have been impressed with my rehab . . . with my steady employment this last year. I guess it boils down to the fact that I didn't need him anymore. Once his money ceased to be a bargaining chip, I was allowed my piece of the rock. Cheers!"

He finished off the fourth round. Then he sat down.

"My sister . . ."

His smile was wicked.

"My sister, on the other hand, was completely indulged, utterly spoiled because (a) she was a beautiful, beautiful little girl and (b) as a child, she was of mediocre mind and wholly without talent. Jeanine is now twenty-eight years old. She has never held a paying job, has never worked a day in her life. She has lived neither with responsibility nor with the consequences of her behavior. I, on the other hand, was not permitted such luxury because I was precocious, I was intelligent, I was *gifted*. There it is. My family saga in its pure, unadulterated form. Have you any more questions for me, suh?"

Webster waited a moment. "Were you on speaking terms with your parents when they died?"

"Yes."

"Visit them often?"

"No. But we were on speaking terms. Occasionally, I played the dutiful son and called my mother." He paused a moment, swallowed hard. "I . . . liked my mother."

Garrison looked away, spoke softly.

"No one . . . including my old man whom I disliked . . . deserves to *die* like that! Slaughtered like a trophy of some demented man's hunt. It is an abomination! The man who did it should be destroyed . . . completely . . . thoroughly . . . without remorse."

Garrison marched back to his bar. With shaking hands, he poured himself another drink. And that's when Webster realized how much Garrison had been hurting. The drinking and the slovenliness, his way of dealing with grief. Gently, he said, "Been gettin' outta bed lately, David?"

"What?"

Webster said, "You've been showin' up to work at all?"

Garrison spun around, drink in hand, "I *told* you I just finished a set."

"Was that before or after what happened at Estelle's?"

Garrison looked down. "I've got a gig lined up in a week. Not to worry, Detective." He gulped down a shot. "I'll pull myself together."

"Your parents were founding members of Greenvale Country Club, correct?"

He stared at Webster. "This is leading somewhere, I hope."

"Am I correct? They were founding members?"

"You are correct, suh!"

"In your teenage years, you spent some time at the club?"

"I despised the club. And everyone in it."

Webster paused. "Didn't hang out there much then?"

"I believe I used the word *despised*, Detective."

"So you never visited the club as an adult . . . maybe to meet your parents for dinner there or something like that?"

"Never." Garrison hesitated. "You're asking about Greenvale for a reason. Must have something to do with what . . . what happened at Estelle's. Does it?"

"The murderer, Harlan Manz . . ."

"Yes?"

"He worked at Greenvale before going to Estelle's."

There was a moment of silence. Garrison's face was unreadable. "What does that mean?"

"We're not sure it means anything," Webster said. "Just trying to get a fix on Manz, hoping to figure out why he busted loose. Thought maybe you might have spoken to him at Greenvale . . . could give us a clue about what made him tick."

"When did he work at the club?"

"'Bout two years ago."

"No . . ." Garrison shook his head. "No, suh, I wasn't around two years ago. I was working off a drug sentence at County. I assume you're aware of that?"

Webster nodded, hoping his embarrassment wasn't

showing. Stupid of him not to commit the dates to memory.

Garrison sat down. "This murderer . . . Harlan Manz . . . he had worked at Estelle's, right?"

"Yes."

"He had been at Greenvale, then he went to Estelle's. My parents were members of Greenvale and they often went to Estelle's." His face went white. "Was this monster *stalking* them?"

"I have no evidence—"

"Then *why* are you implying a connection?"

"If I am, I don't mean to do that. I told you, we're just trying to figure why Manz freaked. You seem like a real perceptive fellow. I was hoping that maybe you knew him from Greenvale . . . could lay a little insight on him."

"I've never met the man in my life. You doubt me? Give me a lie detector test."

Webster chuckled. "That won't be necessary. You're not a suspect."

*Not yet.*

*Because a sudden seven-figure inheritance really did sound like a right fine motivation for a hit.*

Garrison said, "What did this Manz do at the club?"

"Tended bar—"

"Ah, so I can see why you thought . . ." Garrison lifted his tumbler of booze and laughed. "No, in my past, I was a coke fiend. I assure you my friendship with Mr. Scotch is of a quite recent nature." He appeared pensive. "My father drank . . . he wasn't a drunk, but he drank. It is conceivable that he ran into this Manz at the club. You might want to ask my sister."

"Has she spent some time at Greenvale in recent years?"

"She plays tennis there just about every afternoon. She's a fanatical player, though she isn't very good. She's clumsy actually. Although you'd never believe it to look at her. Because she truly is gorgeous."

"Harlan Manz also taught tennis at Greenvale."

Garrison's eyes widened. He gave off an overly loud laugh. "Perchance is someone asking questions of my sister?"

"Someone is talking to her, yes." Webster looked up from his notes. "Think she might have met Harlan?"

"Detective, if Manz taught at Greenvale, Jeanine not only knew him, but she slept with him."

Webster waited a beat. "You're pretty sure about that?"

Garrison raised his glass and grinned. "To paraphrase your boyhood Suthen lingo: Suh, ah gar-run-*tee*!"

# ❧13

**_With a wave_** of her hand, she invited Decker into her personal office. Fabulous view, art on the walls, handsome furniture, and a big desk. A state-of-the-art computer, but nothing on the screen other than the screen saver, a whirl of geometric shapes gliding across the monitor. She took a seat behind her desk, giving no explanation for her delay.

"Thank you for seeing me," Decker said.

She spoke in a moderated voice. "Why'd you come here? Out of courtesy? Or was it guilt?"

"Guilt?"

"Crime in the city has become rampant. The police have completely lost control. How else could you explain what went on in that place?"

Decker waited. Jeanine made a pair of fists, knuckles whitening. But her eyes remained steady. "How can I help you?"

Decker met her gaze. "I'm very sorry for your loss, Ms. Garrison. I hope my questions won't be too intrusive or too painful."

"But perhaps they'll be both."

Decker reasssessed the situation. Her demeanor had abruptly changed since their first encounter, leaving him to wonder if she had taken legal advice in his absence. Best to keep it brief. "Certain inconsistencies have come out during our investigation of the tragedy at Estelle's—"

"Inconsistencies?"

"Yes, ma'am."

Jeanine's gaze was still on him, eyes never wavering. "Go on."

Decker made a conscious effort not to squirm. "We're interviewing a number of people. Your parents belonged to Greenvale Country Club, correct?"

Jeanine waited a beat, lips slightly parted. "Why are you asking me this?"

"Pardon?"

"Why are you asking questions about my parents? Why are you dragging them into your investigation?"

A long pause. With a planned casual manner, Decker leaned back in the chair. "It's a simple question, ma'am. We both know the answer is yes."

"So why are you asking me the question if you know the answer?"

"Do you know how long they've been members?"

"I suppose you know the answer to that one as well."

"I was under the impression they were founding members . . . which means they've been there for fifteen years."

"You can count."

"You spend some time there growing up, ma'am?"

"How do you quantify time?"

"Did you spend weekends there, for example?"

"Sometimes."

"Doing what?"

"I don't see how that's your business, either."

Decker tapped his pen against his notebook, put on edge by her sexuality and sudden hostility. He had come for simple information. For some reason, she was perceiving it as an interrogation. "Do you spend time at the club now, Ms. Garrison? I know you have privileges through your father's lifetime membership."

Jeanine observed Decker with appraising eyes. "Are you hiding some kind of crucial information from me?"

Again, under her scrutiny, Decker found it was hard to appear relaxed. He realized he had tensed up, been sitting with erect posture. He relaxed his shoulders, loosened his spine. "I wish I were holding back. Unfortunately, I'm not."

"Then is there a point to all of this?"

Decker rolled his tongue in his cheek. "Is this a bad time for you to talk to me, Ms. Garrison? If it is, I could come back another day."

She stared at him. "I resent these questions. Actually, not the questions but the subterfuge."

"Pardon?"

"You're ostensibly here to ask questions. But in fact, you're shifting the blame from the LAPD to the victims. Like it was somehow their fault for being in the restaurant."

"Ms. Garrison, I'm confused—"

"Typical of LAPD philosophy," she said, dismissively. "My parents were mercilessly . . . *slaughtered* in a crime-riddled city . . . and somehow it's my fault. Or Greenvale Country Club's fault. You know what? Do me a favor. Stop attending funerals where you don't belong. Like I don't have enough grief in my life without the police harassing me."

Decker let her words hang in the air. Yes, her parents were slaughtered. But he was on *her* side. Why was she drawing lines in the sand? Could be she, like some of the others, had known Harlan and felt guilty about it.

Then he thought about the Garrisons. Marge had said they were worth beaucoup bucks. Inheritance— pause for thought.

He started to ad-lib. "I hear you're a tennis player. A pretty good one at that."

Jeanine was quiet. She closed her eyes and opened them, the blue jewels homing in on Decker's face. "Where'd you hear that?"

He stepped over her inquiry. "How long have you played?"

"A long time."

"Do you prefer sod or clay?"

"I only play on clay."

"Yeah, sod leaves too much to chance, not enough to skill."

"Are you trying to establish rapport with me, Lieutenant?"

Decker gave her a boyish grin. "Probably."

Jeanine looked downward, took out a tissue and dabbed tearless eyes. "Do you play tennis, Lieutenant?"

"Not too much anymore. I'm getting too old. You need to be in shape."

Jeanine gave him a once-over, let her aqua-blue

eyes linger on his chest, then his face. "You're big . . . well-built. Of course, if you lost ten pounds, you'd probably be lighter on your feet."

"I'm sure you're right."

"Ah, well, we all battle the bulge."

An attempt to extract a compliment? Because the woman was as thin as lamination. Decker smiled. "Some more than others."

Jeanine smiled back. A sexy smile with healthy teeth . . . just like the newspaper photographs he had pulled up. It was getting hot in her office. Still looking at him, she said, "Do you ever play charity games?"

"Charity games?"

"Play sports to raise money for charity. Specifically, tennis."

"I'm not good enough."

"How about being on an LAPD team? Does the LAPD even have a *tennis* team?"

"I believe we do."

"We should set something up . . . for charity. How about police versus the fire department? Or West Valley LAPD versus West Valley LAFD? Proceeds can go to . . . to building a community center. Or revamping the one we have."

"Sounds great."

"I could get you good press coverage. Maybe even show it on cable TV. I've got pull. It's what I'm known for."

Decker said, "I'm a little dense today. What exactly do you do?"

Jeanine became impatient, but not hostile. "I organize and host charity events. It used to be parties.

But now I concentrate on tennis matches. Brings in the right people."

"The right people?"

Jeanine smiled. "Rich people."

"Ah—"

"Those who can afford to give money. Tennis lovers seem to be of a higher socioeconomic bracket. Hence, more money. And rightly or wrongly, that's the bottom line."

Decker paused. "And you . . . take a percentage of the gross for your services?"

"Oh, no!" Jeanine was offended. "Every ounce of profit goes to the charity. I take nothing other than the costs of rental or catering or . . . whatever. It's called philanthropy—a lost art."

She sighed.

"My father was very philanthropic. But he lacked time to put his good thoughts into deeds. That's where I came in. I made it *happen*!"

"But your father finances—"

"Through his charitable foundation, which pays the bills, pays the payroll including my salary. Which is generous. My dad was a very generous . . ."

Again, she lowered her head, patted at her eyes with a tissue. "I'm sorry . . ."

"Ms. Garrison, I'm sorry to be opening up wounds—"

"I know. You're doing your job." She looked up. "You were the one on TV. The one who said the inside of Estelle's was your worst nightmare." She looked solemn. "That was so insightful."

"Thank you."

Still grave, Jeanine said, "So . . . maybe we should

set something up? Show the world that we survivors of that terrible tragedy hold no animosity toward the LAPD?"

Decker paused. From the grieving daughter to the society hostess in five minutes. He said, "Let me talk to my captain."

"I'll call him if you'd like."

"Sure. I'll give you his number in a min—"

"Oh, I have his numbers." She pointed to her electronic Rolodex. "I've been doing this for a while. I have lots of contacts."

Decker took in her words, wondering how much of it was bravado. Then he remembered the newspaper picture with Jeanine standing between Strapp and the mayor. Casually, he asked, "How long did you take lessons at Greenvale?"

"Years," Jeanine answered. "I had some talent, but not enough. In the world of professional tennis, you learn your limitations quickly. Instead of moping, I directed my energies into fund-raising. And in that, my friend, I am a star. Do you know that just last month our culture committee's celebrity-studded party in our library raised over thirty thousand dollars for the new West Valley Art Museum?"

"Really?"

"Yes. I believe your captain was there. Because the mayor was there. And where there are mayors, there are police officials."

Decker made a mental note to watch his words. Because this one was not only sexy but *sly*. Seductive was the word. Ms. Femme Fatale wrapped in a cloak of charity.

"Have you been there yet? To the museum? We're

strong on the California pleinairists. We've opened with two special exhibits right now. Grandville Redmond and Edgar Payne. Both painters are extraordinary."

"Have to get over there."

Jeanine glanced at Decker's hand, at his wedding ring. It didn't seem to deter her. "If you'd like, I'll be happy to give you a guided tour."

Decker smiled. "Thank you, but—"

"How about . . ." Jeanine pulled out her calendar. "I can do it tomorrow. Twelve or oneish?"

Again, Decker smiled. "I'm booked this week."

"I'm sure I can call your captain and tell him—"

"No, Ms. Garrison, that's quite all right. I'm old-fashioned. City pays me to work, I work."

"Very refreshing." Again the sexy smile. "How about after work? I could arrange a private tour after the museum's closed."

"Thank you, but my family likes me home for dinner."

"How about after dinner?" Jeanine's smile turned to a grin. "You can bring your wife and kids if you'd like. I'm assuming you have children. Most married men do."

She was toying with him, *vamping* him. And getting the upper hand. He looked directly into her eyes. "Thank you for the invitation. I'll take you up on it sometime."

"Do that."

"Who'd you take tennis lessons from, Ms. Garrison? Someone at Greenvale?"

Jeanine stared at him, slowly put the calendar away. Her face had suddenly turned gelid and unforgiving.

"You can call me Jeanine. Why are you so interested in my tennis years?"

Decker shrugged, still holding her eye. "Just wondering if anyone famous ever taught at the club."

"Famous?" Jeanine's tone was condescending. "Oh, yes, at one time, I learned with Martina and Jimmy and Chris and John and—"

"I get the point." Decker was quiet. She wasn't giving him an inch to work with. "I was just wondering . . . if anyone remotely known might have ever taught there . . . spurred your interest in the game." He stood. "Not important. Sorry to bother you. And I'll try to get to the museum. Thanks for the tip."

Jeanine's eyes turned distant. "You know who *used* to play at Greenvale?"

"Who?" asked Decker, still standing.

"Wade Anthony."

Decker sat back down, trying to conjure up an image of a face. Nothing. "Don't know him."

"I know," Jeanine said softly. "And that's too bad. Once, he was a rising star. He was . . . in his teens when he played at Greenvale. Sixteen to be exact. I was fourteen. I had a mad, mad crush on him."

She smiled sadly.

"Me and all the other teenyboppers. He was simply gorgeous. Outrageous as well. He had sex with at least two of my friends. Rumor had it that he had sex with some of their mothers as well."

"Sounds like a tennis player."

"Yes, he was strictly *bad boy*. My father ordered me to stay clear of him. Of course, I did the opposite. I watched him play almost every day. He was wonderful to watch."

She was quiet. Decker waited. When she didn't continue, he prodded further. "What happened to him?"

"Though he was a master tennis player, he was still a sixteen-year-old. He got drunk one night. Took out Daddy's Ferrari and smashed up the car with him inside. He's now confined to a wheelchair."

Decker paused. "That's very sad."

"It was more than sad, it was terrible. I was heartbroken. He stopped coming to the club. Just dropped out of sight."

She faced him.

"I hadn't thought about him in years. Then about a year ago, I saw an article on him in the sports pages of the *Times*. Not the front of course, page two or three."

"Really? What's he doing?"

"Apparently he's a top-seeded player in *wheelchair* tennis."

"Wheelchair tennis?"

Jeanine nodded. "Played on a regulation-size court. Only difference is the players in the chairs get two bounces instead of one. Fascinating to see how fast they can move."

Her mood had suddenly darkened. Decker knew he was treading dangerous ground. "What'd they say about him in the article?"

"It was a write-up on some charity games in New York—a major fund-raiser for the physically challenged. Five hundred fifty a ticket. Do you know who his partner was? *Ivan Lendl*."

"That's incredible!"

"It brought back a flood of memories, Lieutenant. I'm glad he's doing well."

Decker said, "I don't mean to sound thick-headed but . . . did Lendl play in a wheelchair?"

"No." Jeanine raised her eyes. "It was Wade and Lendl against John McEnroe and some other paraplegic. It drew a huge crowd." She stared into space. "Wade and Ivan won. They showed a picture of them . . . of him. He still looks good . . . great to be exact!"

Decker looked at her. "Ever think of asking him to play for one of your charities?"

A wistful smile. Jeanine said, "I think we're a little small-time for him. I had tried to convince Dad to go out for better, more major causes—things like AIDS—but Dad was *so* conservative."

"A terrible tragedy that took your parents' lives," Decker said. "Lots of victims including yourself. Maybe you could host a game for the victims of the shooting."

Jeanine opened and closed her mouth. "I . . . I don't know. I hadn't thought about it." Her sculptured face took on an animated glow. Again, she threw open her calendar. "That is a *marvelous* idea. I could arrange something magnificent, something that would rival the Open."

*Dream on.* He said, "Maybe you could hold the event at Greenvale."

"Another good idea." Jeanine's body language was suddenly exuberant. "Listen, I'm so sorry I jumped down your throat. It's just this thing with my parents . . . it's thrown me for a loop."

"Of course."

"Did . . . did you have any other questions you needed to ask me?"

He had lots of questions to ask her. Originally, he had wanted to know if she or the family had known Harlan Manz, if she or the family had ever taken lessons from him, could have offended him in any way. But her odd behavior had sent his antennae quivering overtime.

*Be honest, Deck. She quivered other things as well.*

Brushing that aside . . . which took some effort . . . he knew, as a professional, that she was acting strange. Her hostility, her flip attitude, her vamping, her summing up the Estelle's tragedy by calling it a "*thing* with her parents," her evasive answers when it came to her past teachers, her strong passion for tennis, her sudden enthusiasm at the thought of hosting a big event tied to the deaths of her parents. Bizarre. Left Decker wondering if she had perhaps known Harlan in an intimate way.

Yet, he sensed he had gained some kind of rapport with her. He knew that implying any kind of relationship between this eerie but beautiful woman and a mass murderer would blow the trust to smithereens. He was reminded of what a psychologist friend had once told him about his field.

*Good therapy is an art. Timing is everything.*

Decker kept his manner professional but warm. "I do have a few questions, but they can wait until later."

*Until he found out more about her.*

*Until he could calm himself down.*

"Really, it's all right."

Decker stood. "Some other time. We'll be in contact."

"I certainly hope so."

Jeanine's smile was brilliant. "Nice to have met you."

"Same."

She offered him her hand. Gently, Decker shook it.

# ❧ 14

*Some would call* him obsessive. Decker referred to himself as thorough.

More digging. Trying to find some *personal* information. After an hour he found it—columns in the locals entitled "Milestones." A small sentence about a failed marriage two years ago. Brent Delaney. No picture. Decker backtracked, tried to find a wedding announcement. Indeed it existed, but not in the local throwaways, in the *LA. Times.* Brent had dark hair, thick brows . . . handsome features. Slick. Striking resemblance to Harlan. Brent's occupation was listed as actor. His hobbies were car racing and tennis. Their marriage had lasted a total of seven months.

Then nothing. Still, Decker continued to search and search. For any little telltale hook that could formally tie her to Harlan Manz. He never did find the mother lode. But his prospecting wasn't a total bust.

Farrell Gaynor let go with a congested cough. The elder statesman of the five-person Homicide team had the floor and was making the most of it.

"The kids stand to inherit . . ." Another spasm. "Inherit a lot of money . . ."

He was now hacking dry. Decker pounded his back, said to Oliver, "Get the man a drink of water."

Oliver made a face. "I'm his personal valet?"

"For godsakes, Scott!" Marge stomped out of the room.

Oliver said, "I was going to go . . ."

"You okay, Farrell?" Decker asked.

"It's the season." He brought up mucus, spit it into a handkerchief.

"Christ, Farrell!" Oliver said in disgust.

"Quiet, or next time I'll aim it at you."

Marge came back with the water. Gaynor drank it greedily. He was in good health other than his allergies. Overweight, yes. Old, yes. In need of a lube job in the morning, yes. But considering where some of his peers lay, he was in *very* good health. His wife had knitted him a new cardigan—the hunter-green one he had on today. He liked it. Went with his gray slacks. He thanked Marge for the water, cleared his throat.

"You were saying . . ." Martinez prompted.

"What was I saying?"

"Garrison kids are gonna inherit . . ."

"Money," Gaynor said. "Now, they don't get their inheritance all at once. David gets about a third of his share now and the rest at thirty. Jeanine also gets a third now and the rest at thirty-two."

"About four years from now," Oliver said.

Marge said, "Does Jeanine work?"

"Not according to her brother," Webster stated.

"So as of right now, she has no income?"

"She arranges charity events," Decker said. "Said

her father's foundation gave her a salary and expenses came out of profits."

"What kind of expenses was she talking about?" Oliver asked.

"The catering, the hall, the setup—I don't know the details." Decker looked to Farrell. "Maybe you could help me out on that."

"I could try."

Marge said, "So what happens to her now that her father is gone?"

"Her inheritance should keep her well afloat," Gaynor said. "Ray Garrison was worth ten to twelve million—"

Marge said, "How do people amass that much *money*?"

Oliver held out his hands. "Don't look at me."

Decker said, "The age for dispersal in the trust. Can that be changed? Or is the trust irrevocable?"

"In theory, it is irrevocable," Gaynor said. "But that doesn't mean much if one chooses to contest it."

"Is anyone contesting it?"

"Not so far."

"Who's the executor?" Oliver asked.

"Executor of the will?"

"No, of the trust."

Gaynor said, "There's no executor for the trust, only a trustee."

Oliver held his temper. "So who is the trustee, Farrell?"

"Jeanine Garrison on behalf of herself and her brother, David. I don't know how the money is divided. I don't even know if they inherit the entire estate. I couldn't push my mole that far without skirting the bounds of legality."

Webster said, "David seems to think his inheritance is something in the lower seven-figure range."

Oliver said, "Which means Jeanine gets something in the higher seven-figure range?"

Gaynor said, "If the estate was divided . . . let's say . . . sixty/forty. That means Jeanine would get around two million now, David would get a cool mil."

Marge said, "I call that rich."

Decker said, "Millionaires, to be sure. All the same, there are estate taxes, lots of hidden costs. Did Ray and Linda Garrison have any insurance?"

"Like a *second to die* policy?"

"Exactly."

"Nothing I could find."

"So she's going to have to fork out some cash to the IRS for death taxes. What is it now? Around sixty percent?"

"Something like that."

"She'll live well," Decker said. "But she isn't going to live like a princess."

"I ain't crying for her," Oliver said.

Martinez said, "What'd this guy do to earn all that money?"

"He was a corporate lawyer—his own firm. Seven partners. Seems to have invested wisely—real estate, stocks, bonds. Some risky stuff—futures, derivatives, commodities. Obviously, he came out on top."

"And son David was a druggie." Oliver smiled. "Another American tragedy, yawn yawn."

"Stop being so smug," Marge said.

"And why not?" Oliver grinned. "I may not have millions but my kids are earning their own keep." His grin turned malicious. "Hey, how's Cindy doing, Loo? Still forking out those tuition bills for her schooling?"

Decker's face went dark.

Instantly, Oliver knew he had hit a nerve. Maybe the guy was broke. Decker *seemed* well heeled, but tuition could stretch any wallet. "Hey, I'm just kidding. You've got a terrific kid. Smart, too. I'm threatened by her . . . by your whole family . . . especially by—"

"Oliver, shut up," Marge said.

The room went quiet. Webster broke it. "David Garrison is troubled. But he's nobody's fool. He's talented and bright."

Oliver said, "Then why did he do eighteen months in County?"

"'Cause people screw up," Decker said.

Webster said, "From David's perspective, he got the short end of the deal. Because Jeanine was beautiful but *ordinary* in the brain department, nobody ever made demands on her. David, on the other hand, had lots of demands made on him. Mostly from his father. Probably wasn't strong enough to stand up to Papa directly so he did it in other ways."

He turned to Decker.

"You ask Jeanine if she knew Harlan Manz, Loo?"

Decker said, "I kept trying but she kept changing the subject. Clearly didn't want to talk about her tennis instructors at Greenvale."

Webster said, "David was sure that Jeanine not

only knew Harlan Manz, but had probably slept with him." He related everything David had told him.

"But he has no proof that Jeanine and Harlan knew each other," Oliver said.

"Jeanine knew him." Decker pulled out a newspaper photograph, gave it to Oliver. A snapshot of a charity tennis match with the proceeds going to New Christian Hospital. For the infirmary's diagnostic radiation division. It was a couples game—Jeanine Garrison and Harlan Manz alias Hart Mansfield against Sonia Eaton and Terrance Howell. The four of them, smiling in a frozen capsule of time.

Oliver passed the picture around, each one taking their turn, studying the photo in silence.

Finally, Decker said, "Now we know that Jeanine knew Harlan. How well?" He shrugged.

Again, the room was quiet.

Decker said, "We've got a mass murder that produced excessive bullets for the number of empty magazines found. We've got a man who committed suicide by shooting at his head, but the gun was held at least two feet away from his temple. We've got Ray and Linda Garrison, probably among the first victims to be gunned down, riddled with entrance and exit wounds that defy logic. We know that Garrison's son has or had a drug problem, and daughter Jeanine has an office and secretaries and no visible means of support other than Dad. Now Gaynor tells us that they stand to inherit around twelve million bucks. You want to tell me what this smells like?"

Oliver said, "A perfume called Menendez."

Webster said, "Except brother don't like sister."

Marge said, "That's what David told you. Maybe that's what he *wants* you to think."

Martinez asked Decker, "Does sister like brother?"

"Never got that far. I told you, Jeanine's sly. Didn't talk about her instructors at the club, never mentioned Harlan Manz by name. The woman is also a roller coaster of emotions. First time I met her, she was all sweetness and light—overly touchy-feely. You know . . . holding my hand, looking me straight in the eye. Like some inspirational guru. She asked me if I'd return later in the day because something had come up. I said sure. I came back and suddenly she was cautious . . . wary. Gave me the feeling that she'd consulted an attorney in my absence. Asked what to say to a police lieutenant."

"Maybe she did call up counsel," Marge said.

Oliver raised his brow. "You call your lawyer when you've got something to hide?"

"I'm not saying she did," Decker clarified. "Just that the shift in attitude was strange. *She's* strange. Referred to the murder as 'this thing with my parents.'"

"Can't arrest someone for filial indifference, Pete," Marge said.

Webster said, "Didn't one of the French existentialists write a book along those lines? The one where they had him arrested and tried for murder because he didn't cry at his mother's funeral?"

The group stared at him.

Gaynor said, "Maybe the character was in shock. You know people have different reactions to grief."

"That wasn't the point of the book, Farrell—"

"Can we get back to the case?" Oliver interrupted.

Martinez said, "Does this woman look as good in life as she does in the picture?"

Marge said, "You know we've completely ignored Wendy Culligan. Harlan actually went *out* with her."

"Who's Wendy Culligan?" Farrell asked.

"Real estate agent." Oliver went through his and Marge's interview with Brenda Miller, leaving out the dinner date he made with the veep. Marge had left it out as well.

"But Culligan isn't dead," Webster said.

"No," Marge said. "But maybe Harlan was trying to prove a point with her. 'This is what you drove me to!' That kind of thing."

"Was she seated near the Garrisons?" Decker asked.

"Other side of the room."

"The businessmen with her . . . were they shot in their seats?"

"Under the table."

"Garrisons were murdered in their seats. I'm assuming they didn't have time to duck."

"You're still leaning toward Jeanine and David?" Marge asked Decker.

"I'm not leaning toward anyone or anything because we still may have a random murder here. A simple case of a disgruntled employee looking for revenge."

Oliver said, "Don't know about you, but twelve million bucks makes me skeptical of the lone killer theory."

"Okay. Try out this hypothesis. Assume Estelle's was a hit gone bad. If we see Jeanine and David Garrison as setting up Estelle's as a murder for hire, then it would be nice to establish a *close* relationship between Jeanine Garrison and/or David Garrison and Harlan Manz."

Decker held up the newspaper photo.

"We need *concrete* evidence first. Something that ties Jeanine to Harlan in a personal way. I'll have a little talk with Sonia Eaton and Terrance Howell. See if they can tell me something."

"Say you establish a close relationship between Jeanine and Harlan," Marge said. "Then what?"

Decker smiled. "One step at a time."

Oliver waited until he was the only one left in Decker's office. Then he closed the door and sat down.

"I was out of line with the remark about college tuition. Cindy's a bright kid and I know you're proud of her. It's good that you're keeping her in school. More education, the better. My ex would have done anything to keep our boys in college. It just wasn't their thing."

"You've got good sons, Scott."

"Thanks." Oliver turned grave. "I did something dumb, Deck. I asked a woman out, someone I questioned in the case. Brenda Miller, the veep at Ashman/Reynard. Actually, she asked *me* out for dinner. Took me by surprise. But I did accept."

Decker looked at Oliver. "How'd you fall into that?"

Oliver sighed. "She was holding back information. She used dinner with me as an excuse to spill about Wendy Culligan dating Harlan. Once Brenda did talk, I guess I felt obligated to go through with my end of the bargain. Stupid. Anyway, you know how some women are. They don't get what they want, they can make trouble. I could cancel it."

He paused.

"Or now that I told you, I could go ahead with it and pretend that I'm doing it for work. Maybe I'm better off just . . . going out—"

"Cancel it."

Oliver was quiet. "All right. Can I tell her I'll call her after the case is resolved?"

Decker exhaled. "She seem like the vindictive type?"

"Who can predict?"

Decker exhaled again. "Yeah, go ahead. Tell her you'll call her after . . . do you even want to call her up after everything's resolved?"

Oliver turned rosy. "Yeah, I'd like to see her. She's not beautiful like Jeanine Garrison. But she's lively. Probably be an animal in bed."

Decker said, "Watch yourself, Scotty."

"I'll be more careful."

"Marge know what you did?"

"Yeah, she was right there when it happened."

No one spoke.

Decker chuckled. "She didn't say a word to me. She's a good partner."

"Yes, she is."

Decker stood and so did Oliver. He placed his hand on Scott's shoulder, then slapped his cheek. "Keep it in your pants, guy."

"Such simple advice. So hard to follow." Oliver smiled. "Thanks."

"Your shoe's untied," Decker said. "Don't trip."

As Oliver bent down to reknot the laces, pocket change tumbled from his pants pockets.

Decker retrieved the silver, handed the metal to Oliver. "Your meter money, Scotty."

"More like total worth." Oliver counted the coins. "At least I know I'm safe. My sons ain't gonna pop me for a haul of seventy-three cents."

# ❧15

*It was after* ten, but Rina was still up. More than up. She was working, had spread junk all over the dining-room table—pens, pencils, ledgers, papers, receipts. Gnawing on the back of a pencil, staring down at columns and rows of numbers. She did look up when Decker kissed her, gave him a peck on the cheek. But then she returned her attention to her books.

"Dinner's in the oven."

Distant. Preoccupied.

Well, that was some hell of a greeting. Decker said, "We're doing self-service tonight?"

Rina stopped what she was doing, her expression surprised. She dropped the pencil on the tabletop. "Would you like me to serve you, Peter?"

"Not if you put it *that* way."

Neglected, Decker stormed into the kitchen, threw open the oven door, then pulled out the warming plate, burning his hands in the process. He dropped the plate on the floor. It crashed into bits, spewing around food and pieces of pottery.

"Shit!" he screamed. Ran to the tap and threw his hands under a blast of cold water. "Shit, shit, shit!"

Rina walked in. "I'll get you some ice—"

"I can *manage*, thank you."

Rina said nothing, got out the ice tray and tapped it on the counter. She wrapped the loose cubes in a towel, then cleaned up the floor. Prepared another plate with leftovers from the refrigerator, and placed it in the microwave.

Decker turned off the tap. "I don't expect the red carpet treatment . . . which is good, because I don't get it. But you could actually seem glad to see me."

"I am glad to see you."

"If that was your being glad, I'd hate to see you when you're angry."

"Here's your ice."

Decker stared at his wife, then took the ice bag. "Thank you."

"You're welcome." Rina opened the cutlery drawer, retrieved a knife and fork. But Decker snatched the implements away. "Don't bother. I can do it—"

"Peter, if you want to make an issue of this, you can do it by yourself, all right?"

Rina left the kitchen, but Decker dogged her heels. "Is it too much to expect a little TLC?"

Rina studied her husband. "It looks like you've had a hard day."

"Don't be shrinky on me."

She stood on her tiptoes, brushed her lips against his. "Go back into the kitchen and we'll try it again, all right?" He didn't move. She gave his rear a pat. "Go on. I'll be there in a moment."

"Fine." He stomped off into the kitchen. Rina heard soft laughter and pivoted around. Sammy shaking his head. Rina placed her finger on her lips. "He'll hear you, Shmueli—"

"Is he being a butt—"

"Don't talk that way."

"Okay, is he being a jer—"

"I get the point, Shmuel. Please. You'll make it worse."

"Why don't you have that kind of patience with *me*?"

"Has this date been codified as 'pick on Rina day'?"

Shmuel went over to his mother and kissed her cheek. "I'll go in with you . . . deflect the whole situation."

Rina kissed him back. "Actually, that's a good idea." She looked at him sternly. "Just behave yourself."

They came into the kitchen together. Sammy appeared casual. "Hey, Dad. Nice to see you." He kissed his stepfather's forehead. "How was your day?"

Decker regarded his son, stared at his wife. "What'd you do? Bring in the reinforcements?"

Rina smiled brightly. "How's your hand, *dear*?"

"Hurts."

"What happened?" Sammy asked.

"I burned it . . . being a jerk."

The microwave beeped. Rina took Decker's dinner out and set it before him.

"Thank you," Decker muttered.

"You're welcome." She sat down. So did Sam. Both of them staring at Decker, watching him eat. He felt as if he were undergoing a taste test. Finally, he asked, "Where's Jake?"

"Over at a friend's," Sammy said. "I'll pick him up in a few minutes."

Rina said, "It's wonderful now that he can drive.

So liberating not to have to schlepp the baby everywhere. To have backup—"

"Because I'm never home, right?" Decker said.

"Poor, poor Peter. Overworked and underappreciated."

"You mock but it's true." Decker looked up from his dish. "What am I eating?"

"Lamb curry on basmati rice. Do you like it?"

"It is absolutely delicious!"

"Would you like more?"

"Definitely."

Sammy said, "I think he was just malnourished, Eema. His color looks better."

"I believe you're right."

"Stop talking about me in the third person," Decker grumped.

Sam said, "I think you can take it from here. The code red has been averted."

"Go ahead. Have fun at my expense."

Sammy kissed his parents. "I'm going now. Can we stop off at Berger's and get some dessert, Eema?"

"It's after ten, Shmueli."

"No school tomorrow morning. Teachers' curriculum conferences. We can sleep in. C'mon. Everyone's gonna be there. We'll be home before midnight, I promise."

"Don't you guys ever have school?" Decker asked. "I should be paying tuition per diem."

"Don't blame me," Sam turned to his mother. "Please?"

She turned to Decker "Eleven-thirty?"

"I think that's fair."

Sam grinned. "Thanks." A shake of his car keys and he was gone. The kitchen became silent. Decker continued to wolf down his dinner.

"You're quite the gourmet."

"Curry's wonderful. The more you cook it, the better it gets."

"I suppose you're wondering why I'm so testy."

"Actually, it's become quite the norm."

"Humorous, Rina. Just for that I won't tell you."

"Up to you." She stood up. "Would you like something to drink?"

"Beer would be great, thank you."

Rina brought out a bottle of Michelob, poured it into a glass . . . watching the head spill over the rim. Rina sat down, stared at her husband, smiling when he looked at her.

He said, "Am I keeping you from something?"

"Not at all."

Decker put down his fork. "Someone got the better of me today. Only person who's allowed to do that is you."

Rina said, "Who was the woman?"

Decker smiled tightly. "How do you know it's a woman?"

"A sixth sense."

Sixth sense? Decker wondered if she had smelled his pheromones.

"Who was she?"

"Not important." Decker pushed his food away. "This tragedy at Estelle's . . . horrible enough to think of it as some maniac's vision of going out with a bang. Unfortunately, I'm getting the feeling it's more complicated."

Rina became attentive. "In what way?"

"Certain bullet angles contradict a lone killer theory. And certain individuals have a lot to gain from some of the untimely deaths. You know, murdering an individual for profit is vile enough. But to take out thirteen other innocent lives just to cover your tracks—it's truly monstrous . . . bestial."

"You have evidence of this, Peter?"

Decker looked at his wife. She sounded upset. She *was* upset. Dunce that he was. Can't just lay the job on civilians. He tried to sound matter-of-fact. "Just a sixth sense. Kind of like yours, I suppose. I'm sorry I jumped on you. I'm feeling misogynistic today. First, I got an earful from Cindy last night. Then Jan's been calling me at the station house all day. Then, this woman . . . giving me a hard time . . . playing games—"

"Why would she do that?"

"Because she's probably *hiding* something." He picked up his fork and speared another piece of lamb, feeling his face turn red. Hopefully, Rina would assume it was from anger, not from embarrassing sexual feelings. "Anyway, none of this is your fault. Go back to work. What are you doing, by the way?"

"The yeshiva's books—"

"Oh, that's right. How's it going?"

"Frankly, it's a mess. Contributions from institutions I've never heard of. Stocks and limited partnerships in exchange for tuition. The yeshiva supposedly owns real estate holdings and has bank accounts in foreign countries. At least, on the books."

"What's going on?"

"Well"—Rina scrunched up her brow—"I know

the place went through quite a few in-house accountants, each one with a different agenda. Some of them obviously went in for creative bookkeeping . . . not that I found anything illegal."

"But . . ."

Rina sighed. "The books were not as neatly kept as they should have been. Because the yeshiva used *kollel bochers* instead of professionals. You know, a man would do the books for the place in exchange for room and board for himself and his family. Then he'd leave after a few years and another one would take over. No consistency."

"Just like now."

"What do you mean?"

"Why is he asking *you* to do the books instead of a professional?"

"Yes, a professional is definitely going to have to be brought in. I think Rav Schulman knows the books are in terrible shape. He wants me to organize things *before* he hires a professional. Just to make sure everything's . . . kosher."

Rina stood up.

"Old-time Europeans are another ilk. Always bartering. In this case, stock instead of cash for tuition."

"Meanwhile, someone gets a free ride along with a nice write-off."

"My, *you're* feisty today. Why don't you give it a rest and go to bed?"

"Is that a nice thing to say?"

"Well, I'm grumpy now. *You* made me grumpy."

"So why don't *you* go to bed?" Decker brightened. "Better yet, I've got a great idea. Why don't we both go to bed?"

Rina eyed him. "The boys'll be home—"

"They'll be gone at least an hour." He raised his brow. "How about it?"

"We're both too cranky."

"So how about a little cranky love? 'Not so slow, not so fast, not this way, not that way, watch the back, my knees are locking, watch the hair—'"

Rina whacked him. "You're impossible!"

"I'm making fun of *myself*!" Decker laughed. "You don't have bad knees *or* a bad back."

Rina chided, "Listen, Lieutenant Geriatric, may I remind you that one of us is still a youthful thirty-four—"

"Low blow—"

"However, she is quickly aging from the stress of an overworked and very *moody* mate."

Decker said, "True. In spousal stress years, you've got me beaten by a mile. To bed? I promise I'll behave myself the rest of the night."

"Not good enough. You've put me in a bad mood."

"So I'll make it up to you."

"How? I don't see any flowers."

"How about if I tell you I love you?"

"Not good enough."

"Then how about if I do the dishes?"

"No dice—"

"And wake up for Hannah tomorrow—"

"Nope."

"I'll be home early tomorrow night."

"Don't feel like delaying gratification."

"Give you a back rub?"

"We've already established that I don't have a bad back."

"A foot rub?"

"My feet are fine."

"Run you a bubble bath?"

"I've already showered."

Decker was running out of options. "Hey!" He snapped his fingers. "I *got* it. The ultimate female aphrodisiac. How about if I tell you you're *right*!"

"Right about what?"

"About . . . everything. Anything you say, you'll be right. Unconditional rightness."

"For how long?"

"Twenty-four hours."

"Forty-eight hours."

"Deal—"

"Starting Friday night. I want it over a *weekend*. When you're *home*. And *around*."

"You drive a hard bargain."

Rina shrugged. "I'm worth it."

"Yes, you are." Decker scooped her up in his arms. "How's this for being romantic?"

"It's a start." Rina put her arms around his neck. "And a good one at that."

Abruptly, he awoke—eyes popping open, heart beating, head pounding, a ringing in his ears, and the dead bodies in his brain as clear as daylight.

A Nam dream.

Something he hadn't had in many moons. At least he roused himself before the thrashing, before he woke Rina up. He realized he must have had some kind of control over his reactions even in sleep. Otherwise, how could he have lived in hell so quietly?

The routine was second nature by now. Tiptoeing

into the kitchen, turning on the light over the stove, putting the kettle on the fire. A minute later, he sat down at the table, sipping a hot mug of tea that steamed his face.

He glanced up at the kitchen clock.

It was only eleven-fifteen. Boys had fifteen minutes.

He was glad Rina hadn't heard him get up as she usually did. Sex had knocked her out. A good night. The juices had been flowing for both of them. Pure fireworks. Afterward, Rina seemed joyous . . . a word that hadn't been in her vocabulary for quite some time.

She needed escape more than he did. Though she tried valiantly to hide it, she'd become a different woman since Bram had died. Difficult because she had never confided to Decker the depths of her feelings for him. On some level, she had loved him. But it had to be more than that. He'd come to the conclusion that Bram had been Rina's last link to her late husband, Yitzchak. In Bram's untimely demise, she had relived both deaths at once. Been hell for her. For him and the boys as well.

Maybe this would signal good times.

*If* Decker could ever exorcise his own demons.

Eleven-twenty.

Late. But not too late for a night owl like Cindy. She picked up immediately. He asked her how her day had gone.

"Nothing exciting." She paused. "I did speak to my ex-professor of Criminal Sciences. Told him about my decision to enlist with the LAPD. He said I should have signed up with the FBI—"

"You've *got* to be kidding!"

"He says LAPD are a bunch of clowns—"

"Oh, fu—for *this* kind of advice, I was forking out twenty grand a year?"

"He says that the FBI is a more professional outfit with a more highly educated crew—"

"A bunch of yahoos—"

"They've lifted their hiring freeze, Dad. I'm just the type of person they're looking for. Young, female, well educated, with a parent in law enforcement—"

"Congratulations. You've succeeded in really *aggravating* me."

"The thing is, Father, I really want to *solve* crimes, not wear sunglasses."

Decker laughed so loudly he was afraid he'd wake up Rina. "Now I know why I love you, Cin."

"Although there are some good agents out there."

"Maybe one or two."

"So why are you calling at eleven-thirty at night? No, I'll tell you. Like most men, you never use the phone for chitchat. You use it to make appointments or to do business. You want to do chitchat, you invite me over for dinner or out for breakfast. So what do you need to know?"

Decker was surprised by her perceptiveness. "Which French existentialist wrote the book about a guy getting arrested for not crying at his mother's funeral?"

"Camus. *The Stranger*. Why?"

"I take it you read the book, then."

"In French actually."

Decker broke into soft laughter.

"What?"

"A Columbia graduate who reads Camus in French becoming a cop. Maybe you *are* better suited for the FBI. Sit around all day musing about life while constructing serial-killer profiles. They certainly don't *solve* any serial killings—"

"You're being very insular and petty."

"Your ex-Criminal Sciences professor is a jerk. What is existentialism anyway?"

"Everything is random . . . purposeless. Each person for himself."

"Sounds like the FBI—"

"Daddy—"

"Kinda like a dog-eat-dog philosophy?"

"Not exactly. Since the world is purposeless and meaningless, it's up to humankind to impart humanism into it through *free will*. Ultimately, our job is to civilize our societies."

"*Human*kind?"

"Columbia was very PC. Why are you asking about Camus?"

"Just wondering if I got my money's worth from Columbia."

Cindy laughed. "There's more to it than that. But I won't press. However, if you'd like to tell me . . . take me out for breakfast—"

"You're on."

"Great. When and where?"

"Gotta be somewhere kosher. How about Noah's bagels? I'll meet you halfway in Sherman Oaks. Six-thirty on the dot."

"Six-thirty? You mean A.M.?"

"Some of us have jobs. Six-thirty at Noah's. Are we on?"

"Yes, *if* you promise to tell me about your case."

"No dice. This isn't business, just chitchat."

"But maybe you'll accidentally let a few things slip?"

"At six-thirty A.M., this is a real possibility."

She laughed, hung up, and so did he.

But his thoughts weren't on Cindy. They were glued to a mental video camera that was in rewind. Back to Jeanine Garrison's office. The moment he first saw her. Again, he felt a jolt of lightning in his groin. In his head, he went through the interview, slowly . . . deliberately. Her initial anger, her sudden display of inappropriate sexuality, her animation when she talked about tennis.

A stunning, erotic woman in black. Dabbing her eyes with a tissue.

Another jolt hit him. But this one came straight to the brain.

Jeanine patting her eyes. Then she had looked up. Decker had seen her face, had seen those eyes.

They had been totally clear—bright blue and shining like diamonds.

Completely dry.

# ✥16

*A pleasant breakfast* with Cindy followed by a morning of meetings, paperwork, and crime. Decker took his lunch break at two-thirty, eating his sandwiches, going over the articles from yesterday's computer search on Jeanine Garrison. A half hour later, he heard a knock on the door. Scott Oliver entered the office, noticed the clippings on Decker's desk.

"You're kinda fixated on this—"

"They knew each other," Decker sat up, stretched. "Something she didn't admit in the interview."

"Why should she? Who'd want to be associated with a mass murderer?"

"That's the point, Scott. If she didn't know him well, she would have admitted it openly . . . *wondered* about it. At least, she might have brought it up. Because it's weird not to."

"Wendy Culligan didn't bring up knowing Harlan."

"But she brought it up to Brenda Miller. Besides, Wendy had nothing to gain by anyone's death . . . as opposed to the Garrison offspring. Harlan Manz takes out thirteen people and suddenly Jeanine Garrison's a millionaire."

"Along with her brother." Oliver paused. "Why do you think it's *her* and not David Garrison?"

"Picture shows Manz with Jeanine, not Manz and David."

"Can I play devil's advocate for a moment?"

"Shoot."

"Deck, why would she do it? And don't just say for the money. Obviously, Daddy took *good* care of her. Even her brother admitted that. Besides, a piece of ass like Jeanine . . . she could marry money in a snap."

"But in both cases, she'd still be dependent on someone else's goodwill."

Oliver said, "All I'm saying is, her addict brother has as much to gain as she does."

"Absolutely." Decker stretched. "And according to Webster, David had lots of animosity toward his parents . . . his father. But . . ." He organized his ideas. "Webster saw David as a talented but troubled individual. David's a *successful* artist. You see him hanging out with a loser like Manz?"

"Not hanging out with him, Pete. *Using* him."

Decker thought about that. Oliver had a good point. "So give me something that links David Garrison with Harlan Manz, and I'm all over his ass, too." He stacked the printouts, laid them neatly on his desk. Focused his attention on Oliver. "How'd that call to Brenda Miller go?"

Oliver smiled—a white crescent of teeth. "She was great! Understood completely. Even said she *admired* my integrity." He rubbed his hands together. "Can't wait until this case is over. At this point, I don't care *how* it's resolved, just as long as it *is* resolved." He paused, eyed his boss. "Jeanine got to you, didn't she, Rabbi?"

Decker felt his face get hot. "She's dangerous, Scott. A knockout bitch with an ice-queen smile that gets you rock hard. Not too many of those around."

He paused.

"Men'll do incredibly dumb things to get laid by a gorgeous piece of ass. Something tells me she knows how to use that fact for her own purposes."

Oliver's eyes fell on the pile of articles. "So if you can't fuck her in the flesh, you'll fuck her over instead."

Decker smiled. "Believe me, I'm *not* interested in fucking her. And even though I think she's hinky, I am *not* out to get her. But then I examine what we have. So far, things are . . . well, they're not pointing *to* Jeanine. More like . . . revolving *around* her."

"You want to revolve around her, Deck?"

"No, Scott, I'd like to keep my marriage intact."

"But she did get to you."

"Yep. She's got a Svengalian quality to her . . . the voice, her manner. Very rhythmic, very intoxicating. She's the type of woman who could get even honest men to do hinky things . . . let alone slackers like Harlan Manz."

"Things like pop her parents? Then pop himself?"

"Who said he popped himself?"

"Ballistics."

"Not exactly. Ballistics says that the bullet in Harlan's head came from the gun at Harlan's side. It never said that Harlan actually fired that *specific* gun."

"You're stretching."

"Yes, I am." Decker laughed. "Aw, well. Maybe I'm doing this because it's better than attending a lunch meeting with some brass from Parker Center."

"Now that I can believe." Oliver paused. "An ice queen, huh? I gotta meet this woman." He produced a sickly smile. "Then again, my track record with the opposite sex ain't too hot."

"You're showing some unusual insight."

Oliver squirmed. "Loo, you're so straight, at times I think you've got a rod up your ass. She makes *you* poke your zipper . . . man, that scares the shit out of me."

Before Decker signed out, he made two quick calls. First one was to Terrance Howell, who wasn't in or wasn't answering. Decker left a message on his machine. As luck would have it, he caught Sonia Eaton right as she was leaving. She couldn't talk now. Perhaps they could talk tomorrow evening. Could she ask what it was about?

Decker hedged, then said something about Harlan Manz aka Hart Mansfield. As he understood it, Sonia had played tennis with him a couple of times. Just wanted to ask her a few questions about him and the matches. The police were trying to get a lock on the mass murderer. Maybe insights could prevent tragedies like this in the future.

Sonia's voice turned cold. "Lofty ambitions. I didn't know the LAPD cared."

Decker was silent.

"Look, I barely knew Hart. Maybe I spoke a dozen words to the guy."

"You played a doubles match with him for the

New Christian Hospital charity games. About two years ago?"

A long pause. "Where'd you dig up that? *Why'd* you dig up that? You aren't going to publicize it, are you?"

She sounded horrified. Decker was soothing. "Not at all."

An impatient sigh. "I swear I barely remember him."

"But you did play tennis with him."

"Just that once. And that was at the behest of one of my friends."

"Maybe I could talk to your friend, then?"

Sonia snorted. "I'm not about to give out names and numbers over the phone. I don't even know if you're for real."

"I can give you the number here at the station house—"

"I'm a busy woman. I don't have time for this nonsense! What's your name again?"

"Lieutenant Peter Decker."

Sonia said, "Look, Lieutenant, *if* you know about that tennis match, *and* you know about me, you probably know about my friend. So what's this all about?"

Decker weighed his options. He decided to be truthful—at least partially truthful. "I found a photograph of you with Harlan from the local newspaper— *The Valley Voice.* There were two other people in that match. Your partner, Terrance Howell, and Manz's partner, Jeanine Garrison. And yes, I'm going to phone both of them. You could help me out by telling me which one of them asked you to play with Manz."

A long pause. She said, "I suppose you'll find out soon enough. It was Jeanine."

"Thanks. Were they an item, ma'am?"

"That's all I'm going to tell you, Lieutenant Peter Decker from the LAPD."

Decker laughed. "Thank you for your time. I really do appreciate it." He tried one more time, doing the sympathy ploy. He sighed deeply into the phone. "This terrible ordeal at Estelle's . . . I don't know . . . we were all affected by it."

The line was quiet.

Decker continued, "I would really like to prevent things like that in the future."

"How *can* you?" Sonia sounded upset. "How can anyone *prevent* monsters from going crazy?"

"Well . . . we talk to people." Decker was really winging it now. "We try to get profiles, ma'am. On who may be likely to do this kind of thing."

"I hope you conclude that it's not *too* many people."

"No, no, no," Decker reassured her. "No need to be alarmed. But if we, as law enforcement providers and protectors, get . . . even a tiny, tiny insight into what makes these guys tick . . . what can I say? I think it's worth the intrusion."

"Maybe."

Sonia sounded wary. But she continued to talk anyway.

"Look, I wish I could tell you more. But I'm not going to talk behind Jeanine's back. She's not a close friend, but she is a . . . an acquaintance. A very formidable person. You'll know what I mean once you meet her."

"I'm sure you're right." Decker paused. "Formidable, huh?"

"You don't want her as your enemy."

"Ah! Can you tell me if she and Hart dated?"

"Jeanine doesn't date." Sonia's voice had turned flat. "She has . . . admirers. Shuffles them around like cards in a gin game."

"She likes tennis players, doesn't she?"

"She likes . . ." Sonia paused. "I've really talked too much. I've got to go."

"Ms. Eaton, let's do us both a favor. I won't say anything about this conversation, if you won't say anything. Strictly confidential?"

"Fine with me."

"Can you do me another favor?"

"What?"

"Since this is just between the two of us, can you just complete your sentence?" Decker asked. "Jeanine likes . . . what?"

Faint laugh. Sonia said, "Jeanine likes anything that doesn't stand in her way."

It was only six-thirty. Surely some florist would still be open.

Decker got off the freeway, started cruising the boulevard for an open shop. If he didn't find one, he could always go to the market. Smiles carried flowers. Not very nice ones. Dyed mums in a terracotta pot. Emergency flowers. Like if you forgot the secretary's birthday. Not for the wife. Rina would see through it. Besides, he really did want something extra special . . . something that conveyed what years of being a man had taught him to repress.

Lord, he was tired. Weary and disappointed in himself. He used to think he was impervious to women's wiles. After his divorce, he had developed a hard shell, a seasoned air, and a wizened attitude. No bitch was ever gonna fuck with his brain again, thank you very much.

When he met Rina, he had known immediately that she was a jewel—a rare, precious diamond. Still, he had taken his time. Hadn't stopped dating other women until it had become clear *she* was committed. That she wanted him as much as he wanted her. And even when she wanted to go to New York to think things over . . . well, that had been cool with him. Though when she had returned, he had been glad to see her.

Glad, but cautious.

He doubted his blood pressure rose beyond a notch.

Everything on an even keel.

The courtship had proceeded nicely. She placed no demands on him—other than religion.

Religion.

Yeah, that had been a biggie. But once that was resolved, things ran smoothly. Of course, he had to become the type of Jew she wanted. An Orthodox Jew. Keeping kosher, keeping the Sabbath, keeping family purity. Had to do it. Otherwise, marriage would have been out of the question. And he had wanted to get married . . . very, very badly.

But he never felt compromised. Because Rina was a traditional woman herself. She took care of the house and children, he took care of *everything* else.

An old-fashioned family and that was fine with him.

And he was in *charge* . . . the illustrious *paterfamilias*.

Man, had he been fooling himself. Meeting Jeanine, being bowled over by her sexuality, realizing what a sensual woman could have done to him. If Jeanine carried the moniker seductive kitten, Rina would have been tagged a full-fledged man-eating tigress. There had been times when Decker had thought about her . . . times late at night. His lust had been so overwhelming, so damn powerful, he had needed no physical contact to achieve orgasm. Only had to close his eyes . . . picture her face . . .

He would have done anything to *get* her. Anything at all. And had another man entered the picture, he would have done anything to *keep* her. Lie, cheat, steal . . .

Maybe even murder.

He broke out in a sweat.

All of his macho posturing . . . a facade maintained by Rina's indulgence. After Jan, he hadn't become any smarter. He had just been lucky. Really, really lucky. He had met a femme fatale, but thank God she turned out to be as beautiful on the inside as she was on the outside.

Thank you, God. Thank you, thank you, thank you!

# ❧17

*The message was* on his desk when Decker walked into his office.

*See me immediately.*

Not a good omen. What could Strapp want with him at seven-thirty in the morning? He went around the corner to the captain's office.

Strapp waved him inside. "Shut the door."

Decker complied, regarded the man. In his thin face sat intense, angry eyes and a hard mouth. But his hands . . . fingers kneading one another. He was anxious.

"Sit down."

Decker sat without speaking, eyes scanning the room. Walls filled with diplomas and certificates as well as pictures of the captain with VIPs—the mayor, the governor, the president. Still, the furniture was strictly departmental issue. A serviceable desk and standard chairs. Metal file cabinets. The man had an ego, but he wasn't peacock vain.

Decker directed his eyes to his superior. "What is it, sir?"

"Do you have hard evidence against Jeanine Garrison?"

Decker continued to stare, said nothing.

Strapp met his gaze. "I got a wake-up call this morning. You've been implying an involvement between her and Harlan Manz—"

"So much for keeping confidences," Decker muttered.

"You toss Jeanine Garrison's picture around with Harlan Manz to Garrison's friends, you think it's *not* going to come back on you? Are you out of your mind? She's furious, screaming police harassment. Threatening a lawsuit."

"I didn't toss anyone's picture around. I mentioned the picture to a mutual friend, trying to get a fix on Garrison's relationship to Manz. I'm running an investigation, Captain—"

"That's right. You're running an investigation, not a witch-hunt."

Decker looked at the ceiling. "Get a call from the mayor, Cap?"

"You're fucking outta line, Decker!"

Decker was quiet and so was Strapp. The captain was breathing audibly, cheeks and the tip of his nose bright red. But there was more than that. Decker knew that someone had tied Strapp's hands. It didn't sit well with him.

Quietly, the captain said, "We've got a society woman, Pete. She's hosted umpteen charity events for some very good causes. A philanthropic woman with a lot of contacts. And she just lost her parents in a horrible, devastating tragedy—"

"Ah, yes, the *thing.*"

"What?"

"Never mind."

Strapp glared at him. "You go around talking about a newspaper article that's over two years old, implying that she played a part in her own parents' murder—"

"Not at all. You want to hear the truth?"

"Not particularly. I want you to stop whatever the hell you're doing until you get evidence. Good, solid, concrete, carved-in-stone *evidence*."

"If I stop what I'm doing, I won't get evidence—"

"You don't have evidence, you quit pestering her. You can go now."

Silence.

Decker said, "At least Jeanine's not a liar. She does have her connections—"

"Decker—"

"An O. J. and Menendez rolled into an eye-pleasing package."

"Are you done with the sarcasm?"

"Yes, I suppose I am."

"Then get back to work."

Decker took a deep breath, let it out slowly. "Cap, you tell me how I'm supposed to get evidence against *anyone* if I can't conduct an investigation."

Strapp said, "Harlan Manz came into Estelle's and mowed down thirteen people, maimed thirty-two others, then shot himself. We got forensics, we got witnesses, we got a cut-and-dried case. Why are you turning this into a conspiracy?"

Decker was about to speak.

Strapp blurted out, "She said you came on to her. She refused you and now you're seeking revenge."

Decker kept his face flat, his heart suddenly pounding in his chest.

Strapp said, "You want to tell me about it?"

Decker said, "She's a very sexy woman."

"And?"

"And that is it."

Strapp rubbed his temples. "You didn't come on to her?"

"No."

"Let anything slip out?"

Decker was about to respond, then laughed at the unintentional double entendre. They both did. "No. I was completely professional. I was aware of her attraction. So I was especially conscientious."

"Maybe you're going at her because of your strong attraction to her?"

"I didn't say *strong* attraction—"

"Don't argue semantics with me, Decker. Are you out to get her?"

"No, I am not, sir. I am out to explain some gross inconsistencies in a very puzzling case."

Strapp eyed his man. Quietly he asked, "She come on to you, Pete?"

"Looked straight at my wedding band, then invited me to a private tour of the new museum."

"What'd you say?"

"I told her thanks but no thanks. My family likes me home at night. Would you like me to reconstruct the conversation verbatim?"

"Don't get smart-assed with me."

Decker blinked a couple of times. "Is she slapping me and/or the LAPD with a formal suit?"

"Not yet. But I got a call from her lawyer . . . among other people. He made noises, Pete. Told me to control my men."

"Christ!" Decker reminded himself to unclench his jaw. "Okay. *What* do you want me to do?"

Strapp said, "If it was anyone else . . . anyone else . . ."

No one spoke.

"The fact that I believe you doesn't mean squat. If she presses charges, I'm hogtied. You go through the whole routine."

"I know."

"Do you think she's doing this to keep you from doing your job? Or is she a spurned woman who's getting even? *Or* is she just a nutcase?"

"Maybe all three."

"What do you have?"

Decker paused, then pulled out his notebook and began to recount the case, item by item. He told Strapp about the suicide position, about the inconsistent bullet trajectories, about the number of bullets per number of empty magazines. Then he discussed Jeanine: how she had put him off the first time. Later, when he returned, her friendly attitude had turned hostile. He spoke about how she stood to inherit millions, her interest in tennis, and her acquaintance with Harlan Manz. How close, no one knew. At the moment, that's what Decker was trying to figure out.

"What you have isn't conclusive of anything."

"Of course not. That's why I'm running an investigation. If I had *conclusive* evidence, my job would be over."

"What you have doesn't give you the right to accuse victims of murder."

"I don't point fingers, I gather evidence. Accusations are for the District Attorney's Office. Would you like to hear what I have so far?"

Strapp was quiet. "Go ahead."

"I've got witnesses claiming that gunshots were coming from every direction—"

"Because they were hysterical."

"Granted. They were all hysterical. And if that's all we had, I would have dropped it. But then Forensics comes back . . . we got bullet trajectories inconsistent with the position of the shooter *and* a suspicious suicide."

For the first time, Strapp's interest was piqued. "In what way?"

"Harlan apparently held the gun about two and a half feet from his head."

"Some people have problems putting a gun to their temple."

"Six inches, maybe . . . but thirty? I got long arms . . . but even I would have problems bringing my arm out two and a half feet, then precisely aiming the gun at my temple."

"How long is Harlan's arm?"

"About three feet from the shoulder to the tip of his fingers. But you've got to remember that to shoot himself, he would've had to flex his wrist backward to aim the gun at his head. Which takes away his hand as part of the distance. I'm not saying it's impossible. But it *is* an unusual angle."

"What else?"

"I've got more shell casings than magazines—"

"In all the hullaballoo, we lost magazines."

"Sir, everything you're saying is possible. But all these glitches . . . they have a cumulative effect,

Captain. So I took it a step further. I asked myself the logical question. What could explain the inconsistencies?"

"A second gunman."

"Exactly." Decker tried to hide the excitement in his voice. "First thing I zeroed in on was Harlan Manz. Estelle's wasn't a robbery, we know that. So if it wasn't a robbery, and if it wasn't the work of a lone madman who committed suicide, what was it? To me, it was beginning to shape out as a hit."

"Keep going."

Decker paused. "Here's the speculation part. I'm thinking that the person who hired Harlan to do the hit also hired a second gunman. Two people to do the job. And then the *second* gunman did a double-cross—either on his own or as part of the plan."

The captain spoke in a flat voice. "A conspiracy worthy of Oliver Stone."

Decker went on, ignoring the skepticism. "If we assume a hit, then someone who died in that restaurant was set up."

Strapp said, "So you went through a list of the victims, looked up their loved ones and friends and enemies. Figured out who had the most to gain by the victim's death."

"You got it."

"Narrowed it down to those who had a lot to gain *and* those who might have known Harlan Manz."

"Right on the nailhead—"

"Came up with Jeanine Garrison."

"Actually I narrowed it down to three parties because all the victims belonged to Greenvale Country Club, where Harlan had also worked." Decker began ticking off the list on his fingers. "A real estate broker and her entourage, Walter Skinner and his date, and Ray and Linda Garrison. Marge and Oliver took the real estate group, Martinez took Walter's widow, Webster took David Garrison, I took Jeanine. I went into the interview expecting nothing. *Nothing.* Then, out of *nowhere*, she started going hinky on me."

"You hit a nerve—"

"The whole damn spinal column."

"So she wasn't the only one being looked into?"

"No, she wasn't the only one. Captain, I didn't know this woman from Adam. There was no hidden agenda."

"Webster questioned the brother?"

"Of course."

"That's good . . . strengthens your case . . . our case." Strapp made a tepee with his hands. "Still, you have nothing on her. And even if there was a connection between her and Manz, it doesn't mean she ordered anything."

"You know, sir, we're talking thirteen homicides. The woman lost her parents. I think she'd be thrilled to hear about an investigation—if she were innocent."

"Not an investigation that implicated her. Even innocent people don't want to be *associated* with a mass murderer. Use your brain, Deck."

Oliver had said the same thing. Decker said, "She's *lying* about the harassment. So you've got to ask what else she's lying about. And why does she want me out of the picture?"

"Because you're implying nasty things about her. She claimed she rolled out the red carpet for you, took time out of her busy day, was civil and answered all your questions. Afterward, you were slow to leave. She didn't know what to do, offered you something to drink—a soft drink, a glass of wine—"

"I don't drink while I'm working."

"You took the glass of wine, had a couple of drinks, then asked her out. She was shocked, tried to be nice, but you were insistent. Finally, she flatly refused your advances and you became angry. Next thing she knows, you're spreading rumors about her."

"Her allegations are patently *ridiculous*! I didn't come on to her, I wasn't slow to leave, and I didn't have a glass of anything, let alone wine. I don't drink on the job. It's grounds for dismissal. Why would I do something so stupid?"

"Because we think with our cocks."

"Sir, I'm not impervious to sexual feelings. Still, I keep my mouth shut, my hands to myself, and my zipper closed at all times. Because I love my wife, I love my children, I love my marriage. Bottom line, sir. What do you want me to do? You want me to back off, I'll back off."

"Until we work things out with her lawyers, stay away from Jeanine Garrison."

Decker made a fist. "Crazy bitch—"

"I didn't hear that," Strapp said. "These are direct orders. Stop showing that picture you have of her and Harlan Manz together. Makes us look like the tabloid press. And stay away from Garrison's friends."

"What about her enemies?"

"Decker—"

"*Who* can I talk to?"

"You talk to anyone you'd like about Harlan Manz.

And if Jeanine Garrison's name happens to come up in the conversation . . . someone wants to talk about her . . . I suppose you can listen."

Quietly, he walked through the door, heard Rina's distant hum. The gentle soothing song of a mother to her baby. She was putting Hannah down for a noontime nap. He could picture them mentally . . . his wife's smile, Hannah's little head peeking out from the covers of her bed, carrot-colored curls over her forehead, Rina brushing them aside. Such pure love. It almost brought tears to his eyes.

He swallowed dryly, sat down at the dining-room table. Waiting. Waiting some more. Head in hand, his stomach in a knot. His brain played the bongos against his cranium. Finally Rina came into the room, surprised and delighted to see him.

"First roses, then this . . ." Suddenly, she became alarmed. "You're ashen, Peter. What's wrong?"

Decker paused before speaking. "Remember that woman I interviewed a couple of days ago? The one who got the better of me?"

Rina turned pale, sat down herself. She exhaled deeply. "Yes, I remember."

"Well . . . there's a possibility that I might get slapped with a sexual harassment suit."

She brought her hand to her chest, whispered, "Thank God."

Decker stared at her. "Thank God?"

"No, I mean . . . that's terrible. What happened?"

Decker was quiet. Then he said, "Am I misreading you . . . or did you just think I was about to confess something . . . like an affair?"

"Well, I don't know." Rina took a deep breath, let it out slowly. "I mean, first the roses out of the clear blue sky. Then you come in all white and hangdog."

"Thank you for the trust." He got up and walked into the kitchen.

Rina followed. "I'm sorry, Peter," she said softly. "I'm really sorry. But I can't help my feelings."

"Do you trust me?"

"Of course I do."

"Then how could you *think* a thing like that?"

"Peter, I love you so much . . . and things have been kind of tense around here. I guess I just got . . . scared." She wiped tears from her eyes. "Also, you blushed when you talked about her."

"I did not."

"Yes, you did."

He paused. "Okay, I did."

"She's beautiful?"

"Yes."

"Sexy?"

"Maybe to the unsuspecting." Decker felt his mouth go tight. "Right now, I'd like to kill the crazy loon."

"So you found another woman attractive—"

"*Found* is right. *Found*. As in the *past* tense."

"You don't have to sugarcoat it. It's okay. Because I know you, Peter. Her mind must have been inventing things. You're much too professional to let an attractive woman get in the way of your work."

Decker stared at her.

Rina shrugged. "The whole allegation's frivolous. Don't worry about it. How about some coffee? You want regular or decaf?"

"Decaf." Decker eyed her suspiciously. "You're taking this very well. Much better than me."

"Than I." Rina fetched a bag of coffee. "If this woman's crazy, is it your fault? As a matter of fact, I bet she came on to you. Just like Lilah Brecht, right?"

"God, I forgot about her." Decker raised his brow. "Obviously, you didn't."

"Obviously. Did she make a pass at you?"

"Sort of."

"So you rejected her in a very professional manner. Which probably made her mad. Who is she anyway?"

"Jeanine Garrison."

Rina scrunched up her forehead. "Why does that name sound familiar."

Decker gave her some background information.

Rina scooped out coffee and put it in the drip machine. "Then I've probably seen her picture on some society page."

"I can't believe how calm you're acting. I was a nervous wreck driving over here."

"Well, you needn't have been worried just for being a healthy man."

Decker couldn't get over her attitude. So dispassionate! It was worrisome. Was she keeping her anxiety inside for his sake? Or was there more? He stared at her. "Rina, are you keeping something from me?"

Her cheeks took on a rosy hue. "Now, what would I be keeping from you?"

Decker studied her, said nothing for a long time. Then he said, "It was Bram, wasn't it?"

Rina was quiet. "He's dead, Peter. Can we change the subject?"

"When you two were alone together here . . ." Decker rolled his tongue in his cheek. "Nothing happened, right?"

Rina turned to him, her face angry. "Thank you for the trust." She stalked out of the room.

Decker followed, his heart thundering in his chest, his head pounding. "Well, you have to admit there was a little history behind my question. I saw the way he looked at you. I saw the way you looked at *him*."

Rina picked up a magazine, sat down at the dining-room table and began to scan it angrily, turning the pages with force.

"Don't ignore me!"

"Why not?"

"Because I'm your husband, for Chrissakes."

Rina said nothing.

Decker ripped the magazine from his wife's grasp.

Rina looked up in shock. "Excuse me. Where I come from we don't bully people into having conversations."

Decker felt his emotional thermostat going haywire. He looked at his hands, realized they were shaking. He took a deep breath, closed his eyes. "Look, I'm sorry, all right? Here." He offered her the magazine. "Take it back . . . please."

Rina saw her husband's trembling hands. Something was terribly wrong. She didn't move; tears rolled down her cheeks.

Decker put the magazine on the table. Clasped his hands together. "I'm sorry, Rina. I'm sorry for the accusation. I know nothing happened. We're going through a rough period. It's been sticky around here since Bram's death. We'll weather it. Let's just work together, all right?"

Rina nodded, her face crumbling. Decker raised her up, swept her into his arms, and rocked her as they stood. "It's okay, honey. It's okay. I know you loved him. He was a very good man. You have good taste in men."

Rina talked through tears, hugged Peter tightly. "Very."

"I didn't mean to extract a compliment, but I'll take it anyway."

Rina broke away, dried her eyes. "You want that coffee now?"

"Fine." Decker followed her into the kitchen, sat down at the table. "Man, what a week."

Rina retrieved mugs from the cupboard. "What a year."

"That, too."

Rina said, "I haven't been easy to be around."

Decker was quiet.

"His death hit me hard, Peter."

"I know. I'm sorry."

"I feel so . . . *guilty.* Like it was divine retribution or something."

Decker was taken aback. "That's ridiculous!"

Rina was quiet.

"That didn't come out right," Decker said. "I don't mean to minimize your feelings—"

"It's all right," Rina wiped her eyes again.

Decker said, "Neither one of you did anything wrong, Rina. There's no reason to feel guilty."

"Except that my husband was barely cold, not much more than three months in the ground, I was a religious woman. And Bram was a *goy*. Not just any goy, mind you. A seminary student studying to be a priest *and* my late husband's best friend. I felt like I *violated* everything that I held dear. Such betrayal—"

"Yitzchak had died, Rina. Betrayal is for the living, not the dead."

"You can betray a memory." Rina poured coffee into the mugs. "Bram didn't feel too good about it, either. It was horrible—the mixture of love and guilt. We shouldn't even have started." She plunked a mug in front of Decker. "So now you know. Are you any richer because of it?"

"Maybe I am. Because maybe now I understand why you've been so upset. Rina, God didn't strike Bram dead. A very disturbed person lashed out and he happened to be in the way."

"Maybe she was just an instrument in God's plan."

"And maybe we're just protozoa under a microscope."

"What does *that* mean?"

"They're both equally absurd thoughts."

"Not that you're minimizing my feelings."

Decker felt his jaw tighten. He willed it slack, weighed his words. "Darlin', I'm just trying to ground you. Keep you from going further into your blue funk. Bram was a *wonderful* man, Rina. A brilliant scholar and a caring individual and good-looking to boot. He was also very complex and troubled coming from that dysfunctional family."

"Yes, he was."

"Take my word for it, honey. You were the *best*

thing that ever happened to him. Man, he would have jumped bridges for you, he loved you that much. And there you were, a young, young widow who had just lost her husband to a monstrous, lingering illness. You had two small children and not much in the way of support."

"My parents were around."

"I *know* your parents, Rina. They're wonderful people, but they're also camp survivors and very emotional. I know you didn't unload on them like you did on Bram."

Rina was quiet.

"You were lost and lonely and so was Bram. You took each other through transitional periods in both your lives. And that wasn't a bad thing. It paved the way for me."

Rina sat down with her coffee, leaned over, and kissed her husband tenderly. *Poor Peter. Dealing with my past upheavals while your own dam of troubles is cracking.* "Don't worry about this Garrison woman, okay? You're a very attractive man who's in a very attractive profession—"

"I thought the LAPD ranked behind a leper colony in attractiveness."

"Despite the press, cops still carry cachet. And a detective . . . well, he has even more clout. If she tries to make these fatuous allegations actually stick, you'll fight it. And you'll win because the truth will prevail."

"If it were only that simple." Decker ran his hand over his face. "Thanks for not being angry—"

"Why should I be angry? You may have had thoughts, but you didn't *do* anything."

"No, I didn't. Still, it's a load off my mind." Decker gave her a sheepish look. "So you'll support me?"

"All the way."

"The little woman standing behind me?"

"You mean standing in *front* of you, chump. They want to talk to *you*, first they go through *me*."

# ❧18

*Marge said, "I* can't believe they *did* this to you."

Decker said, "It's not that bad. Jeanine's screwy reaction shows we may be on to something."

Oliver said, "Fucking bitch—"

"We'll just have to find another way," Marge said. "You can't stay on her ass, *I'll* do it. Like to see her slap *me* with a sexual harassment suit."

Webster said, "Reckon I could tote a few pictures around of Jeanine and Manz, ask her friends and ex-husband a few questions—"

"No, no, no!" Decker said. "No pictures of Jeanine Garrison with Harlan Manz. Strapp made that clear."

Martinez said, "So how are we going to make a connection between them if we can't talk about them in the same breath?"

Decker said, "I'll tell you what we're going to do. We're going to take a connection between Harlan Manz and Jeanine Garrison as a *given*, okay? *We* are going after a phantom: the second shooter—who may or may not exist."

"What's the game plan?" Oliver asked.

"Find out who Jeanine might have been dealing with *prior* to the shooting." Decker turned to Farrell

Gaynor. "This is your specialty. I want a complete paper trail on Jeanine—every phone call, every credit card slip, every bank account, every withdrawal slip, every will or legal document—"

"I'm foaming at the mouth."

"But we also have to work on the sly," Decker said. "Quietly. No slipups. Because Jeanine is a liar . . . and a connected one. It's just a small step from slapping me with charges to slapping all of you with police harassment. Ergo, I want an equal investigation of her brother. Not only because it will play well for the lawyers, but also because he's a suspect—a former drug user with a record, who hated his father. Harlan Manz turned him into a millionaire, too."

Webster said, "Want me to lean on him, Loo?"

"Not just yet. First, let's get paper on him." He turned to Marge. "Dunn, you're on target with Jeanine. She can't claim sexual harassment against you. If we need to question her, you'll be the one."

"Agreed."

Webster said, "Since y'all're trying to figure out this unknown second hit man, reckon it might be a good idea to try to profile him?"

Decker said, "What do you have in mind, Tom?"

"Examine what we've got and come up with a composite of this phantom."

"Don't like profiles," Oliver said, "They're misleading."

Webster said, "I'm talkin' generalities. For instance, this phantom killer . . . if he were one of *Jeanine*'s beaux, I reckon he'd be young and impressionable, rather than an old experienced hit man."

Martinez said, "Why do you say that?"

"Because this woman uses her sexuality to get things. Younger the guy, the faster the boner."

"Experienced hit men don't get hard-ons?" Martinez asked.

"She's into *power*, Bert," Webster said. "Easier to have power over a young untested stud than an experienced racehorse."

Marge said, "He's got a point. Look at the kind of woman Jeanine is. She sets things up, takes charge of events, and *coordinates* everything."

Webster went on. "Then just look at what she did to the Loo here. Using her sexuality to mess with his brain. When that didn't work out, she went straight for the jugular. She's into power . . . power over men."

"Manipulating men," Marge said. "Couldn't do it to Daddy, so she offed him?"

Martinez said, "That's a leap. But I like it."

Oliver turned to Webster. "So you're thinking she roped some young stooge into doing her dirty work by fucking him?"

"Or by promising to fuck him," Webster said. "It don't even have to be the real thing. I know lots of women like that. Southern belles who are steel magnolias. They love to dangle things and I don't mean worms on a reel."

Oliver said, "So Jeanine was working on Manz and some other jerk at the *same time*?"

Marge said, "Why not? She's good at organizing things."

"Men aren't things."

"True. They're easier to manipulate. All you got to do is *moan*."

Oliver threw her a dirty look. Marge gave him the peace sign.

Webster regarded Decker. "You're awfully quiet."

"Just thinking about what Sonia Eaton said about Jeanine. That the woman has admirers . . . shuffles them around like cards in a gin game . . ."

Martinez said, "Look, I don't want to lose her. Let me *tail* her. Even if she should notice me, I'm completely harmless-looking. Blend into crowds."

Decker said, "I'd love for you to tail her, Bert. Problem is, you've got a heavy current caseload that can't be neglected for a 'what if.'"

Martinez rubbed his stomach. "You know I'm not feeling so hot, Loo. I really wouldn't mind taking the day off."

"No dice," Decker said.

"It's already two o'clock, Loo," Martinez said. "Let me go take a peek. Especially now that you've made her nervous. She might do something stupid."

Decker sat back in his chair. "I take any of you off your cases and put you on Garrison without some very strong indications of guilt, we all become vulnerable to lawyers."

"Who's running the investigation here?" Oliver asked. "Some slick Beverly Hills eagle or Strapp?"

Marge looked at Webster. In unison they said, "The slick eagle—"

"That's not entirely fair," Decker said. "Strapp's getting squeezed. If he really wanted his ass protected, he would have pulled me off the case entirely."

Martinez said, "Loo, I got a light day tomorrow. I can do my paperwork and phone calls from the car. It's my idea, not yours, okay?"

"How about if we all take rotating code sevens tomorrow," Marge said. "I'll do a couple hours, Bert'll do a couple hours, Oliver'll do a couple hours—"

"I'll go first round." Webster sat back in his seat. "Reckon I'll be in the mood for a long lunch break."

"At eight in the morning?" Decker smiled.

"A breakfast break then," Webster said. "Y'all know it's unhealthy to work without proper nutrition. Besides, stakeout is pleasant for me. Put a couple of Bach cantatas in my CD player, I'm not only happy but very *alert*."

Martinez said, "Hey, it's our problem, Loo. Not yours."

"I may regret this, but . . ." Decker nodded.

Martinez gave his hands a clap. "Great. I got a couple of court reports to finish up. I can knock off around . . . maybe three, three-thirty."

"Y'got a video camera, Bert?" Webster said.

"I'll check one out from supplies."

Oliver said, "Overtime work without overtime pay! What the hell! Can't let the bitch push us around." He looked up and grinned. "Only wives get to do that."

"You ain't bitter, are you, Scotty?" Marge said.

"Me?" A finger in his chest. "Never!"

This time, it was Marge who was the last to leave. Stalling until she was alone with him. She closed the door, tried to smile supportively. "How's Rina taking the bad news?"

"Well. Thanks for asking."

She waited for more. When nothing came, she smiled again and said good-bye.

Decker said, "Margie, I really appreciate your support. Thanks."

"Of course. The bitch is out of her mind."

"Yes, she is. And that makes her . . . formidable." He stood. "I'll walk you out."

"Where are you going?"

"A couple of errands to take care of. And no, I'm not going anywhere near Jeanine Garrison."

Marge studied him. Decker knew she was leery, but she remained quiet. A smart lady. He left the station house, drove the unmarked about a half mile, then stopped at a pay phone. The phone rang twice, then Cindy picked up. He said, "I need your expertise."

"My *expertise*?"

"Can you come over to the house? If you can't, I'll meet you."

"No, I can come over. Can you give me a hint?"

"Later. Come over for supper. Afterward, I'll fill you in on the details."

They had been going at it for over an hour without interruption. Quietly so as not to disturb Rina or the baby. The boys were out as usual. Decker studied his daughter, feeling a mixture of love, admiration, and curiosity. Slowly, he was making his way over that interminable hump . . . viewing his daughter as an independent adult rather than his charge.

Cindy perused her notes, her father's notes as well. Piles of them. Brow wrinkled in concentration, she said, "To prevent any misunderstandings, maybe we should review at this point."

"A good idea."

"You've got this guy—Harlan Manz—who by newspaper and witness accounts went postal at Estelle's."

"Right."

"But *you* think he was just some hired gun."

"Maybe."

"Daddy, I've read your own case notes, the *original* assessment you took at the time of the shooting."

"You can read my handwriting, that's pretty good."

"I can not only read your handwriting, I can forge your signature."

Decker's eyes widened. "What?"

"That's a separate issue." Cindy grimaced. "Using your own notes as a backdrop, Harlan Manz does fit the standard profile for a mass murderer . . . whatever that means."

"Which is?"

Cindy began to count on her fingers. "He was male, he was under thirty, he used a firearm, he worked and was terminated from his employment at the location of the shooting, he talked about revenge to some of the coworkers—"

"Only right after he was fired, Cin. Subsequently, no one remembered his belaboring the point."

"That's not unusual. Many times, these things are premeditated. So if he had been planning the shooting, he would have kept it quiet."

"Cynthia, I combed Manz's pad. Didn't find anything there to suggest he was out to get Estelle's. No letters, no notes, no pictures of his ex-bosses on which he was doing target practice, nothing to imply a man on the edge."

"Dad, you didn't find much of anything in his

apartment period. You wrote that down right in your notes."

"Where?"

Cindy showed him the pages. "See? Right here. A loner's apartment. Also consistent with mass murderers."

"Or consistent with the fact that someone got to his apartment first and removed all his personal effects." Decker clenched his jaw. "Harlan was no loner. A slacker, yes, but no hermit. He was good-looking, a sharp dresser, had girlfriends, made the social scene, taught tennis, tended bar, went to auditions—"

"More like the Ted Bundy type," Cindy answered. "Used his wiles to get his victims. Except he wasn't a serial killer. But there might be some similarities here. I bet you he used drugs or alcohol before his final act. Something that lowered his inhibitions, calmed his nerves. Did you do a gas chromatography on his blood?"

"I'll call Pathology in the morning and find out if one was done. If not, I'll order it. They still have his blood, so it shouldn't be hard to get a complete analysis."

"Daddy, it's not that I completely disagree with you. Manz was not your typical schizoid. It does appear that he was able to maintain an outward social facade."

She paused.

"He was also an actor of sorts. He could have been better than average at emotional deception."

A very good point. Decker told her so.

Cindy smiled. "So let me get this straight. You

think that Manz was hired by Jeanine Garrison to kill her parents and he covered his tracks by committing mass murder at Estelle's. And then, someone else—also hired by Jeanine Garrison—was chosen to shoot up Estelle's as well as kill Harlan Manz with the same type of double automatic?"

"Maybe. Ballistics lab can't do a weapons match on each and every shell. Just too many bullets. They don't have the time or the manpower."

"But the gun at Harlan's side was the gun that killed him."

"Appears that way, yes."

"So if it wasn't suicide, how'd that gun get there?"

"Someone exchanged weapons at the scene."

"O-kay." Cindy was dubious. "And then this mystery killer fled the scene, leaving a dead Harlan—the disgruntled employee—to take responsibility for all the killings."

"Yes."

"Pretty darn artful."

"And pretty darn cold."

"I'll say." Cindy thought a moment. "A perfect crime."

"Except forensics doesn't lie." Decker briefly explained the inconsistencies of the weapon angles.

"Ah . . ." Cindy nodded. "So, obviously, Harlan Manz didn't know about this other mystery killer."

"Or maybe he did, Cin. Maybe Harlan thought they were in it together. And the other person double-crossed him."

"So then they both would have gone into the restaurant and opened fire at the same time."

Decker thought a moment. "No . . . that's not how the witnesses described it. They only noticed Harlan. No one mentioned a mystery killer."

"But you did write that people claimed that the bullets were flying all around them . . . indicative of more than one gun going off. Maybe it makes more sense to assume that Manz didn't know about a second shooter."

"Maybe."

"Then Jeanine was working with them both independently."

Decker said, "Possibly."

Cindy looked at her father. "I don't quite understand how that would work."

Decker said, "Suppose Jeanine was doing a number on Manz, getting him worked up over the loss of his job and the need for offing her parents. When Jeanine finally convinced Manz to do it, they set up a date. Then she hired another guy to murder Manz and mop up her parents' killings—in case Harlan screwed up."

"At the same time, Harlan was murdering everyone else?" Cindy shook her head. "Wow."

Decker smiled. "Pretty far-fetched. Then again, Jeanine Garrison is one hell of an organizer."

"By your definition, she'd have to be."

"What I'm looking for is a profile on the *mystery* killer. Any ideas, hon?"

Cindy shrugged. "If she indeed did use Manz to kill her parents, she probably would have used someone similiar to Manz for the second kill. Because most killers are pretty unoriginal. They use roughly the same methods unless they're serial murderers out to play games. But you're assuming Jeanine is not a serial murderer."

Decker said, "No, I think she's just a greedy woman out to get an inheritance."

"I agree with Detective Webster's assessment. That the phantom killer would be a young guy, someone she could psychologically and sexually manipulate. Maybe even a teenage boy in her sexual thrall. Teenagers are very high on the impulse scale." Cindy made a face. "I wonder how she coordinated it all."

Decker sipped coffee. "I'm probably over-psychologizing. Maybe she's actually . . . dare I say it? . . . innocent."

Cindy thought a moment. "Except she did react very strongly . . . accusing you of sexual harassment. That's typical of people who kill for inheritance. They view themselves as victims, think everyone's out to get *them*, standing in the way of what *rightfully* belongs to them. *Or* she could just be a nutcase. Able to maintain on the outside, but fragile once you peel off that protective layer."

"What else can you tell me about Mr. Phantom Murderer other than that he's likely to be young?"

"Well, like I said, most people aren't too original. If she recruited someone from her club first time out, she could have gone back to the club for number two. Maybe another tennis teacher or a bartender or the pool maintenance man or a waiter at the restaurant."

She thought a moment.

"If you want me to probe further, I can call up my professor tomorrow. See if he'll let me use their computers."

"Is this the professor who told you to join the FBI?"

"The very same one. Actually, he's a nice guy. We dated, you know."

This time, Decker paused before he spoke. "No, I didn't. Then it's over?"

"Yes. But we're still friends. I'm sure he'll let me hook into his data banks with my modem. I'll input the information and see if it jibes with anything. I'll also try to pull up profiles of femme fatales who've convinced men to kill for them. There're lots of those around. I can work from a much bigger sample size . . . a bigger pool of people."

She thought a moment.

"I don't recall a case where a woman used two men at the same time for the same murder. But there's always a first."

"You've been very helpful Cindy. Thanks."

"For you, I'd do anything."

Decker felt a warm glow in his heart. He kissed Cindy's forehead. "You look tired. You *are* going to sleep here tonight, correct?"

Cindy checked her watch. "Yeah, it is a little late. I'll bunk down in Hannah's room. Baby's rooms always smell so sweet."

Decker looked into his daughter's eyes. "You take care of yourself, okay?"

"I will." She studied her father. "Your color's better, Dad. You look happier. Must be my positive influence."

"That—and the fact that I'm finally getting something back from all that tuition."

Cindy whacked him. Just like Rina.

Why were women always hitting him?

Must say something about their own helplessness. Or maybe something about dominance needs.

Even Jeanine. She had hit him, too. Only in her case, she had hit him where it hurt.

# ❦19

***All dressed up*** with nowhere to go. But it didn't matter much. With stakeouts, image was everything. Dark suit, striped silk tie, white shirt, and a bulging briefcase with a gold clasp. The ensemble stated that Webster *belonged*. Because even without looking at the directory, he instinctively knew that Jeanine Garrison's building had to contain law offices.

He rode the elevators, a portable CD player stowed in his pocket, earphones indiscernibly tucked into his outer canal. Chopin. Piano études. They didn't get in the way. In his breast pocket was a Dictaphone, which he used instead of a notepad. Less conspicuous. Because lawyers did lots of dictation. He kept watch over who punched Jeanine's floor, who entered her office.

She didn't have many visitors. The mailman, the Federal Express guy, the UPS lady. Someone brought up coffee—cappuccino from a local coffee bar. When he wasn't riding in elevators, he loitered in the bathroom, listening to the rolls and frills of keyboard exercises. Time passed. Ten-thirty. He went back to the unmarked; Marge was already waiting for him. Within a minute, he had reviewed his two hours for her: Jeanine had come in around nine. She wore a red jacket with black trim over a black skirt and high heels. Great-looking legs. Great-looking ass.

"Her face wasn't too bad, either," Webster said. "The kind of woman who'd produce some interesting fantasies. *If* she wasn't so crazy." He shook his head. "I reckon therein lies the rub."

Marge said, "Were you in the building?"

"Whole time."

"How'd you go unnoticed?"

"Just the anynomous West Valley lawyer."

Marge studied her clothing—black rayon pants, white blouse, black bomber jacket. She tapped her foot. "I'll stand out if I go in like I am."

"Agreed."

"Any ideas?"

"Uh, I hate to say this but . . ."

"What?"

"There's a weight-loss clinic up there—"

Marge hit him.

"Lots of ladies going in and out."

"And I'll just blend in perfectly, huh?"

"There's also a gym." He winked. "You can go for the burn, babe."

"What got into you?"

"Just cutting loose." He clicked off his CD, threw his tissue paper-stuffed briefcase in the back of his unmarked. "Glad to get rid of that thing."

Marge frowned. "You wouldn't happen to have a pair of sweats on you?"

"In the trunk of my car. Might bag on you a bit, but now's not the time for vanity." He retrieved the gym clothes, smelled the fabric. "It's livable."

She took the sweats. "Thanks. Watch the car door while I change?"

"Be glad to, sugar."

"And don't get so familiar with me."

Webster grinned. "Anything you say. I never argue with a lady. 'Specially if she's toting a gun."

Martinez was waiting in the parking lot, a smirk on his face. "How many calories a day did they put you on?"

"Yuck, yuck, yuck." She wiped her sweat-soaked forehead. "First, they weighed me in, then I got counseled by some yahoo thin person. Then they sent me over to the gym for a free introductory workout. Step aerobics on this stool thing. On, off, on, off, on, off. Talk about going nowhere. And all I'm gonna show for it is a monster-size charley horse tomorrow."

"Get a chance to work at all?"

"For your information, I took a stool near the window, could see the office the entire time. Very quiet place. Nobody in, nobody out. I wonder what she does all day? Probably preens in the mirror."

"Or tortures men." Martinez shrugged. "Well, I brought a good costume." He reached into a bag, pulled out a janitor's uniform. "No spee . . . inglaze."

"Except what are you going to clean, Bert? You don't have keys to the office."

Martinez held up a finger, opened the trunk of the car. Out came a vacuum cleaner. "Tommy said the halls were carpeted."

Marge laughed. "But what are you going to do if

she suddenly takes off in her car? You can't follow her unnoticed, lugging a vacuum cleaner."

"Yeah, I thought of that. See, that's why I put a locator under the chassis of her car."

"That's illegal."

"I suppose it is."

Marge covered her face. "Are we breaking every rule in the book?"

"Nah, we got a few left."

"Good luck." Marge gave him a wave. "Off to testify."

"Which case?"

"*Tobias* versus *State*."

"Mr. 'I'm sorry, I'm sorry.'"

"Wait till the judge gets through with him." Marge grinned. "He'll give Tobias something to *really* be sorry about."

"So Jeanine has total control over David's trust money?" Decker asked.

Gaynor said, "Well, she can't commit fraud or embezzle. Things like that would jump out if she were ever sued. But there are subtle things she can do to siphon off David's portion into hers."

"Like?"

"As trustee of the fund and executrix of the will, she can take modest up-front fees for managing the cash. And she's allowed to invest the remaining portion of his inheritance in whatever she wants."

"That's a lot of leeway. There have to be some restrictions, Farrell."

"Anything she wants, Loo. As long as she's not

reckless. She is liable if she goes beyond what's considered standard investment practices. But that's still miles of rope. She can get to him in a number of ways."

"Such as?"

"Something simple . . . like tying up his money. Ironically, all the safe and sound investments are *long-term*. Things like munis and T-bonds."

"There's a secondary market for them."

"Yeah, but historically bonds drop over the long run. They're terrible for quick cash. And in the trust, there is a proviso for that."

"Quick cash proviso?"

"It's called a one-time emergency dispersal. Works like this. If David needs instant money, he can go to his sister. At her discretion, she can grant him his request if it is determined that it is a true emergency."

"Who determines that?"

"There's room for debate here."

"He could say it's an emergency, but she could say no?"

"Exactly."

"And then they'd take it to court?"

"Yes." Farrell coughed. "Anyway, if she were so inclined, she could give David a one-time payout of a percentage of his own money based on the fund's assets at the time. Now here's where a borderline rip-off could occur."

"Okay."

"Jeanine could claim that his assets are tied up with no liquid money. But . . ."

Gaynor held up a finger.

"Being a kind, caring sister, she could do him a favor. She could buy out a portion of his investment at current market value. Now if David's bonds happen to be lower than face value . . . which is usually the case with long-term bonds . . . then Jeanine gets a break."

"Still she's stuck with discounted bonds."

"Thing is, she can afford to do market timing. Either wait it out or sell if there's a sudden drop in interest rates. Because she controls her inheritance. She doesn't tie up *her* assets in long-term bonds."

"So she buys his money at a fraction of its worth."

"Exactly."

"And if David protests?"

"If Jeanine used standard prudent care when investing, he wouldn't have a case. Municipal bonds and T-bonds are definitely standard prudent care." Gaynor frowned. "If I were David, I wouldn't feel too secure. If Jeanine murdered her parents, I don't think she'd hesitate at murdering her brother if he got in her way."

"Except that it would start to look mighty suspicious." Decker thought a moment. "Of course, David could always meet with an accident in the form of a drug OD."

Gaynor said, "Carry that one step further . . . if Jeanine worked quickly, before the initial cash dispersal from the trust, his cash inheritance would probably go to her."

They were quiet.

Gaynor said, "We could tell him our thoughts."

Decker said, "But then if he goes ahead and tells Jeanine . . . that makes us liable for slander."

Gaynor said, "Not to mention setting us up for an invasion of privacy. I sort of skirted some legality here."

Decker thought a moment. "Still, we should talk to David again. Send Webster over there and see if he can slip it in subtly. Better yet, I'll send Scott to talk to him."

Gaynor laughed. "Scott? I thought I used the word subtle."

Decker laughed, too. "Oliver's interview could give us a different perspective, Farrell. Besides, maybe a second interview would jog his memory about other things."

"I suppose Scott couldn't hurt too much." Gaynor gave out a friendly chuckle. "And just maybe, he'll even help."

So much smoke that the window view sat behind a jaundiced cloud of nicotine. The guy had downed enough cigarettes to put R. J. Reynolds in the black. Even so, Oliver liked David Garrison, his matter-of-fact manner when it came to his inheritance. He expected nothing. Anything he got out of it would constitute gravy.

"Generous brother," Oliver said.

"Practical brother," Garrison retorted.

Today he was dressed in a black silk tee and baggy black chinos. On his feet were suede loafers without socks. He sat on his sofa, legs crossed, arms crossed, puffing away. On the coffee table was an empty highball glass.

"Sure I can't get you anything?" Garrison asked Oliver.

"Nothing, thanks."

"Murine for your red eyes?" Garrison smiled, smashed out the cigarette in a mountain of butts. "Terrible vice."

"I know," Oliver said. "Pisses people off like you wouldn't believe." He grinned. "Don't you love it?"

David broke into unrestrained laughter. "One of my true pleasures. Irritating people." He regarded Oliver. "Obviously one of your pleasures as well. Is that why you became a cop?"

"One of the reasons."

"And another?"

"I do like putting scum in jail."

"Ah! So you *are* noble."

"Tarnished nobility . . . impoverished as well."

Garrison smiled, then turned contemplative. "One interview with the cops . . . now I would assess that as police standard practice. But *two* interviews?"

"We're thorough."

"No, you're redundant. I have two questions. Why are the police so interested in my inheritance? And . . . are you asking Jeanine these same questions?"

Oliver played with the knot in his tie. Today, he chose to wear a brown glen-plaid sport jacket over a white shirt and khakis. "I take it you haven't had much contact with your sister since the funeral?"

"My contact with her has been through her lawyers."

"You don't get along with your sister?"

"No, although we're not openly at war. We each just pretend the other doesn't exist. Now that my parents are . . . gone . . . ." He sighed. "It just makes everything that much easier."

Oliver said, "No reason to have contact with her."

"Exactly." Garrison lit another cigarette. "You know, the fact that I'm smoking is a very good sign. It means I'm waxing productive."

"Congratulations."

Garrison sat back, inhaled, then exhaled a billowing cloud of tar. "Yes, a very good sign. I've actually taken a job. F/X for an upcoming Van Grek movie. Sort of a remake of *The Blob*. I saw the original just to get a feel for what had been done." He laughed. "It's ludicrous from a technical standpoint, but it has its moments. When that shit suddenly pours from the projection room into the movie theater . . . well, it took me aback."

Oliver smiled. "Scared the bejesus out of me when I was little."

"Yes, I can completely understand that." Garrison smoked in silence, his thoughts far away. "All these computer graphics . . ." He shook his head. "The guy next to me has been working on one story-board frame for *three* months. Van Grek's upper torso melting into a flaming sea of lava-crusted furniture." He looked at Oliver. "I wonder if the end result won't be so dazzling that it will cease to be scary."

Oliver was quiet.

Garrison smiled. "Ah, well. Silly musings. You never answered my first question. Why are you interested in my inheritance?"

His attitude was so nonchalant, Oliver couldn't help but wonder if Jeanine had gotten to him . . . offered him immediate bucks to keep a low profile.

"Insurance companies," Oliver lied.

"Pardon?"

"It's really absurd to waste police time with it," Oliver said. "But LAPD has been on the hot seat for so long. Anyway, seems insurance companies have had lots of requests for payouts."

"Of course," Garrison said. "People *died* at Estelle's."

"Well, they're doing lots of probing." Oliver sat up, talked to Garrison as if he were confiding in him. "They just want to make sure that Estelle's is what it is. You know—a crazy murderer gone berserk. That it wasn't a planned thing for someone to collect money."

"But the guy committed suicide."

"It's nutty to me, too. But I'm just doing my job, making sure that the police don't overlook anything."

"Did my parents even have life insurance?"

"I thought maybe you'd know."

"I don't. I was shocked when I heard I stood to inherit money . . . a lot of money."

"Do you know how much?"

"Something around a million dollars. I tell you I was *floored*." Garrison thought a moment. "Actually, I think I ceased being the scapegoat once Dad saw that Jeanine was less than perfect."

Oliver paused. "In what way?"

Garrison laughed. "Well, the girl was completely overindulged. Always had to be center stage. I do believe even Dad was growing weary of her tantrums, her incessant demands for him to fund her charities."

"He told you this?"

"No. But Mom . . . hinted all was not perfect between Dad and Jeanine." He sighed. "Still, he set Jeanine up as Queen Bee. You want to know about our finances, talk to her."

"She's kind of difficult to reach."

"Yes, she does surround herself with worker bees . . . drones, as well."

"Lots of boyfriends?"

"Pu-leeze."

"Tennis players?"

"Are you asking a rhetorical question?"

Oliver shrugged.

"Yes, tennis players. Mainly because tennis attracts wannabes and hangers-on. And that's what she likes. Men who hang on to her . . . admire her . . . think she's something *special*. Because growing up, though she was the pretty one, I was the *special* one. Little did she know I would have loved to change places with her, to have nothing expected of me except to smile. Ah, well, seems as if nobody is ever happy with his or her lot in life."

"So you two have never been close?"

"Never. Our father did an excellent job of programming us to hate each other." Garrison lit another cigarette. "He boxed us into categories."

He started ticking off on his fingers.

"Jeanine's pretty, I'm average-looking. Jeanine's smart, I'm brilliant. Jeanine's social, I'm shy and snobbish. Jeanine's caring, I'm distant and cold. Jeanine's organized, I'm in constant disarray."

He laughed.

"At least I was always my own person. Jeanine was always dependent on my father's good graces for her fun. Of course now, with my parents gone, she's independent. Maybe now she'll finally do something with her life besides leech off others' talents."

He smiled wickedly.

"But probably not."

# ᖁ 20

*Sipping coffee, Decker* flipped through the morning papers at four in the afternoon. *The Valley Voice* still had Estelle's as one of its hot items—a side column analysis on Harlan Manz. But the *Times* had relegated it to the back: a Hollywood tribute to Walter Skinner.

The one article that did grab his interest was found on page three of the sports section. More specifically, a photograph of Jeanine Garrison standing at the side of a handsome man dressed in tennis whites. A handsomely carved face. High forehead, a prominent chin. Clipped, curly hair, penetrating eyes, and a neatly trimmed five o'clock shadow.

He was also confined to a wheelchair.

Jeanine's hand resting on his shoulder.

Wade Anthony.

Both of them looking like models. Gorgeous but grave. A small caption underneath the snapshot. Their names. Their purpose. A wheelchair tennis tournament for victims' rights. A round-robin affair with stars promising to attend or lend support. But it was Wade Anthony who was the true star—a top ten seeded player in wheelchair tennis. He promised a big draw for a very important cause.

Decker stared at the photo, then broke into laughter.

At least it was for charity.

The knock distracted his attention. Decker looked up, told Gaynor to come in. He showed Farrell the photograph.

"This ditty was *my* idea."

"And then she slams you. A real sweetheart."

Gaynor sat down.

"Jeanine for victims' rights. Kinda like O. J. hosting a charity for domestic violence." He paused. "Come to think of it, O. J. *did* host a charity for domestic violence. What's this world coming to?"

At that moment, Marge and Oliver walked into his office. Decker looked up. "Someone call a meeting?"

Gaynor said, "I took the liberty."

Oliver pulled up a chair. "Figured it's a good time to recap, right before the weekend."

"Recap what? Jeanine's harassment?" Decker showed Oliver the newspaper.

"Ah shit!" He threw up his hands. "Now we'll *never* get to her!"

Marge read the caption. "So *this* is why the mayor put the vise on Strapp's balls."

Webster and Martinez came in. Oliver tossed Bert the newspaper. "Take a look at that."

"Ker-rist!" Martinez said.

Webster read over Bert's shoulder. "Fuck it. We'll find a way."

"She's makin' it harder and harder," Oliver said. "And I ain't talking about my shlong."

Webster turned to Oliver. "Whaddaya think 'bout David Garrison?"

"He smokes a lot."

"Talk about his sister?" Marge asked.

"Yeah. He hates her."

"You think it's genuine?" Webster asked.

"I'd say it was the real article," Oliver answered. "What about you?"

"My take as well."

"So you don't see brother in cahoots with sister?" Marge asked.

"Unless the guy's doing a right fine job of playacting," Webster said. "I think he really despises her."

"I agree," Oliver said. "Resents her Queen Bee status as Daddy's favorite." He hesitated. "He said something that was kinda telling."

"What?" Webster asked.

"He said once he stopped being the family scapegoat, his father began to see Jeanine in a different light. Said Dad was growing tired of Jeanine's tantrums, getting sick of paying for her parties." Oliver turned to Decker. "Remember we were talking about a motivation for Jeanine popping her parents. That she wasn't independently wealthy. I'm beginning to like that theory."

"Why?" Decker asked.

"The mother . . . Linda Garrison . . . she had hinted to David that all was not well between Pop and Daughter. Maybe Jeanine became homicidally resentful."

"Yeah, it sounds pretty," Decker said. "Too pretty. Remember that David's a former druggie and ex-convict. A notoriously dishonest combination. He could be setting her up."

Marge said, "How do we get to either one of them?"

"Forget about them," Decker said. "We're going after the phantom killer. I've spoken to some people, come up with a crude profile of who this ghost might be."

Decker summarized Cindy's findings. If Harlan was recruited from Greenvale, someone like him might also have been recruited from Greenvale as the number two killer. The guy might be similar to Harlan but possibly younger—angry, impressionable, unstable, grandiose in his thinking, a big one for blaming life, and in a one-down position from Jeanine.

Martinez said, "So this is all we have to go on?"

Gaynor raised his hand. "I think I might be able to help you out here."

All eyes turned to him.

"I just happened to get hold of some reservations books from Greenvale—"

Decker exploded. "Farrell, why didn't you *say* something when we began?"

"I didn't want to interrupt you." Gaynor shrugged. "When my boss talks, I listen. Maybe this old dog can learn something new."

Oliver glared at him. "Can I ask you something?"

"What?"

"How do you come up with these tidbits?" In a mocking voice, Oliver said, "'I just happened to get hold—'"

"The seniors grapevine. Good place to make

connections. Old people love to talk. And to help out. And there are quite a few old people at Greenvale—"

"How'd you get through the door?" Marge asked.

"My wife's sister's brother-in-law is a member. Elwood Halstead. Nice guy. Made his money in plastics, has this big mart—"

"Farrell, we don't need the details," Marge said.

Gaynor smiled benignly. "Suit yourself. Anyway, I asked El for an invitation; he took me out to lunch. I try to maintain good relationships with the family."

Oliver hit his forehead with disbelief. "Bully for you."

"It got me somewhere, didn't it?" Gaynor retorted.

Oliver said, "I don't know that yet because I haven't *heard* where it got—"

Decker said, "Stop squabbling." He looked pointedly at Gaynor. "Farrell, I've got to get out of here in an hour."

"No problem, Loo." Gaynor said. "Anyway, while I was there, I took a massage. Good for the old muscles. The masseur was my age, had been working at Greenvale from the beginning." He paused. "But he didn't remember Hart Mansfield."

The room was quiet.

"And . . ." Decker prodded.

"Oh . . . sorry, lost my train of thought." Gaynor cleared his throat. "Anyway, he was . . . cooperative. And I sort of helped myself to the older reservations books. Some of them went years back. Anyway, Jeanine takes a weekly massage with a woman named Jane. Has been taking it for at least four years."

Martinez said, "Did this Jane act suspicious or anything?"

"Anyone can point a gun. But no, there's nothing suspicious about her."

A pause.

"So?" Webster asked.

"So nothing," Gaynor said. "I crossed Jane off the list. Jeanine had also made other appointments— with the restaurant, with the beauty shop, hair salon, aromatherapy, makeovers and nails . . . Jeanine's really into her nails."

Again, there was silence.

Gaynor said, "All of it looks perfectly normal—"

"Will you please speed it—" Oliver interrupted.

"I'm getting to it, all right?" Once again, Farrell cleared his throat. "Well, like I said, the bad news is that nothing looks suspicious. Because most of her cosmetic and therapeutic appointments were with women—"

Webster said, "Like you said, anyone can point a gun."

"That would be interesting," Marge said. "Jeanine working on a woman and a man at the same time."

"I think we're really *jumping* the gun," Martinez said. "Not only are we assuming she's involved— which is still an if—we have her sexual proclivities mapped out."

"No, her massage appointments really didn't pique my interest," Farrell said. "Not like her court appointments."

"Court appointments?" Webster asked. "Is she being sued?"

"No, not legal court appointments. I couldn't find any of those—"

"Farrell, spit it *out*!" Decker said.

"Her reservations for the tennis court. She's been playing with the same partner for the last six months."

Again, all eyes drifted to Gaynor's face. Farrell was quiet.

"And . . ." Decker waved him to continue.

"A gentleman by the name of Sean Amos."

Decker clenched his teeth. "Who is . . ."

"A very rich boy."

"Boy?" Marge said. "How old?"

"Sixteen . . . oh, wait." Farrell scanned his notes. "Just turned seventeen."

Oliver clapped his hands with joy. "Statutory rape here we come."

"Won't wash," Marge said. "Kid's too old."

"But this isn't peer sex," Martinez said. "Jeanine's twenty-eight."

"How do we know they were even having sex?" Martinez said.

"You have eyes, Bert," Oliver said. "You've seen Jeanine."

"Yeah, you're right."

"What does the kid look like?" Oliver asked.

Farrell said, "The reservations books didn't have pictures, Scott. But I did ask a couple of discreet questions about the family." Again he faced Oliver. "Through the seniors grapevine."

Decker opened his pad. "Go."

"The father's name is Lamar Amos. He's sixty-two. From Texas oil. Owns a chemical processing plant in Long Beach."

"And he lives in the West Valley?" Martinez made a face. "That's almost fifty miles away."

"No, he doesn't live in the West Valley. He lives in Palos Verdes Peninsula with his twenty-two-year-old fourth wife, Amber."

"Then who is Sean's mother?" Decker asked.

"Lily Amos. She's forty, lives in West Valley Estates. She's the one who's a member."

Decker thought about Cindy's profile . . . a club member, maybe even a teenager not big on impulse control. "You find out where he goes to school?"

"Of course. Westbridge Prep—"

"Love those spiffy blue blazers," Oliver said. "Should I have a chat with the lad?"

"On what basis?" Marge said. "That he plays tennis with Jeanine Garrison? She files something ridiculous on the Loo, she's going to file police harassment if we start questioning her underage tennis partner."

Decker said, "Farrell, how long has Mrs. Amos been living in her current house?"

Gaynor rummaged through his notes. "Six years. Member of the club for five."

"Good. So she has established a routine. Kid's not going anywhere over the weekend. We start fresh on Monday." Decker turned to Webster. "I'll need someone who talks in Ivy League language. Can you pull it off?"

Webster answered, "Tell me your approach, Loo."

"Sean's a tennis player, right?" Decker said. "His mom was a member when Harlan was an instructor there two years ago. So let's assume Sean has been taking lessons for a while. Let's also assume that maybe . . . just *maybe* . . . he remembers a summer tennis teacher named Hart Mansfield."

Oliver said, "So we ask Sean about *Harlan*, not about Garrison."

"Exactly," Decker said. "Ask Sean about Harlan Manz/Hart Mansfield. You know teenagers. Love to be the center of attention. Even if Sean has only had a glimpse of Harlan, he'll play it to the hilt."

Webster said, "What kind of questions, Loo?"

"Does he remember Manz, remember anything weird about him, ever remember him being angry . . . any kind of bullshit? Let's just get the kid *talking*."

"And if he brings up Jeanine on his own?" Webster asked.

Decker waited a beat. "If Sean happens to mention Jeanine casually. Says something like . . . 'You know you should be asking my tennis partner these questions. Because she's played longer than I have.' Then maybe his tennis games with Jeanine are just that. Simple tennis games with a partner."

"And if he doesn't say that, Loo?" Marge asked.

Decker shrugged.

Webster said, "Can I ask him about his tennis partners without mentioning names?"

"Too pointed," Martinez said.

"I agree," Decker said. "First priority is to protect you people. Last thing I want is for Jeanine to slap Tom with a police harassment suit."

Oliver said, "Then what's the purpose of interviewing Sean in the first place?"

Decker said, "Jeanine didn't pull the trigger, Scotty. I told you we're going after the phantom, number two shooter—if he exists."

Martinez said, "Loo, even if Sean was screwing her, it doesn't mean he was involved in Estelle's."

Decker grinned. "No. But if they *are* having sex, it does show Jeanine's character. And that's good news for me in case she presses charges."

Before Decker could make it out the door, Strapp called him into his chambers, closed the door to his office. No preamble. Just straight talk. "We heard from Jeanine's lawyer again. She says you're harassing her brother—"

"That's ridiculous. They hate each other. According to David, they're not even in contact."

"That's what *he's* telling *you* to your face. Behind your back may be another story."

"Captain, is David Garrison complaining about harassment?"

Strapp shook his head no.

Decker spread out his arms as if to say, so there you have it.

Strapp said, "She thinks you're putting your men up to it. All part of your plan to get revenge."

Decker reminded himself to speak slowly. "Of course, I've assigned David to my people. We both agreed on that. I'm running an *investigation*."

"Yeah, but from her point of view—"

"Her point of view is bullshit. She's trying to stifle the investigation."

"Yes, it is beginning to seem that way."

Decker said nothing, feeling a little calmer. "You know, I had a team tail on her almost the entire day. I know that Jeanine didn't visit David. And she didn't call him—"

"How do you know that?"

"I'm thorough, sir. Just got off the horn with the phone company. No calls logged between them."

Strapp was silent.

"She must have had someone watching his apartment. Saw Oliver go inside . . ." Decker shook his head in awe. "She really is one hell of an organizer."

Strapp said, "Do you have anything concrete on David Garrison?"

"No."

"Any hot leads that might pan out?"

"Nothing."

"So I'm not creating any problems by telling you to keep away from him until we work out a plan with the lawyers."

"No, actually that's okay. At least for right now." Decker stood. "Can I go? I'd like to make it home for my Sabbath."

Strapp eyed his lieutenant. "You've got something up your sleeve, haven't you?"

"Come again, sir?"

"Don't play dumb, because you're not. I'm talking about Jeanine Garrison. If you're trying to get to her in a roundabout fashion, you'd better fill me in."

Decker told him about Sean Amos.

Strapp started pacing. "Quash the plan. I don't like it. You see the paper today?"

"Sports section, yes."

"So you see what we're up against. Besides, what's your reasoning for going after this Sean Amos— other than the fact that he's Jeanine's tennis partner."

"That is the reason, sir."

"You've got to come up with something better than that."

"Sir, right now we're assuming that Harlan worked with an accomplice. I'm trying to find a candidate. Look, sir, I'm not going to question Sean Amos about his relationship with Jeanine Garrison. I'm going to question him about *Harlan Manz*. Simple point-of-information interview because Amos was a member of the club when Harlan taught."

"So you're questioning this boy about Harlan only?"

"Yes. No one's going to mention Jeanine." Decker waited a beat. "Of course, if he brought her up, we weren't going to prevent him from talking."

Strapp didn't speak for a while. Finally, he said, "Okay. This is what we'll do. *I'll* order the interview. Take the heat off you."

Decker was stunned. "Thank you."

"But if *I'm* ordering the interview, you do it my way. If we question Sean Amos, we're going to have to question at least half a dozen other boys and girls his age who played tennis at the club when Harlan taught."

Decker grinned. "What a great idea. If Sean Amos is having an affair with Jeanine, he won't talk about it to us. But he might have bragged about it to one of his teenage friends. One of them might let it slip out to us."

"Okay, so Sean Amos is taken care of."

Strapp paused.

"Now here's the bad news. Jeanine is doing more than making noises. Our guys want to talk to you. I've set up a meeting at nine Monday morning."

"A Fact Sheet?"

"Yeah."

Decker nodded. Normally, when a complaint was filed, the presiding lieutenant took down the detective's story. Since he was a lieutenant, he'd probably be questioned by Myerhoff—the patrol lieutenant. Or by the Internal Affairs Department if Jeanine actually decided to file a 181 personal complaint. "Is Myerhoff doing the questioning?"

"IAD."

"Terrific." Decker rolled his eyes. "Why?"

Strapp shrugged. "Maybe Jeanine had her monkeys call them as well."

"Who's Jeanine's lawyer?"

"Guy by the name of Silverberg. Know him?"

"No."

"Neither do I. I'll have PPL look into him."

Decker asked, "Police Protection League going to send me someone good . . . as in competent?"

"You'll have a defense rep, of course."

"I repeat . . . a *competent* one?"

"We won't know until Monday. You want to think about hiring a private lawyer, that's up to you."

"Let's see how far it goes." Decker exhaled angrily. "This is a shitty deal."

"It's standard procedure, Peter."

"I don't have to like it."

"Do you have any other complaints against you on your record?"

"One. About ten years ago. A hype claimed I roughed him up."

"How'd the complaint resolve?"

"Unfounded."

"Good."

"That one was easy. He was a hype, lying was his native tongue. Jeanine isn't going to go down as easily."

"No chinks in her story?"

"Believe me, I've been racking my brains. So far, it's her word against mine. At this point, best I can hope for is an Unsustained. Unless we show her involvment in the murders at Estelle's."

"Wouldn't that be wonderful." Strapp paused. "You tell your wife?"

"First thing."

"How's she reacting?"

"Rina's been great. More than I deserve considering how testy I've been lately."

"So you've been completely honest with her about this?"

"Fortunately, there's nothing to be dishonest about. I didn't do anything."

"You told me you found Jeanine attractive, Decker. What if they offer you a polygraph?"

"I'll say go ahead."

"Then they hook you up to a machine, ask you lots of questions. Personal ones. About you and women. About your sex life. Ask you about Jeanine, if you found her sexy, if you wanted to fuck her. How are you going to answer that?"

"I'll tell the truth."

"What if this goes to a grand jury? They might ask the same questions. Your wife's going to hear things."

"It's not a problem."

"So you told Rina you found Jeanine a turn-on?"

Decker bristled. "Not in so many words, but yes, the gist came out that way."

Strapp raised his eyebrows. "And?"

"I'm not concerned." Decker sat back in his chair, pounding his fist to his forehead. "God, how can you find a woman so attractive one moment, then absolutely despise everything about her the next?"

"Don't let that attitude leave the office. It sounds vengeful."

"I know. Got to be stoic."

Strapp was quiet for a moment. "If you think Rina can handle it, it might be a good idea if she was with you at your questioning."

Decker was taken aback. "You're kidding."

"No, I'm not. She can't help you legally. But she can't hurt you, either. Because a wife can't testify against her husband."

"So why should I drag her into it?"

Strapp said, "I'll be blunt. Your wife is beautiful, Peter. And she's *young*. Quite a bit younger than you—"

"Twelve years."

"This kind of charge is a subjective thing. Like you said, it's Jeanine's word against yours. I know these jokers from IAD. Jeanine's a looker. They'll have no problem believing that you came on to her. You need to counteract that notion. Show them *your* side—your sterling record *and* your beautiful, charming wife who *isn't* at all concerned. It's going to influence the way IAD thinks. It isn't supposed to work that way. But it does. Think Rina could handle personal questions about your thoughts on Jeanine? Personal questions about your sex life?"

Again, Decker rubbed his face. "I'm not saying she'll view it as a cakewalk, but Rina's tough. She can handle it."

"She's got to play it right, Pete. Casual. No tears, of course. But she can't present a defensive posture, either."

"Okay."

"No snit fits or hysteria."

Decker smiled wryly. "No, sir, that's my department."

# ᘒ21

*No doubt Rina* noticed how antsy he was. But she chose not to mention it. Instead, they ate and waxed festive, the kids monopolizing the dinner conversation. Which was as it should be. Dinner topics were the machinations of the school's student council and Sammy's rules of the road. As a week-old driver, the boy was now an expert. During the lectures, Rina served up a "modest" Shabbos meal—puree of carrot soup followed by chicken breasts stuffed with wild rice and broccoli Dijonnaise on the side. Dessert was a fresh apple cobbler. When Decker questioned her definition of the word "modest," she replied that she hadn't served a salad.

Decker sipped coffee. "The meal was wonderful."

"Top-notch," Sammy added.

Rina said, "Anything would taste wonderful after eating cafeteria food for a week."

"It's a compliment, Mom."

"I'm glad you liked it."

Jacob said, "Are we walking over to the yeshiva tomorrow?"

"Yes, of course."

"Are we walking back?"

"I'm sure I could wangle you a lunch invitation at Rav Schulman's if you don't feel like walking back."

The boy was quiet. He pushed black hair from piercing blue eyes, looked at his parents. "We should move," he announced.

Rina and Decker exchanged glances.

"We're in the middle of nowhere," Jake said. "It's an hour's walk to the yeshiva and an hour and a half walk to visit anyone from our school. You know, Hannah's four. Eventually she's going to want to go to shul. We can't leave her with a baby-sitter forever. Either we should live closer to the yeshiva or move into the West Valley community."

No one spoke.

Decker closed his eyes and opened them. "You're right."

Jake grinned. "Really?"

"Really." Decker put down his coffee mug. "I'm sure it hasn't been easy for you being so isolated these past six years."

"It hasn't been bad." Sam took another piece of cobbler. "Actually, it's been okay. After Abba died, I didn't feel like being social on Shabbos. All those pitying looks. And then it was good to have some time alone with . . . you know . . . with Dad."

Decker felt his throat constrict. "Thank you. I felt the same way. But now it's different."

"What would you do with the horses?" Rina asked.

"We hardly ride at all anymore," Jake said. "Just sell them."

Rina said, "Slowly, Yonkie. It's not that easy."

Decker said, "Give your mother and me a few days to mull it over. We'll come up with something."

Jake tapped the table. "You know, we can fit into a smaller house. It doesn't have to be fancy. Whatever's convenient."

Decker smiled. "It would be very convenient if you two would clear the table and watch your sister for a bit. I need to talk to your mom."

Sammy said, "I'm still eating."

Everyone stopped talking, watched Sam eat. He pushed the plate away and got up. "Talk about being center stage. I know when I'm not wanted."

"Hannah, help us clear." Jake gave his little sister an empty soda can. "Bring it into the kitchen."

The girl broke into a smile, ran into the kitchen holding the can. The boys gathered up the dirty dishes.

Decker turned to his wife. "How's tricks?"

"Nothing too much other than going blind from looking at numbers."

"Oh, yeah." Decker sat up. "The yeshiva's books. What's going on?"

"The yeshiva looks to be richer than I originally thought. Lots of paper profit. The yeshiva owns a ton of stock."

"Who's been investing for them?"

"No one. Most of the stock has been given to them. From what I can figure out, it seems that the donors probably bought the stock years ago."

"At cheap prices."

"Exactly." Rina handed Hannah another empty soda can. Again the little girl took flight into the kitchen.

Decker said, "Buying ten thou worth of stock and it's now worth twenty thou—"

"More like a hundred thou."

"What's worth a hundred thou?" Sammy asked.

Rina said, "Take the baby to her room, boys. I'll get the rest."

"Trying to get rid of us?"

"In a word, yes." Rina smiled brightly. "Good-bye."

Jacob scooped his sister into his arms. "What do you want to do, Han?"

Hannah said, "Well . . . how 'bout playing dinosaurs."

"Okay."

"And play Barney, too."

"Okay."

"Then read books!" Hannah kicked until Jacob lowered her to the ground. She took Jake's hand in her right and Sam's hand in her left. "Swing me."

The teenagers complied. Decker laughed. "Who really runs the house?"

"That's not even debatable."

"Unlike the yeshiva's books." Decker smiled. "Actually, donating stock is quite a common ploy in estate planning. You buy a stock, hold on to it. The shares increase in value. Then you donate the stock to a charity. Not only do you avoid capital gains tax, but also you get the deduction for the shares' increased value."

"The amounts are startling. Lots of blue-chip certificates just sitting in a drawer in Rabbi Schulman's office. They've been there for years."

"Does Rav Schulman know what he has?"

"I don't think he has a clue. I can't understand why he never put all these assets with a money manager." Rina shrugged. "Although maybe it's better.

Somebody might have sold the stocks a long time ago. Instead, the shares have been splitting and growing and splitting and growing."

"Just going up and up . . ." Abruptly, Decker appeared pensive. "Has Jake ever mentioned moving before?"

Rina sighed. "He's hinted. He's a very social kid. You know how it is, especially in the teenage years. He really is away from the action on Shabbos."

Decker wrapped his hands around his coffee mug. "He's been a good sport."

Rina bit her nail. "How much do you think we can get for this place?"

"Not too much," Decker said. "I built it on spit and a promise. It's up to code, but it's sadly lacking in anything but basics. We'll take what we can get and buy what we can afford. Obviously, Jake doesn't care about luxuries."

Rina stroked her arms. "You know, I have money."

Decker felt his jaw tighten. "I don't need my wife's money to pay for my family's house."

"It's not *your* family, it's *our* family. You're being old-fashioned. What good is the money if we don't use it for things like this?"

Decker didn't say the obvious. Yes, he had life insurance, but it wasn't nearly enough to sustain a family and put three kids through college. Rina's trust from her parents was *emergency* money—in case something happened to him. And having been shot twice, he wasn't doing theoretical estate planning. He said, "We have savings. I make a good living. We'll work it out."

Rina looked away. "Why do you take everything on your shoulders, Peter? Why don't you let me help?"

"You do help. You run the house, take care of the family. You do *all* the finances. I haven't paid a bill since we married. You could be parking all of our money in a Swiss bank account, getting ready to leave me high and dry. And I wouldn't know the difference."

"That's an odd thing to say." She stared at him, placed her hand on his. "What's going on with you? It's that stupid harassment suit, isn't it? Is she charging you?"

Decker pulled his hand away, buried his head in his palms, then looked at his wife. "Strapp got a call from IAD. I've got to go through what they call a Fact Sheet on Monday."

"Which means?"

"IAD asks questions about the alleged incident."

"And?"

"They compare your answers with the charges brought against you . . . come up with a decision. Not right away . . . all this takes time. There are three decisions they can come up with. First, the charges are sustained. Which means they believe the charges against you are true. For that to happen, you have to have dates and witnesses—"

"Motel receipts."

"Even less than that. Just witnesses who confirm that they saw you two together outside the bounds of work. Like in a restaurant or at a movie. Corroborating evidence. I'm not worried about a Sustained verdict. It's the second conclusion they could reach.

An Unsustained. Which is like a no-contest. There's not enough evidence to sustain *or* refute the charges. Third verdict is Unfounded, which says the charges are false. That would happen if we caught her lying, found a chink in her story."

"Such as?"

"Such as if she said . . . oh, I don't know. If she said I had drinks with her at four o'clock and I have proof and witnesses that say I was in my office at four o'clock. Something like that."

"And that's not likely to happen, either."

Decker averted his gaze. "Correct. That is not likely to happen, either."

Rina said, "So the best you can hope for is an Unsustained?"

Decker's fists were clenched. "Unless I can prove what I already know. That Jeanine had some involvment in Estelle's. You know, I don't even *care* about these ridiculous charges. I care about thirteen deaths and thirty-two wounded. I care about the trauma and mayhem that an evil, evil woman inflicted upon innocent people. I'm going to nail her, Rina. I swear, if it's the last thing I do, I'm going to *bury* that bitch where the sun don't shine."

The room turned silent. Quietly, Rina said, "I admire your passion, Peter. Your unquestionable drive to do the right thing. But . . . but if you show emotion when you're questioned . . . it's going to look very bad."

He bit his lip. "You're very perceptive. Strapp said the same thing." He looked her in the eye. "He wants you there for the questioning."

"Me?"

"As an ornament. The charming, beautiful wife.

To show IAD that I had absolutely no reason for wanting to stray."

"The fact that you have an attractive wife would make a difference?"

"Strapp thinks so. I do too."

"To have your unblemished twenty-five-year reputation hang on what I look like . . ." She shook her head. "That's *nuts*!"

"Whole thing is nuts. But despite themselves, people are influenced by what they see. They see someone young and gorgeous and brilliant . . . Rina, they see you, they don't see a logical reason for me to cheat."

"As if men were logical. You must know countless men who have strayed with women much homelier than their wives."

"Not countless—"

"Scott Oliver is a perfect example. You used to say his girlfriends were dogs. And his wife was very attractive."

"Yes, she was."

"Why did he do it then? Explain it to me, please."

"Mid-life crisis, maybe."

"Except he'd been doing it for a while."

"I don't know, Rina. Some people have a hard time growing up." Decker unclenched his fists, laid his hands on the table. "I'm sorry to drag you into this."

"If you want me to be there, I'll be there."

"I think it's a good idea." He smiled weakly. "Besides, it'd be nice to see a friendly face."

Rina's eyes started watering. She took his hand and kissed it. "I love you."

"I love you, too." Decker swallowed hard. "They're

going to ask lots of personal stuff. Maybe . . . it would be a good idea if I wrote down some of the possible questions. So we're both prepared. So I won't be embarrassed answering them in front of you."

She held back tears. "This is really a violation, isn't it?"

Decker smiled softly. "Hey, like your mother says, as long as you got your health . . ."

Rina said, "Let's go over the questions together. Then tell me what you want me to wear, tell me how I should act, tell me what I should say."

"Just be yourself." He threw his head back, sighed. "Ah well, instead of feeling sorry for myself, I should learn a little. Put my mind into something cosmic. Maybe I could even pick up a pointer or two from the holy books. Surely they must have something to say about a man being hunted down by an evil woman."

Rina thought for a moment. "Sort of like Elijah the prophet. Hiding out in the desert in a cave, depending on ravens for sustenance."

"Who was he hiding from?"

"*Izevel* . . . Jezebel."

"What happened?"

"To Elijah?" Rina said. "He went out with a bang. Taken to heaven alive in a chariot of fire—"

"Ah, yes . . . Sunday school's rearing its head. Elijah was a fanatic, wasn't he?"

Sammy entered the kitchen. "All the prophets were fanatics."

"Where's Hannah?" Rina asked.

"Fell asleep—"

"Shmuel—"

"Don't freak, Mom. I put her in a diaper and her pajamas."

Rina was shocked. "You actually had the foresight to dress her for bed?"

"No, he didn't," Jacob said. "But I did. Are we interrupting anything?"

Sammy said, "Just talking about fanatical prophets."

"They weren't fanatical," Rina countered. "They just said things that people didn't want to hear."

Decker squinted, trying to bring back ancient memories. "I remember Elijah. I don't remember reading about Jezebel . . . other than the fact that she's been immortalized as an evil temptress."

Rina said. "She was married to—" She stopped, looked at her sons. "Who was she married to?"

Sammy said, "It's 'know your prophets' time."

Jacob sang, "A-hab the A-rab—"

"He wasn't an Arab, he was a Jewish king," Rina clarified. "King of Israel to be specific. And who was the king of Judeah?"

Jacob and Sammy shrugged.

Rina looked disapprovingly. "You boys don't learn *Navi*—Prophets—in school?"

Sammy said, "*Navi*'s for wimps. Real men learn *gemora*—"

"Just answer the question."

"Students shouldn't show off in front of their teachers. You can answer the question, Eema."

Rina smiled. "Yehosophat was the king of Judeah."

"I don't know *what* you're talking about," Decker said.

Jacob said, "The Kingdom of Israel split into two

after Solomon died. Rehovam was the King of Judeah, the legitimate king. The tribes of Levi, Judah, and one half the tribe of Benjamin remained loyal to him. The other ten tribes went with Jerovam—the king of Israel. Judeah was more righteous than Israel. Hence the other ten tribes were eventually lost in the Diaspora." He glared at his mother. "*Happy*, Eema?"

"Getting there."

"What happened to Jezebel?" Decker asked.

Sammy said. "She died. They all died. *Navi* are books about dead people—"

"Shmuel—"

"She was pushed out a high window," Sammy said. "Fell to her death, then was trampled by horses and finally eaten by dogs."

"Lovely," Decker said.

"It was a very fitting death," Rina said. "*Middah ken-neged middah*. 'Measure by measure.' She bribed some men to bear false witness against a man in order to seize his vineyard. The poor guy was stoned and dogs lapped up his blood. Because of this, it was prophesied that in the end, dogs would do the same to her."

Jacob said, "They did more than lap her blood, Eema. They devoured her."

Decker asked, "They ate everything?"

"Except for her cranium, hands, and feet," Rina said. "Actually, just the palms of her hands and the soles of her feet remained intact." Again, she focused in on her sons. "Okay, guys. Now what's the logical question."

Decker said, "Why wasn't she eaten completely?"

"Exactly," Rina said. "The cranium you can understand."

"Too hard," Decker said. "But why the palms of the hands and soles of the feet? It's soft flesh. It's the first part dogs would have eaten—"

"This is real sick," Sammy said.

"That may be but your father is absolutely right." Rina looked at her husband. "You've really got a scholar's head, Peter."

"What's the answer?" Decker asked.

Rina homed in on Sammy. "Why did Hashem spare her hands and feet? Because she did a mitzvah with them. A righteous deed from the heart. What deed could she have possibly done?"

No one answered.

Rina said. "What do you do with your palms?" She clapped her hands. "What do you do with your feet besides walking and running?"

Again no one spoke.

Rina said, "You dance."

"*Kaitzad merakdim lifnai Hakallah?*" Jacob said.

"I'm *impressed*, bro!" Sammy said.

"I win the prize, Eema?"

"You win the prize," Rina answered.

"What is . . . whatever you just said?" Decker asked.

"*Kaitzad merakdim lifnai Hakallah?*" Sammy said. "It means, 'How do you dance before a bride?' There are actually laws on what you should do before a bride . . . how you prepare her for her wedding, what to say to a groom."

Rina said, "The one and only nice thing Jezebel ever did was dance with a gladdened heart before a bride. Ergo, God spared her hands and feet."

Decker nodded, then abruptly burst out laughing, turning red in the process.

"What?" Rina said.

"Nothing."

"Uh-oh," Sammy said. "This must be good."

"No, it's really nothing," Decker said.

"Come on, Dad," Jacob piped in. "You usually don't laugh like that. What is it?"

Decker looked at Rina. "No, I think I'd better not push my luck."

"C'mon, Eema," Sammy said. "Give the man a break."

"I'm not his mother," Rina shot back. "He can say whatever he wants. And he often does."

Decker turned scarlet. "Well, I was just pondering what would be left if the only good deed a man ever did was being fruitful and multiplying—"

The boys broke into unrestrained guffaws.

Rina stifled a smile. "Is this Shabbos talk?"

Decker said, "*You* set me up."

"I was assuming you'd use good taste."

Sammy chortled, "That's where you went wrong."

Jacob had tears running down his face. "C'mon, Eema. You've gotta admit it's a funny image."

She started to leave.

"C'mon, Rina," Decker said. "Now where are *you* going?"

"To check on Hannah. I'll be right back." She left the boys to their infantile humor. When they were out of earshot, she exploded into unrestrained laughter. It soon turned into tears.

# ❧ 22

*Choosing and discarding* a number of outfits. Among the rejects: the brown "no-nonsense business" suit, the red "foxy lady" dress, and the "Bohemian" flowered ankle-length sarong skirt. In the end, Rina decided to be true to herself. A black long-sleeve sweater over a black A-line skirt, the hem falling below her kneecaps. She tucked her ebony waist-length hair into a large black net that stretched to the tips of her shoulders. Attached to the net was a black silk scarf adorned with gold trim. The scarf covered her scalp, the gold band running across the crown of her head like a tiara. Her makeup was light, her earlobes highlighted by pearl studs.

Walking into the station house, into the interview room. A conference table and lots of folding chairs. All eyes upon her. A nod to Peter. He nodded back. Three other men, all of them in dark suits. She recognized Strapp, nodded to him as well. There was one woman. She had short dark hair, focused brown eyes that scanned her intensely. Disapproving eyes, Rina thought. Her impulse was to look away. Instead, she met the stare and smiled. Habit made the woman smile back. Only half a smile actually, before she caught herself.

Strapp invited her to sit, introduced her. First to Jack Nickerson—a defense rep from the Police Protection League. Peter's lawyer, so to speak. He was in his forties, solidly built. Square face, big shoulders, and a gut. He wore his jacket open, displaying a tie too short for his stomach. A football player past his prime.

The younger suit as well as the woman were from the IAD: James Hayden and Catherine Bell. Both looked to be in their thirties and were more stylishly dressed. The man had on a double-vented, three-button wool crepe suit. The woman wore a double-breasted jacket and her pants had been tailored—straight leg and vented at the ankle.

Rina sat away from the others, at the far end of the conference table. She lowered her purse onto the ground, kept her hands loose but in her lap. Her posture was straight, but not stiff. Her eyes remained alert, taking in everything.

Peter, Nickerson, and Strapp were seated toward the middle of the table. But Hayden and Bell stood. Hayden was positioned behind Decker, Catherine in front of him, on the opposite side of the table. Strapp spoke first, telling the others that it had been his idea to invite Rina. Were there any objections?

There were none. So they went forward.

Turning on a video camera, the lens pointed at Peter's face. Preliminary identification statements akin to name, rank, and serial number. What this inquiry was all about. That all parties questioned were under oath. Then Hayden read from the "sheet."

The charges made by Jeanine. He and the woman, Catherine, had some questions to ask Decker. At that point, Nickerson spoke up.

"My client claims the Fifth Amendment, reserves the right to refuse to speak on grounds that he may incriminate himself."

In a calm voice, Strapp said, "As the captain of the Devonshire Division of the Los Angeles Police Department and as Lieutenant Decker's immediate superior officer, I am ordering Lieutenant Decker to answer all questions regarding the charges made against him or risk immediate termination from his position."

Nickerson said, "Responding to a direct order from his captain, Lieutenant Decker will speak for the purpose of this inquiry only. It is therefore agreed upon by all parties involved that nothing said here can or will be used against Lieutenant Decker in any court of law or at any future court proceedings should the charges advance to that level."

"Agreed," Catherine stated.

"Agreed," Hayden said. "May I remind Lieutenant Decker that he is still under oath."

"He is duly reminded."

All standard procedure, Peter had told her. Rina remained calm. Nickerson turned to Peter, nodded. "You may answer their questions now, Lieutenant."

Catherine started first, leaned forward, trying to invade his sense of space. "How old are you, Lieutenant Decker?"

"Forty-six."

"How many years have you been a police officer?"

"Twenty-five years."

"How long have you been with the LAPD?"

"Seventeen years—"

"How many years as a detective?"

"Sixteen years as a detective."

"Have you ever had charges other than this one brought against you?"

"Yes."

"How many times?" Hayden asked over Decker's shoulder.

"Ever made the list of forty-four?" Catherine shot out. "You know about the list, don't you?"

"Yes—"

"Forty-four policemen with the worst track record," Catherine broke in.

"How's your track record, Lieutenant?" Hayden pushed.

"Can we *please* have one question at a time?" Nickerson asked.

Decker turned his head to look at Hayden. "As an LAPD officer, I've had one other charge brought against me. And *no*, I've never been on the list of forty-four."

"Positive?" Catherine said.

Decker looked at Catherine. Before he could speak, Hayden said, "What charges were brought against you?"

Decker craned, looked up at Hayden.

"*Alleged* charges," Nickerson broke in. "They were dismissed."

Hayden said, "Why don't you let the lieutenant tell the story."

Decker's eyes went to Nickerson. "Should I answer?"

Hayden was annoyed. "Yes, you should *answer*!"

Decker said, "Can you come around into my line of vision, Sergeant? I'm getting a kink in my neck."

Hayden moved slowly, exaggeratedly. He stood to Decker's side, leaning forward. "Better?"

"Much, thank you."

"What charges were brought against you, Lieutenant?"

Decker said, "Assault."

"Don't you mean police *brutality*?" Hayden asked.

"Yes, he did falsely claim police brutal—"

"Did the charges warrant an interdepartmental Fact Sheet? Were you questioned about the incident?"

"Yes."

Catherine said, "Did you go to court?"

"No, it never went that far—"

"But there were charges brought against you—"

"A Fact Sheet and an inquiry."

Nickerson said, "Why don't you ask him how the charges were resolved?"

Bristling, Hayden said, "I believe we ask the questions, sir."

Catherine said, "*Were* the charges resolved?"

"Yes."

"By who?" Hayden said.

"By whom," Decker corrected.

Strapp glared at him.

"By *whom*?" Hayden said, red-faced.

Decker said, "By the department."

"What was the resolution?"

"Unfounded."

Hayden said, "Are you sure you don't mean Unsustained?"

"No, not Unsustained. *Unfound*—"

"How long ago was the incident?" Catherine broke in.

"*Alleged* incident," Nickerson said.

"Answer the question, please, Lieutenant," Hayden said.

Decker said, "Ten years ago."

"Were any other charges ever brought against you?"

"No—"

"You said you worked for twenty-five years as a police officer," Catherine said.

"Yes."

"Seventeen years with LAPD?"

"Yes."

Hayden sat down, leaned into Decker. "*Whom* did you work for other than LAPD?"

"*Who* did I work for?"

"Decker . . ." Strapp warned.

Rina also shot him a "cool it" look. Still, she admired his spunk. The interrogators were jerks. But it didn't help his case to make them mad at him. Hayden leaned into Decker's face, waited for an answer.

Decker's expression remained flat. "I was employed by the Gainesville and Miami Police Departments in Florida. I worked three years as a uniformed officer, two years as an undercover agent in Narcotics, and three years as a detective in Sex Crimes."

Catherine faced him with intense eyes. "Were any charges ever brought against you while you were employed on the Gainesville force?"

Decker paused. "I have to think a moment—"

"It's a simple question, Lieutenant," sniped Catherine. "Yes or no."

"It was a while ago." Decker remained placid. "During my first year as a patrol officer, I think a complaint was filed but immediately drop—"

"What were the charges?" Hayden said.

"The complaint—in the singular—was police brutal—"

"So you've had two incidents of police brutality brought against you?"

Nickerson said, "Sergeant Hayden, may I remind you that the allegation against my client as a member of the LAPD was resolved as being Unfounded, which means—"

"I know what it means—"

"Why was the Gainesville charge against you dropped?" Catherine asked Decker.

"It was a complaint." Decker smiled, then stifled it. "I don't know why it was made, I don't know why it was dropped."

Hayden touched his shoulder. "Something funny, Lieutenant? You were smiling. And may I remind you that you're still under oath?"

"I realize that."

"And you still contend that you don't know why the charge was made?"

"I *suspect* the complaint was registered by one of the *many* people I arrested during the *many* anti-Vietnam War demonstrations that took place during that period."

"Are you a vet?" Hayden asked.

"Yes."

"Made you mad to have those punks spit in your face, didn't it?"

Nickerson spoke before Decker could. "Can we go on with the immediate inquiry, please?"

"So you don't know who filed the complaint?" Hayden persisted.

Nickerson said, "Sergeant Hayden, Lieutenant Decker was not brought here today to answer questions about a twenty-five-year-old *resolved* incident—"

"He didn't say the incident was resolved—"

"He said the complaint was dropped."

"That doesn't mean it was resolved," Hayden went on. "For all I know he could have harassed the complainant just like he harassed Jeanine Garrison—"

"*Allegedly* harassed," Nickerson said. "Speaking of which, why don't you ask him about the Jeanine Garrison incident?" He turned to Decker. "They've read you the charges against you, Lieutenant. Would you like to respond?"

"Yes."

The room was quiet.

Catherine gave him the go-ahead. Unhurriedly, using his notes, Decker took them through his interview with Jeanine Garrison. Rina was impressed by Peter's organized mind, by his simple language. His recounting was followed by more questions. Specific questions about her charges. Procedural questions. Then, of course, came the personal questions.

"Jeanine Garrison is an attractive woman," Hayden said.

Decker said nothing.

"Did you hear me, Lieutenant?"

"Yes, Sergeant. You made a statement. I didn't think it required an answer."

"Do you agree with my statement?"

"Yes."

"Did you notice that she was an attractive woman when you met her?"

"Yes."

"Did you think she was beautiful?"

"I noticed she was good-looking—"

"Answer the question, sir."

Decker squirmed slightly. "Yes, I thought she was beautiful."

"Sexy."

"Yes."

"Very sexy—"

Nickerson interrupted, "Sergeant Hayden—"

Hayden shot him down. "Lieutenant Decker has agreed to answer questions for the purpose of this inquiry. Let him answer the questions."

Hayden waited.

Decker said, "What was the question?"

"Did you find Jeanine Garrison very sexy?"

"Yes."

"Were you sexually attracted to her? Remember you're under oath."

"And may I also remind you that you've offered to take a polygraph," Catherine added.

In other words, lying made no sense.

Hayden said, "Did you find Jeanine Garrison sexually attractive?"

Decker sighed. "At that time, yes."

"At that time, did you fantasize about having sex with her?" Hayden asked.

Rina winced at the directness. Decker glanced at her, at Hayden. "I don't remember—"

"Lieutenant, you're under oath," Hayden said. "Did you want to *fuck* her—"

"Sergeant Hayden," Strapp broke in, glanced at Rina. "Show a little courtesy, please."

Hayden said, "Did you want to have *sex* with her, Lieutenant?"

Rina nodded to her husband, telling him to answer the question.

Decker said, "Maybe."

"Maybe?"

"That's correct."

"Are you sure you don't mean *yes*, Lieutenant?"

"No, I mean maybe."

"You were attracted to her?"

"Yes—"

"Extremely attracted?"

"I wouldn't say extreme—"

"You're telling me—under oath—that no sexual thoughts about Jeanine Garrison entered your mind?"

"I had some sexual thoughts," Decker said.

"Such as?"

Decker said, "That she was attractive."

"I think my mother is attractive." Hayden laughed mockingly. "Doesn't mean I have sexual thoughts about her. You wanted her, didn't you, Lieutenant?"

"Sergeant . . ." Nickerson admonished.

Decker spoke calmly. "I don't remember my exact thoughts because they came and went very quickly. Then I was all business."

Catherine said, "During your interview with her,

you never *once* entertained the thought of getting Jeanine Garrison into bed?"

"No."

"A moment ago, you said maybe," Hayden corrected.

Decker said, "I said *maybe* I had those thoughts when I first *met* her. During the actual *interview*, I had no thoughts other than my business."

"Amazing you can turn yourself on and off so quickly." Hayden's smile was mean. "You must be a man of considerable control."

He hadn't asked a question so Decker said nothing.

Hayden glanced at Rina, "How old is your wife, Lieutenant?"

"Thirty-four."

"And you're forty-six?"

"Yes."

Catherine said, "She's quite a bit younger than you."

"Yes."

Hayden said, "First wife?"

"No, she's—"

"Second, third, fourth—"

"Second."

"You're forty-six?" Hayden said.

"Yes."

"Mid-life crisis time, Lieutenant?"

Decker smiled. "No, I already went through that. Hence the age difference between my wife and me."

Again, Rina shot him a "behave yourself" look.

Hayden gave a sly smile. "You were married when you met your current wife?"

"Divorced."

"What was the reason for the divorce?" Catherine asked.

"Irreconcilable differences."

"Were you having an affair while you were married to your first wife, Lieutenant?" Hayden asked.

"No."

Catherine said, "You're under oath."

"I know that. No, I was not having an affair."

"Ever had an extramarital involvement?"

"No."

"Not even a one-nighter during your marriage to your irreconcilably different first wife?"

"Nothing until we were legally separated."

Hayden said, "Was your second wife married when you met her?"

"Widowed," Rina spoke up.

Abruptly, Hayden faced her with stern eyes. "I was asking a question to your *husband*, ma'am."

"My apologies." Rina's voice was sincere, her soft eyes upon Hayden. Immediately, he looked away. Her interruption seemed to throw his rhythm off. As he faltered, Catherine picked up the slack.

"How's your sex life, Lieutenant?"

"Fine."

"How would you rate it? Excellent, very good, good—"

"Excellent."

"How often do you have sex?"

"Meaning?"

"Once a week, twice a week—"

"Must be more than that if he rates it excellent," Hayden broke in. "How about it, Lieutenant? How many times a week do you have sex?"

Decker looked at Rina.

Hayden said, "Why are you looking at her, Lieutenant? Can't you answer the question for yourself?"

"It's complicated—"

"It's a simple question," Catherine said.

"With a complicated answer."

Rina broke in. "We're Orthodox Jews." She paused. "*I'm* an Orthodox Jew. The religion prohibits sexual encounters during a certain period of every month—during the woman's menses and for seven days afterward. Then she undergoes ritualistic purification by bathing in prescribed waters. When she is done, she is permitted to resume relations with her husb—"

"This is for real?" Hayden spoke derisively.

"Yes, sir, this is for real," Rina answered without malice. "If you'd like, I will bring you some beautifully written books explaining the sanctity of this ritual more clearly than I have done."

Hayden averted his eyes, quieted his voice. "Thank you, but that won't be necessary."

Rina let his admission hang in the air. Then she said, "Generally, it works out to two weeks of abstinence followed by two weeks of sexual activity. In our specific case, it's a little shorter—more like twelve days off and eighteen days on—"

"Why's that?" Catherine asked.

"You get some kind of special dispensation?" Hayden butted in.

"In a manner of speaking—"

"What was the reason?" Hayden grew a sneer. "He couldn't *wait*?"

Nickerson said, "Sergeant Hayden—"

"She brought it all up!" Hayden defended himself.

"Medical factors," Rina answered. "Anyway, there was a reason I bothered to tell you all this. It explains why my husband couldn't answer your simple question about a *weekly* sexual allotment."

Her eyes lowered, then rose to meet Hayden's head-on.

"A point of information. During the times of activity, *all* forms of play between husband and wife are permitted." She gave him a serene smile.

A blush coursed through Hayden's cheeks. Again, he looked away. *Son of a bitch*, Decker thought. Rina's modest dress notwithstanding, the jerk had the hots for her.

And why not?

Decker regarded his wife, studied her sculpted face, her open eyes shining like jewels, her red, moist lips. The band of gold fabric arcing across the top of her head, her hair tucked into a net, giving it the appearance of a Cleopatra cut. Just like the alluring Egyptian queen, Rina exuded confidence.

Hayden tried to regain his aggressive stance, stuttered out, "So you consider yourself a religious woman, then?"

"Yes."

"And you follow this . . ." He waved his hand in the air. "This . . ."

"Religious ritual?" Rina tried.

Nickerson broke in. "Sergeant Hayden, no charges have been brought against Mrs. Decker—"

Hayden said, "She's claiming religion to be an integral part of her husband's sex life."

"And . . ." Nickerson asked.

Hayden hesitated, eyes darting from Rina to

Decker. Catherine glared at her partner, said, "Lieutenant, during the period when charges were brought against you by Jeanine Garrison . . . were you abstaining from sex with your wife?"

They say timing is everything. Decker smiled to himself. "No. We were involved during that period."

"So you were having sex with your wife?" Hayden said.

"Yes." Decker refrained from adding, "You wanna hear details, guy?"

"When was the last time you had sex?"

"Last night."

"With your wife?"

Strapp interrupted this time. "Sergeant Hayden, was that really necessary?"

"We have serious charges brought against your lieutenant," Hayden countered. "We'll do what's necessary—"

"That's what you think," Decker said.

Hayden zeroed in on Decker. "What did you say?"

Decker shrugged. "That's exactly what I was doing, Sergeant. Running an *investigation*. What started as a mass murder began to look like murder for hire. And no simple hit at that. Thirteen people dead, thirty-two wounded, many more traumatized for life. I'd say the stakes were pretty high."

Catherine said, "High stakes or not, no one in this department has a right to harass anyone else."

"I agree, Officer Bell. I assure you no one was harassed, sexually or otherwise. Jeanine Garrison is making noise because she's got something to hide."

Hayden said, "And you have proof of these allegations, Lieutenant?"

Rina asked, "Forgive a layman's ignorance, but why would Lieutenant Decker be investigating if he had proof? I thought that was the purpose of an investigation. To gather evidence."

Catherine said, "We've run far afield."

"No, we haven't," Strapp said. "As a matter of fact, Mrs. Decker is right smack in the center of the damn ballpark. We're trying to run an investigation and Jeanine Garrison's ludicrous charges are slowing everything down—"

Hayden said, "It's for us to determine whether or not the charges are ludicrous."

"Hook me up to a polygraph," Decker said. "Ask me the same questions. Draw your conclusions. You call the shots."

Hayden and Catherine exchanged glances.

Decker said, "Is there a formal one eight one complaint being pressed?"

Hayden said, "Yes."

Decker closed his eyes and opened them. "Then I can only help myself by taking a polygraph. How about this? If I pass, department rules it as an Unfounded. If I *don't* pass, I'll go along with the departmental ruling of a Sustained."

Catherine finally took a seat at the table. "We can't base our ruling on a polygraph. But you can take one."

"Set it up."

She pulled out a notebook from her jacket, flipped through some pages. "Possibly we can hook you up with a polygraph in two weeks."

"Why so long?" Strapp said.

"The examiner I use is on vacation."

"So get another examiner," Decker said.

"I like this one."

Strapp said, "My man has to cool his heels for a couple of weeks because your examiner is basking in the sun?"

"If he's innocent, it'll keep," Hayden said.

Decker said, "I can wait. Can I get back to work now?"

Catherine glanced at her partner. Hayden nodded, turned off the video camera, and removed the cassette. "I'll call you with the details."

Decker smiled. "I'll be waiting."

Strapp got up. "I want a copy of the cassette."

"Certainly," Catherine said. "Despite what you've been led to think, IAD is very up-front."

"A bastion of honesty," Strapp said. "Two weeks. You go longer than that, I make noise."

Hayden nodded deferentially. Even though he wasn't under Strapp's jurisdiction, the captain's rank still demanded respect. As soon as they were out the door, Strapp shoved it closed. "Bastards!" He turned to Nickerson. "What do you think?"

Nickerson yawned. "They're lightweights. All sound and fury signifying nothing. Brilliant stroke to bring the wife in. Kept it civil." He turned to Rina, smiled. "You were very good."

"Thank you." Rina paused. "Good at what?"

Nickerson laughed. "The way you explained your religious beliefs about sex. Open. Unembarrassed. Straight out. Even . . ." He smiled. "Excuse me, Lieutenant, for my candor, but your wife is very . . . appealing. At least Hayden thought so. See him blush?"

"Blush?" Rina asked.

"You'd better believe it," Decker said. "Frankly put, he had the hots for you."

"He did *not!*"

Nickerson said, "It was the sex talk combined with the dowdy dress. The quiet ones. Gets 'em every time. Good move, Mrs. Decker."

Rina said, "I always dress like this, Mr. Nickerson."

Nickerson stuttered, "Well, yes, of course . . ."

"Not always this somber," Decker remarked. "But she does always dress modestly. Can I have a few moments with my wife in private?"

Nickerson stood up. "I suppose you deserve that." He saluted. "We'll be in touch."

After the defense rep left, Strapp laid a strong hand on Decker's shoulder. "Despite what they say, the polygraph means a lot to IAD. You beat that, we'll be fine."

"Thanks for your support, sir."

"Can't let the bastards get in our way."

Decker nodded.

Strapp looked at Rina. "Mrs. Decker."

"Captain."

Strapp went out of the room, closed the door. Immediately, Decker let out a gust of air, slid back in his seat.

"Are you okay?" Rina asked.

"Fine, fine." He pulled her onto his lap. "You were *wonderful*. People say they love one another. But you did more than words could ever convey. You came through for me. I'll never forget this, Rina. Never."

"It wasn't hard." Rina grew misty. "I love you."

"I love you, too." Decker grew tense. "Bastard! Probing like he did." He imitated Hayden. *"What was the reason? He couldn't wait?"*

Rina smiled. "For a moment, I considered telling him about my hysterectomy—"

"Don't you dare! None of the bastard's business!"

She shrugged. "I didn't because I thought it would work against you. Make me look . . . less desirable—"

"That would be *impossible*!" Decker said.

"Besides, then I'd have to explain why I got a period at all. And how a period is defined by Jewish law. In reality, I didn't think the sergeant was up to grasping the intricacies of remnant endometrial tissue sloughing from a subcervical hysterectomy. Hayden is just not very clever."

"He's an idiot!" Decker pulled her close, kissed the nape of her neck. "Know how I feel right now? Like the luckiest man alive. To be honest, it was harder than I thought it would be. I actually told a little fib."

Rina dried her eyes, turned around to face him. "What kind of fib?"

He pulled her back into his arms. Kissed her neck again. "Hmmm, you smell nice."

"What was the fib, Peter?"

"The complaint against me while I was on the Gainesville force. It was justified." He kissed her again. "Hayden had my psyche nailed, darlin'. I *was* caught up in the whole antiwar thing. But from the unpopular side. I had just come back from Nam. Confused, scared, full of self-doubt . . . but mostly angry. I had an ugly temper, Rina."

"You?"

"You don't become this controlled a person unless there's something to control. Most of the time, I could hold it in check. Then . . . I don't know. There was this typical college demonstration. Nothing unusual. Just wimpy, little know-nothing jerks spouting off . . ."

He looked away.

"Something snapped. I lost it. I took the loudest, most obnoxious one and dragged the kid, stomach down, over a hundred feet of rocky, newly laid asphalt—"

"My God!"

"By the time I was done, the kid's stomach looked like raw meat—"

Rina shook him off. "That's terrible."

"Yeah, it was bad. It's hard to understand unless you've been there."

Head pounding, Rina took in a deep breath, let it out slowly. Obviously that had been a long time ago. Right now, Peter didn't need a morality lesson. "I suppose you're right."

Again, Decker kissed her neck, which he noticed had visibly tensed. "I acted out of anger and that was wrong. But honestly . . . the release of such raw . . . fury . . . it felt good."

Again, Rina broke away, stared at her husband.

He met her gaze, thought for a moment. "Don't worry. It'll never happen again."

"Why are you telling me this?"

"I trust you to know the truth."

Rina tried to relax but failed. "As long as it's true confessions, how'd you get him to drop the charges against you?"

"It was a her," Decker said. "I did a big no-no. After the complaint was filed, unknown to my superior, I *contacted* her. Went to her dorm. I remember putting on a T-shirt and jeans . . . sandals. Tried to look as uncoplike as I could. I apologized profusely. Just about went down on my knees. Offered to make amends any way she saw fit. Laid on the charm and hoped for the best. Much to my astonishment, the next day she dropped the complaint."

"And?"

"And the rest, as they say, is history."

Rina stared at him, openmouthed. "Jan?"

Decker laughed. "The one and only complaint against me that she's ever really *dropped*."

# 🐦23

*Tricky business, talking* to teens. Authority figures left them frosty and distrustful. The "cool" grown-up approach was also out. They were suspicious of anyone who tried too hard.

How to manipulate them?

Webster figured he'd play into their overinflated sense of importance. Their opinions about Harlan Manz *really* mattered to the police.

He parked the unmarked about a block down, hit Westbridge Prep just as the four-thirty dismissal bell rang out. The campus sat on acres of lawn, a Federalist-style complex, complete with bell tower. Behind the main four-storied structure were wings and extensions. The buildings were herringboned in brick, unsuitable in L.A. earthquake country. No matter. To parents, New England architecture connoted New England universities. The physical image fueled the Harvard dream.

For the role, Webster had donned a black silk jacket, black T-shirt, and jeans. Professional but not off-putting. The school gates had opened, and adolescents swarmed out. Noise. Lots of it. Males letting off steam, shouting and cursing and posturing bravado. Estrogen-ladened girls, flailing their hands with exaggerated movement, while rattling off Valleyspeak between nervous giggles. The parking lots roared volleys of cars: four-wheelers and Jeeps as well as sports car convertibles—Mustangs, Camaros, Thunderbirds, as well as older Jags, BMWs, a Mercedes, and a Porsche Carrera. The driver of the Porsche was pitted with acne. Who knew? Maybe the wheels helped him get laid.

Webster's eyes panned over the scenery, spied an average-looking group congregating on the sidewalk. Three blue-blazered boys, and two white-shirted, plaid-skirted girls. The boys were big and thick—football players or wrestlers. One of the girls had blond hair; the other lass had tresses of garnet red. Webster ambled over, presented his badge, watched them grow wary. Then he spoke.

"Any of y'all happen to be members of Greenvale Country Club . . . through your parents, maybe?"

The tallest of the boys stepped forward, eyes focused on Webster. Around six two with a refrigerator chest. Simian-featured. Bushy hair, swarthy complexion, hooded eyes, and the ever-present adolescent gaping mouth. "What's going on?"

Webster said. "We're doing a little follow-up on the tragedy at Estelle's. On the shooter—"

"Harlan Manz," the redhead broke in. She had been bronzed by the sun, her ruby mane tied back in a braid.

Webster took out his notebook. "And you are . . ."

"Kelly Putnam."

"Don't tell him your name," the blond girl scolded. Long straight hair, blue eyes, creamy skin, and legs that didn't quit. A nice young package. Then Webster thought about the Loo's Fact Sheet earlier in the day, Decker being raked over the coals . . .

Blondy said, "Can I see your badge again?"

"Sure." Webster showed it to her. "Detective Thomas Webster, LAPD, Homicide Division."

The blond stared at the shield, wetting her lips with the tip of her tongue. "How do I know that it's for real? You could be a perv in cop's clothing."

"Good to be cautious," Webster said. "None of you have to talk to me. I'm just trying to get a fix on Harlan Manz."

"Why?" Simian asked. "He's dead."

"We're trying to understand the situation. Give some closure to the victims of this terrible tragedy. Any of y'all happen to know him? Harlan?"

"Why would we know him?" Simian asked.

"That's why I asked if any of y'all happened to be members of Greenvale. He worked there . . .'bout two years ago."

One of the boys spoke up. He was a tad shorter than Simian. Pug features, straight dark hair, and green eyes. He held out a meaty hand. "Rudy Wright." He pointed first to Simian. "Jack Goldsteen." Then he cocked a thumb at the last male friend. The smallest but only in relationship to the other two. He was fair and had the finest features but was far from delicate-looking. "He's Dylan Anderson."

"Pleased to meet you boys." Webster shook hands all around. "And thanks for talking to me. We're pretty upset 'bout Estelle's. Figured taking it to the public might help."

He turned to Blondy.

"I didn't catch your name, miss."

"It's ms. to you and that's because I didn't tell you."

Kelly the redhead let out an exasperated sigh. "It's Sarah Amos—"

"Kelly!"

"Stop being so nasty, Sarah."

"Screw you!" Sarah turned to Webster. "What do you want to know about Harlan?"

Webster looked into her eyes, hoping his excitement wouldn't show.

Sarah *Amos.*

In one school, how many Amoses could there possibly be?

"Did you know him, Ms. Amos?"

"Sure, I remember him."

"We all do," Kelly interrupted. "Hart Mansfield. I realized who he was right away. When I told my parents I thought it was the same guy, my dad didn't believe me. Said I was just being an . . ."

She sighed.

"An overly emotional, hormonally driven, hysterical female adolescent. Dad equates enthusiasm with hysteria. To Dad, excitement means an eagle on the eighteenth hole."

Jack said, "Yeah, your old man is pretty grave." To Webster, he said, "He's a sports lawyer. Negotiates multimillion-dollar deals for free agents." He turned back to Kelly. "Maybe it's me, but I think he's looking me over."

Kelly said, "Wouldn't doubt it, Lug. Despite your Neanderthal appearance, you do have solid raw talent."

Webster said, "Your dad belongs to Greenvale, Kelly?"

"But of *course!*" She spoke in a French accent. "He belongs to all the *right* places."

"You know, I had a hard time believing it myself," Rudy said. "About Harlan, I mean. What a shock! You don't expect a normal-looking guy with a good backhand to suddenly kill twelve people."

"Thirteen," Webster corrected.

Rudy grimaced. "God, that's awful!"

"You should be talking to Amy Silver," Jack said. "She was there. At the restaurant."

"She was one of the girls at the Sweet Sixteen," Webster said. "She's been interviewed."

"She hasn't come back to school," Kelly said. "I'm not good friends with her, but I did visit her. She's really a basket case, poor thing."

Webster said, "So you remember Harlan Manz, Ms. Sarah Amos? Did you ever meet him?"

She shuddered. "Couple of times."

"Take lessons from him?" Webster asked.

"Nope," Sarah said.

Kelly added, "I don't think he taught teens. More like worked with women my mom's age."

"He taught teens," Sarah said. "He taught my brother."

Webster counted one one thousand. "And who might your brother be?"

"Sean Amos," Dylan said. "Mr. Studmuffin—"

"Fuck off!" Sarah whined.

"Don't tease her, Dyl," Kelly said. "Ain't her fault that she has the bad luck to share progenitors with *him.*"

Sarah had become edgy. "Sean doesn't like to talk about Estelle's. I mean, he was really freaked when he found out about Harlan."

Jack said, "I was freaked, too."

Rudy said, "Speak of the studmuffin, that's him in the red Acura convertible."

Webster's eyes went to a blond boy wearing a white shirt and sunglasses. His hair was down to his shoulders. Webster said, "Nice wheels."

Dylan said, "Yeah, if you don't mind changing tires every five thousand miles."

Jack added, "Tread wears out faster than a virgin in an army barracks. Something screwy with the alignment and balance."

Dylan said, "Wasn't there a recall on the car, Sarah?"

"Beats me," Sarah said. "I don't talk to Sean about his car." In an undertone, she added, "If I can help it, I don't talk to Sean, period!"

"Would he mind if I spoke to him?" Webster asked.

Sarah shrugged. "Probably. Sean doesn't like anyone to invade his *personal* space."

Sean honked, but Sarah waved him over. The boy frowned, blasted the horn. Sarah, God bless her, remained rooted, continued to motion to him. Finally, he killed the motor, double-parked, and got out. Jogged over to his sister. "Whaddaya *doing*? I gotta go!"

Sarah said, "Sean, this guy's from *Homicide*—"

"What?" Sean took off his sunglasses. Glanced at Kelly, then at Webster with midnight-blue eyes. "Who are you?"

Kid spoke with a very slight Texas drawl. Webster

took out his shield, introduced himself. Sean's expression turned dark. "Whaddaya doing talking to a cop, Sarah? You outta your *mind*?"

Sarah turned red. "I didn't say any—"

"Just shut up and get in the car."

"Sean, I—"

He grabbed her arm. "Just *shut* up and get—"

"Drop her arm *now*!" Webster ordered.

Immediately, Sean let go of his sister's biceps, raised both his palms in the air. "No prob . . . *sir*."

Webster glared at him. "You know the drill, son?"

"I don't know *what* you're talking about."

"How 'bout this? You keep your hands to yourself. Is that clear enough?"

"Fine. Can I go now . . . *sir*?"

To Sarah, Webster said. "You okay, Ms. Amos?"

"She's *fine*!" Sean sniped at his sister. "Now look what you've done. Get in the car."

Sarah hugged her books tightly, didn't move.

Webster said, "I'll take you home if you want, Sarah."

Red-faced, Sean silently mouthed, "Get! In! The! Car!"

Sarah blinked back tears and ran toward the Acura. Again Sean gave Kelly a sidelong glance, then turned his stormy eyes to Webster. "Is that what you do for kicks, Detective? Hassle *minors*? Your *superior* will hear about this!"

Webster said, "Uh-huh. In the meantime, quit grabbing girls, including your sister."

Sean bit his lip, spoke to the group. "You guys are stupid fucks. You're playing into their bullshit. You know how cops twist words. Go home." He slipped on his shades, muttered, "Bunch of retards!" and jogged off.

Webster let out a gush of air. "Whew! What's his problem?"

But the kids had turned silent. Sean had done his job. Finally, Rudy said, "Sorry. I've gotta go."

"We all do," Jack said. "Weight-training practice."

Rudy said, "That's not a problem, is it?"

"Not at all," Webster said. "Thanks for your help."

Dylan shrugged. "We really didn't do anything. You coming, Kelly?"

"In a minute."

Rudy paused, then said, "Sean's an asshole but he has a point, Kel. We shouldn't be sticking our noses where they don't belong." He turned to Webster. "No offense."

"None taken. Thanks again."

When the boys were out of earshot, Webster said, "You don't have to talk to me, either."

Kelly was silent.

Webster said, "You used to date Sean, didn't you?"

"Why do you ask that?"

"He kept looking at you."

"He dated my older sister, Tara."

"And?"

"Why do you think there's an 'and'?"

Webster looked around. "Kelly, it's not real private here. Can I meet you someplace public but more discreet? I'll call my female partner to come join us. Her name is Detective Marge Dunn. Phone the police station at Devonshire and ask for her and about me, too. We're both legitimate."

"It's okay. I believe you."

"Tell me a place."

"It's not necessary." Kelly fiddled with her plait. "I don't have anything to say."

"You don't like Sean much, do you?"

"Why is that relevant?"

"He seems . . . cautious around you."

"Why are you asking about Sean? I thought you wanted to know about Harlan Manz."

*She's gotcha, Tom.* "Well . . ." Webster's mind raced for a logical retort. "Sarah said he freaked when he found out about Manz. That he acted strange—"

"So?"

Webster stalled. "Maybe he knew something about Harlan. Something that made him feel guilty when the shootings at Estelle's went down."

Kelly played with her braid.

"Were they tight?" Webster asked. "He and Harlan?"

"How should I know?"

He was probing too deeply. "Yeah, that's true. Anyway, thanks a heap for your time—"

"I hate him," Kelly blurted out.

Webster paused. "Harlan?"

"No, Sean. I hate his fucking guts." Kelly's voice dropped to a whisper. "He knocked up my sister. Paid for the abortion, of course. Then dumped her. As if that wasn't bad enough, he spread rumors about her. Horrible lies. He said she was . . . she was *diseased*."

"That's despicable."

"My sister hasn't been the same since. She was a straight-A student. Now she's lucky if she pulls C's. He ruined her. Just . . . buried her self-confidence."

Her eyes moistened. But she held the tears in check.

"Your parents know about the abortion?" Webster asked.

"Of course not."

"How old is Tara?"

"Seventeen."

"And you are?"

"Fifteen and a half." Kelly paused. "I saw him shove Tara once. After he dumped her. She just wanted to *talk* to him and he . . . he pushed her away like she was *rancid* or something! I became infuriated!"

"I don't blame you."

"Yeah, well, listen to this. Later that day, I caught him alone. I told him that if he ever, ever dissed my sister again, I'd go straight to his *mother*. He tried to scare me, grabbed my arm just like he did to Sarah. I took my other hand and slapped his face. Hard! I *stunned* him. He's been nervous around me ever since. He's all bluff and no bite."

"So his mother never knew about the abortion?"

"No."

"How'd he get the money?"

"Detective, obscenely rich boys like him *always* have money."

"And you think his mom would be upset about the abortion?"

"She'd have a fit and a half because she's a *real* right-to-lifer. Card-carrying protestor with pictures of aborted fetuses and all that crap. Never mind that she dresses like the whore of Bourbon Street. When it comes to politics, she's Madame Reactionary."

"Bourbon Street." Webster paused, "She's from Louisiana?"

Kelly nodded.

"But Sean's from Texas."

Kelly faced him. "How'd you know that?"

*Shit*, Webster thought. Sometimes a little learning is indeed a dangerous thing. Smoothly, he said, "I recognized the accent."

"You think Sean has an *accent*?"

"To my Southern ear, it screams Dallas, Texas."

"Ah." Kelly smiled. "Guess it takes one to know one. Accents, I mean. Are you *really* from the South?"

"Biloxi, Mississippi, if you please. Home of the Dixie Mafia."

"But you're college educated, aren't you."

"Tulane University." Webster smiled. "Ever thought of a career as a detective?"

Again Kelly smiled. Then she checked her watch. "I really gotta go."

"Out of curiosity," Webster said, "who's Sean dating now?"

Kelly shrugged. "Don't know. Why?"

Again, Webster was forced to ad-lib. "If she's young enough, might be helpful to warn her about Sean's temper."

"Oh." Kelly nodded. "That's nice of you." She thought a moment. "Could be he's seeing someone from Greenvale. He's there all the time practicing his backhand. He's on the school's varsity tennis team."

"Ever see him there with anyone specific?"

Kelly shook her head no. "Just his tennis partner, Ms. Garrison."

"Garrison . . ." Webster paused. "Why does that name . . ." He stared at Kelly. "Now that wouldn't be *Jeanine* Garrison, would it?"

Kelly nodded. "Her parents were murdered at Estelle's."

Webster said, "And she and Sean are *tennis* partners?"

Kelly nodded.

"Maybe that's why Sean's so freaked out about Harlan. That this monster killed his partner's parents."

Kelly looked at Webster. "Good observation."

"Thanks." Webster appeared to be thinking. "Jeanine Garrison. She's a bit older than Sean."

"She's in her late twenties, I think. Why?"

"Any chance that maybe she and Sean are . . ."

"*What?*"

Webster backtracked. "Just a thought."

Kelly laughed. "Sean may be hot stuff for high school. But Ms. Garrison is like . . . God, she's *beautiful*! And she always has like a ton of men hanging around her. Sean is *way* out of her league."

"I see. Thanks for talking to me, Kelly. Can I ask you a favor? Keep what we talked about confidential? It would make my life easier."

Kelly smiled sadly. "I've kept a zillion secrets in my life. One more ain't no big deal."

# ❧ 24

*"Hassle minors,"* **Decker** repeated.

"Yes," Webster said.

"You're sure Sean used the word *minor*."

"I'm sure. And then he said that my superior would hear about it. 'It' meaning the conversation I was having with the kids."

"Hostile little bugger," Oliver said. "Probably thinks that a good defense is an offense."

"Reckon that about sums it up."

Decker sat back in his chair. "Jeanine prepped him."

"My take on the situation," Webster said.

Marge said, "You know, she might have messed herself up. By Sean making a case of his being a minor . . . if she and he are screwing . . . well, then she can't plead ignorance of his age."

Oliver said, "She can always claim he told her he was eighteen."

"But the onus is on her." Martinez turned to Webster. "You think he's spouting idle threats?"

"Maybe."

Decker sipped cold coffee. "My opinion? We're going to hear about it. Probably first thing Sean did when he got home was give Garrison a ring."

"She's calling the shots," Webster said.

Oliver said, "Probably told Seanny boy to call the police and make a stink."

"Not call the *police*," Decker said. "Call the *school*. Have them make the stink." He looked at Webster. "Where were you when you talked to the kids? I mean physically. Where were you standing?"

Webster thought a moment. "'Bout fifty yards from the front entrance of Westbridge."

"On school property?"

"On the sidewalk."

"Public domain," Marge said.

Decker said. "But you were still standing in front of school buildings, correct?"

"Yes."

Without preamble, Strapp walked into Decker's office.

"We've been expecting you," Oliver said. "Get a call from a kid named Sean Amos, Captain?"

"Westbridge Prep." Strapp's eyes locked on to Webster's face. "You were out there today, Tom?"

"Yes, sir."

Decker said, "Captain, we agreed to interview the kids about Harlan Manz—"

"Not on school property, Pete."

Webster said, "I wasn't on school property. I was on the sidewalk."

"You didn't enter the school?" Strapp asked.

"No." Webster grew tense. "And last I heard interviewing kids politely didn't constitute police harassment."

Strapp said, "Tell me what happened."

Webster recapped his conversations with the teens

for the second time in twenty minutes. Strapp listened carefully.

Afterward, Decker said, "When did the call from Westbridge come through, Captain?"

"About five minutes ago."

Decker said, "And when did you leave the school, Tom?"

"Around five-fifteen."

Decker's eyes swept over the wall clock. Six-thirty. "Okay. Sean waited before he called the school to register the complaint. First, he called Jeanine, asked her what to do—"

"Got their stories straight," Oliver said.

"So what do we do?" Marge asked. "Look for outgoing calls from Sean's number to Jeanine's. Or if he's involved, would Sean be stupid enough to use his own phone number?"

"People do stupid things when they panic," Oliver said.

"I say we look for incoming calls to Jeanine," Martinez said.

Decker looked at Strapp. "What would it hurt?"

"Go ahead."

Decker picked up the receiver, dialed the phone company, gave out his badge number, and waited.

Martinez said, "You know, it doesn't say much even if he did call her. They *are* tennis partners."

Marge said, "It's the timing, Bert. Sean hassles Tom, goes home, then *waits* to call the school. First, he calls Jeanine. You're telling me he's more interested in a tennis date than in registering a complaint?"

Strapp said, "It proves nothing, Dunn."

"Yes, I'm still here." Decker picked up a pen, wrote down the telephone number. "Thank you."

He hung up, held the slip in the air. "West Valley prefix."

Martinez said, "I'll look it up."

Decker said, "If it isn't in the backward directory, Bert, call up the phone company."

Martinez took the slip with the phone number and left to work at his desk.

"Even if Sean did call Jeanine," Strapp said, "just what exactly are you trying to establish?"

Oliver said, "That Sean's involved as the number two shooter—"

"If there even *is* a number two shooter," Strapp interrupted.

"If Sean was involved in Estelle's," Webster said, "I don't picture him as the number two shooter. Kelly Putnam summed him up as all bluff and no bite, and I agree. Sean's hotheaded, but a coward. Backed off immediately when I came on strong."

"He called the school on us," Oliver said.

"A phone call avoids direct confrontation."

"Tommy, if he's a red-blooded teenager, he'd do anything for pussy."

Webster said, "I don't think the little snot has the balls to pull a trigger."

Martinez came back into the office. "Phone call was made from a pay phone about a half mile from the Amos house."

Marge said, "We should send someone out right now. Dust it for prints."

Strapp said, "Since when is it against the law for Sean Amos to use a pay phone?"

"C'mon, Captain," Decker said. "A kid like that is bound to have either a cellular phone or a car phone or both. Why would he bother with a pay phone unless he's trying to hide something?"

Strapp said, "If Tom doesn't believe that Sean was involved in the shooting, why are we *hassling* him?"

"Sir, I think he was involved in the shooting," Webster said. "Just not as the triggerman."

"So how was he involved if he didn't shoot?" Martinez asked. "Orchestrated the thing? Brokered it out?"

"Maybe both."

Strapp threw up his hands. "I don't like this at all. You're chasing ghosts. Go back to standard investigating procedures."

Marge said, "So let me go out to the phone booth and dust for prints, Captain. That's standard detective procedure from the get-go."

"I'm putting myself on the line here," Strapp said, "allocating detective time without a decent reason. You know you're going to find Sean's prints on the phone. So what?"

"Sir, we connect Sean to Jeanine," Oliver said. "Then, twenty minutes later, the school calls us on a harassment charge—"

"That's reverse police harassment," Marge said. "You know, we should check incoming calls to the school. Find out if any of them match Sean's number."

Strapp said, "This is really skirting the law."

Oliver said, "He's a suspect—"

"Suspect in *what*, Scott? You don't have an atom of proof of Sean's involvement."

"That's what we're trying to establish, Captain," Webster said.

"But first you need reasonable cause, Tom! Right now, you don't have shit!"

"How about this, Captain?" Decker spoke calmly. "Sean roughed up his sister."

"He grabbed her arm—"

"According to the law, it's assault," Decker said. "True or false?"

"Go on." Strapp was irritated.

"According to Kelly, Sean has a history of roughing up girls. Now after Tom spoke to him, he was angry . . . hotheaded. Maybe we should put a tail on him. Just to *make sure* he doesn't do anything to his sister or Kelly or anybody else."

Webster grinned. "The Loo has a point, sir. Sean's a bully. I think he bears watching. What do you think?"

Strapp said, "You're stretching longer than a hippo's condom."

Decker said, "Of course we're stretching. We're doing everything back door—"

"*Why* do you really want to tail him?" Strapp was annoyed.

Decker said, "Because Tom thinks he's immature and impulsive. And Bert made a good point. Maybe Sean is the broker for the hit. The middle man. The kid's already registered a complaint against us—"

"Westbridge never said it was Sean," Strapp said.

"Sir, we could check that out," Martinez said. "All it would take is a quick call to the phone company."

Marge said, "Hate to be a broken record, but I'd still like to go dust the pay phone for prints."

Strapp scowled.

Webster said, "What would it hurt to see where Sean'll take this?"

Marge said, "Scare him bad enough, maybe he'll lead us to a candidate for number two shooter."

"Or to Jeanine," Martinez said.

"And maybe he'll sit tight," Strapp said. "If Jeanine Garrison has half the cunning we think she has, that's exactly what she told him to do. Sit tight. Don't do anything because they have no proof. And she's right."

Marge said, "All the more reason to scare him."

"And how do you propose to do that without making contact with the boy, Detective Dunn?"

"I agree," Decker said. "No contact with Sean because he's a minor. But it's easy to shake him up, sir. Just make the tail obvious."

Oliver smiled widely. "Two-car tail. First for show. Second for real."

"What do you say, Captain?" Decker said. "Do we run an investigation or do we run?"

"That's not fair."

Decker was quiet.

Strapp swore under his breath. "All right. Go for it."

Gaynor threw up his hands. "Sorry, Loo. I checked through six months of receipts. I couldn't find any large sums of money debited from any of Jeanine's accounts."

Decker rubbed his eyes, looked at his wall clock. Seven-thirty. He had hoped to make it home a half hour ago . . . take Rina out for dinner and a movie. If he hustled, they could still make a movie . . . maybe have ice cream afterward. He said, "What are your criteria for large sums of money, Farrell?"

"Any lump sum over twenty-five hundred," Gaynor said. "During the past week, she has made several withdrawals of around a thousand each. But I've traced them to deposits—for a caterer and for the arena for her upcoming wheelchair tennis tournament."

"Don't talk to me about that!" Decker picked up an eraser, threw it across the room. "If she hired a hit man for Estelle's, she had to pay him somehow!"

"Hidden cash," Gaynor said. "Withdraw a couple of hundred one week, a couple of hundred the next . . . pretty soon she'd have a tidy sum."

"A couple of hundred a week?" Decker looked at Farrell. "Take her a while to save up enough to pay off two hit men."

"Two hit men?"

"I'm counting Harlan Manz as a hit man."

"So maybe she didn't pay out in money," Gaynor said. "Maybe she paid in sex."

"If Sean Amos hired a second shooter, she couldn't have paid *him* with sex. Money had to have been exchanged somehow."

"So maybe Sean paid and she paid Sean back." Gaynor frowned. "No, that wouldn't work. There'd still be cash out from her accounts." He paused. "She could have a secret account somewhere. I couldn't tap into everything."

Decker ran his hands through his hair. Marge walked into his office, her nose and cheeks blackened with print dust. "The good news is I have solid whorls. The bad news is Sean Amos doesn't have anything resembling a record. So I have nothing to match them against."

Decker said, "Label them and put them under Jeanine Garrison's file for the time being . . . until I figure out what to do with them."

Marge said, "Are both Scott and Tom watching Sean?"

"Just Oliver right now. Because the kid hasn't moved. Holed up in his manse." Decker blew out air. "Strapp's right. The kid's gonna sit. Whole thing's a bloody waste of time."

Suddenly, he stood and put on his jacket.

"It's been a long day for me. I'm packing it in."

Gaynor said, "Save my wife a trip if you took me home, sir."

"Be glad to."

"I'll take you home, Farrell," Marge offered. "If you don't mind waiting until I've finished some paperwork."

"Nah, I don't mind."

"Nonsense," Decker said. "I'll take you home now, Farrell."

"It won't take me long, Pete."

"It's not a problem for me, Marge."

"This is nice," Gaynor said.

Decker stopped talking. "What's nice, Farrell?"

"Being fought over." The old man smiled. "Been a long time since I've felt wanted."

# ❧ 25

*Prayer in front* of a mirror was forbidden.

Which was fine with Decker. At six in the morning, the last thing he wanted was to look at his haggard face. Of course, that wasn't the reason for the prohibition. The eyes were supposed to be focused inward to God, not outward, seduced by vanity. Yet every so often Decker caught his reflection in the living room's bay window. A large figure wrapped in a *tallith*—a long fringed religious shawl—and *tephillin*—known by the clumsy English word "phylacteries." They were small prayer-filled boxes which were secured to the body by leather straps. One set of long thin strips of hide had been wound down the length of his right arm; another set encircled his skull, then dangled past his shoulders. A black leather box rested on his forehead; a second was perched on his biceps.

Weird.

Still, the primitive ritual worked. Every morning as he girded his arm and head, Decker thought about God even if only for a twinkle of time. Thinking about Rav Schulman's explanation . . . the beautiful allegories he had used. The box on the forehead representing God's gift of intellect to man, the other on the biceps connoting man's brute strength tethered to the spiritual.

But he looked strange. As he removed the paraphernalia, he wondered what his fellow professionals would think if they saw him bound in leather, as if embroiled in an S&M sex game. He pondered this as he undid the straps, freeing himself of symbolic servitude.

The phone rang. The business line. Still partially tied, he picked up the receiver. "Decker."

Strapp spoke. "David Garrison was found dead in his apartment ten minutes ago. Looks like an OD."

Decker refrained from cursing. He still had God's name resting on his forehead. "Who found him?"

"Cleaning lady."

"She's sure he's dead?"

"As cold as Russian vodka."

"An OD. Okay. Let me guess. There was a needle conveniently gripped in Garrison's fingers."

"By his side."

"Jeanine's slipping—"

"There's no evidence that Jeanine was anywhere near the place."

"There's where you're wrong, sir. We've got concrete, carved-in-stone evidence that Jeanine *was* there."

"What are you talking about?"

"David Garrison's body. *There's* your evidence."

"Decker—"

"I'm coming down."

"I'll meet you there."

\* \* \*

He ducked under the yellow crime-scene ribbon that had been stretched across the door.

The first detective at the scene, but not the first cop. Four officers, one of them talking to a young Hispanic woman in a white uniform, who was rubbing her arms. Beside her was a pail filled with bottles of cleaning solutions and brushes. The cleaning lady. She'd keep for a moment. He flashed his badge to the uniforms, went over to the body.

Stretched out on the floor, Garrison's arms and legs were bent at all angles. He had landed or had been positioned on his back, his head arched back, white lips apart. Clean blond hair framed a gray face, fell across open dead eyes, the pupils already fixed. A knocked-over chair was at his left side, the needle and tourniquet at his right. He wore jeans and a short-sleeve T-shirt. Two puncture wounds in the cubital fossa—the triangular depression below the elbow crease. The common plexus of veins where junkies first shoot up—until those vessels collapse. Then they go for the backs of the hands, the legs, the feet, the stomach, finally settling on anywhere with a pulse.

Such ugly business.

He heard a grinding sound, looked up. Out of nowhere, a wheelchair broke through the yellow ribbon, as if it had just won a race. The machine's occupant was very muscular from the waist up. Blond curly hair, manicured three days' growth of beard.

Wade Anthony.

Behind him was Jeanine. Wide-eyed. Her mouth agape. Dressed in loose sweats.

"I got a call from David's landlady!" she shrieked to no one in particular. "What's going on?"

Decker stepped in front, blocking her view of the body. "Ma'am, can you step outside for just a moment?"

Instant anger in her eyes. "What are *you* doing here?" she snarled.

"Ms. Garrison—"

"Get out of my way! Now!"

Anthony spoke up. "Can someone tell us what's going on?"

"Be glad to tell you, sir, once we're outside—"

"Get out of my way!" Jeanine charged him, bounced off his chest. It was then that Decker noticed she was wearing makeup—including foundation. Because it had come off on his shirt. She also wore earrings and had put on perfume.

Two uniforms—a man and a woman—rushed over. Injected themselves between Jeanine and Decker. Stood their ground, legs apart, arms folded across their chests.

"Back off, ma'am!" the woman ordered.

Arms flailing, Jeanine started screaming. "You goddamn son of a bitch, bastard—"

"Back off!" the female officer insisted.

Jeanine screamed, "I want to see my brother and this bastard won't let me through!"

Decker shouted over her, "Ms. Garrison, can you let me talk?"

"You son of a bitch! Get *out* of here!"

Strapp chose that moment to make his entrance. Jeanine whirled to him. "Get this monster out of my way. He won't let me see my brother! He's trying to brainwash him against me! That's what David told me. The police were brainwashing him—"

Strapp said, "Ms. Garrison, the police are here because we received a call. I'm sorry to say that your brother has reportedly died of an overdose!"

Jeanine's hands gripped long blond hair. "Oh God! Oh no!" She yanked at her tresses. "My parents, then this! It can't be! It just can't be!"

Hate-filled eyes turned to Decker, advanced toward him. "You *killed* him, you bastard!" Abruptly, she drew back her hand, smacked him hard across the face.

Decker's fingers went to his stinging cheek as fury clouded his senses. The female officer—Heather Morgan—grabbed Jeanine's arm, turned her, and pushed her face against the wall. "Calm down this *minute*!"

"I'm going to *get* you, Decker!" Jeanine struggled against the officer's grip. "I'm going to get you *all*!"

Decker said, "Take her *out* of here!"

Anthony hoisted himself upward until his rear was off the seat. He yelled, "Let her go, man! She's just had a terrible shock!"

Strapp said, "Let her go, Officer Morgan!"

Decker's eyes grew in shock. "*What?*"

"I *said*, let her go, Officer!" Strapp reiterated. "That's an order." To Decker, he said, "Take a walk, Pete!"

A second slap across the face. Not a physical one but much deeper and harder. "I don't friggin' *believe*—"

"Now!" Strapp gripped Decker's arm, pushed him forward. "Take a *long walk*!"

Jeanine shook off Officer Morgan, smugness stamped across her face. She shrieked, "You'll hear from me in court, Lieutenant. By the time I'm done with you, you'll be begging on street corners!"

"Is that a *threat*?"

"It's a *promise*—"

Strapp pushed Decker forcefully. "*Out*, Lieutenant!"

Jeanine screamed, "I'll ruin you, you *bastard*!"

Decker stepped toward her. "The sentiment runs both ways, lady!"

"*Out* now, Decker!" Using an interlocking finger grip and body leverage, Strapp was barely able to contain him. He slowly managed to inch the big man away from the scene, away from the apartment. Using maximum exertion! Maximum effort!

And Decker wasn't even *fighting*. Just passively resisting. The guy must have the strength of a bull elephant. Which gave Strapp pause for thought. Had Decker wanted to lash out, there could have been real problems.

Onto the street. Decker was soaked in sweat . . . panting . . . shaking . . . ready to strangle the next asshole who got in his way. Seething at Jeanine, boiling over at Strapp. Angrier at *him* than at *her*!

Goddamn son of a bitch!

As soon as Strapp had taken him to a secluded spot, Decker shook off the captain's arm as if it were a gnat. He spoke quickly and furiously. "You just cut off my balls in front of that cunt—"

"Go back to basics, Decker!" Strapp snapped back. "First de-escalate the situation—"

"Bullshit!" Decker spat out. "Bullshit, *bullshit*!"

"You're skirting the border of insubordination!" Strapp cut in. "Take a walk, Lieutenant, and cool off!"

Decker felt his head pounding, exploding fireworks of white light. He closed his eyes, forced himself to count to ten. Heard Strapp speaking softly.

". . . been through the mill, Pete. Why don't you take the day off? Spend some time with that beautiful wife of yours. We'll talk about this tomorrow."

Again, Decker counted to ten. He opened his eyes. With physical sight came the focus. Clarity of purpose. He laughed bitterly. "This is unbelievable. You're shutting me down!"

Strapp blinked. "Pete, you're the best lieutenant I've ever had under my command. Incredibly hard-working, dedicated, not only book smart but street clever. Believe it or not, I'm trying to save you—"

"Thank you, Jesus—"

"—get you away from that bitch before she makes you react . . . giving her a *real* reason to sue you."

Decker's hand involuntarily went to his cheek. He didn't speak.

Strapp blew out air. "Go home, Pete!"

Decker waited a beat. Then he said, "I'm a good soldier, Captain. But I'm not a mindless one." He took his badge from his pocket, unharnessed his gun. Presented the package to his captain. "Here you go."

"Put it away, Peter."

"I mean it—"

"I know you do. Put it away."

Decker didn't move.

Strapp tightened his fingers into fists. "Don't draw lines in the sand, Pete. You have too much to lose."

"Fine. I lose. Take my job. I'll keep my pride."

"Don't be a schmuck, for godsakes. You've got kids to support."

"I quit now, I'll retire with half-time pension. My wife has skills. And a trust fund. A big one. Besides, I'm not exactly without resources. I've got twenty-five years of police experience behind me and I'm still licensed as a lawyer. So screw you—"

"Decker—"

"You want to cut off my balls, this is what you get. Take my damn badge. Either take it or stay the hell away from me!"

A standoff.

Strapp's jaw working overtime. "Just hear me out."

Decker didn't answer.

Strapp glanced around, over his shoulder. "Put your badge and gun away. We have our differences. But we don't advertise them in public."

"Yeah, I forgot. This is Hollywood. Image is every—"

"Fuck you!" Strapp blurted out.

Decker expected Strapp to stomp off. But he didn't. Decker stalled but eventually pocketed the equipment. "Make it quick, Strapp. My bullshit meter is about to blow."

Strapp glared at him. "You asshole, don't you dare push me any further! I am still your *superior* officer. You talk to me, Decker, you call me *sir*."

Decker held up his palms, took a step backward in mock retreat.

Strapp caught his breath. "Pete, I did what I just did for your sake. And I'm doing what I'm doing for your sake as well. I've *got* to take you off the case—"

"Fuck this noise—"

"I can't give the bitch any more fodder for her suit! And I can't have David Garrison's death ruling tainted by shouts of police conspiracy. The poor guy is dead! We owe him the truth—"

"What the *hell* do you think I've been looking for!"

"Jeanine's suit is a stumbling block to your involvement. You're off the case. *But*—"

"Ah, the *but*."

Strapp continued. "Pete, it doesn't mean all your prior work on Estelle's has been shitcanned. It doesn't mean Jeanine's off the hook. It means we continue the investigation, it means you have input. But officially, I'll call the shots. Ergo, I take the heat. You have nothing to lose except aggravation. And maybe a little credit if we ever get to the bottom of this fucking mess!"

No one spoke.

Strapp sighed. "Can you live with that?"

"I don't give a flying fuck about credit."

"Then you have nothing to lose. Lieutenant, you are a busy man. *You've* got a squad room to run. I refuse to allow that cunt to distract you any longer."

Decker didn't answer, his head still buzzing like a jackhammer. He forced himself to breathe normally, to listen to ambient sounds—birds chirping, dogs barking, the faint rotors of a helicopter, the distant rush of morning traffic.

Strapp said, "We'll discuss the case daily. All you have to do is stay out of it *officially*. Let me direct."

"I have no problem with you directing. I don't give a rat's ass who directs as long as we get bottom-line results. I firmly believe that thirteen . . . *fourteen* people died because of that bitch. She's got to pay!"

"If that accusation turns out to be backed by solid evidence, she'll pay big time. Just let me handle it."

Whatever that was worth. Decker regarded his superior. Tense. Nervous. Angry. Upset. Was he telling the truth? Impossible to know.

Strapp took out a kerchief, wiped sweat from his forehead and face. "Call up Dunn and Oliver. You trust them, don't you?"

"Very much."

"So we'll let them secure the scene, gather evidence, and talk to the ME. Let David Garrison's death be their baby, okay?"

Decker paused. "Fine."

Again, Strapp wiped his brow. "You know, Decker, as much as you don't want to believe it, it could have been an OD. David had a history of drug abuse."

"How convenient for Jeanine."

Strapp didn't speak. Decker closed his eyes and opened them. "It's a good point . . . *sir.*"

Strapp jerked his head up. "Go home."

"I'm going back to the station house."

"Fine with me. Go back to the station house, go run your division. We *both* have jobs to do."

With that, Strapp turned around and jogged back to the apartment.

# ❧ 26

*Oliver said, "We* ordered a full toxicology, including a blood-gas chromatography. See if David Garrison had any tranquilizers in his system—things like roofies or ludes—"

"Things that might have put him under," Marge said. "We'll also test to see if the junk was cut with cyanide, arsenic, thallium, or any other heavy metal or poison."

Oliver raked his hair with his hands. "I don't think we're going to find anything unusual though."

"Why's that?" Decker asked.

"First off, from our search, it appears the guy had his own private stash. Yeah, it could have been planted, but to my eye, it looked like it'd been dipped into before."

"Also Garrison reeked of booze," Marge added. "We did a quick blood analysis at the scene. BAL was point two five."

"Jesus!" Decker rotated his shoulders. "Guy was a pickled specimen."

Oliver nodded. "He probably did half the dirty work for her. Drinking himself comatose. Then all

Jeanine would have to do is come in the house and pop him in the vein."

"No forced entry," Marge said. "But that doesn't mean anything. Jeanine has a key."

"She admitted it?"

"Right away."

Decker rubbed his forehead. "You have a point two five BAL, you can't focus, let alone find a vein."

"He had two pokes in the arm," Oliver said. "Maybe he didn't get it on his first try."

"He wouldn't have gotten it *period*!"

Marge said, "Maybe he shot up first. Then he started knocking off the shooters. Scott and I were going over this very thing. We both decided that Jeanine would have to have been really stupid to pop him at this moment—"

"Casting even more suspicion on herself—"

"And we know Jeanine's not stupid," Marge said, "so if she *did* do it, she must have had a pressing reason."

"Like what?" Decker asked.

"Maybe David stumbled onto something," Oliver said.

Decker perked up. "Such as?"

Marge said, "Maybe David found out that Jeanine was planning shenanigans with his trust."

Oliver paused. "Like what if Garrison wanted the money invested one way and Jeanine wanted to invest it another way?"

"Or what if she just wanted his money before he got a chance to spend it?" Marge said.

Decker said, "Farrell Gaynor and I talked about that. That's why I sent Scott out to see David Garrison in the first place."

"Talked about what?"

"That if Jeanine worked quickly—meaning if Jeanine offed David quickly—before the cash from the trust was distributed, she would probably inherit his cash as well as her own."

Webster walked into Decker's office, pulled up a chair next to Oliver. "Maybe she figured it like this. Her cash would go to her, his cash would pay her estate taxes."

"And the fact that she got away with Estelle's . . ." Marge paused. "That kind of lust for power . . . makes you arrogant."

"We all know about Jeanine's arrogance!" Oliver whispered. "And that bastard Strapp feeding right into it."

"Whole thing sucks!" Marge said.

"Sucks big time!" Oliver agreed. "Cunt may be able to shut *you* down. But she can't shut down the entire Homicide Division." He paused. "Though she's making a gallant effort."

Webster said, "Jeanine's getting pretty brazen . . . popping her brother like that."

"Or maybe the OD was a lucky accident for her," Marge said. "They do happen, even to evil people."

Decker said, "Neighbors see or hear anything suspicious?"

"Nothing."

Decker turned to Webster. "What's going on with Sean?"

Webster said, "He went to school, he went home."

"Did he pick up on your tail?" Decker asked.

"If he did, I don't reckon he cared much. The boy just went about his business . . . buried in school most of the day. He could have been plotting murders, but I wasn't privy to his conversations."

Decker sank into his chair. "We're going nowhere fast."

Martinez walked into the office. Webster was annoyed. "Where've you been, Bert?"

Martinez stood against the wall. "Checking out the license numbers. How're you doing, Loo?"

"All right," Decker said. "Thanks for asking. What license numbers are you talking about, Bert?"

Webster said, "Sean chatted with half a dozen kids after school . . . as he walked to the parking lot."

Martinez said, "At that point, we split assignments. Tom took Sean, I checked out some of the other kids."

"And?" Decker asked.

Martinez said, "Tracked down three of them. First, the buxom blond girl who drives a Mercedes three hundred. She and Sean gabbed for a few minutes, he gave her something, she drove off. Then Sean talked to another girl for a minute or so. She was part Asian and maybe part black. Beautiful thing. She drives a Range Rover. He held the door open for her and she took off. The last person Sean talked to was a guy—a rangy Caucasian kid wearing jeans and a ski cap. He drives a ten-year-old Saab."

Oliver said, "A ten-year-old Saab? I didn't think Westbridge allowed them."

Martinez said, "Ran all the plates through DMV. The Mercedes belongs to Barry and Susan Door. Range Rover is registered to a Jane Highsmith—"

"Jane Highsmith . . . why do I know that name?" Oliver snapped his fingers. "Got it! Family dispute ten years ago. Terence and Jane Highsmith. He's some kind of English lord, she's also from Brahmin background. Literally. Some upper-crust Indian family—"

"Upper caste," Webster punned.

The group groaned.

Oliver clucked his tongue. "Man, they were both skunk drunk . . . throwing things at each other— plates, dishes, flower vases, magazines. More things flying in that room than at O'Hare. And the kids." He shook his head. "Two little girls. Hiding in bed together, covers pulled up over their faces. Hugging each other. Scared shitless. Big blue eyes poking out of dusky skin. Beautiful girls."

"One of them still is."

"What about the Saab owner?" Marge asked.

"Doctors Kenneth and Elizabeth Rush," Martinez said. "But they're not MDs. Mr. Doctor is a professor of mathematics at Northridge, Mrs. Doctor is a professor of physics at UCLA. Their son, Joachim, is a senior at Westbridge. He's on scholarship."

Oliver said, "And you found this out from DMV?"

"Not quite." Martinez smiled. "Since Tom was on Sean, I figured I'd go for Joachim. Only I didn't know he was Joachim then. I followed the kid to My- croft and Cranepool—"

"The new bookstore on Devonshire," Marge said.

"The one with the café and espresso bar," Oliver added.

Marge stared at him. "You've actually been to a bookstore, Scott?"

"Stick it in a dark place, lady," Oliver snapped back. "Yes, I've been to a bookstore."

"Singles night, Marge," Webster said.

"Fuck you, Uncle Tom," Oliver said. "And for your information, lots of hot-looking babes were at the Jack Kerouac reading."

Martinez went on, "I followed Joachim to Mycroft and Cranepool. Kid got out of the car, carrying a bunch of papers. I didn't follow him into the store, but I could see what he was doing because the entire front is one big glass window. He didn't go there to browse. He left the papers on the store's counter, then came out again. I tailed him back to his house. Rather than just hang around there, I returned to the bookstore . . . picked up one of the leaflets."

Martinez took a breath.

"An advertisment for a Scrabble tournament. I asked one of the clerks about it—a kid named James Goddard, who goes to public school. But he knows Joachim from the Scrabble matches. Once a month, they're held at Mycroft's. But games are hosted at other places as well. Seems that Joachim's a hot dog in the National Scrabble Association. A ranked player and an absolute fanatic. At the matches, he's known as Cyberword because he plays like a computer. Goddard was the one who told me about Joachim being on scholarship at Westbridge. He also told me that Joachim was accepted to Yale under an early admissions program. That's supposed to be impressive."

"I'm impressed," Webster said. "A formidable kid."

Decker said, "Is James Goddard a good friend of Joachim's?"

Martinez shook his head. "Didn't get that impression. Just that they knew each other. Then again, I didn't want to pry too deep. Mostly we chatted.

Talked about the store's special events." He looked at Oliver. "Like singles night—"

"Fuck you!" Oliver said.

"Stop being defensive, Scotty," Martinez answered. "He told me that except for major author signings and children's bedtime story evening, the singles night is the store's biggest draw."

Oliver didn't say anything, appeared to be mollified.

"Anyway, that's how I found out about Joachim's parents," Martinez said. "They're not only regular customers but also faithful members of Mycroft and Cranepool's sci-fi book club. You join, you get discounts on sci-fi books and a monthly newsletter talking about upcoming sci-fi events, the whole nine yards."

"Beam me up, Scotty." Immediately, Marge followed with "That's a trekkie saying, Oliver, not a come-on."

Oliver looked crushed.

Webster asked, "Is Joachim a member of the sci-fi book group?"

"James didn't say, I didn't ask."

Marge said, "Is Sean a Scrabble player?"

"I didn't ask that, either. Sounded too inquisitive."

Webster loosened his tie. "You got Sean Amos. Mr. Hip Guy with the hip clothes and the hip convertible. Mr. Tennis Player who roughs up women . . . knocks up his girlfriend, then dumps her—"

"He paid for her abortion," Marge said.

"The kid's rolling in dough," Webster said. "Besides, betcha the boy's philosophy is God giveth, God taketh away. Because guess who he thinks *is* God."

"Tommy, tell us how you really feel about Sean," Marge said.

"You should have seen the way he treated his sister. Like garbage."

Decker said, "So you're thinking, why is a hip guy like Amos talking to Cyberword Joachim Rush? Mr. Poor Boy with the torn clothes and the old Saab."

Webster said, "The two don't exactly seem like blood brothers."

Martinez added, "Who says they're friends? I just saw them talking to each other."

Decker said, "So why did you bother looking into him, Bert?"

"Good question." He gathered his thoughts. "I think it was the fact that Sean approached Joachim instead of the other way around."

Decker pulled out his notebook. "And?"

"Nothing much. They walked to Joachim's car together. Talked for maybe a minute with Sean doing most of the speaking—"

"Sean look nervous?" Marge asked.

"More like animated," Martinez said. "He talked with his hands, with his face. Joachim, on the other hand, appeared lost in thought except for the occasional nod. Apathetic. When the boys got to the Saab, Sean kept talking, even after Joachim was inside the car. But the driver's window was rolled down. Finally Sean reached into his pocket and pulled out an envelope, passed it through the open window—"

"A transaction?" Marge was animated.

"Looked that way to me," Martinez said. "Because afterward, Sean stuck his arm back into the car. I guess they shook hands. Then Joachim drove off."

"A payoff," Webster said.

Oliver said, "Okay. Here's what we got. We got Joachim, who's a nerd—"

"More like a weirdo," Webster interjected. "A guy called Cyberword, who's a Scrabble fanatic—"

"My kids play Scrabble," Decker said. "I play Scrabble. I'm not a nerd, I'm not weird, and I'm not a hit man. We don't know a friggin' thing about this kid. We've just made leaps that could traverse the Grand Canyon."

No one said anything.

Decker gave a slight smile. "Still, if I were TV typecasting for an outcast, theoretically Joachim Rush would fit the bill—a scholarship boy in a rich prep school. A loner because he's out of the social loop. Then both of his parents are not only math and science professors but also fanatic sci-fi readers. He's a fanatical Scrabble player. I'm always skeptical of fanatical anything—"

"Even religious fanaticals?" Oliver said.

"Especially the fanatically religious," Decker countered. "The Rushes don't sound like part of the typical Westbridge population. Neither the kid nor the parents."

Oliver said, "You add to your pot that a wad of money was exchanged between Sean and Joachim."

"Who said it was money?" Martinez said. "I just said an envelope."

"What else could it be?" Webster said.

"Lots of things—"

"Including cash for a hit made to look like an OD that happened just last night—"

"Whoa," Decker said. "We're getting *way* out there with our theories. But it *is* an interesting postulation. Too bad we won't be able to check it out."

"Why not?" Martinez asked. "I can tail Joachim for a couple of days, Loo."

"It's okay by me except I'm off the case now." Decker felt his jaw tighten. "You've got to take it up with Strapp."

Oliver frowned. "You know what he'll say, Loo."

Martinez said, "Just let me tail him tomorrow."

"I'm not authorized to give you the go-ahead, Bert. Talk to Strapp."

"He'll bury it," Webster said.

"Probably."

Oliver said, "That means all our work—hell, all *your* work—it's all gonna be shitcanned. You know that."

"I know that," Decker said.

Marge said, "Aren't you frustrated?"

"I'm very frustrated."

"So what are you going to do?"

"At this moment, I'm grinning and bearing. But as for the future . . ." Decker shrugged. "I hear Montana's beautiful at this time of year."

Marge said, "If you don't mind militia men and Nazis."

"Margie, I've been a cop for twenty-five years," Decker said. "I'm used to nutcases with guns."

Freed by Strapp from the Estelle's shooting . . . the tragedy's persistent nagging . . . Decker polished off his paperwork by seven. He thought about his work, he thought about his life. What had happened to all the dreams? All the vacation fantasies? Hand and hand with Rina, running barefoot on empty beaches, toes tickled by the waves. Or hiking through pristine mountains, smelling clean air. Why had he allowed himself to become mired in the muck? His words to Strapp this morning crystalized his dissatisfaction. Openly admitting that the end might be near.

And maybe that was a good thing.

Because there was life beyond the LAPD.

Someone knocked on his doorjamb, jogging him out of his reverie. Marge said, "A woman named Tess Wetzel is waiting outside. She wants to talk to you."

"What's it about?"

"She wouldn't say."

Decker paused, the name pricking at his memory cells. "Tess Wetzel?'

"That's what she said." Marge looked at her watch. "It's kinda late. Tell her you left?"

"No, you can bring her in."

"You're the boss."

Decker laughed. "Right."

A moment later, a plain-looking woman of around thirty limped into the office. She walked with a cane, wincing at every step. Burdened beyond her years. She was on the heavy side, but still had curves. She wore baggy jeans under a loose cable-knit sweater. No makeup. No jewelry. A basic woman, yet there was something about her that connoted strength. Decker stood, held out the chair opposite his desk.

With effort, the woman lowered herself into the seat. Her voice was soft. "Thank you very much for seeing me."

"No problem." Decker sat, held out his hand. "It's Mrs. Wetzel, is it?"

"Tess." The woman laced her fingers around his, squeezed his hand, then quickly placed hers in her lap. Her eyes grew moist. "You don't remember me, do you?"

Decker stared at the face . . . the pained expression . . . the iron will. He blinked, then said, "That entire night was a blur, Tess, but I remember you clearly. Although I don't think we were ever properly introduced." Again he held out his hand. "Lieutenant Peter Decker. Pleased to meet you."

She smiled, then started crying. Buried her head in her hands. "I'm sorry."

Decker leaned over, about to place his hand on her shoulder. Thoughts of Jeanine's harassment suit flitted through his brain. Aw, *screw* that! He patted her arm gently, offered her a tissue. She took it and wiped her eyes.

He said, "It's wonderful to see you up and about."

"Of sorts."

"Can I get you something, Tess?"

"Nothing." She blew her nose. "I came to thank you."

"You're very welcome, although I didn't do anything more than my job."

"I didn't know cops were trained to splint legs."

"I had some medical training when I was in the army. Amazing. It came back to me in a second."

"You should have been a doctor," Tess said. "You have a great bedside manner."

Decker smiled. "Thank you. How are you coping?"

Tess looked away. "Not too awful. Been so busy

thinking about myself I haven't been able to think much about . . . about Ken."

Decker nodded.

Tess blinked tears. "We weren't getting along so hot, you know."

Decker waited.

"That night . . ." Tess cleared her throat. "That night . . . Ken was telling me it was over . . . between us. That he was gonna leave me for some little . . . floozy he was messing around with . . . at the office."

"I'm sorry."

"I remember sittin' there, Lieutenant. Just sittin' there like a piece of wood. Not feelin' anything. Still, the tears wouldn't stop comin'."

Decker nodded.

"I remember thinkin' . . . thinkin' . . . I wish I was dead. I wish *he* was dead. Next thing I knew, he was."

Tears streamed down her cheeks as she cried silently, her gaze fixed on his wall.

Softly, Decker said, "You didn't mean it, Tess. Don't you even give it a second thought because you didn't *mean* it. You think about yourself now— yourself and your kids. You have children, right?"

"Two."

"You had *nothing* to do with your husband's death. There's only one man to blame for what happened that night."

"Harlan Manz," Tess whispered.

"He's the only one responsible for your husband's death," Decker said. "Is that clear?"

Tess didn't respond right away. Then she said, "At the hospital . . . we formed a group . . . those of us who were hit but weren't on the critical list."

"A survivors' group?"

"Yes. We started talking among ourselves. Because only we knew what it was like."

"I think that was a great idea."

"I'm still in contact with a few of the women. The waitress there named Carol. We became friends. We have kids the same age and all. I was thinking like . . . maybe you could come talk to us one day."

"Anytime." Decker paused. "What do you have in mind?"

"Just talk about . . . what happened. And *why*."

"That's tough. Because we really don't know why. We have theories, we have suspicions, we have profiles and psychologists and criminal experts—all of them yakking about this kind of thing. But that's all we really have, Tess. Just talk. Still, I'd be happy to address your group and answer any questions you people might have."

Decker pulled out his calendar.

"Did you have a specific date in mind?"

She shook her head no. "I've got to call some of the others first. Can I get back to you?"

"Absolutely."

She started to rise. Decker bolted out of his chair to aid her, but she stopped him. "I can manage."

"Okay."

She stood, leaned on the ball of her cane. "This is gonna sound crazy . . . but . . ."

Decker nodded encouragement.

She started to talk, then stopped. She tried again. "The shooting . . . there was a lot of shooting."

"Yes, there was."

"Ken and me . . . it seems like we was hit right away." Her eyes moistened. "Right off the bat."

"I understand."

"There was all this shooting. Even after we was hit."

"Yes, there was lots of fire."

"I got this bad habit . . . of being curious . . . too curious. Even after I was hit . . . instead of just staying down like a normal person, I had to look."

Decker's heart started racing. "What'd you see, Tess?"

"Lots of very scared people. Somehow . . . seeing them so scared . . . it made me less scared. Does that sound crazy?"

"Not at all."

Tess grew silent. Decker tried to hide his disappointment. Well, what did he expect? "No, it doesn't sound the least bit crazy."

Tess dropped her voice to a whisper. "Suddenly it stopped . . . the shooting. After it was over . . . everyone moaning and crying . . . but nobody dared to move. Too afraid that it would . . . you know . . . start up again."

Decker nodded.

Tess said, "So no one moved . . . even after it was over . . . except that one guy."

*One guy?* Decker tried to keep calm. "What guy was that, Tess?"

"Some guy in a heavy green jacket . . . it was cold that night."

Decker sat up. A *green* jacket? Harlan was found dead, wearing a *green* jacket. "You saw a man in a green jacket walking around *after* the shooting stopped?"

Tess appeared confused. "He was more like standing around. But I'm not *positive*. Because the one time I mentioned him, no one knew what I was talking about. But like I said, I have a bad habit of being curious. That's how I found out about Ken and his floozy."

Decker forced himself to talk slowly. "Tell me about this guy. What did he do?"

"He didn't do anything really. Just bent down, then stood up, put his hands in his pocket . . . he looked around, then walked out the door. Isn't that odd?"

Decker agreed. It was very odd. Casually, he told her that he'd look into it.

# ❧ 27

*Placing his hands* on his desk, Strapp made a tepee with extended fingers. To Decker, he said, "And how many of Estelle's people did you interview?"

"All of them. But that doesn't—"

Strapp interrupted. "Tell me if I'm wrong about this, Lieutenant."

The captain's eyes went from Decker to his Homicide team minus the old guy, Farrell Gaynor. Dogs encircling him like prey. Well, fuck that. He'd run *his* investigation in *his* own way, at *his* own pace. Less chance of errors—procedurally as well as politically.

"Any of you in this room," Strapp addressed them. "I *welcome* the chance to stand corrected. Now you people interviewed every single patron and employee at Estelle's. Correct?"

The question was rhetorical so no one answered.

Strapp said, "How many were there, Lieutenant?"

Decker could see where this was leading. "One hundred forty-eight—"

"And not *one* of them mentioned a phantom man—"

"In a *green* jacket," Marge interrupted.

"Yes, Detective, I know the details. Can I finish?"

"Sorry, sir," Marge replied.

Strapp said, "So I'm right about this, am I not, Decker? That no one mentioned a *phantom* guy . . . in a *green* jacket?"

Oliver spoke up, "Sir, many of the witnesses mentioned that the shooter wore a green jacket."

"Harlan Manz wore a green jacket, Detective." Strapp grew irritated. "Forget about the jacket. I want to know *which* of your one hundred and forty-eight witnesses mentioned this phantom guy?"

Decker said, "Captain, it was right after—"

Strapp held up his hand, signaling quiet. "Yes, I know, I know. Everyone had been in shock. And it takes time for the shock to wear off . . . for the memories to come back. This is all true. And I'm willing . . . to entertain Mrs. Wetzel's . . . what was her first name, Pete?"

"Tess," Decker said.

Strapp clasped his hands together. "All right. Let's say Mrs. Wetzel's observation was more than a figment of her imagination. Before we proceed any further—with our outer-space conspiracy theories and teenage hit men postulations—we go back to *basics*. How about doing a little *police* work?"

Decker said, "I had every intention of having my team reinterview every single person at Estelle's that evening—"

"Good," Strapp said. "Because now it's an order! Just damn well make sure you don't *push* anyone. If they don't want to talk, we come back. Because it's only been what . . . about three weeks since the incident. We're still dealing with open wounds. So that's what we do. We concentrate on interviews."

The captain looked pointedly at Martinez.

"We forget about tailing a gawky teenager whose only crime is playing Scrabble." His eyes turned to Webster. "And we forget about Sean Amos, whose only crime is being a schmuck."

"He roughs up women," Webster said.

"He grabbed his sister's arm, Detective," Strapp said. "No, it's not *nice*. But if we arrested every older brother who manhandled his younger sibling, we'd have no civilian population."

"It's different when you do it in front of a cop," Webster said. "It makes a statement."

"It says nothing, Webster. More important, it means nothing with regard to the murders at Estelle's. Lay off Amos, is that *clear*?"

"Very."

"Good." Strapp faced the others. "We also forget about Jeanine Garrison—"

"What about David Garrison?" Marge interrupted. "Do we forget about him as well?"

Strapp's face turned red. His hands clenched into fists. "Detective Dunn, you're here by my good graces, not by *his*." He cocked a thumb in Decker's direction.

"It was a legitimate question, Captain," Decker retorted. "Do we view David Garrison as a plain suicide or do we hunt around?"

"For now, it's a suicide," Strapp said. "If Forensics tells us differently, we barrel ahead into a homicide investigation."

Strapp looked at his watch.

"It's eight-thirty. No sense bothering people at

night. All the interviewing is to be done during work hours, but not at the expense of your other investigatory duties. Is that clear?"

"Couldn't be any clearer," Oliver said.

"Are you being snide, Detective Oliver?"

"I'm always snide, sir," Oliver answered. "It's part of my personality."

"It's a rotten part."

"I'm sure my ex-wife would agree with you, sir."

Decker smiled, looked down.

Strapp caught it, started to sneer, but smiled as well. He threw his head back, exhaled slowly, then looked at the group. "You should see yourselves. Like a bunch of hyenas ready to pounce. And for what reason? Because I'm telling you to do sound police work."

He turned to Decker.

"Lieutenant, given Tess Wetzel's revelation, what would you do?"

Decker ran a hand over his face. "I'd handle the investigation more or less the same way. Because at the moment, we have nothing on Jeanine Garrison other than a photo of her and Manz. And that's not indictable evidence. I do believe Tess Wetzel's disclosure. So maybe I'd make the interviewing more top priority. But basically, the captain and I are in agreement."

Martinez said, "So then we don't have a problem."

"I have a problem," Webster said. "We're sidestepping a killer because she's connected."

"So get me evidence." Strapp became suddenly angry. "I can't *believe* you people. A bunch of asses. Finally, you get a big break . . . some outside confirmation that maybe there was a second shooter . . .

and you're mired in shit. Stop blowing smoke through your butts and start asking the right *questions*. And maybe you'll even get the right *answers*."

He turned to Decker.

"I don't want you questioning anyone, but you can draw up the list of people to be interviewed and divide them any way you see fit."

Webster said, "Then I reckon you don't want us questioning Jeanine Garrison . . .'cause she wasn't there."

"That's right, Webster," Strapp said. "I reckon you don't do that. It's not only *pointless*, it's *stupid*."

"Aren't pointless and stupid the same thing?" Oliver asked.

Webster said, "You can be pointless without being stupid."

"Well, your idea, Webster, was both." The captain turned to Decker. "Anything else you want to discuss?"

Decker shook his head.

"Meeting is over." Strapp turned back to Decker. "I need to talk to you alone. The rest of you . . . *out!*"

Slowly the group got up, left the captain's office feeling depressed and put down. Strapp found their resentment palpable. Too bad. You want to bolster the ego, get yourself a whore. Strapp waited until the last of them had filed out, then closed the door a little too hard. He took a deep breath, let it out slowly. "You want coffee, Pete?"

"You're offering me coffee?" Decker paused. "Gotta be bad."

Strapp sat down, buried his head in his hands.

"God, what a mess." He looked up. "What a fucking mess!"

Decker waited. Strapp said, "I got an apology call from Jeanine's lawyer . . . her behavior this morning."

"Uh-huh."

"Quote, unquote. 'She was in shock at her brother's untimely demise, she was hysterical. She didn't know what came over her. She's extremely sorry for her unprecedented outburst.'"

Decker shifted in his seat. "Obviously someone told her that slapping constitutes legal assault. Her lawyer was feeling you out to see if I'm going to file an assault charge against her."

"They realize it's a possibility."

"A *strong* possibility."

"They want to deal. You be gentlemanly, she won't proceed with the harassment suit. Let bygones be bygones."

"And what about my hearing with the IAD?"

"What about it?"

"Does she call them up and tell them she was lying?"

"Decker, if she doesn't pursue the charges, you'll beat the in-house investigation."

"No, that's not true. If she doesn't pursue the charges, I'll get an Unsustained from IAD. Which is what I'd probably get in any case. I want my record to remain spotless. Which is what I deserve. I want her to call IAD and tell them she was lying. I want a decision of Unfounded."

"Decker—"

"You call up her legal eagle, tell him that *if* she

admits she was lying, I won't bring her up on assault charges. Charges on which I—unlike her—have witnesses—"

Strapp broke in. "Pete, *listen* to me. Jeanine is not going to admit that she was lying. Yes, it's unfair. But look at the positive. This is a great chance to rid yourself of an albatross around your neck. Don't be an idiot."

"No dice."

Strapp flung himself against the back of his desk chair, looked up at the ceiling. "Would it help if I ordered you to do it?"

"You can't order away my civil rights."

The captain gazed intensely at Decker. "Don't you think you owe it to Rina to consult her before you make such a blanket decision?"

"Charges are against *me*, not her."

But even as Decker said it, he knew Strapp had him. No way he'd chance going to trial, making it public . . . becoming an embarrassment to Rina and the kids. Backed into a corner like a circus lion, seething with rage . . . lashing out in vain as the devil snapped the whip.

Quietly, Decker said, "Tell her lawyer I'll think about it."

Strapp cleared his throat. "Peter, we both know that Jeanine is unstable. She's giving you a bargain . . . now . . . at this moment. Tomorrow she may change her mind. If I call now, her lawyer will have the papers ready tomorrow morning. I'll have them reviewed by our legal staff, have them sitting on your desk before lunch. You sign them. And when you return from your break, you'll be rid of this whole fucking mess. What do you say?"

"I'll talk to Rina."

Strapp didn't push it. "I'll call the lawyer anyway. You can always change your mind. Be here in my office by eight tomorrow."

Decker forced himself to unclench his jaw. "Okay."

"For what it's worth, it stinks."

"Anything else?"

"Yes, there is something else." Strapp averted his gaze. "She wants to make amends . . . Jeanine."

"Oh, Christ—"

"Not with you necessarily . . . with the LAPD. You've been reading about this wheelchair tennis tournament?"

"Yes."

"I heard it was your idea."

"Go on."

"Anyway . . . if you've been following the articles—which I'm sure you have—you know that the proceeds are going to the Estelle's victims—"

"Robbing Peter to pay Paul—"

"Decker, the massacre made widows. Not all of them were rich women."

"Unlike others who became millionaires overnight—"

"Didn't your friend Wetzel lose her husband?" Strapp broke in. "And she has kids?"

"Yes, she did lose a husband, and yes, she does have kids," Decker snapped back. "So what's the point? Jeanine been elevated to hero status?"

"No. But the tournament is for a good cause."

The captain's voice turned soft.

"She hit upon a real winner, rabbi. A grand a ticket for the courtside boxes. And they're selling like hotcakes because big names in the tennis world are going to be there. And that attracts the press. Major publicity. The mayor's ordered a box. So has the governor."

Strapp pointed to his chest.

"Me, I couldn't care less about that. But I do care about the people I serve."

Once again, Decker felt anger race through his veins. He knew too clearly what was happening.

Strapp said, "Jeanine has a box reserved for us—for the police. Because she has rightly assumed that we'd want to be there to show our support. As the captain at Devonshire, it's my duty to be there as an agent of the community I serve."

Heart and head pounding, Decker glared at him. Slowly he said, "Jeanine whacks me across the face and you cut off my balls in front of her—"

"Decker—"

"Out of respect for *your* authority, I say nothing. I *do* nothing. You tell me to deal with her lawyer, I deal with her lawyer. And you repay me by giving the bitch the honor of your presence—"

"It's not for her, dammit!" Strapp pounded the table. "If you'd get down off your self-righteous high horse for one goddamn second, you'd realize the position I'm in. I've *got* to be there."

"No, you don't."

"Decker, what do I say when the victims' families question why their police captain was absent at their benefit?"

"You tell them the *truth*. That you think Jeanine Garrison is a lying scumbag—"

"That's called slander."

"It's called integrity."

Strapp started to speak, but stopped. He refused to meet Decker's eyes. "I've got nothing more to say. Be here tomorrow. Eight o'clock sharp. That's all. You can go."

Decker rose, stood in place for a moment. "Sir, I'm not as self-righteous as you believe . . . nor am I as righteous as I'd like to believe. I know how things work. So take my words as one political animal talking to another."

Strapp waited.

"Jeanine Garrison was involved in that massacre. And Jeanine Garrison *is* going to fall. Anyone associated with her and her causes—no matter how worthy they are—is going to wind up looking like a dupe."

"I'll take my chances, Lieutenant. Good night."

Decker walked over to the door, opened it, then turned around. "Do yourself a favor, Captain. On the day of the tournament, come down with the flu."

# ✌ 28

*And there was* evening, and there was morning.

On the seventh day, God rested.

With any luck, so could Decker. It always took him a while to slip into Shabbos mode. Gourmet food and fine wine helped the process. As he sipped tea, he watched his wife shuffle papers.

She said, "The first contender's a four-bedroom, three-bath. Around thirty-five-hundred square feet. Center hall plan, living room, formal dining, a den. Central air and heat. Built-ins in the kitchen. And it's got a pool with a Jacuzzi."

"California living," Jacob added with a grin.

"Pools mean maintenance," Decker groused. "A Jacuzzi means lots of maintenance."

Sammy asked, "Can Ginger swim?"

At the mention of her name, the setter lifted her head. Decker told her to go back to sleep. "Yes, she can swim. That's all I need. Dog hairs clogging up the filter."

"I'll clean the pool, Dad," Jacob said. "Just show me what to do."

The boy's offer tugged at Decker's heart strings. So anxious to get out of here and into civilization.

Decker picked up his teacup, eyes on the flickering Shabbos candles. Dinner had been scrumptious, and everyone, including the baby, had been in a good mood. Hannah had lasted until dessert, then announced she wanted to go to sleep. As Rina put her to bed, the boys cleared the dishes, restored a rose-filled vase to its rightful place at the center of the table. Decker stacked the plates, made the tea. For the first time in weeks, he felt at semi-peace.

Rina went on, "The house is a little bruised, but certainly something we could live with for a while. About six blocks from the shul—"

He returned his eyes to his wife. "How much?"

"They're asking three twenty five, but the realtor thinks there's flexibility."

"Should be at that price."

"Also the lot is small."

"How small?"

"Around sixty-five hundred square feet."

Decker winced. "Any yard at all?"

"Room for a swing set, a patio set." Rina showed her husband the tear sheet.

He scanned the vitals of the home. "At least Hannah'll be happy." He paused. "I've got acres here."

Rina sighed. "You must feel like Gulliver being thrown into Lilliput."

Jacob fidgeted, then said, "We don't need such a big house, Eema. Show him the other one. The three-bedroom. The lot's bigger, Dad. It's got room for a pool. Not that I expect a pool. I'm just saying it's got the room."

Jacob was trying so hard. Decker never realized how difficult the isolation had been on him. "We'll find something, Jake." He turned to his other son. "What do you think, Sammy?"

He shrugged. "I don't mind sharing a room if you want the bigger lot. I don't mind having my own room, if you want the bigger house. It's up to you."

Rina paused. "There is this one house—if you could call it that—on a good-size lot. Fourteen eight."

Decker considered the size. "Not bad."

"It's a little farther from the shul . . . about a mile, mile and a half away—"

"After what we've been walking, a mile and a half's *nothing*," Jacob said. "Besides, the house is inside the *eruv* so we can carry on Shabbos. And push a stroller. Which is good news for Hannah. The shul has a toddlers' play group. It's real cute. I'm sure she'd love it. She doesn't like being left behind when we go to shul, you know."

Decker said, "Yes, Jacob, I know that."

Quickly, the teen said, "Not that I'm pushing you. Take your time, Dad."

Decker raised his brow. "What about the house?"

"It's tiny. A fixer-upper—"

"Yeah, like it should be rebuilt," Sammy said, laughing.

"It's salvageable," Rina replied. "But it *is* tiny. Two bedrooms—"

"We have three children," Decker said.

"There's a small den. We could convert it into a room for the boys until we add another bedroom . . . or two—"

"You mean until *I* add another bedroom or two—"

"And a couple of bathrooms, too," Sammy said. "It only has one bath."

"Five of us and one bathroom." Decker nodded. "Rich."

"We can always rent something portable," Rina said.

Decker looked at her. "You're kidding, right?"

She hit his good shoulder. "Of course I'm kidding."

"Actually, that wouldn't be a bad idea," Sammy said. "And while we're at it, we could pitch a couple of tents in the summer. Because the house doesn't have air-conditioning."

Decker groaned.

Rina said, "I thought you loved camping."

Jacob blurted out, "It's a great lot, Dad. Full of big trees. Lots of shade in the summer."

Rina said, "The boy is a hard sell."

Jacob blushed. "I'm just looking at the positive."

Rina kissed her son's forehead. "Good for you. You'll always be happy."

Sammy came to his brother's rescue. "The lot is awesome."

"It's a tenth the size of this place," Decker said.

"Yeah, but it's really well planted," Sammy answered. "This place is mostly dirt."

"I've got an orchard," Decker defended.

"Dad, the new lot's got like about three or four *huge* avocado trees—"

"And orange trees, too," Jacob said. "*Big* ones."

"Valencia oranges," Rina said. "Full-sized trees that they don't plant anymore because they're so tall. Must be thirty or forty years old. It's also got lemon, lime, and grapefruit trees. And giant eucalyptuses. Wonderful menthol smell."

"How much?"

"One hundred seventy-five."

"That's too cheap!"

"Actually, it's about plot price."

"Could we live in it?"

"For as much as you're home, yes," Rina said.

"Funny." Decker glared at her. "You have a tear sheet on this, Lucille Ball?"

"No. It's by owner. Another reason why the price is good."

"This doesn't sound like a house," Decker said. "It sounds like a project."

Rina shrugged. "It would give your father something to do if your parents come out for Thanksgiving. He loves to tinker and build."

"I have to live in a shack to give my father a life?"

Rina muttered, "To give yourself a life."

Decker snapped, "I heard that."

"You were *supposed* to hear that."

No one spoke for a moment.

Sammy cleared his throat, said, "Hey, Yonkie, wanna learn a little?"

"What?"

Sammy cocked his head at his parents, yanked his brother out of his seat. "Let's go."

"Oh," Jake said. "I get it."

Since the boys' bedroom was dark, they went into the kitchen. Decker kept his voice down, but he was peeved. "I'm tired of your digs! I'm doing the best I can!"

Rina took Peter's hand. "I'm worried about you."

"I'm *fine*. I'd be a lot *finer* if I didn't have to think about you being mad at me for the hours I keep."

"I'm not mad at you—"

"Could have fooled me. Think I want to work this hard? Think I like coming home every night having missed dinner and the baby. We have thousands of ongoing cases, Rina—"

"I'm aware—"

"With new ones every day." Decker counted off on his fingers. "There're phone calls, there're meetings, there's paperwork, there's assignments, and lots of people with problems. Not to mention the dees and their problems. I must spend half my time doing counseling to keep them functional. I can't help my hours."

"I know that."

"I'm not stopping off at a bar with the guys. Although there'd be nothing wrong if I did. I'm not stopping off at the gym to play racquetball, either."

"I wish you did."

"What does *that* mean? You want me to spend *more* time away from you?"

"I want you to be happy."

"Then stop razzing me."

"Deal."

Neither of them spoke for a moment. Decker rotated his shoulders. "What are you really trying to tell me, darlin'?"

Rina said, "Even when you're here, you're not here. You're distracted. I talk to you and half the time you don't even hear it. You're thinking about your cases. You breathe and eat your job and that's not healthy."

Decker was quiet.

Rina said, "You used to spend hours with the horses. Now the poor things just languish in their stalls. The horses aren't the problem. We can sell them. It's the fact that you don't seem to enjoy life outside of work."

"It's been a miserable month." Decker rubbed his neck. "I'm very unhappy."

"Is it Estelle's?"

"For the most part, yes."

"It's only been about a month."

"It's getting colder by the day . . . damn near frigid."

Rina tried a cheerful smile. "At least the suit has been dropped."

"I'm very angry about that. I should have fought it. Instead I caved in."

Rina was quiet.

"Stupid to be angry." Decker looked away. "It's over."

Rina kissed his hand. "You didn't cave in. It's called being married." She waited a beat. "Maybe it's the same thing."

Decker's smile was genuine. Again, he moved his wounded shoulder, trying to relieve the dull throb of former battle. "I should move on. Because I'm sure not getting anywhere."

"Nothing productive from the interviews of the patrons?"

Decker rolled his eyes. "Sure there was a man. No, it was a woman. No, it wasn't a man at all. He was tall, he was short. He was blond, he was brunette, he was bald. He was fat, he was skinny. He was wearing a coat, he wasn't wearing a coat, he streaked naked through the restaurant. He had a gun. No, he didn't have a gun, he had an Uzi. No, he didn't have an Uzi, he had a cannon. No, he didn't have a cannon, he had a Sherman tank."

He looked at his wife.

"Garbage in, garbage out. People telling us what they think we want to hear. It doesn't amount to a hill of beans."

He drank cold tea.

"I'm starting to doubt my own instincts. Maybe Jeanine had nothing to do with it. Just a histrionic lady who had the bad luck to be in a picture with a mass murderer. And I had the bad luck to push her button."

"Peter, why don't you hire a private detective? PIs can do things you can't do. Why don't you see what kind of dirt they can dig up?"

Decker stared at his teacup. "Actually, I considered the idea, then nixed it. I can't afford the fees myself. And with the evidence I have, there'd be no way to squeeze it out of the department."

Rina hesitated. "How much do they cost?"

"About two hundred a day plus expenses—"

"Don't they give professional courtesy?"

Decker smiled. "No. Besides the expense, their use in these types of cases is not really effective. They're good for tracing missing persons or tracking down deadbeat dads—doing a paper trail. They're also good for photographing illicit encounters or stalkers or industrial espionage and theft. Things that happen on a regular basis. Things that can be caught in the act. Jeanine's basically a law-abiding citizen who happens to have murdered fourteen people. She's finished with her dirty work. Now all she has to do is hang tight. What's a PI going to tell me? She's hanging tight?"

Decker paused.

"What I really need is a stoolie. Someone who was involved in her plot to drop a dime on her. Or someone from the inside to whom she might have confessed."

"Inside of what?"

"Good question."

Decker got up, began to pace.

"Like this wheelchair tennis tournament she's hosting. Probably lots of handicapped around. Ideally, if money wasn't an object, I'd hire someone handicapped to work on the inside. Someone nondescript and nonthreatening who's a good listener. Someone who could get her trust *and* get her talking. Then I could wire him or her and catch Jeanine's slipups on tape."

"What about Wade Anthony?"

He stopped walking. "If I approached Anthony on this, it would be tantamount to cutting off my own head. First thing he'd do is tell Jeanine. Then she'd slap me with another suit—police harassment. And she'd have a legitimate case!"

No one spoke. Decker took his wife's hand, kissed it. "Rina, this shack . . . it's a good price. Something we can afford. Let me have an inspector out there. See what needs to be done. If it looks okay . . . like something I can handle, let's do it."

She broke into a smile. "You've just made Yaakov's year."

"In the meantime, since it *is* reasonable, we can afford to keep this place for a while. Maybe live *there* over the weekends and be here on weekdays, where it's more comfortable. At least until I can add an extra bathroom. Shouldn't take me more than a couple of months of Sundays if the sewer line's not a problem."

"I was serious about your father, Peter," Rina said. "Buying it would give him motivation to come out. He loves anything that has to do with tools. So does your brother for that matter."

"I'll get me my kinfolk," Decker drawled. "We'll have ourselves an ole barn raisin.' So, little lady, what are you and *your* hands going to contribute to this purchase?"

"I can sew, I can paint, and I can even hang wallpaper."

"A real down-home family affair." Suddenly, he turned serious. "So my folks haven't made a decision about Thanksgiving?"

"Still thinking about it. But I'll get them out here. Especially now. I can work on your dad by dangling the new house in front of his face."

"The new house . . ." He laughed softly. "I love it. We're already talking like we own it."

"All it takes is money."

"Yeah, maybe we can ask Jeanine to float us a loan. She's rolling in it."

Rina grew serious. "Peter, you'll get your resolution from Estelle's. It may take time, but you'll get it."

"The woman's parents die a horrible death, her brother dies a horrible death . . . and she's out being Miss Social Butterfly . . . raising money for poor, poor victims like herself."

Rina said nothing.

"I know," Decker said. "There were *real* victims. And why should they suffer?"

He pushed his chair from the table, threw his head back.

"I'm just . . . frustrated. Because the woman's smart. Suing me like she did . . . immediately deflecting the investigation. Then taking up the cause of the victims. Getting them as a support system. Placing herself behind a barrier of officials and hotshots."

He regarded his wife.

"Still, if we had evidence, she wouldn't be impenetrable. Trouble is, we have nothing. We can't even figure out the basics. Like how she could have bought a hit man. We've surreptitiously examined Jeanine's accounts. No big transfers of money either before or after Estelle's. She doesn't even show little transfers that could add up to big transfers. Of course, she could be hiding it."

Rina paused. "She will inherit a great deal of money from her parents' trust, correct?"

"Yes. We thought about that. We didn't spot any cash transfers from the trust, either."

"You know, Peter, I'm sure her parents didn't keep all their assets in cash. Vis-à-vis our discussion about the yeshiva's finances and its charity donations, people pay using all sorts of assets—"

Decker slapped his hands over his face. "How could I be so *dense*! She made the payoff with stock certificates—"

"Or maybe with bearer bonds inherited from her parents' trust—"

"Jesus! Of course!" He leaped to his feet. "The Garrisons had to have had coupon bonds. They fit the profile to a T. Middle-aged to elderly and *rich*.

Furthermore, munis would be perfect contract money because they're untraceable."

"Not the new ones," Rina said. "They're all registered. To prevent capital gains tax evasion as well as state tax evasion. Instead of coupons, owners get the bond's interest in an annual or semi-annual check."

Decker said, "But there are still plenty of coupon bonds on the secondary market. The Garrisons have been rich for a while, probably purchased bearer bonds years ago. And *those* would be untraceable."

"At least very hard to trace."

Decker sat up. "You *can* trace them?"

"In theory, I suppose you could trace them via the coupon. You'd have to wangle a heap of private information from a broker or from the paying agency. I'm sure it's illegal." Rina looked at him. "Did you have something specific in mind?"

"Not really. We're sadly lacking in concrete evidence."

"What do you have?"

"Not much." Decker raised his brows. "We have Jeanine, who has been playing tennis with a seventeen-year-old male partner for the last six, seven months."

"And?"

"And that's about it."

"You think her tennis partner has something to do with the shootings at Estelle's?"

"Maybe."

"Why? Because he's Jeanine's tennis partner?"

"Yes."

Rina shrugged. "Thank God for due process."

Decker smiled.

"And you think Jeanine manipulated this boy into killing . . ." Rina squinted. "Who did he kill?"

"Harlan Manz."

"And how did Jeanine know that Harlan was about to shoot up an entire restaurant?"

"Two theories," Decker said. "Either she was manipulating Harlan as well, and knew he was about to explode. *Or.* The whole thing was a planned hit masked to look like . . . I don't know . . . a random act of violence. Ostensibly, Jeanine used two hit men. But then she did a double-cross. She got the second hit man to take out Harlan . . . and that made the whole thing look like a mass murder by one insane man."

"This is *very* far-fetched."

"No, I haven't gotten to the far-fetched part. At least *that* part of my theory is backed up by evidence that points to more than a lone gunman."

"Okay."

"The far-fetched part is the second hit man," Decker said. "We were looking at Jeanine's tennis partner. His name is Sean Amos—a snotty rich kid. Webster doesn't think he has the ba—the nerve to pull it off. So we were thinking that maybe Sean contracted the assignment out."

"With or without Jeanine's permission?"

"Don't know."

"And do you have any theories about whom he contracted with?"

"There's a kid in Westbridge Prep—"

"That's where Sean goes to school?"

"Yes. You know the place?"

"By reputation. It's a West Coast prep school. A pressure cooker for the kids of the country club."

"You got it." Decker sipped tea. "There's a senior there named Joaquim Rush. He's on scholarship . . . kind of a loner kid who keeps to himself. He's also a Scrabble fanatic."

"So what? I like Scrabble."

"No, Rina. A real fanatic. Like in tournaments."

"It's still harmless."

"The Scrabble isn't the interesting part," Decker stated. "This kid, Joachim Rush, he and Sean Amos had made some sort of deal together. Martinez saw an envelope exchange hands—"

"Ah, now *that* sounds interesting!"

"Indeed. We were looking into him as a candidate when Strapp pulled the rug out."

Rina sighed, said, "Stonewalled by the good captain. I'm sorry."

Decker laughed. "Maybe it's good he eighty-sixed it. Going undercover to Scrabble tournaments, tailing some cipher whose nickname is Cyberword. Not exactly a righteous allocation of department time."

"Maybe not." Rina smiled. "But heck, it could do wonders for the vocabulary."

In the darkened room, Sammy stared at the ceiling, listened to the medley of the mockingbird. The critter wouldn't shut up, just kept going from trill to tweet to cheep to caw. Yet there was something comforting about it . . . like a lullaby from nature.

Overhearing his parents talking . . . arguing . . . then talking again.

Because although the lot was acres, Peter's house was real small.

Once the arguing had bothered him. Now he shrugged it off and his indifference puzzled him. He thought about the change. Probably had something to do with the fact that now he could drive.

Joachim Rush.

A Scrabble fanatic.

Like Yermie Cohen.

He had once attended a Scrabble tournament with a friend. Didn't place but he did okay. So what would it hurt if he attended another?

And if he found this Joachim dude . . . then what?

And what if Peter was right? What if Cyberword was a hit man?

Frustrating. To have ideas and not be able to use them. Because he couldn't tell his mother. Not just yet. And he didn't *dare* tell Dad. Because . . . well, you just didn't tell Peter things like that. Things that he wouldn't approve of. He loved Peter, but the man was sometimes too much for him to handle.

So different from Abba.

Abba.

The memories kept getting dimmer and dimmer and dimmer . . . except for the few clear ones. The ones that had been played out so many times that they'd taken on legendary proportions.

Abba.

The move to the new house meant a final break from the yeshiva, the padlock that would seal that childhood phase of his life forever.

Time to move on.

Still, Sammy felt his throat clog.

Move on. To current things.

Like Joachim Rush. Simpler to think about him.

No harm in going to a tournament.

Still, he didn't want to do this alone. He felt he should tell someone first. Jacob came to mind. But he didn't want to get his brother involved.

Maybe he *should* tell Eema?

No, that wouldn't work. Sammy realized that he would be putting her on the spot by telling her and not Peter. Getting between them.

So Eema was out.

So who could he tell?

Who would understand?

Nestled in his bed, he thought a while, cooed into near slumber by avian songs and a comforter of night. Then his eyes suddenly snapped open.

As plain as the nose on his face.

He'd make the call as soon as Shabbos was over.

In the meantime, he closed his eyes and went to sleep.

# 🌿 29

*Cindy picked up* her latte, sipped foamy milk. "It's all interesting . . . what you've told me. Still, I'm not sure what you have in mind."

"I don't know myself," Sam said. "That's why I'm talking to you." He took another bite of his bagel sandwich. "I was figuring you for a game plan."

Cindy picked at her cinnamon bagel baked on the premises of Harold's East. A retro New York dairy-only deli. One of the few places where Sam would eat because it was kosher.

She said, "I have no game plan, Sam. Because there's no game. If you have inside information, you should talk to Dad."

"I *can't* talk to Dad, Cindy." Sam grew frustrated. "First of all, I have nothing significant to tell him. Second, I don't want him to know I overheard my mom and him talking. Third, he knows about the Scabble tournaments and he's choosing not to go to them. Or rather Strapp's not letting him go. I thought that maybe we could have a look around—"

"I'll bring the wiretaps and you bring the hidden cameras?"

"Will you just hear me out?" Sam snapped.

"Sorry. Go on."

Sam thought a moment "I don't know. I thought . . . well, since no one under Dad's command can touch this Joachim guy . . . that maybe you could follow him for a couple of days—"

"Well, I've always admired Nancy Drew—"

"Forget it!" Sammy's jaw tightened "It was a dumb idea. Sorry to bother you. You can go whenever you want. I'll pay."

Cindy sighed. "God, I sound just like him. Negative, sarcastic, sharp-tongued." She licked milk off her lips. "Terrible to be shut down. I'm sorry, Sam."

"You're just being honest." He adjusted his glasses. "You're right. It is ridiculous. But I'm not sorry I tried."

Cindy was quiet, observed her stepbrother. A quiet kid dressed neatly in jeans and a long-sleeved white shirt. He had a lean build, a head of sandy hair partially covered by a knitted yarmulke. Dark, intelligent eyes. He was turning into a very handsome kid.

Sam leaned on his elbows. "It's just that you don't know what's going on. You don't live with him every day. He's very frustrated."

Cindy grew annoyed. "I've seen him frustrated more times than you can count."

"Look, I'm not pulling filial rank or anything." Sam looked down. "I mean, biology is biology. I know you're the real kid—"

"Oh, *please*!" Again, Cindy caught harshness in her voice, reflective of her father's cynicism. Biology was biology and more insidious than she had thought. She softened her tone. "Sam, ranking my father's . . . *our* father's affections is silly. He loves *all* his kids.

And yes, I know he's very frustrated. And I'm sure if he knew of our meeting, he'd appreciate the concern. But I don't see how we can help."

The boy blurted out, "What would it hurt if we showed up at one of the tournaments?"

Cindy said, "Say we show up. Say we see this Joachim guy. Say we even *talk* to him. Then what? Do you even know what Joachim Rush looks like?"

"Not a clue. But I'm sure we wouldn't have any trouble identifying him. According to Dad, he's well known in Scrabble circles."

"Yes, I suppose finding the sucker would classify as the easy part." Cindy's mind was racing. "Suppose we get a best case thing here, Sam. Suppose I go to the tournament and wind up talking to him. Suppose I can get him alone . . . invite him out for coffee. What then? I can't just drop names like Sean Amos or Jeanine Garrison into his lap. You just told me that this Joachim Rush was accepted on early admission to Yale. The guy isn't a moron."

"This is all true."

"Even if I could get him to talk to me . . . to get him into my confidence . . . Sam, that step could take weeks, *months*. I'm starting the Academy soon. I'm going to run out of time."

"Move quickly."

"Then what if I get him talking and find out he's completely innocent. Not only did I chance exposing confidential information crucial to Dad's case, but also I toyed with a kid whose sole crime is being a little nerdy."

Sammy drank club soda from a bottle. "Hate to say it but you are making sense."

Cindy finished her coffee. "I suppose I could tail him. See if he does anything weird. But let's face it. If he has anything to do with Sean, he's going to talk to him either over the phone or at school. Chances of me catching him doing something naughty are extremely remote."

"That's why I wanted to show up at the tournament. At least that way, we'd get a chance to observe him in the flesh."

"And . . ."

Sam smiled. "Never underestimate the powers of simple observation."

Cindy shook her head. "This is against my better judgment." She sighed. "When is this shindig?"

"Next Thursday."

It was Saturday night. Cindy had less than a week to hone her skills at the word game. She said, "We're also ignoring an essential fact. I'm not a good Scrabble player."

"I know someone who could help you—"

"Nuh-uh. We're *not* bringing a third party into this mess. Really blow Dad's case to smithereens. You can't talk about this with anyone else but me. That's a given."

Sammy waited a beat. "I could show you a few tricks. Nothing fancy, but hey, you're smart. You should pick the game up pretty easily."

"I know how to play. I just don't play well."

"It's a matter of practice," Sam said. "And memory. You're gonna have to learn all these oddball two- and three-letter words. Plus all these screwy words that start with K and Q and X—"

"This really isn't my forte—"

"Plus, competitive tournaments are timed."

*"Timed?"*

"Usually like fifteen or twenty minutes per person per game. Both you and your opponent punch a clock. They're obviously connected to each other. You finish your word, you punch your clock, it starts *his* seconds ticking away—"

"I'm terrible at timed tests. I hate pressure."

Sammy looked at her. "Then why in the world are you becoming a cop?"

Cindy opened her mouth, then closed it. Quietly, she said, "Touché."

The boy said, "I'm not trying to score points. Just asking a question."

"I have my reasons."

Sam looked away. Her tone of voice told him not to pursue the topic. So he ate his sandwich and drank club soda.

Cindy nibbled on her food, her face hot with embarrassment and truth. The kid had scored very valid points. She might have furthered the conversation, but Sam seemed so oblivious to her mental anguish.

Sam finished his sandwich. "Cindy, you'll ace the game once you get the hang of it. Look, you're a Columbia grad—"

"That proves nothing."

"Well you took the SAT. That was timed."

"I had more than fifteen minutes."

"It's the same thing . . . only sped up. Trick is, do your thinking on your opponent's time. It's not hard once you get into the rhythm. You'll do great."

Cindy regarded the boy's earnest face. "Okay. I'll

give it a whirl. Just to see if I can do it, if for no other reason."

"Besides, what could possibly happen at a Scrabble tournament? The contestants aren't the rowdy type." He checked his watch. "It's after eleven. I have to be home by midnight or else Eema will send out the National Guard. Worse, she'll send out *Dad*." A pause. "How about if I drop by your house tomorrow at ten?"

"Don't *drop* by the house. Don't go *near* my house. Don't even *call*. We've never been best friends—"

"We're not enemies, Cin—"

"No, of course not. But we haven't had much to do with each other except for the obligatory family affairs."

"True."

"If my mother sees us together for no visible reason, she's going to start asking me questions. That's all we'd need. For Dad to hear about this little escapade from my mother."

"Where then?"

Cindy said, "McGregor Park. Eleven o'clock. You, me, and all the old Russian people. Be there or be square. Call it a night, Sam?"

"Sure. You go on. I still have to *bench* ... to say grace." Sammy's hand reached for the bill, but Cindy was too quick.

"A division of labor," she said. "You thank God for the meal; I'll pay for it."

# ❧ 30

*It seemed to* Rina that Hollywood got uglier and dirtier with each passing year, that the gentrification that was always being touted was just a word in the dictionary. And now with the Metro rail . . . all the construction and soot and dust and microorganisms being thrown into the air. Not to mention the bizarre parade of human flesh. Hard to believe this place was still a major tourist spot. But there they all were, all nationalities, wearing short-sleeved Hawaiian shirts even in the winter, toting cameras around their necks. And the local inhabitants. Unisexual sleaze with greasy hair, torn jeans, vests, and tattoos. What wasn't covered in ink was studded with pierces. They must never fly commercial airlines, Rina thought. Because they'd never make it through the metal detectors.

She found the address with no problem, parked her twelve-year-old Volvo in a pay parking lot. Sweaty hands. A pounding heartbeat. She hoped he wasn't home, but feared he was. He didn't get out much.

She had dressed simply. Black sweater over a denim skirt. Her hair was braided and covered with a kerchief. She knocked on the door, heard the uneven clomp of his compromised walk on the other side. It took a while for him to answer. His face registered instant surprise.

He leaned on his cane and grinned. "I b'lieve I know you."

"Believe you do." Rina smiled. "You were at my wedding."

"Ah . . . I remember the wedding . . . the food. Right fine Peking duck, ma'am. Think I ate enough to last me a year."

"Then we'll have to throw another wedding. Because it appears you haven't been eating much since then."

He patted his thin stomach. "I get by."

She glanced at him, then looked away. Abel Atwater. Peter's war buddy over in Vietnam. Hard to fathom that this man was ever fit for combat. Unbearably thin. A gaunt face given the illusion of fullness by a gray beard. His hair had turned silver, still fashioned in a long braid. His sweats hung on his emaciated body. Only giveaway of life was his eyes . . . clear . . . aware. She said, "Your clothes are literally falling off."

"You don't like the sagging look." He hiked up his pants. "Old person's move. The pants hike."

"Can I come in, Abel?"

"Absolutely." He swept his cane over the threshold, bidding her enter.

Rina walked into a room stuffy with heat. Small. The place overlooked the pay parking lot, had a kitchen the size of a closet. Thin gauzy curtains, a threadbare brown carpet. Furnished with junk.

Faded, lumpy pieces. Formica table with two plastic orange chairs. But the place was clean. Spotless.

"Offer you a beer, Mrs. Decker?"

"It's Rina."

Abel smiled. "Rina . . . a pretty name. For a pretty lady. Would you like a beer, Rina?"

"No, thank you."

"I don't got much else beyond beer." Abel opened an ancient icebox, stuck his head inside. "Would you b'lieve I've got orange juice? Want some orange juice?"

"Nothing, thank you."

Abel straightened up, closed the door. "An easy customer." Again, the cane pointed, to the couch covered in something that might have originally been red and gold. Rina sat. Abel plunked down on the opposite side. "You showin' up like this. I'd be a mite concerned about the big man. But you're actin' too calm for there to be serious trouble."

"Peter's fine."

"Glad to hear it. Should we continue with the chitchat? Or do you want to tell me why you're here?"

"Actually, it has to do with the big man."

"You throwin' a party for his birthday or somethin' like that?"

"No. Peter hates surprises."

"Don't we all," Abel said to himself. "What's up, then?"

"I need help, Abel."

The thin man smiled, then grinned, then laughed. A spindly finger pointed into his sunken chest. "You want help from *me*?"

Rina sighed. "Maybe it wasn't such a good idea coming. When I first met you . . . I didn't treat you very nice. Perhaps I was jealous of your relationship with Peter. So it's really hypocritical of me to ask you for help."

"I put a gun to your head, Mrs. Decker," Abel said. "It made you cautious around me."

Rina lowered her eyes, remembering the incident. The "big get-even" Peter had called it. "I suppose I did have my reasons for being reserved."

Abel laughed, hobbled over to the window, and opened it. "Sorry about the stuffiness. I wasn't expecting company. Wanna tell me what's going on?"

Rina said, "It's about one of Peter's cases. The mass murder at Estelle's—"

"I read about it, read his quote 'bout the shootup being your worst nightmare." He looked upward. "Guess he don't have any more Nam dreams."

"Oh, he's had his fair share lately. All the carnage . . . it evoked terrible memories for him."

Abel nodded.

Rina said, "He's obsessed with the case, Abel. One of the victims in the shooting . . . actually the daughter of two of the victims . . . Peter feels she had something to do with it."

"With the shooting?"

"Yes. He questioned her. The next day she charged Peter with sexual harassment—"

"Doc?" Abel made a face. "It's a lie, ma'am."

"I know. The suit was frivolous and was eventually dropped. But the charges made it hard for him to do his job. He had to tiptoe around her. Eventually it got very complicated. His captain pulled him off the case entirely."

Abel limped back to the couch, lowered himself slowly, using his walking stick for support. "I thought the mass murderer committed suicide at the scene."

"That's the official story."

Then Rina told him all she knew. Abel listened, legs stretched out, crossed at the ankles, hands buried in the folds of his sweatshirt. When she was done, he sat up, drew his right leg upward so it folded at the knee. His left leg followed without help. He waited a moment before speaking.

Abel said, "A woman manipulatin' two men to shoot up a restaurant. Gettin' one of 'em to blow the other's brains out—"

Rina said, "That's the wild card. The second shooter. One of the victims remembers a man leaving Estelle's right after the shooting stopped. Just walked right out of the door. A very strange behavior unless he was involved, don't you think?"

"Don't matter what I think." He cocked his head. "And Doc thinks this second shooter is a seventeen-year-old Scrabble player?"

"I know . . . it sounds ridiculous."

Abel scratched his beard. "The ice Pete's skating on is thinner than Saran Wrap." He hoisted himself up. Went over to the window. "Still, Doc is an intuitive sort. I don't discount that. Woman gives him a hinky feelin', she's hinky."

"I'm glad you feel that way." Rina fidgeted with her kerchief, then dropped her hands in her lap. "He was stonewalled, Abel. She's been using her connections to obstruct him. He needs someone to get around her." A pause. "This is where you come in."

Abel waited a moment. "I'm not what you'd call 'high society.' Exactly what did you have in mind?"

Rina blushed, blurted out, "Peter seems to feel that if he had someone on the inside, he could maybe get information."

"Inside of what?"

"This wheelchair tennis tournament she's hosting." Again, Rina turned red. Her speech faltered. "It's filled with handicapped people. If Peter could place someone . . . you know . . . someone on the inside . . . someone Jeanine would never expect . . . he felt that maybe she'd let something slip up about the case . . . and Peter could learn something that way . . . about Jeanine . . . and about the case. Am I making sense?"

"Indeed you are. You're sayin' you need a gimp—"

"Abel—"

"Because you think that all us gimps have this Masonic brotherly bond with one another—"

"Abel, please don't make this even more nauseatingly hard on me."

No one spoke.

Abel said, "I'm sorry. That was rude."

Rina said, "I was thinking of people I knew who could maybe pull this off. You're the only one who could do it *and* the only one I could *trust*. Because you love Peter almost as much as I do."

Abel's eyes misted. "I take exception to the word almost, lady." He scratched his face, furrowed his brow. "Rina, these tournaments are ritzy things. You don't just walk in . . . or hobble in . . . and announce your availability for a job based on the fact that you're handicapped. I mean, even if I wanted to do it, they ain't gonna hire me . . . even for manual labor. They got their own crew."

Rina considered his words. "You're right."

"Besides, the paraplegics don't consider amputees among the real physically challenged. Because we can walk. There's an unspoken hierarchy among us gimps. All the quadraplegics want to be paras, the paras want to be amputees, and we amps want to be able-bodied. And I'm not even a bad amputee—only half of one of my legs. To them, I'm barely crippled . . . the lowest gimp on the totem pole."

"Of course. Forget the whole thing." She got up. "Abel, don't be a stranger, please.

"Invite me for dinner if it'll ease your conscience."

"How about Sunday night?"

"You don't think Doc'll find that a mite suspicious?"

"I can say I ran into you."

"I don't run into anything." Again, Abel scratched his beard. "I'll take a rain check, Mrs. Decker." He started to talk, then stopped, then said, "You're right 'bout one thing, ma'am. I do love that son of a bitch." He sighed. "He's a good man. I owe him big and I suppose it *is* payback time."

"Abel, it's not necessary—"

"Even so, give me a couple of days to think. I know a few people in the network. Find out if any of them is working for this tournament. Ask them to throw some scut work my way."

Rina bit her lip. "Thank you for hearing me out. It's hard to see someone you love so frustrated. I'm trying to help, which is probably a mistake—"

"Most likely a very big mistake. Your devotion, although overwrought, is touching."

Rina smiled. "Thank you for the backhanded compliment."

Abel looked her over. "You're a very pretty woman. Doc's one lucky guy."

"You like pretty women, you'll love Jeanine."

"She's pretty?"

"A knockout."

"But a real Jezebel, huh?"

"Jezebel . . ." Rina waited a beat. "You went to Bible school, Abel?"

"Kentucky Appalachian poor, ma'am. We lived on dust and God. Bible was the only book in the house. That and the Sears catalog. Learned how to read using the both of them. Then when I got hold of some *real* books, I couldn't figure out why people didn't use words like hast and doth and makest . . ."

Rina smiled softly.

Abel said, "Yes, I know who Jezebel was. She was a very evil woman."

"Yes, she was."

"So be it." Abel stroked his beard. "I've dealt with my fair share of evil women. Reckon one more cain't do me much harm."

# ❧ 31

*The Scrabble tournament* was set up on the second floor of the bookstore, all the way in the back, sandwiched between the video/audio section and the game department. Lots of board games. Old standards such as Monopoly, Life, Clue, Scrabble, chess, checkers, backgammon, and go. But there were also lots of the exotic and/or erotic adult games. Lots of "Host Your Owns." Host Your Own Murder Party, Host Your Own Stock Market Party, Host Your Own Baseball League Party, Host Your Own Strip Party. Host Your Own Sex *Party?*

Cindy wondered what *that* was all about.

Sam tapped her on the shoulder. She spun around. He said, "He's the one wearing the knitted cap and the orange jacket."

Cindy's eyes moved to the boy. Tall and thin. A pale but clear complexion with freckles thrown across the forehead and the nose. Patches of brown fuzz above his upper lip and under his chin. Dark eyes that skittered across the room, sizing up the crowd. Long, delicate fingers. Tapered nails. He wore an oversized white T under a tangerine cotton zip-up jacket, and old jeans. On his feet were Docs or facsimiles thereof.

"Doesn't look like a hit man to me," Cindy said.

"Yeah, he does seem pretty ordinary," Sam waited a beat. "Whole idea seems so stupid now."

"Nothing ventured, nothing gained."

"You sign up yet?"

"Nope."

"Come on. I'll show you where."

"You know, Sam, if we're gonna make headway, we can't be hanging around each other."

Sam didn't move. "I don't know about this. What if you talk to him afterward? What if he gets you alone and wham—"

"I'm not going anywhere," Cindy said. "Anyway, now's not the time for cold feet. I'll go sign up and you make yourself scarce. We'll meet up later."

Sam paused, then nodded. "Take care."

"Bye." Cindy walked away, studied the surroundings.

Folding chairs and card tables were scattered throughout the aisles, bordered by bookshelves on Games Strategy—Chess, Bridge, Whist, Go, Backgammon, Poker, Craps. Not to mention the tomes on Game Theory, Logic, and Probability. Math subjects that Cindy had assiduously avoided at Columbia.

About sixteen tables in all. Most held playing boards and timers. One table had been designated for snacks—bowls of pretzels, popcorn, potato chips, several water pitchers as well as paper cups and napkins. Another held the sign-up sheets for the tournament. Divided into three categories—two players, three players, and four players. Prizes and points were awarded to the highest score in each category.

Ambitious ones signed up for all three. Joachim was ambitious.

Cindy did the same. That way she knew she'd get to meet him at least once during the one-on-one. With any luck, she'd be assigned a three- or four-person match with him, too.

She poured herself a cup of water, felt a tap on the shoulder, and turned around. Tried not to act surprised.

Face-to-face. Eyes that bored into her. She bit her lip, sipped water. She cocked her hip in his direction. "Yes?"

"Are you the Cindy on the sign-up sheet?"

"Yes. Is that a problem?"

"No, not at all." He spoke in a soft voice. "Just need to know if you have an ISN?"

"A *what*?"

"An International Scrabble Number."

Cindy said, "How about a Social Security number—"

He smiled. "Sorry—"

"Driver's license?"

Joachim said, "This is an ISN tournament. You have to have an ISN number to play."

Cindy said, "And where would I get one?"

"I can give you one. But it's five bucks—"

"*What!*"

"Sorry. Their rules, not mine."

"The man leaves me no choice." Slowly, Cindy locked eyes with him. His cheeks turned a shade of pale pink. She smiled pointedly, pulled out her wallet from her jeans, ruffled through its contents. "I've only got two . . . no, three dollars—"

"I'll give you the two bucks." Joachim held out his hand.

Cindy slapped three ones into his palm. "If you give me your address, I'll pay you back."

"Forget it." Joachim pocketed the money. "Wait here. I'll get you your number."

Cindy watched him, studied him. Nothing to suggest that he was anything other than a typical gawky teenager. He returned a moment later. "Here."

The slip was made out to Cynthia Cohen. As a precaution, Cindy had used her mother's maiden name. She said, "Four-seven-eight-two. My lucky number."

Again he smiled. "Have fun."

He walked away. Cindy turned, exhaled forcefully. To herself, she said, "That was cool."

It took three uneventful matches before she hooked up with him. A two-person game. He smiled when he saw her, sat down across the table, and checked the timers.

"How're you doing?"

"Not too good."

"You play a lot?"

"I played in college," Cindy said. "But nothing like this. It's a no-brainer to bowl over a bunch of stoners bummed out on William Burroughs and weed grown from their windowsills."

"I like William Burroughs," Joachim said.

"That's because you're still young and impressionable."

"As opposed to you, Grandma?"

"Give me a rocker, I'm a happy woman."

He smiled. "You can go first."

Cindy looked at him. "That's not playing by official rules, bud."

"Yeah, I know. But I'll beat you anyway. Wind up with . . . oh, let's say, twice your score. For William Burroughs's sake."

"Arrogant little sucker, aren't you?"

"I just know my strong points. Go."

Cindy picked her letters. And suddenly the push of competition made her fierce. No way she could ever win him fairly. Go for the groin, she thought. She punched her clock, put down her first word, punched it again.

Punch, it was her turn again.

She let her shoe drop off. Made her word, punched the clock, then brushed her bare foot against his calf.

He looked up, looked back down. Said nothing and made his word.

Punch, it was her turn again.

Punch his.

Punch hers.

Punch his.

Again, she brushed his calf with her foot. Did it twice.

"You're kicking me," he said, red-faced.

Her voice was light. "Sorry."

Punch her turn.

Punch his turn.

Another brush. He turned red but said nothing, played his tiles, blinking back embarrassment.

The game was over in eighteen minutes. Cindy grinned. "You won. But not exactly twice my score, bud."

"That's because I played like an amateur." Joachim stood, his eyes shot with anger. "See you."

"You're mad," Cindy said.

Joachim said, "You *did* that on purpose."

"So?"

"So?" He glared at her. "It *distracted* me."

"It was *supposed* to distract you." Cindy grinned. "How else could I get a fair shot?"

Joachim continued to stare, then broke into laughter. "I don't believe . . ." He turned red. "Next round. Gotta go."

Cindy went through the rest of the evening without another chance to play him face-to-face. Joachim came in first in all three categories, graciously declined the gifts, which went to the next three highest scorers.

Trying to catch Joachim's attention. When she got it, she looked away. He waited a while. But eventually he walked up to her. He said, "You seem bored."

"This is true."

"You want to get a cup of coffee or something?"

"That's your answer to alleviating my boredom?"

He blushed, rocked on his feet, started to back away. Cindy took his arm. "I'm just funnin' with you, guy. Now the proper comeback would have been something like . . . 'So *this* is what I have to look forward to in college?'"

He let out a soft laugh. It matched his voice.

Still holding his arm, she said, "I'd love a cup of coffee except some gremlin took away my last three bucks—"

"I'll pay."

"If you pay, I'll come."

"I have to close up a few things first," Joachim said.

"That's okay. Meet you at the bookstore café in . . . ten minutes?"

"That would work."

"Good," Cindy said. "I'm glad it would work." She dropped his arm. "See you."

When she was downstairs, away from him, she made a fist and whispered, "Yes!"

Sammy appeared a minute later. "What'd he say?"

"He admitted he did the murders—"

"Cindy—"

"He didn't say anything!" Cindy said. "We're going to get some coffee in a few minutes. Go home. I'll call you later—"

"Nuh-uh, no way," Sam said. "This wasn't part of the deal."

"What wasn't?"

"You being alone with him."

"Sam, how can I find out information if I can't *talk* to him."

"The evening was supposed to be purely observational—"

"So it turned into something more—"

"This isn't what we talked about."

"I'm improvising. Now go home before he sees us talking to each other."

"I'm not leaving you alone—"

"Sam, did you get a good look at the kid? Could they make them any more harmless?" She patted her stepbrother's yarmulke. "Look, bro. No way we can ever prove Joachim's a hit man. But maybe I can prove his *innocence*. Find out where he was the night of the shootings. At least that way, if Strapp ever loosens the screws, Dad won't be spinning his wheels, wasting time on someone useless."

She was making sense. Still, Sam wasn't completely convinced. "I don't like it."

Cindy tried a different approach. "Didn't you tell your mom that you'd be home by eleven?"

"Oh sh—!" The boy stamped his foot in exasperation. "Look, Cin, you've got to call me. Let me know you're okay."

"You don't have your own line. What do I say when your mother picks up the phone?"

"You press two and then the pound sign. That makes the phone ring in my room and nowhere else. Deal?"

"Fine, fine. I'll call."

"When?"

"I'll call by . . . twelve," Cindy said. "Will you still be up? It's a school night."

"Yeah, I'm a night owl." Sammy rubbed his hands together. "So by twelve."

"Yeah. Twelve. And if I'm a little late, don't panic. I'm not going to turn into a pumpkin, all right?"

A pumpkin would be fine, he thought. Just so long as it wasn't a corpse. He kept his thoughts to himself. His hands had turned icy. He was spookin' himself. Stupid. Because Joachim did look harmless. Trying to calm himself down, Sam told himself to go home. Go home and pray. At least talk to Someone who could do some good.

"I went through like this voices of American literature phase. You know, Fitzgerald, Hemingway, Faulkner, Eudora Welty, Steinbeck . . ." Joachim dipped a chocolate-covered biscotti into a cup of espresso. "I was doing fine until I got to *Light in August*. Like I knew it was some kind of allegory for the expulsion from Eden and original sin. But man, it was so heavy with the prose—"

"That's his style," Cindy said.

"Yeah, but there's nothing wrong with making it readable. I mean I've waded through *The Magus* and *Clockwork Orange* and *Beowulf*. I'm not averse to experimenting with word origins and syntax. I'm talking about the actual phrases. I guess Faulkner's theory is why use one adjective when you can use twenty."

"He's a Southern writer, Joachim. They drip atmosphere. Something to do with all the humidity near the Gulf Coast."

"Could be." Again Joachim took a bite of his biscotti. "You ever read it?"

"Way back when."

"How old are you anyway?"

"Twenty-one," Cindy lied.

"So you're a senior then?"

"Just graduated."

"Ah. And now what?"

"Loose ends."

"Grad school isn't in the picture?"

"Nope."

Joachim said nothing.

Cindy said, "I'm sick of school. You'll understand when you get to where I'm at."

"You're too young to be patronizing," Joachim said.

"Four years of college puts us worlds apart," Cindy said. "Not in intellect, Joachim. I'm just saying you get tired of all the academic pettiness. All the profspeak and the braggadocio and the tired lines they use to get you horizontal—"

"Did they work?"

"Not on me."

Joachim blushed. "Sorry. That was rude."

"S'right." Cindy studied him. "You turn red a lot, you know that?"

Again he blushed. "I don't get around girls much. Or should I say women? What's the proper nomenclature anyway?"

"Females will always do in a pinch." Cindy sipped her caffe latte. "Yeah, you seem a little—"

"You can use the N word."

"Naive?"

"That was nice." He smiled. "You wanted to say nerdy, but didn't. It's true. I'm a little nerdy. But I'm not bothered by it." His face darkened. "Rather be nerdy than be like my snot-nosed, drugged-out, weak-willed, spineless, brainless, rich-kid classmates."

"So how do you really feel about your school?"

Joachim remained grave. "School's fine. Just the inhabitants whom I loathe."

"They give you a hard time?"

"I can handle them now. Brains do have their lucrative compensations. But there was a time . . ." He gobbled his biscotti, gnashed his teeth. "Not entirely their fault. I don't fit in . . . never did. You think I'm weird, you should meet my parents."

Cindy said, "I don't find you weird. You're just ill-suited for high school because you're bright."

The boy looked down, his face a primary color. And at that moment, Cindy saw how easy it was to manipulate teenage boys. And she wasn't exactly a femme fatale. Not like Jeanine Garrison. Man, she must have them dropping like flies.

The boy checked his watch. "It's getting late."

Cindy looked at her wrist. Eleven-fifteen. "Go ahead. I'm gonna stick around here for a while."

Joachim licked his lips. "You don't have to be home or anything?"

"I'm twenty-one, Joachim," Cindy said. "I don't *have* to be anything."

"You live by yourself?" he asked, shyly.

"With my mom. I'll find my own place as soon as I'm gainfully employed."

He drummed on the table. "You . . . want to come over my house? Watch a late movie or something?"

She stared at him. "Your parents wouldn't mind?"

"Actually, my parents are out of town." He squirmed in his seat. "I'll make some popcorn. Turn on the Monster Cable Station. It ain't much, but at least you won't have to worry about me feeding you sorry lines. I'm completely innocuous."

Cindy waited a moment. "You're gay?"

"Oh, no . . ." Again, he became scarlet. "No, that's not what I meant at all. It's just nice to talk to someone. That's all."

*Cindy's* brain went into overdrive. *What an opportunity. But what a dumb thing to do.* She shocked herself when she heard her lips utter, "Sure. Why not?"

The boy's face lit up. "Great. You can follow me home."

"Sure. But I've got to make a phone call first."

"Make it from my house. I live a couple of blocks away."

They both rose. Joachim left a twenty on the table.

Cindy's eyes went to the bill. "That's a very generous tip."

"I've got a good racket going."

"Racket?"

"Uh . . . tutoring . . . thirty bucks an hour." He grinned. "Sometimes it actually pays to be smart."

# ❧ 32

*She had a* strange feeling. But the .22 in her purse made Cindy feel bold. Reflecting upon the situation: A poor boy who could suddenly afford to leave a twenty on a six-dollar tab. A boy with a good racket? He said it was tutoring. But where did he *really* get his money?

Asking herself more questions. What did she hope to discover?

Information, she guessed. Some event that would link Joachim to the nefarious Sean Amos. Either that or an alibi that would prove his innocence. She thought about this as she followed him home.

He drove a ten-year-old Saab, did a series of quick turns, pulled into the driveway of a one-story wood-sided ranch house. A scrub lawn, a few bushes in front. She pulled her Camaro in back of his car. They both got out at the same time. He fiddled with his keys, opened the front door, allowing her to enter first.

"Thanks."

She gave the room a quick once-over. Basic living-room furniture—a couch, a couple of easy chairs. Old gray carpeting. Wood shutters on the windows.

Framed posters on the wall—Maxfield Parrish and Peter Maxx.

Joachim threw his jacket on the sofa. "Make yourself comfortable."

Cindy asked, "Were your parents hippies?"

"Hippies?"

"The artwork."

"Ah . . ." Joachim looked at the walls. "Actually, they're sci-fi buffs, although they're not averse to a good fantasy novel, either." He paused. "Better taste in novels than in artwork."

"Parrish is okay."

"If you like kitsch. You can take off your jacket, you know."

"I need to use the phone."

"Oh . . . right." Joachim pointed to the clear plastic phone on one of the sofa's end tables. "Help yourself."

Cindy picked up the phone. "Welcome to space age—"

"Actually, my father fitted it with this chip. You tell it the number and it'll dial automatically."

Cindy looked at him, at the phone. "I think I'll pass. Why don't you go nuke some popcorn? I suddenly have the munchies."

"Sure. Be right back."

She punched the numbers quickly, pressed two and pound. As soon as Sam picked up, she whispered, "I'm here, I'm fine, I'll call in later."

Sammy felt his heart go into his throat. "You can't be serious—"

"I gotta go—"

Sammy whispered, "You're insane. Get out of there *now*."

In the background, Cindy heard Rina's voice. "Sammy, get *off* the phone and go to bed now!"

Cindy said, "Looks like *you've* gotta go—"

"Cindy, get out of there—"

"Later." She hung up, heart doing the steeplechase. This *was* insane. All this intrigue, and for what purpose? What did she think she'd find? She felt her handbag, felt instantly relieved when her fingers pressed hard steel.

Calming herself. What could possibly happen?

She regained her composure, found the kitchen. Popping sounds were coming from the microwave. He said, "You want anything else?"

*Keep him occupied.*

"Got any veggies?" she said.

"I can cut some up if you want."

"If it's no problem."

"It's no problem."

Cindy stalled. "How about some nachos?"

Joachim turned around. "You want a banquet hall for this, King Henry?"

"Look, if it's too much work—"

"No." Joachim turned serious. "No, I'll rustle something up."

"That would be great."

"Anything else?"

"A Coke."

"You want some wine? You're over twenty-one."

"A Coke is sufficient, Mr. Innocuous."

He said, "I'm not trying to get you drunk. It

was an earnest offer. My mom drinks wine all the time."

"A Coke is fine. You spike it with a roofie, I'll kill you—"

"Not a chance." He went to the refrigerator, took out a can of Coke. Opened it and guzzled. Then offered it to Cindy. "I'm a card-carrying member of drug-free America."

Cindy took the can. "You got a TV in your bedroom?"

He blushed instantly. "Yeah. Wanna watch in there?"

"Why not be comfortable?" Cindy said.

"Why not indeed?" Joachim whispered. But his tone was tight. "Go ahead. I'll be there in a few minutes."

Cindy hesitated. "Are you okay?"

"Uh, yeah." He saluted her with a carrot. "I'm fine."

Hesitating a moment. Then she left the room, hooking her purse over her shoulder. As soon as she shut the door to his room, she threw the purse on his bed and went to work.

His lair resembled her stepbrothers' bedroom. A huge desk upon which rested a computer, fax, phone, answering machine, something that looked like a digital sound board, other gadgets she couldn't identify. A couple of movie posters on the wall. Weird stuff . . . distorted images of faces and mouths.

She attacked the desk drawers first. Rummaging through them, looking for a gun, looking for phone bills, recent purchases, even a stash of heroin that could have been the junk used to murder David

Garrison. *Anything* that might link him to Sean or Jeanine. She worked quickly and quietly.

And found nothing. Which was to be expected.

She opened the bedroom door, listened for a couple of seconds. He was still in the kitchen.

She tiptoed inside his closet, started going through the pockets of his jackets. A few receipts from bookstores, another from a computer store. She searched the upper shelf of the closet. Came up dry.

Next in line was the bedding—mattress and pillows. Looked under them, inside the covers. Gave them a few pushes. Nothing in there but foam. She dropped onto her stomach and looked under the bed. Nothing.

Then she heard his voice.

"What are you doing?"

On her knees, she peered over the mattress. He stared at her, holding a plate of veggies and another plate of nachos. She smiled benignly. "I dropped my earring—"

"You're not wearing earrings."

"Did I say earring?" Again, she smiled. "I meant my ring."

His face darkened. He placed the food on top of his bed, licked his lips. She got to her feet. "You look upset. What's wrong?"

"Nothing. Here's your food."

"Thanks."

Again, she felt her heart beat. Made a move for her purse, but he got there first. Lifted her handbag in the air out of her reach and stuck his hand inside.

Pulled out her gun.

Cindy froze.

Fingers around the trigger. A two-handed grip as he sighted down the wall. Showing her he knew how to use firearms. Then he lowered the barrel toward the ground, checked the safety clip. "Why are you carrying a twenty-two?"

"That's my business."

"With all due respect, I disagree." His voice had become gelid. "You carry a gun into my house, it's my business, too."

*Think of something!* Quietly Cindy said, "I went to school in New York. I got used to packing."

"You could get arrested for this, you know. Carrying without a license."

"Are you planning on calling the cops?"

He shrugged, hefted the firearm. "Not much weight to it."

"It can do damage—"

"That it can." He spoke more to himself than to her, examining the gun as he talked. "Bullets go in but don't always come out. Especially when you're talking about head shots, the ammo entering dense, solid bone like the cranium. Mostly . . . they bounce around, turning the brain to hamburger with each pass."

Cindy said, "You're making me nervous."

Joachim looked at her as if he had suddenly become aware of her presence. He lowered the gun, stuffed it back into her purse, and threw the purse on the bed.

It took all of Cindy's strength not to make a quick grab for her bag. But she managed to resist the urge.

Joachim said, "You like guns, let me show you some real weapons."

He removed a movie poster. Behind it was a safe. A few quick spins of the dial and the door popped open. He pulled out a revolver.

"You want real protection, you should be carrying something like this. Know what it is?"

"A Smith and Wesson thirty-two caliber Saturday night special. Snub-nosed front. Easy to pack, easy to carry—"

"I'm impressed—"

"Put it away, Joachim—"

"My parents . . ." He cleared his throat, stared at the gun. "Like I said, they're *weird* people. They're not white supremacists, but they do subscribe to a certain . . . pioneer mentality. The each-man-for-himself kind of thing. Their idea of fun is playing survivalist. I spent many a summer in arid, isolated mountains, hundred-degree heat, munching on roadkill and squeezing water from cacti with cracked hands."

"That's awful."

"Yeah, it was pretty bad. Still, I preferred the summers to the freezing winters in the Great Divide. While my classmates went skiing, I pitched a tent on snowpacked ground in twenty below." He paused. "Oh, we had heat . . . little sterno things that prevented frostbite. But as far as being like . . . warm . . . or even just cold . . ."

His face was expressionless.

"I don't know. Made me strong, I guess. Sure as hell made me a crack shot." Joachim stared at the revolver. "One thing I like about these suckers . . . they never jam." He put it back in the safe, then pulled out another weapon.

"Unlike this. Bet you know what this is."

"A Beretta semi-automatic. Eleven rounds."

His eyes locked with hers. "Preferred weapon of policemen . . . people like Peter Decker."

Cindy felt her stomach drop. She said nothing.

"Suppose you're wondering why I brought that up."

"I'm a bit curious."

Joachim said, "Our phones are hooked up to a central computer. Any one of our ten terminals can give me an instant list of outgoing calls made from this number. When you made your phone call, I checked it against the computer's backward directory. I suppose you know what that is."

"How'd you get hold of one?"

"Survivalists have their ways." Joachim paused. "Of course, the directory only told me the name. Peter Decker. It didn't tell me he was a cop. But I read papers, Cindy. Mass murders in this area aren't everyday occurrences. Lieutenant Decker was quoted a lot. I'm a top-ranked Scrabble player. Remembering words, even proper names, is something I do naturally."

Cindy's eyes traveled to her bag. Joachim caught it. "Go ahead. Pick up your purse. Pick up your gun. I won't stop you."

"You have a Beretta in your hands. That stops me."

Joachim put the gun back in storage. Eyes boring into her face. He said, "You've been after me since the beginning of the tournament. From the moment you looked at me, I knew something was up. Because girls don't look at me that way. Especially older . . .

attractive girls who are college graduates. You think you were being subtle, but you weren't. Still, I was willing to give you the benefit of the doubt. Because I enjoyed talking to you—"

"Joachim—"

"Just save it, okay?"

Cindy became quiet.

The teen said, "You're using a floppy bag purse. You hook it over your shoulder. I can't quite make out the outline, but I can see it's weighted down by something heavy and inflexible. That, combined with the phone call to Lieutenant Decker . . . I just knew it was a gun."

He sat down on the bed, averted his eyes.

"You're obviously a cop. What I can't figure out is why you're *spying* on me. This can't be a police matter 'cause I haven't done anything." He stared at her. "Maybe you're moonlighting. Did Krieg send you? Is he *paying* you to do this to me?"

Cindy tapped her foot while stalling for time. Trying to come up with something. "Paying me to do what, Joachim?"

"To *torture* me! Because I refused to take the SAT for him. Idiot doesn't realize they have *proctors* checking out things. I should screw up my entire future to get the asshole into the Ivies?"

*Think of something* quick, *you jerk!* She blurted out, "But you've taken the SAT for other people—"

"That's an outright lie!" Joachim's face had turned beet red. "Who *told* you that? Where are you getting your information? I've never taken any standardized tests for anyone. Think I'm crazy?"

And then the lightbulb went on.

*Sometimes it pays to be smart.*

His *racket*! Sam had told her about an envelope passed through the open window of his car. Cindy said, "How about for Sean Amos? You took the SAT for him—"

"Never—"

Cindy fired out, "But you've been writing essays for him, haven't you? For him and Krieg and all the others. We know this for a fact, Joachim. So there's no sense denying it!"

The boy had turned ashen. He whispered, "Who's . . . *we*?"

Cindy balled her hands in fists, eyes glued on the boy's face. She lied, "Joachim, I've been hired by your school to root out cheaters—"

"Oh, God!" Joachim moaned out.

"They've hired me to get to the bottom of all this deception. It's been a black mark on the school—"

"I'm gonna be sick!" He beelined for the bathroom.

Cindy felt her own stomach rock. It was now obvious how Joachim had kept the rich boys off his back and earned bread. Money for tutoring, money for homework. And money for term papers and essays. The big question was . . . did he do other more heinous things for cash as well? Cindy wasn't ready to write him off as completely innocent. Not just yet.

The boy came out a moment later, his complexion gray, eyes and nose leaking water. "Sorry about that." He smiled weakly. "Not too good for a survivalist, huh?"

Cindy handed him a can of Coke. "Drink."

"I'm not—"

"Drink!"

Joachim took a tiny sip. "Did the school hire you as part of a general crackdown? Or was this specifically against me—"

"Let me ask the questions." Cindy tried to appear official. "If you hope to get out of this, I'd better have some cooperation—"

"Whatever you want."

"Let's start at the beginning. Tell me about Sean Amos."

"What about him . . . specifically?"

"How long have you been doing his work?"

Joachim's voice was a whisper. "Maybe four years ago."

"Four years ago?"

"Yes. For him, for Krieg, for Denny, for all of them. How do you think I got the assholes to leave me alone?"

"And you charged them money to do . . . what?"

"Homework, essays, science projects, you name it." Joachim looked at her. "And yes, I charged them money."

Cindy asked, "How much?"

Joachim said, "Depends. Everything was negotiated."

"Is that why you were talking to Sean Amos in the parking lot of the school about a month ago? An envelope was given to you by Sean Amos. Were you negotiating a price for something?"

"A month ago?" Joachim sighed. "I haven't the faintest idea what I was doing a month ago."

"It was on a Tuesday. You talked to Sean . . . rather, Sean talked to you. Then you left, put notices in the local bookstore about the Scrabble tournament—"

"God, you people are thorough." He paused. "Who exactly do you work for?"

"Just answer the question, Joachim!" Cindy barked. "Why were you talking to Sean Amos?"

Joachim said, "A month ago . . . honestly, I don't remember. I could look up the date in my daily planner—"

"Go ahead. Do that!"

Joachim took a leather pouch from his desk drawer. From it he removed a small electronic device. Turned it on and began pushing keys. "A month ago, Tuesday . . ."

He paused.

"Here we go. Yeah, we had an English assignment. A three-page paper on comparing and contrasting the English versus the American Transcendentalists. Could be I was talking to Sean . . . about it . . . offering to help him out—"

"Cut the crap."

Joachim stiffened. "Look, Cynthia Cohen, or whatever your name *really* is, all I do is write a damn paper. And then I show it to him. If *he* chooses to put *his* name on it, is that my problem?"

"It's called plagiarism—"

"Is it any different from looking up the information in an encyclopedia?"

Cindy said, "And when you talk to Yale's Office of Admissions, you can tell them just that—"

"What do you *want* from me!" Joachim cried out. "Please. I swear I'll never do it again. Please, please, please. My whole life depends on this. Just give me another chance—"

"What else do you do for Amos?"

Joachim's eyes darted in their sockets. "What do you mean?"

Cindy picked up her bag. "He ever hire you to help him out in other ways?"

"What other ways? What else would I do for him? I *hate* the son of a bitch! I hate them all. Fucker bastards. Fucking users." He laughed bitterly. "Literally, as well as figuratively."

Cindy's brain started racing. *Computer users? No, jerk, the other kind. Users as in drugs. David Garrison's OD.* "They indulge, do they?"

"Boy, do they—"

"You ever buy Sean's drugs for him?"

Joachim's eyes got big. "If he told you that, he's lying! Guy's a fucking liar!"

"Just answer the question—"

"No!" Joachim said. "No, no, no. I've never bought drugs for Sean or anyone. I don't do drugs. I have nothing to do with drugs or Sean or any of them. Especially *Mal.* I tutored him a couple of times. That guy is psycho! I avoid him like the plague."

The mind sped into overdrive. She improvised. "You're referring to Mal Miller?"

"Who's Mal Miller?"

Cindy looked at him pointedly. "Which Mal are *you* talking about?"

"Malcolm Carey."

"Ah, yes . . ." Cindy nodded, knowingly. "Who does he sell to besides Sean and Krieg and the others?"

"Anyone who asks. But I don't really know. I told you, I don't go near him. Please. You've got to believe me."

Kid was pale, sweaty. Cindy's heart went out to him. She backed off. "You're willing to swear to that in a court of law?"

"Yes, of course!" The teen's face was a study in confusion. "Can you please, *please* tell me what's going on?"

"In a minute." Cindy steadied herself. Now or never. She took a calculated risk. "Let me see your planner."

Joachim's eyes went to his pocket computer. He handed it to her, but she didn't take it.

"Turn it on," she said.

The teenager did as told.

She said, "If I scanned through that planner, I wouldn't find any appointments between Malcolm Carey and you, would I?"

"Not a one. I swear—"

"So if I looked up some . . . random dates . . . I'd find nothing incriminating?"

Joachim looked ill. "Nothing I could go to jail for."

"But I might find something like . . . *essay for Sean is due?*"

The kid wiped perspiration off his brow, nodded.

She said, "You don't have to let me look at it, Joachim. Legally, I can't force you without a warrant—"

"It's okay." Again, he offered her the planner. His hands were shaking. "Just . . . I don't know. It's okay."

"I'm going to pick out some random dates," she said. "You look them up for me, show them to me. Got it?"

The teen nodded.

"Then show me your schedule for . . . a week ago Tuesday."

Quickly, he brought the date onto the small screen. "Here. Take a look."

She did. A couple of school tests, a doctor's appointment, nothing for the evening. And nothing of significance.

"How about two weeks ago Saturday?"

Joachim punched keys, offered her the monitor. Nothing.

Heart drumming in her chest, Cindy gave him the date of the Estelle's executions. Without a pause, Joachim brought up the date on his planner and showed it to her. She looked at the demarcated hours, scanning the time until she hit eight P.M.

At the time Estelle's was being riddled with bullets from a madman, Joachim was at a Scrabble tournament at the local YMCA. Cindy pointed to the appointment. "Did you actually attend this event?"

Joachim looked at the tip of her finger. He thought a moment. "Uh . . . I've got to think. The YMCA match? Yeah . . . yeah, I was there, too. Why?"

"Let me ask the questions."

"Sure. Whatever you want."

"Your presence at this tournament . . . it can be verified by witnesses?"

"Of course. Why?"

Cindy waved her hand. "That's all for now."

Joachim stood frozen. "What do you mean, *that's all*? What are you going to do?"

Cindy said, "Nothing for the time being."

Joachim paused. *"Nothing?"*

*"If* you promise never to write another essay for anyone else but yourself . . . I suppose I could let the matter drop."

"I swear, I'll never do it again. Let the bastards drown for all I care."

"Okay. I won't report you. But you're not entirely off the hook. I've got a couple more questions."

Joachim slumped, looked visibly relieved. "Sure. What?"

"I want to talk about Malcolm Carey. Where does he operate from? Where does he peddle his merchandise?"

Questioning eyes went to Cindy's face. Joachim said, "Are you a narc—"

"Answer the question, Joachim."

"I don't know where Mal gets his shit. But I could find out if you want—"

"Joachim, I *don't* want you going around asking questions. Is that understood?"

"Sure—"

"Because Malcolm Carey is trouble. These questions are just between you and me."

"Whatever you want, Cindy ... can I call you Cindy?"

She held back a smile. "What does Sean buy from him?"

"I imagine everything. Uppers, downers, coke, roofies, scag—"

"Sean buys heroin from Malcolm?" Cindy interrupted.

"I suppose."

"But you're not sure."

"I know Sean occasionally smokes the shit. Where else would he get it from? I mean Malcolm *owns* Westbridge."

"How do you know that Sean uses heroin?"

"Everybody knows. Sean brags about it, among other things. Guy has a big mouth."

Cindy paused. "What else does he talk about?"

"What doesn't Sean talk about? What drugs he's taking, which girls he's screwing—"

"He talk about . . ." Cindy swallowed. "Sean talk about that *older* woman at all?"

"Jeanine Garrison?" Joachim nodded. "Yeah. All the time. He keeps telling people not to tell anybody. In the meantime, everyone knows they're screwing. At least that's what *he* says."

Cindy nodded. "Tell me more about Sean and Jeanine."

He paused. "You mean the rumors?"

Cindy felt her chest pound. She played along. "Yes, I mean the rumors. How valid are they?"

"Who knows?" Joachim paused. "God, you know *everything*—"

"I have my inside information," Cindy lied. "But right now I'm talking to you. So give me your take on the rumors."

Joachim said, "I think they got started because Sean's been acting so weird lately. Especially after Estelle's. You know about Jeanine Garrison's parents?"

"Shot dead at Estelle's. Go on."

"Okay . . . then . . . when Jeanine's brother OD'd . . . you know about that?"

"David Garrison. Found dead of an OD in his apartment. Continue."

Joachim looked grave. "I mean, the woman loses her parents . . . well, no one thought too much about that. Because we all thought it was just a lunatic doing target practice. But after her *brother* bought it . . ."

Joachim kneaded his hands.

"See, she came into lots of money after her parents were murdered. Sean was saying that Jeanine was resentful about sharing her inheritance, especially since her brother was a hype."

Cindy nodded. "Go on."

Joachim sighed. "Rumor was that Sean . . . paid Mal to stick a needle into David Garrison's vein. To make it look like an accident."

"Sean hired Malcolm to off David Garrison?"

"That was the scuttlebutt. And, you know, that Mal's psycho enough to do it." A pause. "It's probably just bullshit. But you know, once things get said out loud—they take on a larger-than-life scale. All of it . . . made Sean look like a real badass."

Cindy sat down on the bed. She said, "Joachim, it is of the utmost importance that you don't repeat this conversation to anyone. All of this, it's just between you and me. You can't breathe a word of it. For your own safety."

Joachim stared at her. "You're not really from the school. You're a narc, aren't you?"

Cindy didn't answer. Instead she said, "Now I want you to repeat what you just told me about Sean Amos and Jeanine Garrison and Malcolm Carey. Talk about the rumors and Sean being a user and Malcolm being a pusher and a bad guy. I want you to repeat all of it."

"Repeat it to you?"

"No. Repeat it to Lieutenant Decker."

"When?"

"Now."

"Now?"

"Now!"

Joachim looked at her. "He's your superior, isn't he?"

For once, Cindy didn't have to lie. "Yes, Joachim. Lieutenant Decker is my superior."

# ❧ 33

*Reading yesterday's paper* at one in the morning. Decker wondered why he bothered. The news was never uplifting. Sitting in his pajamas and bathrobe at the dining table, sipping weak coffee, wishing the nightmares would vanish. Still, he couldn't complain. Only five weeks since Estelle's and he made it through the night about half the time.

He heard a bedroom door open, turned around. Sammy froze in his tracks, an odd smile on his face. "Hi."

"Hi." Decker put the paper down. "Trouble sleeping?"

Sammy shrugged. "I guess. Thought I'd get something to drink."

"Anything specific on your mind?"

"No, I'm fine." The teen rubbed his hands together. "Are you always up this late?"

"Sometimes. I like it when the house is quiet."

"So then . . . no one's called here in the last half hour?"

Decker's eyes bored into the boy. "What kind of phone call would come through at one in the morning?"

"Yeah, silly question, huh?" The teen looked away. "I'll be in the kitchen. Bye."

The boy scooted out.

*Now what the hell was that all about?*

Within minutes, Sam materialized. Again, that funny smile. "I'm going back to bed."

"Good night, Sam."

" 'Night."

Decker watched his stepson disappear behind his bedroom door, went back to his paper. A few minutes later, an engine purred, headlights shining into the house. Then silence and darkness. A door opening and closing. Again, he put the paper down, got up, and peered through the bay window.

What in the world?

A shadow resembling his daughter. He opened the front door and in walked Cindy. Decker's eyes shot down to his naked wrist where his watch usually sat.

"It's one-fifteen," Cindy informed him. "Glad you're up. I've got someone in the car you need to talk to as Lieutenant Decker. I'll give you a few minutes to get dressed."

Then she walked out. Decker was stunned. Resisted the urge to bolt after her. Instead, he went to get dressed. By the time he was back, Cindy had brought in a boy. Way too young to be a date. A gawky kid of around seventeen, garbed in baggy clothes. Peach fuzz sat on the face. But the eyes were alert and well focused . . . anxious as well.

Decker nodded. The boy nodded back. Unnoticed by his stepfather, Sam had tiptoed in, stopped, stared open-mouthed at Cindy and Joachim. Cindy's eyes drifted over her father's shoulder to Sammy, who was making gestures at her. Slitting his throat with his finger.

Still, she plowed ahead. "Lieutenant, this is Joachim Rush. I believe the name is familiar to you. Joachim, this is Lieutenant Decker."

Instantly, Decker's chest started pounding. That was all he needed—a heart attack at one in the morning. The boy extended his hand.

"Sir."

Decker shook it, managed to keep his expression neutral, hoped he could do the same for his voice. "Have a seat. I'll be with you in a moment."

Decker crooked a finger at his daughter. Cindy looked past him at Sammy, who was gesticulating frantically, swinging his arms out, mouthing the words: no, no, no.

"What are you looking—" Decker turned around.

Sammy gave him a little wave.

Cindy said, "Good night, Sam—"

"Hold on a minute," Decker said. "You're not going anywhere. Can someone tell me what's going on?"

Cindy spoke to the teen. "We'll get down to business in a moment. Sam, why don't you keep Joachim occupied for a little bit? Take out a Scrabble board."

Her stepbrother had the same sick grin on his face.

"Do it *now*, please," Cindy said.

Sam tightened his bathrobe. "Sure."

Before Decker could speak, Cindy took her father's arm, steered him into the kitchen, out of Joachim's earshot. Still, she whispered. "Dad, give me a chance and I'll explain everything."

He was a fraction of a second away from exploding. But his daughter's expression held him back. A look of intensity, of purpose. He spoke quietly. "You've got thirty seconds. Make it good."

"Joachim knows nothing about your suspicions regarding Jeanine Garrison, that she had planned Estelle's as a front for her parents' hits. My opinion? Joachim had nothing to do with Estelle's, period. He was at a Scrabble tournament when the shooting went down. I'll tell you how I found that out later. Actually, this isn't about Estelle's at all. It's about David Garrison. There have been rumors at Westbridge Prep that Sean Amos might have hired someone to ice David Garrison with a needle. Make it look like an accidental OD because everyone knew David was a hype. Prime candidate as hit man is a student/dealer named Malcolm Carey. I'd say more but my thirty seconds are up."

Decker stood speechless, then forced words from his throat. "Good Lord, what have you gotten into?"

"Me? Nothing. I'm just a conduit—"

"How'd you . . ." He glared at her. "Sammy drag you into this?"

She returned his fiery expression. "Does it matter, Dad? The point is, you've finally got a way to get to Jeanine Garrison—"

"Estelle's isn't even my case anymore—"

"Oh *screw* that—"

"Shhh. Give me a moment to think. To absorb what you just threw at me." Decker's brain was awhirl. "What kind of rumors?"

"Might be better if you heard it from Joachim."

"Cindy, how do you know the kid's not onto you, snowing you with lies?"

"I have my reasons. But talk to him yourself. If you disagree, I'll defer to you."

"But you don't think he's involved in any crime?"

"Dad, far as I can tell, his only *crime* is dishonesty. He sells his brain, writes papers and essays for people like Sean Amos."

"For a price."

"Yes, for a price. Matter of fact, Joachim was negotiating a paper with Sean Amos when Martinez spied them in the school's parking lot. The envelope that he saw exchange hands . . . money for an English essay."

"You *asked* him about that meeting?"

"Of course not. Everything was done indirectly. Daddy, he didn't tell me about the plagiarism scheme. I guessed it. That's how I tripped him up. Joachim not only cribs for Sean, but for others. I told him I was Cindy Cohen, hired by the school to investigate a big homework deception scandal—"

"You figured out that cover by yourself?"

Cindy nodded.

"Just . . . made it up? On the spot?"

She smiled. "You're impressed?"

Decker was *very* impressed! But he didn't tell her. Instead, he said, "And he fell for it?"

"No, not completely. Now he thinks I'm a narc. He thinks I'm working under your command. Actually, I sense that he doesn't know *what* to believe. Except he knows that you really are a police lieutenant. So he's scared enough to talk. I suggest you take advantage."

Decker cocked his head over his shoulder. "What's Sammy's part in all of this?"

"He overheard you and Rina talking about the

Garrison case, had some ideas of his own. He didn't know how to broach you, so he called me." Cindy waited a beat. "He did it because he cares about what matters to you. So do I."

No one spoke.

Cindy said, "Dad, Joachim might not be the break you need. He might not pan out. But he *is* an in to Westbridge. If you had hired your own private detective, you couldn't have done any better, correct?"

Decker didn't answer.

Cindy said, "Malcolm Carey's got a lock on Westbridge. You want chemicals, you go to him. Deals in pot, rock cocaine, powdered coke, roofies, ice, and heroin. He's a bad boy. Certainly Joachim is entitled to talk to the police about criminal activity at his school. Just hear him out. You know I'm making sense."

"Yes, I know. But I'm not objective right now." Decker spoke to himself. "I need a third party."

"How about Rina?"

"Better yet, I'll call Marge. Go take care of your charge and I'll be out in a few minutes."

Cindy said, "Thanks for keeping your cool, for not playing irate parent—"

"That'll come."

"No doubt." She kissed her father's cheek. "But nothing I can't handle."

Marge had brought Oliver. Martinez and Webster had wanted to come as well, but Decker had nixed the idea. Too many people. Might make the kid choke.

The burst of activity in the house had awakened Rina. She walked into the brightly lit living room, eyes squinting, a dazed look on her face. More than anything she wanted to know why Sammy was playing Scrabble at 1:45 in the morning. Cindy took her into the kitchen, tried to explain things. But it left Rina even more confused. Still, she didn't argue. Instead, she made a pot of decaf, deciding to sort it out later.

Sam finished his game with Joachim by two, put away the board and tiles, then retired. Rina went to sleep ten minutes later, leaving the group sitting around a table, coffee mugs in hand. Decker gave Joachim center stage. He told his story, speaking slowly and carefully.

Marge was the first one with a question. "Has Sean heard these rumors?"

"Yes, ma'am."

"What did he say about them?"

"Shrugged them off."

"Did they bother him?" Oliver wanted to know.

"No," Joachim said. "At least, that's my perception. I told Cindy . . . is that really your name?"

"Yes. Go on, Joachim."

"It seemed like Sean enjoyed the notoriety," the kid said. "Made him look like a hard case. Because up until then . . . he was just another whiny rich boy. No one took him seriously."

Cindy said, "He's popular. You told me that."

"You have that kind of money, you're superficially popular. But that doesn't prevent people from talking behind your back. Sean's a first-class slacker."

"He's on the tennis team," Cindy argued.

"Yeah, he does athletics," Joachim said. "But mostly he parties—gets drunk or stoned, then screws around. Also, he and his friends like to tag on the weekends.

Mostly street or stop signs. Their big forays into criminal activities."

Joachim made a face as if to say Amos couldn't even cut it as a felon.

"Sean did get some brownie points when he started doing Jeanine. Impressive at first, but even then people started poking him behind his back."

"Could be they were jealous," Oliver said.

"Yeah, I'm sure they were," Joachim said. "Still, he was getting a rep of being pathetic, that she treated him like a trained dog—'Fetch, boy, roll over and play dead.'"

He paused.

"*I* never saw it. But you'd hear things."

The teen licked his lips.

"I've known Sean for a while. Seen him react to all kinds of situations. The talk about Jeanine . . . it got to him. He started acting weird. Especially after Estelle's. Because the dissing got worse."

"Why?" Oliver asked.

"Because everyone kept saying that Jeanine was going to dump him now that she'd inherited money. See, up until then . . . no one could figure it out . . . him and Jeanine. I mean, no one had any trouble understanding his attraction to her. But why would she be interested in Sean? They figured she had to be after his bread."

"Wasn't Jeanine rich in her own right?" Marge asked. "Even before her parents died?"

"I have no idea. But I do know that Sean's dad is really rich . . . Texas oil money. Sean has lots of toys."

"What kind of toys?" Oliver asked.

"Typical Westbridge stuff—the sports car, the

skis, the wet suit and surf boards, the five-eight-five PC with CD-ROM, the winter vacations in Switzerland, the summers on the Riviera. Plus the private tennis lessons. Sean plays the local circuit. He's not very good. But I know professional instruction doesn't come cheap."

Marge asked, "Do most Westbridge boys belong to Greenvale, Joachim?"

The teen nodded.

"And most of them are rich?"

"Yes."

"Then Jeanine could have had her pick of boys."

"Probably."

"So why do you think Jeanine chose Sean?"

"I don't know."

Decker said, "After Jeanine's parents were killed, you said kids began to razz Sean."

"Yes, sir."

"And he began acting weird?"

"Yes."

"Define weird?"

Joachim thought a moment. "Short-tempered. Also physical. Apparently, he'd gone psycho at a couple of parties, got into a few shoving matches. Also . . ." He sighed. "He raped a girl. Sean claims it was a party thing . . . that everyone was drunk and the girl consented. But she claims it was rape. You know . . . rophynol . . . roofies."

"Any charges filed?"

"Not that I know of."

"So you have no way of knowing whether any of it is true or not."

"No. But when you hear the same story over and over . . ."

"What about Sean's drug use?" Decker asked.

"I tutored him," Joachim said. "I've seen him use."

"What does he use?" Decker pressed.

"Pot, coke . . . heroin. He used to smoke it. After he hooked up with Jeanine, he started chipping."

"Mainlines?"

"Don't know." He was quiet. "You know, you get a rep as a real badass if you use a needle. That and doing hookers without wearing skins. It means you don't give a shit. Viral Russian Roulette. They're all *crazy*. I mean, they've got *everything* and all they can think about is frying their brains. I don't *get* it."

The room went silent.

Joachim said, "That's when the rumors about Sean popping David Garrison got started. When Sean started using a needle."

Again, the boy paused.

"You know, it worked. The badass image, I mean. People stopped razzing Sean after David Garrison OD'd. I think they were . . . afraid of him."

Decker said, "Tell me about Sean and Malcolm Carey. Are they buddies?"

"Malcolm's kind of a loner. But he and Sean did start hanging out together after David Garrison died."

Decker said, "Malcolm is in charge of Westbridge's drug distribution?"

"Yeah."

"Does he have any competition?"

"Not that I know of."

"Who does he buy from?"

"Don't know," Joachim said. "But he speaks fluent Spanish. And he took French in school. I know this because I've tutored him."

"Is Malcolm a rich kid?" Marge asked.

"His father's an entertainment lawyer who became an agent. I'm sure he makes an obscene amount of money. Still, Mal is *not* in Sean's league."

Marge said, "You think Malcolm would do real nasty things for money?"

"Things like stick Garrison with pure heroin?" Joachim nodded. "Without question. Probably do it just for the kicks. But I don't know this for fact."

Oliver asked, "Did Malcolm suddenly start showing off any new toys after David Garrison died?"

"You mean like buy a new car or something?"

"Exactly."

Joachim thought a moment. "I don't know. But I don't pay attention to Malcolm. I could check it out—"

In unison, the detectives told him *No! Don't check anything out!*

Firmly, Decker said, "Joachim, it's imperative that you *don't* get involved. That you *stay away.*"

Marge added, "That way you don't get hurt and we can run our investigation."

Joachim looked at Cindy. "Your questions . . . they were just a front. This is really about David Garrison, isn't it? I mean . . . my doing papers for other people. You don't care about that, do you?"

"Nah, I don't care," Cindy answered.

"So I'm not in any trouble with my school or with Yale's Office of Admissions."

"Nope."

Joachim sat back in his chair. "God, you're a *sadist!*"

Cindy shrugged.

The boy said, "Don't be too remorseful."

Decker said, "Officer Cohen was just doing her job."

"So you *are* a cop!"

Decker tossed his daughter a surreptitious wink. "And a very good one at that."

Holding back a smile, Cindy said, "Sorry for the subterfuge. And I appreciate your help, even if it was coerced." A pause. "You know, Joachim, being accepted to Yale . . . you might want to keep your nose clean for the next nine months."

"You're absolutely right." Joachim looked down. "It was never the money, you know. I don't care about money. I'm not saying I did it because I *had* to. I didn't have to. No one *made* me write the papers. But . . . sometimes you do things . . . because it makes your life easier."

Decker said, "That's valid. But I agree with Officer Cohen. Keep your nose clean."

Joachim tapped his foot. His eyes grew big. "You know, if you want Malcolm Carey, I could help you—"

"No, Joachim," Decker said. "We don't want your help—"

Joachim blurted out, "Don't you use informants, Lieutenant?"

"Not minors," Marge said.

"I turned eighteen a week ago," Joachim said.

The room went quiet.

Joachim bounced his leg up and down. "I wouldn't even have to be involved in any transaction. Just keep my ears open. I blend into the crowd there. People talk around me—like I don't exist."

Marge said, "Joachim—"

The teen interrupted, "If you wanted to catch Sean doing a buy from Malcolm . . . that would be hard. Probably they deal at Sean's house. But if you want Malcolm . . ." He waved his hand in the air. "That's a snap. First off, he's got more shit in his car than the Medellín Cartel. Second, he deals openly at parties. All I have to do is keep my ears open. All you'll need is a couple of narcs and a warrant—"

Decker said, "I don't like it—"

Oliver said, "Uh, Loo. I think we need to talk—"

Decker said, "What if it got back that the information came from him?"

"How?" Oliver said. "All he has to do is make an anonymous phone call to me or you or Narcotics."

Joachim said, "Lieutenant, I have nothing to do with Malcolm—"

"Exactly," Decker said. "They suspect the one who has nothing to do with the dealer."

Joachim said, "Lieutenant, the entire school isn't on drugs. I'd say over fifty percent of the student body has nothing to do with Malcolm Carey."

Decker said, "Officer Cohen, don't you have to take Joachim home?"

Cindy frowned. Excluding her at this crucial time. Still, she understood her father's dilemma. "How about if we wait outside?"

"Good idea. Be with you two in a moment."

Oliver waited until the front door closed. Then he said, "Deck, you can't let an opportunity like this pass through your fingers—"

"Scott—"

Marge broke in, "Pete, he's right. Worse comes to

worst, we arrest a felon, get a major dealer out of the school."

Oliver said, "Deck, we use Malcolm to get to Sean, we use Sean to get to Garrison. Yeah, there are a lot of holes along the way. So what? Marge is right. Even if we're *completely* off base, even if Sean and Malcolm had nothing to do with Garrison's OD. What's the worst that can happen? We jail a pusher."

"We'll bring Narc in on it," Marge said. "Really make it look legit."

"With the understanding that we get first crack at Malcolm," Oliver said. "It's *gold*, rabbi. The honest-to-goodness twenty-four-karat item. If the kid's willing to make a discreet phone call—"

"I'm worried about the kid going overboard," Decker said.

"So we'll talk to him," Marge said. "He's a legal adult, Pete. We can't get into trouble that way—"

"We're still using a kid," Decker said.

"We're not asking him to wear wires," Oliver protested. "Just to make a simple phone call if he hears something. Face it, Loo. We're not going to get Sean any other way. And if we don't get Sean, we won't get Jeanine Garrison. Think about those innocent victims from Estelle's—thirteen murdered, thirty-two wounded."

Decker said. "This whole thing has nothing to do with Estelle's."

"You don't know that," Oliver said. "Maybe Malcolm's the mysterious second shooter—"

"Or maybe he isn't—"

"Forget about Estelle's!" Marge blurted out. "Estelle's is irrelevant, okay? We're not *investigating*

Estelle's. We're investigating David Garrison. His
death is listed as an accidental OD, but homicide has
*not* been ruled out. If we hear rumors that lead us to
investigate his death as a homicide . . . well, then I'm
gung-ho. Because that's what I do. I investigate
homicides. And as far as I'm concerned, David Garrison is as good a homicide as any. And in the process of my investigation, if I get a rat's ass punk
pusher out of a school, well, then . . . fine with me!"

No one spoke. Decker threw back his head. "God,
what a night." With resolution, he gave his hands a
clap. "We'll do it under two conditions. First, the
reason we're going after Malcolm is to get to Sean
and Jeanine, right?"

They both nodded.

Decker said, "We can't possibly expect Malcolm
to admit to a *homicide* in exchange for a simple drug
charge. Which means we've got to get *multiple* charges
on him—pop him with so many drug felonies that
he's *never* going to expect to see the light of day. To
get that, we're going to have to arrest at least a dozen
students who'll admit to buying from Malcolm.
Which means we can't pop him for a simple buy.
We're going to have to raid a dope party."

"Good point," Marge said.

"Agreed," Oliver said.

Decker said, "Once we have the kid convinced that
we're his only hope, we bring up David Garrison—"

"You mean Sean Amos," Oliver said.

"No, David Garrison."

"But we don't have anything that connects Malcolm to Garrison."

"Then we'll just have to convince not only

Malcolm but his lawyer that we have *compelling* evidence," Decker said. "We'll say we're going to run a gas chromatography on all Malcolm's heroin. Tell him the composition matched the shit found in David Garrison's apartment. Convince him that the odds of any one batch of heroin exactly matching another batch of heroin are extremely minuscule."

"Are the odds remote?" Marge asked.

Decker shrugged. "Who knows? But it sounds good. Let's bring Joachim back in here and explain the situation. Tell him not to call us unless he's sure that there's a big whopper going down. When he's *sure*, we move. And not a moment before. We move too early, we blow everything." He caught his breath. "Now for the second condition. In order to execute the operation, I'll need clearance from Strapp."

Marge frowned, "We can't circumvent him?"

"No, I've got to tell him what's going on." Decker rubbed his eyes. "I just have to figure out how to do it without bringing in Cindy."

Marge said, "I'll take the heat. We'll tell the exact same story except I'll be Cindy."

"I'll cover for you, Dunn," Oliver said. "I'll say I was backup while you were with the kid." He turned to Decker. "You know, your daughter was really clever to come up with that jive-ass cover on the spot."

"Yes, she was." Decker shook his head. "But she was completely out of line . . . taking a chance like that. I don't know whether to brain her or kiss her."

"Why'd she do it?" Oliver asked. "What was in it for her?"

"She was trying to help me out."

Marge said, "Then she accomplished her goal."

Words spilled from Decker's mouth. "She's entering the Academy after the first—"

"*What?*" Marge said.

"When did this happen?" Oliver asked.

"She told me about a month ago."

"Why didn't you *say* something?" Marge demanded.

"I kept hoping she'd change her mind." Decker sighed. "This bit of intrigue certainly dashes *that* hope. You notice that excitement-junkie look on her face? Like she took a vial of adrenaline and shot it through her vein."

"She did a good job," Oliver said.

Marge said, "For what it's worth, I think she'll make a good cop."

But Decker couldn't let go of the image—an hours-old infant nestling in his arms. Soft, red, and so very warm. He bit back mist that had clouded his eyes, said, "Let's go talk to Joachim."

# ॐ 34

*Not much more* than a shed. But it sat in the middle of an enchanted forest.

Decker said, "If you kiss it, will it turn into a palace?"

"Only works on frogs." Rina fiddled with the keys. "Shall we go inside?"

"Sure, let's live dangerously. You're positive this place has a sewer line?"

"Last I checked, it even had cable hookup." She placed the key inside the lock, turned the bolt. "Nice of the owner to give us the run of the place."

"He's probably hoping we'll burn it down so he can collect insurance."

As the door opened, they were spotlighted by dusty rays. Old lumpy furniture sat in an old house. Dirt-coated floors. Decker bounced on the planks. No squeaks. "Sturdy . . . solid wood."

"What kind?"

He bent down, regarded the grain. "Cherry."

"That's good?"

"Our dining-room table's cherry." He scratched the floor with his nail. "Yeah, this is all superficial gunk. It'll come right off." He knocked on the walls. A thud answered. "Lath and plaster."

"Is that good or bad?"

"Good." Decker rapped his knuckles against the walls several more times. "Here's the structural beam." More knocking. "Several of them. Deceptively well built. Bet you could add a second story."

Rina gave off a soft smile. "You like it."

"Just trying to be positive."

Together, they explored the pint-sized den, two tiny bedrooms—between them a connecting water closet. The kitchen, though roomy, looked like it hadn't been touched in fifty years.

Decker stood, legs apart, arms folded across his chest. "A major undertaking."

"Up to you," Rina said. "If it involves too much, we'll keep looking."

"Could you live in this place?"

"As is?"

"As is with another bathroom."

She shrugged. "In Israel, this would be considered a luxury apartment."

"First of all, we're not in Israel," Decker said. "Second, I saw some of the apartments there, darlin'. They had granite and marble."

"I could manage," Rina said. "But eventually, we'd have to have another bedroom." She looked at the worn cupboards. "And a decent kitchen. Can you save any of the cabinetry?"

He examined the doors, gave them a gentle cuff. "I could save it all. This is solid stuff."

"What do you think?"

"With enough elbow grease, it could be something." Decker rolled his shoulders. "Now I could get another bathroom in within . . . oh, a month or so. But the rest . . . the kitchen, another bedroom, expanding the master bedroom if you could call it that." He exhaled. "It's going to take time. My Sundays'll be booked for the next year."

"Too much for you?"

"No, I don't mind," Decker said. "I was thinking about you—and Hannah. Cooped up with a little kid running around."

Rina said, "But, she's in school during the day. And when she's not, there's the yard. It's smaller than you're used to . . . but isn't it beautiful?"

"Yes, it is nice."

Decker's beeper went off. Rina frowned. "Can't you disconnect that thing?"

"It would only come back to haunt me." He looked at the number. "It's Narc's extension." He took out the portable phone. "Niels, it's Decker. What's up?"

"You still looking for that kid, Malcolm Carey?"

"Absolutely."

"Call just came through. Westbridge is having a big party hearty scene at some kid's house. Parents are out of town. Starts around nine tonight. Call said Malcolm should be there with his pharmacy."

Decker felt a jolt. Joachim had actually come *through*. His beeper went off again—Marge. To Niels he said, "Start setting up operations. I'm sending over Bert Martinez and Tom Webster to coordinate with you. It's your baby, but I want Malcolm Carey."

"He's all yours."

"I'll clear it with the captain, then get back to you."

"Got it."

Decker hung up, called Marge. She said, "Guess what?"

"Joachim called. There's going to be a drug party." A pause. "He just called Narc. They got to me first."

"Joachim called Narc?" Marge was surprised. "Kid's real thorough."

"Apparently. Was Joachim invited to this shindig?"

"He said it was an open-invitation bash."

"So his presence shouldn't be missed."

"Probably not," Marge said. "Who's coordinating with Narc?"

"Bert Martinez and Tom Webster. That leaves you and Oliver to pull the warrant for the house and Malcolm's car if we're lucky enough to hit pay dirt. Who's on the bench?"

"Randall."

"Yeah, he's fine." Decker paused, trying to keep excitement out of his voice. "I just have to clear the whole thing with Strapp—"

"You haven't talked to Strapp yet?"

"Why would I have talked to him about it? I had no idea if Joachim would produce. It's only been two, three weeks since we talked to him."

"Something like that."

"I'll ring up Strapp right now."

A long pause. "Pete, I think he's at the tennis tournament."

A knife went through Decker's gut. "That's right. I'll catch him there."

"How about if I go—"

"No need."

"Pete, I think it would be—"

"Gotta go, Marge." He disconnected the line.

Rina said, "Joachim called?"

"Yes."

She smiled. "That's good news, isn't it?"

"Yes, very good."

She hesitated. "You don't look happy."

"I've got to okay the procedure with Strapp. Right now, he's probably gliding into his seat at Jeanine Garrison's wheelchair tennis tournament. Twenty bucks gets you into the place, a hundred lets you have a decent view, and a thousand puts you courtside. FYI, the arena is sold out."

Decker gave a bitter grin.

"But Strapp don't have to worry none. He's been comped."

A cloudless November day, the deep blue sky engulfing the L.A. basin with a gentle autumn kiss. Even though most of the deciduous trees had lost their leaves, the area still sparkled emerald from the perennial landscape and blades of freshly planted lawn. The West Hills Sports Center stood in the middle of parklike grounds.

Even with the official badge and placard, Decker stalled in the event's traffic. Though spacious, the center was not built to host major tennis tournaments. But Jeanine had done a fine job on short notice, setting up tiers of portable bleachers around a central court. He parked in a space marked LOADING ZONE, walked over to the gates, and showed the attendant his badge. She gave it a moment of her time, then allowed him to enter.

As people poured in, Decker's eyes swept across the

scene. The space outside the arena's seating was filled with kiosks. Some were stacked with memorabilia— T-shirts, sweatshirts, visors, sunglasses, and wristbands, all of the items emblazoned with the title TENNIS FOR VICTIMS. Others hawked all types of ethnic comestibles. Diners munched their grub either standing up or sitting on folding chairs beside tables.

His eyes moved back outside, to the parking lot, to a roped-off and guarded area of trailers. Eight of them partnered two by two. The athletes' dressing rooms. Directly in front of the barrier was a crowd of reporters, photographers, and lookie-loos.

Decker thought a moment.

Extremely unlikely that Strapp was holed up inside a trailer. That whole business was really none of *his* business. But curiosity got the better of him. He left the arena through one of the makeshift gates, waded through the throng of fans, and presented his badge to one of the minimum-wage security guards who asked the usual question: What was this all about? Decker evaded with the stock reply of police business. Then he ducked behind the ropes.

Shingles posted on the vans. Names of well-known figures in the game, some of them seeded players. Jeanine had pulled out all the stops. Ramps instead of steps led up to the trailers' doors, which were also guarded. Some of the sentries stood, others were seated in wheelchairs. The paraplegic watchman stared at Decker, said nothing as Decker fast-walked past him. Turned the corner, squeezing between the backs of trailers. Took a step into the seam, then immediately retreated, his heart flying in his chest.

And there they were . . . Jeanine and Sean. Cautiously, Decker peeked around the corner, observing them with intense eyes, trying to interpret the body language.

It wasn't the tongue of love.

Jeanine    looking    away . . . peeved . . . bored. Hands on her hips, foot tapping. Sean talked with his hands . . . with his arms, the appendages flying as his face grew redder. His voice became louder, faster. Still Decker couldn't make out words. Only the sentiment. An argument.

Wishing he were a fly on the wall. He backed up, trying to find a way to get closer. A wheelchair-bound guard stopped him, asked for ID.

Decker took out his badge, which did little to erase suspicion from the watchman's face. The man adjusted his frame in his metal transportation and began the questions. Decker never got a chance to answer because Jeanine had suddenly appeared sans Sean. Frantically, Decker attempted to arrange his thoughts, tried not to stare.

She was as lovely as ever, dressed for the nip of fall in a long-sleeved white shirt that sat under a gray wool blazer and black slacks. The collar of her jacket had been turned up. Golden hair framing porcelain skin. Aqua eyes passed over his face. Quietly she said, "May I ask what you're doing here?"

Decker managed to hold her eyes. "I'm looking for my captain."

"Obviously he's not here."

The guard said, "Everything all right, Ms. Garrison?"

Jeanine's smile was benevolent. "Just fine, Brock. You can let us be."

Decker began to walk away. "I'm out of here."

Jeanine followed. "I'll be happy to escort you—"

"Not necessary." Decker picked up his pace. But Jeanine continued to dog his heels.

"Would you like a seat for the match, Lieutenant? I'd be happy to arrange it." She grabbed his arm, forcing him to stop. A teasing smile on her face. "After all, we're no longer enemies."

*That's what you think, lady.* Decker looked at her hand, gently but pointedly removed it from his forearm. Her touch made his skin crawl. "No thank you."

Jeanine grinned, showing teeth. "His seat is located off aisle four, courtside. Are you sure I can't cajole you to change your mind?"

Decker said nothing, jogged off without looking back. Sweating from the interchange. Nobody had a right to affect him like that. Embarrassed. Angry.

He came back into the arena, now in the final frenetic moments before the event. The anticipation. Tennis talk. Celebrity talk. He made his way to the front rows as cameras flashed, blinding him with bits of light. Not for him, of course, but for the dozens of film and TV stars who had shown up wearing black solidarity ribbons.

Ostensibly for the victims of a very horrendous crime. Yet where were the survivors?

Not the biggest names in Hollywood. But not too shabby either. A couple of stars from a top-rated TV doctor drama, a sexy blonde who played a detective in a cop show, three of a sextet who starred as young but neurotic single/swingles in a weekly cast-driven comedy. Supporting actors and actresses. Drinking bubbly, laughing heartily. And smiling those famous smiles as adoring fans hounded them for autographs.

A tremendous affair for a quiet place like the Valley.

Decker's eyes continued to dust the crowd, falling on twenty or so elderly character actors—men in their seventies and eighties, as aged and weathered as the cowboys they once had portrayed. Sucking on unlit cigars, laughing and hacking about old-time mishaps.

Friends of Walter Skinner.

But Decker couldn't find the widow anywhere. He scanned the crowd, shaded his eyes with his hands until he saw another group sitting a couple of aisles away. They also wore solidarity ribbons, yet they sat unmolested by well-wishers and the press.

The survivors . . . friends and relatives of the victims. Far from being part of the gaiety, they looked out of place—tense, nervous, and angry. Yet they chose to make an appearance. Decker made his way to their seats. Tess instantly stood up to shake Decker's hand. She said, "I was hoping you'd be here." She turned to another woman. "Carol, this is Lieutenant Decker. He's the one who fixed up my leg."

Carol was Carol Anger—the waitress who had suffered a gunshot wound to the arm. Though the limb was no longer confined to a sling, she still held it close to her body. She stood, shook Decker's hand, her face suffused with hostility. "Nice that the police made an appearance."

Decker said, "My captain should be here."

"Well, he's *not* here—"

"Carol, please!" a big man interrupted. He introduced himself to Decker, extended his hand. "Olaf Anderson."

Decker took the hand. "You were one of Estelle's chefs."

"Yes, sir, I *am* one of them."

"The place reopened, I hear."

"Yes. Very busy . . . busier than ever. Customers are . . . curious."

"You mean ghoulish!" Carol shot out.

"Carol, don't be so cross." Tess sighed, looked around. "What a scene!"

Carol said, "Like one big party. As if these dingalings—including *her*—give a hoot."

Tess said, "Carol, don't be so mad. She's doing good stuff and she's not taking a dime—"

"She doesn't need it," Carol broke in. "You might think she'd at least come over and say hello. After all, she lost her parents—"

"People mourn in different ways." Tess looked at Decker. "You must think we're awful. Being so mad and all."

Carol said, "You're not mad. *I* am."

Decker said, "An ordeal like Estelle's would turn anyone into a cynic."

The waitress faced Decker. "Maybe your captain had something more important to do. Something like . . . like a *budget* meeting?"

Decker said, "How's your arm, Ms. Anger?"

Immediately the woman loosened her grip on her limb. "It's fine."

"You look like you're in lots of pain."

"I'm *fine*!"

"Even if it feels like agony, you should try to move it. Keeping it tight against your body like you do . . . the muscles stiffen up. If you can remember, rotate your arm every hour or so. And don't forget the Advil or Aleve. If that doesn't cut it, ask your doc for something *stronger*. You don't seem like the addictive type, so don't be shy—"

"I'm not shy about anything!" Carol countered.

"This is the truth!" Olaf said.

The waitress studied Decker's face. "You've been shot?"

Decker nodded.

"In the line of duty?"

Again, Decker nodded. "Hardly the same circumstances."

"You bleed just the same."

Decker smiled. "Yes, you do."

A woman butted in. "What's going on down here?"

Carol said, "This is Lieutenant Decker. He was at . . . at the scene."

The brash woman stuck out her hand. Petite with short dark hair and penetrating eyes. "Brenda Miller. Nice to meet you."

Brenda was cute. No wonder Scott Oliver had liked her. Decker took the proffered hand. "You're from Ashman/Reynard Realty . . . Wendy Culligan's boss, correct?"

Brenda jerked her head back. "Someone prep you?"

Decker smiled. "I'm good with names. Is Wendy here?"

Brenda cocked her thumb upward a couple of rows. Decker's eyes climbed with her finger, rested upon a frail woman. "She lost a lot of weight."

Brenda said. "That's what happens when you don't eat."

"Who's next to her? Is that Adelaide Skinner?"

"Yeah."

"Maybe I'll go over and give them my regards."

"Better if you left Wendy alone. She's still . . ." Brenda extended her fingers, rocked her wrist back and forth.

"I'm sorry to hear that," Decker said.

"She should take lessons from the Garrison lady." Brenda raised her brows. "Man, that woman knows how to party."

"Photo op, photo op," Carol mimicked.

Tess sighed, shook her head. "What a mob!" She smiled tearfully at Decker. "Wanna know the real sad part, Lieutenant? Kenny woulda loved this . . . just woulda ate it up. Anything that made him feel special."

Brenda said, "Have a seat, Lieutenant. Tell me something. How's Detective Oliver?"

"He's fine—"

"I said sit down," Brenda said. "That means you've got to bend the knees."

"I can't stay—"

"Doughnut break calling?" Carol said.

Tess chided, "Stop being so rude to him. He's the reason I'm walking today."

Carol became quiet, sullen. Decker said, "I'm very sorry I can't stay. But I'll be happy to meet with any of you—anytime, anyplace, anywhere. Just give me a little advance notice, that's all."

Olaf said, "We tank you for your offer very much."

No one spoke. Decker said, "Honestly, I don't know why Captain Strapp isn't here. You people were the *only* reason he had chosen to come."

"Obviously we just weren't that important!" Carol barked.

"On the contrary." Decker took out a portable phone and dialed Strapp's house. A few minutes later, he cut the line, paused, looking down at his feet. He said, "I just spoke to his wife. He's sick at home with the flu—"

*"Right!"* Carol said.

Decker said. "If she says he's sick, the man is bedridden. Trust me on this one."

Again, Carol studied him. "Why do I believe you? I don't *want* to believe you."

Decker said, "You're clenching your arm again."

Carol dropped her arm. "Why can't you stay?"

Decker said, "I have a very *pressing* matter. So pressing, I'm going to drag the captain from his sickbed." He shook hands all around. "I know money's not compensation for human life. But none of you should have to worry about paying the bills. I hope the games raise lots of cash."

"It would help." Tess paused. "I got the job, you know."

Carol said, "You did! When?"

Olaf said, "That's great, Tess! Congratulations."

"No big deal. Just answering phones. But it's better than nothing. And it's simple, too. So I can study for my real estate license when it's quiet." She looked at Brenda. "If the offer's still open."

Brenda said, "Of course. It's an open-ended offer." She stalled a moment. "So how is Detective Oliver anyway?"

"He's fine, Ms. Miller. I'll tell him you send regards."

"Do that." She sighed. "I've got to get back to Wendy."

"Give both Wendy and Adelaide Skinner my best."

Carol said, "I'll walk you out."

"Not necessary."

"I know that. I'll do it anyway."

The two of them left, walking silently as they steered through the stars, fans, and cameras on their way out. Then, as if conjured up by a demon, Jeanine appeared, the smile on her face widening when she saw Carol and Decker. Immediately, she wedged herself between them, linking her arms around theirs. She bubbled, "Photo op!"

A Nikon clicked and flashed.

Decker jerked away from Jeanine's hold, grabbed the camera, slapped open the back cover, and yanked out the roll of film, exposing it to the light.

The photographer was irate. "Da *fuck'er* you doing?"

Decker handed him back the camera, reached into his wallet. Four ones, two fives, and a hundred-dollar bill. He stuffed the Franklin into the photographer's hand.

To a shocked Jeanine, he said, "If you ever, *ever* touch me again, I'll sue you for assault. Like I should have done the first time. And notice that I'm talking in front of witnesses."

He stalked off, forgetting about Carol until she called out to him. He stopped abruptly, took a deep breath, let it out slowly. She was panting by the time she reached him. She breathed out, "Are you okay?"

Decker counted to ten, said, "I'm sorry for stomping off like that. Are you all right?"

"Winded but fine."

Decker shook the waitress's hand. "Call me in a couple of weeks. Let me know how you're doing. Enjoy the matches."

Carol stared at him. "Lieutenant, what was that all about?"

"Not important."

The waitress smiled. For the first time today, it seemed genuine. "You hate her guts, don't you?"

Decker was quiet.

Carol said, "Seems we have more in common than just a bullet in the arm. C'mon, Lieutenant. You've got me curious. What's going on?"

"Talk to me in a couple of weeks."

"That's the *best* you can do?"

"For now, that's all I have to say."

"You sound like you're taking the Fifth."

"It's a good amendment." Decker started to walk off. "Not a bad commandment either."

Carol remained rooted as she yelled out to him. "What *is* the fifth commandment anyway?"

"To honor your parents," Decker shouted as he trotted off. "Go do God a favor. Call up your mom."

# ❧ 35

*The woman stepped* aside, let Decker in. He said, "How are you, Susan?"

She cocked her hip. A tall, shapely woman with auburn hair and bright green eyes. She wore a white blouse, denim capris, and flats. "He's got a hundred-and-three-degree fever. He says you cursed him."

Decker smiled. "I think the fever's gone to his brain. I do need to talk to him."

"He's dressing . . . going to the tournament." Susan eyed him. "I don't suppose you could talk him out of it."

"Me?"

"He respects you."

Decker waited a beat. "How about if I drive him?"

Susan said, "He doesn't need a chauffeur, he needs rest."

Strapp walked into the room, his complexion ghostly, with a sweaty sheen. He had on a black jacket, a turtleneck sweater, and wool slacks. Boots on his feet. Still he shivered. He viewed Decker through sunken eyes. "Marge just called here. She was looking for you. Something about a kid named Joachim Rush who called her. What the hell is going on?"

"I'll tell you on the way over to the tournament, sir. How about a lift?"

Susan scolded, "No shop talk on Sunday."

"This better be important," the captain groused.

"Just ignore me," Susan muttered.

Decker said, "Yes, sir, it's very important." To Susan, he said, "I'll take care of him."

Susan shook her head, adjusted her husband's collar, and kissed his cheek. "Try to make it home in one piece, Strapp."

He kissed her back. To Decker, he said, "Let's go."

Strapp said, "Who's pulling the warrants?"

The light turned green. Decker depressed the accelerator. The Volare shot out. "Dunn and Oliver."

"For where? The party house?"

"The party house, Malcolm Carey's car—"

"How about Carey's house?"

"We don't have enough probable cause to justify a search. After we've pinned something on Malcolm, then I figure we can move to the house. I've got the papers written up, just waiting a signature."

Decker tapped the wheel nervously.

"If things go well, we shouldn't have a problem nailing them. I told Webster and Martinez to hold off with Narcotics until you'd okayed the operation. They're waiting to hear. Sir, I'd like to move on this as quickly as possible—"

Strapp interrupted, "Give me the damn mike."

"Thank you—"

Strapp cut him off with a wave of the hand. Phoned Narcotics and gave permission. Then he handed Decker the mike. "You're clear." He coughed into a tissue. "You got me in a weakened state, you son of a bitch. Otherwise, I'd really be pissed at you."

He paused.

"You'd better pray Joachim is legit. Which brings up another point. Last I heard the kid was a suspect."

"Not anymore. We've cleared him."

"How'd you get the info on him?"

"What do you think? I hired out."

"You spent from your *own* wallet?"

"With my own blood, sweat, and tears." Decker gripped the wheel. "I hope it pans out. If not, we nail a pusher. Good PR if nothing else."

"Also makes us the target of some very rich parents," Strapp complained. "Fuck them. They start making noise, we tell them to keep their own houses in order first. Slow down. Your driving is making me nauseous. You put the whammy on me, you son of a bitch."

Decker said, "Me?"

"Telling me not to show up at the tournament. Telling me to get myself sick . . . to come down with the flu. You help it along with some voodoo dolls?"

Decker smiled, then grew serious. "For what it's worth, Captain, you were right. LAPD did have an obligation to the survivors to show up at the tournament." He sighed. "No matter who sponsored it."

"Swell," Strapp grumped. "In the meantime, I'm feeling like a truck ran over me and you're decking photographers—"

"I didn't deck anyone." He paused. "We'll ignore the pun—"

"Nor do I like your shit fit in front of Jeanine."

"Sir, the photographer isn't going to make noise. I slipped him a hundred . . . in front of witnesses."

"You hire out from your own pocket, you slip some jerk a C-spot in exchange for a roll of film. . . ."

Nobody talked for a moment. Then Strapp said, "Were you planning to interview Malcolm Carey? Because, technically, you're off this case."

"Look, sir, you want to keep me off Estelle's, do that. This isn't about Estelle's, it's about David Garrison."

Decker organized his thoughts. "I realize we have to keep the chain letter going to make this work. Using the busts to get something on Malcolm Carey. Then using Malcolm Carey to get to Sean Amos. Lastly, Sean to get to Jeanine. And then, if we're extremely lucky, maybe . . . just maybe, we'll be able to bring charges against her."

"For her brother's murder only," Strapp said. "Nothing about Estelle's."

"Right. We have nothing to tie her to that . . . so far."

"Maybe she didn't do it," Strapp said.

"Okay. Assume that Estelle's was the sole work of Harlan Manz. Could be that after her parents died, she got greedy. Fine. If that's the case, then we'll box her for the one murder—"

"Of which you have no proof other than rumors."

"Even if the rumors don't play out, we'll have busted a pusher. And if they do play out . . . if she took out her brother, using Malcolm to pump poison into David's veins . . . let her fry."

Strapp shook his head. "Greed. Gets 'em every time."

* * *

For a wild party, things seemed subdued. A couple of dozen cars outside, distant thrash metal music leaking from the windows, an occasional yelp and fit of laughter. No kids heaving on the lawn, no untamed screams of abandon, nothing to suggest a *scene*. Narcotics didn't like it. But something intuitive kept Decker calm, confident.

The hard part had been getting the vehicles inside the gated Community without arousing suspicion. The cars had filtered in slowly to their prearranged spots. Staggered around the streets to make it look more natural. Clandestine meeting places for foot patrol. Waiting for the signal. Waiting to raid.

Quiet streets. Dim lights guarding sinews of private roadway. Lots of black patches amid gray forms. The target was a two-story Colonial sitting on a hill of grass. Magnolia trees cast gnarled shadows. Muted lights coming through the windows. They'd have to move fast. Narc would handle the entry, the initial busts. Decker's team would come in for arrests, evidence, and cleanup.

And Malcolm Carey belonged to him.

The countdown. The signal. The sudden spurt of activity. Officers running, pounding on the doors. Identification.

"Police! Open up!"

The ensuing shouts, the screams, the dull thuds of wood splintering as the hand-held ram butted against the locked door. The final shove. And then they were in.

Decker closed his eyes, prayed. Atavistic response.

But at least it was proactive. He counted to one hundred, sprinted over, charged into the house.

Eyes skittering across the room. A dozen teens sprawled out on the floor, several boys attempting to bolt out windows and through back doors. Hauled in by agents, pinned against the walls.

The screaming.

The crying.

The smell of fresh piss.

A sofa table holding cellophane bags of powder, scattered loose pills, and brown clumps of rock crystal. A hookah oozing fumes. Used needles on the floor along with several handguns for good measure.

Thank you, Joachim.

Thank you, God!

Dashing through the house, Decker shouted, "Where's Malcolm Carey? I need Malcolm Carey!"

Two loud pops.

Gunfire.

Someone grabbed his arm.

Marge shouted, "Upstairs bathroom."

"Christ!"

They raced up the stairs, just as the bathroom door caved in. A body halfway through the second-story window, another figure desperately stuffing junk down the toilet. Narcs pulled him down first—to the ground, kicking open his legs, jerking his hands behind his back, intoning Miranda as they secured him for arrest. He wasn't the challenge. He melted like ice cream in the Sahara.

Decker's eyes went to the floor, to the white face. "Hello, Sean."

The kid retched, gagged. Decker said, "Turn his head to the side. Don't let him aspirate. And careful with his hands. I want them paraffin-tested. See if he fired the revolver—"

"I swear, I didn't shoot—"

His words were drowned out by screams.

The body out the window.

Officers trying to grab on to a set of kicking legs. Fighting with all their strength. The sounds emitted. Animal sounds. Grunts, growls, snarls. Agents sweating as they tried to pull his body back through the window and into the bathroom. As if reeling in the big one. Too bad no one had a gaff. Among the group was Niels Van Gelder, the detective who had called Decker earlier in the day. Big bull of a guy with big hands. All six of them talking at once.

Niels shouted, "Anyone find the gun?"

"Watch the hands! Watch the fucking hands!"

"No gun?"

"Watch the *fucking* hands—"

"Slow, slow . . . slow down!"

"Is he packing—"

"Does he have anything in his hands?" Niels asked.

"It's dark, man. Can't see a fucking thing—"

"Look at the hands!"

"Careful—"

"If you stick your hand out—"

"You wearing a vest, Condor?"

"Yeah, I'm covered."

Condor was Arnold Myerhoff. Five eight, one seventy, and bald. Five years with L.A. Narc, ten years prior with Miami Narc. He grunted, "Someone grab the fucker's arm while I hold the legs—"

"I can't see—"

"Watch your face. Pull back—"

"Go for the arms. The arms. You got the arm?"

Silence.

"Got it?"

"I . . . got it."

"Yank it inside—"

"It's in a bad position. Don't want to break the suck—"

"Just pull it inside, Marc."

Marc Kirby, a fifteen-year veteran Narcotics officer, pulled an empty fist into the room.

Niels said, "Now get the other hand so we can pull—"

"Check the pockets—"

"Hold this hand while I get the other—"

"Shit, bastard's trying to scratch me—"

"Wrap the hand up, Marc."

"In what?"

"Just push it up his back."

"Got the other arm?"

"No."

"Got it?"

"Yeaaaa . . . got it!"

"The hand, the hand—"

Finally, Marc brought up a second empty fist.

"*All right!*" Condor called out. "Pull the fucker up!"

First came the legs, then the torso, then the face.

A feral face. The mouth opened, a gaping hole, like a snake unhinging his jaws.

Decker screamed, "He's gonna bite!"

Marc jerked his face away, swore as he looped his arm around Malcolm's neck.

Coiled muscles popping from the teen's neck. Arms as stiff as wood. He continued to kick and flail, tried in vain to land punches using anything he had—including his head. Though he didn't have a chance against six grown adults, he fought as if he did. The ear-piercing screeches resonated throughout the room as the body was brought onto the floor.

And then it was over, the kid was down. Cuffed and shackled.

Decker recognized the boy. "Yo, Malcolm. What's up, dude?"

The kid's shriek seemed to emanate from his bowels.

Decker said, "Who's doing the booking?"

"Yo," Condor answered.

Decker said, "Arnie, before either one is washed down, paraffin-test the hands to see who fired."

"Where *is* the gun?"

"Fucker probably dropped it."

A sudden stench filled the small room. Decker looked down at Sean Amos's soiled pants. The kid had lost total control.

Niels said, "Who wants to play plumber in the john?"

"It's Gayola's turn," Marc stated.

Gayola Weyman was six one, one eighty, with a size-sixteen neck. Her specialty was hand-to-hand combat. She started gloving up. Malcolm screamed again.

"Will someone shut him up?"

Condor said, "Man, it *stinks* in here."

To Decker, Marge said, "I'll go look for the gun.

Maybe he dropped it on the lawn while he was out there hanging."

Marc searched through Malcolm's pockets. "Got a nice packet of powder . . . two of them—"

Gayola moaned. "God, the toilet's backing up—"

"All the shit thrown inside. Might be needles there. You double-glove?"

"I double-gloved." Gayola stuck her hand down the plumbing, brought up the first load. Looked it over. A couple of packets of rock crystal, some packets of milky liquid—powder diluted by water. She went down for a second dip, brought up some melting pills and crinkled paper.

"What in the world is *this*?"

"What?" Decker asked.

Gayola handed Decker several crumpled, toilet-soaked glossy pictures, a sheet streaked with runny ink.

Decker smoothed out the snapshots. Neck-up portraits. Familiar face. It took a few moments to give it a name.

Wade Anthony.

"What the hell?" Decker looked at the paper, eyes scanning the writing. Appeared to be someone's schedule, the activities listed by the hours.

*1. Eight o'clock: wakes up, dresses, eats breakfast, reads the paper.*

*2. Ten until two . . . tennis practice.* Next to the line was an address. Four, seven . . . maybe a five or a two. With the runny ink it was hard to tell. The street name was clear.

*3. Two to four P.M. . . . . in the spa, then physical therapy.*

Gayola brought up another picture of Anthony. This one was a full body shot. He was sitting on a couch, looking quite content, smoking a big fat stogie. A nice picture except for the dart board bleeding ink over the snapshot. A big red heart drawn over the chest was the bull's-eye.

Suddenly the events of the day came into knife-edge focus. Decker grinned. Couldn't have planned it better had he tried.

Malcolm screamed once more.

Decker said, "Take them back in separate cars. Separate bookings, separate cells, and separate lawyers. No interchange between them. And don't forget about the hands."

To Condor, Marc said, "You want the screamer or the shitter?"

"I'll take the shitter."

Decker said, "Arnie, after you paraffin his hands, give him some jail rags and let the kid clean himself up before you book him. Let him have his shred of dignity."

# ❧ 36

*Savvy kids.*

They all immediately asked for lawyers.

*No prob, man. Just need to take your picture first.*

The station house had become a riot of activity. Twenty-one arrested as pounds of pharmaceuticals were bagged and checked into evidence. The firearms were entered separately. A mammoth-sized bust—children from some very high-powered families. Narcotics was elated. Parents were outraged. Throughout it all, Decker just did his job.

Not nearly enough cell space at Devonshire so the kids were transferred immediately to Van Nuys for booking and arraignment. Between the paperwork, cataloging, and car-pooling, Decker didn't get to Malcolm Carey until hours later, about one in the morning. He brought Marge with him for backup.

Decker found the formerly out-of-control teen sitting comfortably, slouching in his chair, dressed in jail blues. He sipped water, smoked a cigarette. A square face, sporting patches of beard growth. A high forehead, strong jaw-line. Thin arched eyebrows. Pecan-colored hair clipped close to the scalp.

Dull blue eyes. Still, they weren't completely expressionless—not like the eyes of hardened cons. That would come later on.

Since Malcolm was of age, his parents had been excluded from the interview. But Dad had sent along his best wishes in the form of Rupert Flame—a fifty-plus criminal defense attorney, whose haircut budget equaled a month of Decker's salary. He was of medium build, gray hair, brown eyes, ruddy face with the wet complexion of the recently shaved. He wore a superbly tailored double-breasted navy nailhead suit.

Decker took his seat, exchanged glances with Marge, both of them waiting for the lawyer to begin.

Flame said, "He's a kid—"

"Over eighteen," Marge corrected. "Birthday was two months ago."

"He isn't what you're after."

"What are we after?"

Flame said, "You want the big guys, offer me something. He doesn't talk until you lay something on the table."

Decker said, "You know what we have your client on, Mr. Flame?"

"I know what you have—"

"In order of severity, we've booked him on two counts of attempted murder of police officers—"

"Man, I thought you were robbers," Malcolm broke in.

"Mal, we *clearly* identified ourselves," Decker said.

"I didn't hear—"

"Malcolm, you mowed down the door with a semi-automatic," Marge said. "And you did fire the gun. Paraffin tests don't lie."

Flame said, "He was panic-stricken, Detective. His judgment was less than ideal."

Decker said, "Twenty counts of selling illegal substances. Five counts of possession—"

"I was framed, man. The Narcs put the envelopes in my pocket—"

"One count of resisting arrest. Two counts felony reckless discharge of a firearm, not to mention one felony possession of a firearm."

"Nobody likes a pusher," Marge turned to the kid. "Mal . . . can I call you Mal?"

The teen smirked, "You can call me sweetheart—"

"Lieutenant, listen to me. Malcolm *is* over eighteen. But emotionally, he's still a *child*, a dumb kid—"

"A basic retard," Carey broke in.

Flame snapped, "Unless you want your asshole reamed, buddy boy, you shut your mouth!"

Surprisingly, the kid blushed, turned quiet.

Flame took a deep breath, said, "He has a big mouth as you can see. Dumb and brash with a big mouth. But just bark, he turns into a lamb." The lawyer kept Malcolm silent with a stony look. "Just rolls over and takes the beating. And that was what happened to him, Lieutenant. He started selling to be a big man on campus. Nothing heavy . . . maybe just a few joints of marijuana—"

"A regular saint—"

"We concede that the boy sold marijuana on his own. But within a few weeks, he was in *way* over his head, Lieutenant. He got involved with the *wrong* people. People you don't mess with if you want to breathe."

"Uh-huh," Decker said. "Meanwhile, he's racking up a grand or two a month."

"The money wasn't the reason he pushed," Flame said. "Yes, Malcolm continued to push. We concede that as well. But *not* because he wanted to play Mr. Big Shot. He sold only to prevent some foreign animal from cutting off his dick and stuffing it down his throat."

Marge said, "I see. He was *coerced* into making two thou a month. Slick defense, Counselor."

"It's the *truth*, Detective," Flame insisted. "When Malcolm tried to stop, he was threatened. Stalked. Even beaten. We have proof of that."

"Uh-huh," Decker said.

Flame leaned in close. "He's a pawn, not what you and Narc are after."

Decker said, "Actually, Malcolm is *exactly* what I'm after."

"You're missing the big picture," Flame replied. "We can give you names, Lieutenant. Make you and Narcotics very, *very* happy. Just give us something to work with."

"I want to talk about Sean Amos," Marge stated.

Flame was taken aback. "Sean Amos?"

"The kid who was with Malcolm when we took him down." Decker's eyes shifted to the teen. "He's sitting in a cell as we speak. I haven't talked to him yet. But that can be remedied—"

Flame broke in. "What are you talking about?"

Decker said, "Specifically? The pictures Amos

tried to flush down the toilet. What was the deal, Mal? Things flew so well first time out, you decided to do a repeat?"

Flame's face was the picture of confusion. Malcolm turned pale, said nothing. But he was no longer smirking.

Flame stumbled, "Lieutenant, what are you *getting* at?"

Decker said, "Ask your client."

"Then give me a minute with my client."

"You take your minute now, you might as well make it an hour. Because you know what I'm going to do, Counselor? I'm going to talk to Sean Amos. He wants to go state's witness against your client—instead of the other way around—it's fine with me—"

"State's witness?" Flame stuttered out.

"He's bluffing," Carey blurted. "He's bullshitting—"

Decker lied, "I never bluff. I never bullshit. I want Sean Amos's head, Malcolm. Either his or yours. So either you talk or we'll talk to him."

Marge said, "You talk to us now, Mal, maybe we can cut you a deal with the DA. You play mute, then Sean'll do your talking for you—"

Flame cut in. "If you're planning to bring new charges against my client, you have to come clean. You can't conceal evidence."

"I'm not concealing anything," Decker said. "Counselor, we're not at the discovery phase of this case because as yet, I haven't charged him—"

"Lieutenant, you hold back, you're in procedural error. Which messes up your entire case."

"Now you got me quaking."

"What are you *talking* about?"

Decker said, "We're planning to charge your client and Sean Amos in a murder-for-hire scheme—"

"*What!*" Flame glared at Carey. "I thought you said you told me *everything*!"

The teen started to speak, instead looked down and stubbed out his cigarette.

Marge said, "The intended victim is a man named Wade Anthony. That's why there were pictures of Anthony stuffed down the toilet along with Anthony's daily schedule—"

Flame stuttered, "Who is Wade Anthony?"

"A paraplegic tennis player."

Flame said to Carey, "Do you know this Wade Anthony?"

Carey whispered, "He's talking shit."

"Actually, it was probably Sean Amos's idea," Decker went on. "He felt that Wade had stolen away his girlfriend. Looks like Sean got desparate, was in the process of hiring your client as a hit man when the bust went down."

"We hadn't agreed on anything yet," Malcolm said to Decker.

"Shut up!" Flame ordered.

Coolly, Carey said, "Can I just talk for a moment?"

"No, you may not!" Flame ordered.

Malcolm discounted his counsel. "Since when is it against the law to talk about things? Even things like murder? I mean, how many times have you said you'd like to kill someone?"

"It's isn't against the law to talk," Decker said, "but it is against the law to *contract*. More important, it's against the law to *act* on that contract. And you've climbed that mountain before, son. In the form of sticking dope into people's veins. And we both know what I'm talking about."

The teen blanched.

"What are you *talking* about, Lieutenant?" Flame asked.

Marge said, "If Sean drops first, you go home without a pot to piss in."

The boy stumbled, "You have no proof—"

"We have fingerprints," Decker lied.

"That's fucking *impossible*! I used glov—"

"*Shut up!*"

The room fell quiet.

Decker went on. "Not to mention the dragon we collected from you, Malcolm. It has the exact same gas chromatography spectrum as the heroin pumped into David Garrison's veins. Know what the odds are of that, son?"

"Evidence doesn't lie," Marge fibbed.

"Who's David Garrison?" Flame demanded.

The teen broke out in a sweat. "You're trying to freak me out—"

Marge interrupted, "Sean or you, Malcolm?"

Flame stood up. "Before you two go *any* further, I need to consult with my client. Obviously, we're in a different league now."

"We don't have all night," Decker said.

Marge said, "And Sean's awaiting—"

"No!" Carey protested.

"I insist that I converse with my client privately." Flame's voice had become as wound up as a catapult. "But, please, I am asking both of you to hold off talking to this other party. Just give me a few minutes."

"You know what? I'll give you five of them." Decker

started for the door, turned around, looked at his watch. "Starting now."

Outrage was stamped across the defense lawyer's face. But he maintained an even voice. To counteract Flame, Decker had brought in Morton Weller—a man who had packed in over twenty years with the DA's office. Scrawny, with a narrow face, deep-set eyes, and a long neck bisected by the node of an Adam's apple. White downy fuzz sat atop his head. He had on a gray single-breasted suit, white shirt, and red tie. He shook hands with Flame, sat down.

Calmly, Flame said, "Give me a show of good faith."

Weller scratched his ear. "No death penalty—"

Carey screamed, "Fuck that! I didn't kill anybody!"

"Malcolm, calm down. He's trying to rile you."

"I assure you, Rup—"

Flame talked over him. "You want me to start, Mort, I'll start. For turning witness, you drop everything except the murder two. Twenty-five with a minimum of five years—"

Carey screamed. "I'm not going to *jail* for five years!"

Decker said, "Penitentiary, Malcolm. Not jail."

Weller said, "Murder one, life—"

"No—"

"*With* possibility of parole—"

"I'll take my chances on a jury." Flame stood.

Weller said, "Rup, be reasonable. How can I deal effectively unless I hear what your client has to say?"

Flame said, "You take a chance here or take a chance with a jury."

Decker said, "Murder two, twenty-five to life, minimum fifteen years—"

"Seven," Flame said.

Weller said, "Counselor, he'd get a harsher sentence from the drug charges alone."

"Not after I finished with the jury."

Weller said, "Murder two, twenty-five to life, minimum twelve—"

"Seven."

Decker said, "Now he's bluffing. Morton, I *know* I can get the other kids to turn against him—"

Flame interrupted. "Murder two only, twenty-five to life, seven minimum before possibility of parole, no time off for good behavior. Do we have a deal or not?"

Morton and Decker traded glances. The assistant DA nodded.

Carey banged the table. "No way I'm spending *seven* years in jail!"

Decker said, "Penitentiary."

"Fuck you!"

"And it may even be longer than seven—"

Flame shot out, "Malcolm, you refuse, they talk to your friend and *he* takes the deal. Then look at what you have. The same evidence, the same charges against you . . . except now they have a witness to back up a first-degree murder charge. You want me to go to court with Sean Amos as state's witness, I'll take the money. But you'd better believe in miracles, son, because that's what you're going to need."

The room became silent. Flame broke it. "We'll take the offer."

This time the teen didn't argue. All eyes went to him.

"Go on," Flame said. "The worst is over. You have nothing to lose. Tell them what happened."

Carey spoke softly . . . deliberately.

"Sean came up to me one day . . . said he had a problem. There was this guy . . . a hype . . . who was harassing his girlfriend. He wanted the problem taken care of. Could I help him out?"

He scratched his fuzzy chin.

"I asked him what he had in mind. I figured maybe he wanted me to spook him or something like that. But as he kept going, I figured out he wanted something more permanent."

Weller said, "What did he ask of you specifically?"

"Sean asked me to whack him." Carey looked up. "I was shocked, man. I wasn't in the business of murder. I told him he should watch who he talked to, man."

He stopped, fidgeted.

"Go on," Decker said.

"Then . . . then Sean starts asking . . . 'Well . . . do you know anyone who'd want to do the pop?' So I'm like playing along. I ask him . . . how much? He told me ten grand. Then I asked him how he could produce that much cash."

"And?" Marge prodded.

"He told me he had this trust fund with over two hundred and fifty grand coming to him in a couple of years. Now, I'm making, on my own, like one to two grand a month. So why would I risk my ass for only ten grand? But there are people out there . . . ten grand would be a lot of money."

Marge arched her brows. "Hard to believe, but I suppose that's true."

Weller passed her a look, then said, "Then what happened?"

"So then Sean . . . see, he knows that I know certain people." A small smile formed on Malcolm's lips. "He says that if *I* don't want to do it, maybe I can ask around. I'm still like playing along . . . I said sure. Then I forgot about the whole thing."

A pause.

"Month later . . . Sean comes back to me, asks . . . did I find someone to do the job? I say no. 'Cause I never asked about it. I forgot the whole thing—"

"You already said that," Decker interjected. "Go on."

The boy seemed riled, took a few moments to find his footing. "Sean got nasty. You wouldn't believe how pissed he can get. Tell you the truth, he spooked me."

*Right*, Decker thought.

Malcolm became animated. "He started getting agitated. Like . . . really aggressive. Said I gotta help him out."

He hesitated.

"Now this was where I fucked up. Like Mr. Flame said, I got a big mouth. I talk without thinking sometimes. So I told Sean this. I said, 'Look! If this guy's a hype, why are you bothering to pop him? Why don't you play it natural?' Sean looked at me, asked me what I had in mind. I told him I don't have anything in mind *personally*, but if I was going to do the pop, I might want to just . . . put him out in a blaze of glory."

Carey stalled, went on.

"That's exactly how I said it. In a blaze of glory. Sean . . ." The teen smiled. "Now he can be a little dense. But I could see his brain working. He stuck out his arm and made an injection into his vein with his finger. Looked at me questioningly. I nodded. So he asked how. I told him, 'Man, you've stuck yourself. How do you think you do it?' "

The boy took a sip of water.

"Sean thought a little bit. Then he told me that the hype was also a drunk. I say, 'Man, what's the big deal? It's a sure thing. You get the key from your bitch, wait until he gets plastered, then stick him where it counts.' "

Malcolm tapped the table with his fingers.

"I could tell Sean liked the idea. But he didn't have the balls to do it alone. So he asked me to come along as backup."

Weller raised his eyebrows. "You went?"

"It was something to do." Malcolm shrugged. "I told him backup will cost. Ten grand. I never thought he'd go for it, but I was wrong. Sean was real serious about this thing—"

"You mean murder?" Decker clarified.

Carey looked away. "Sean told me the ten grand could be arranged. But for that price, I'd have to supply the dragon. He wanted pure scag. I told him it was stupid to use pure scag. Pure anything in a hype's vein looks suspicious. I told him I'd have to cut it. But I could deliver."

The teen licked his lips.

"Sean got a key . . . we waited for the right time. Garrison got drunk almost every weekend. We did a couple of practice runs . . . to see the layout. And we had to make sure the hype was under big time . . . sleeping off a real bender. Third time we checked, the guy was out cold. I put the scag in the medicine cabinet while Sean shot him up. I was out of the room when it happened. I never touched the guy."

Weller said, "Did you get the money, Malcolm?"

"Yeah, he paid me." The boy's lips turned upward. "Sucker wouldn't *dare* stiff me."

"Where's the money now?" Decker asked.

Malcolm sipped water. "Spent it."

"You went through ten thousand dollars in one month?" Weller said quietly.

A sly smile played upon his lips. "Fine wine and good women cost a bundle. I also bought things."

"Like what?" Decker asked.

"Coins, stamps . . . guns. Same kind of shit my dad buys. He'd be real proud."

"You're just a chip off the old block," Marge said in an undertone.

"Detective . . ." Flame warned.

"S'right," Carey said. "It's true. White-collar crime, blue-collar crime, violent crime . . . it's all the same. Dad and I *are* one of a kind. Only difference? I don't mind getting my hands a little dirty."

# ❧ 37

*Strapp coughed. "Good* news. Sean Amos is being held without bail." He checked his watch, let out a small shiver. "It's almost three. My head's about to explode. He'll keep until the morning. See you here at eight tomorrow. Now go home."

Decker hesitated. "All right."

Strapp studied his lieutenant. "Christ, Decker, what is it *this* time?"

Decker said, "Something was off with Carey."

"What are you talking about?" Strapp shot back. "I was behind the one-way. Saw and heard the whole thing. What was off?"

A long pause. "Didn't it sound . . . rehearsed?"

"No, it didn't sound *rehearsed*! It looked and sounded like a psycho kid getting a thrill out of telling us how bad he was."

Decker rubbed his eyes. "Maybe it's fatigue."

"I think so. Good night, Lieutenant."

"'Night, Captain."

Strapp muttered, "By the way . . . good job."

"Thanks." Decker left, feeling very unsatisfied.

\* \* \*

A kid who had everything—money, looks, connections—and that *still* didn't stop him from screwing up.

What Martinez could have done with any *one* of those advantages. He smoothed his black mustache, his cheeks still stinging from an early-morning shave. He wanted to look good in front of the captain.

Pulling out his notes, he appraised the situation. Sean Amos in jail blues, head down, lips smashed together. No eye contact with his parents. Mom was a rail-thin bubble blond on his left. Sitting on the right was a big-boned, ultra-good-ole-boy Texas lawyer named Edgar Ray Trit, wearing a three-thousand-dollar Brioni suit and a string tie.

Dad was at the lawyer's right. Lamar Amos tried to hide his beer gut under a black suit and white shirt, but to no avail. Ruddy complexion, veiny nose, slicked gray hair like a silverback gorilla.

No ten-gallon hat.

With Martinez were Webster and Katherine Villard, a fortyplus, good-looking deputy DA. Black hair, black eyes, serious expression. A no-nonsense woman. Behind the one-way mirror were Strapp, Decker, Marge, and Oliver.

Webster got the ball rolling, made the preliminary statements. Identification of all the parties in the room. Then the current charges against Sean Amos starting with the murder one of David Garrison.

Trit interrupting, his voice booming, "Now, Kate, we're all friends here. So I'm going to open up the discussion with plain, old-fashioned honesty. I just don't understand where you got the gumption to take up on this murder one." He screwed up his face. "Now if you're relying on the word of that psychopath, Malcolm Carey . . . if you're planning to go to court with that, well, you're going to end up looking like a fool—"

"It's Katherine," the deputy DA answered curtly. "Has the bailiff forwarded you a copy of the statement?"

"Not yet."

The prosecutor opened her briefcase, took out several sheaves of papers. Handed them to him. "Here you go."

Again, Trit grimaced. "Reckon I could use a good laugh right now."

"Edgar, we're standing behind his statement. You want to go to court, we'll bring him to court on a murder one—"

Sean broke in. "I didn't *kill* anyone—"

"Hush up!" Trit snapped as he flipped through the pages, eyes racing over the document.

Katherine said, "I'm sorry you didn't get the statement sooner. You'll need time to look it over. We can reconvene at two—"

Sean said, "Malcolm Carey is a fucking liar—"

"Boy, close your mouth—"

"Oh, fuck you—"

An arm reached out and backhanded Sean across his face. Lamar Amos had turned beet red. "You just sit there and shut yo damn mouth and listen to yo lawyah, y'hear?"

Trit stuttered out, "Lamar, I'll handle—"

"Are you contradictin' me, Edgar Ray?" Lamar broke in. "I hope not lest y'foget who's payin' yo bills."

Sean held his cheek. Breathing hard, he said, "See what happens when you got a balloon inside your dick."

Veins bulging, Lamar charged. Mom screamed as Trit and Martinez held Daddy Lamar back, the Texan screaming obscenities until he was purple. The shrieks brought in a posse of backup. After a moment, Lamar stopped rushing, shook loose. He stalked out of the room. Mom's eyes went to her son, then to the open door. She rose, then raced out.

"Gee. Thanks for the support, Mom." Sean sighed. "Hasn't been married to him in ten years and she still licks his boot heels . . . goddamn bitch!"

Webster said, "'How sharper than a serpent's tooth—'"

"Yeah, well, all the better to *bite* with, my dear," Sean retorted. "And I know that's from Shakespeare. I'm not as dumb as you think."

"Sean, we think you're very bright—"

"That's enough." Trit stood. "We'll reconvene at two—"

"I'm not going anywhere until this is hashed out. Malcolm Carey is a *crazy* fucker—"

Webster said, "Then why were you with him on the night David Garrison was murdered—"

"David Garrison wasn't *murdered*! He OD'd!"

Martinez said, "Sean, let me tell you so you know what you're up against. We have witnesses that put you with Malcolm Carey on the night of David Garrison's death."

Webster named the date. "First you went with Carey to shoot some pool, then you went back to your house to smoke some dope, then you went over to David Garrison's house—"

"I've *never*, ever been to David Garrison's house. If Malcolm told you that, he's lying!"

"Are you saying you didn't shoot pool with him?"

"Yes. I mean no. I mean yes, I shot pool, but—"

"And you smoked dope—"

"But—"

Trit said, "Sean—"

"I didn't *kill* anyone—"

"Why were you stuffing pictures of Wade Anthony down the toilet?" Webster asked.

Sean broke into a cold sweat. "What are you talking about?"

"When we busted you," Webster said. "You were flushing pictures of Wade Anthony down the toilet."

"Along with a daily schedule of Anthony's activities," Martinez added.

"I didn't know what I was doing," Sean said. "I just panicked—"

"What were you doing with those pictures of Wade Anthony in the first place?" Martinez asked. "Starting a fan club?"

Trit said, "We're not talking anymore—"

"What does Wade Anthony have to do with this?" Sean said.

Trit said, "He's a minor. Don't even *try* to use any of this."

The DA broke in. "Edgar, he's been Miranda'd—"

"He's a minor—"

"He's seventeen. Old enough to understand—"

"Wade Anthon—" Amos turned pale. "Oh, my God!"

"What?" Martinez asked.

"Let's go, Sean," Trit insisted.

"The asshole set me up!" the boy blurted out. *"Again."*

"What asshole are you talking about?" Webster asked.

Sean slapped his cheeks with his palms. "How could I be so *stupid*!"

"*Who* set you up?" Martinez asked.

"Malcolm Carey! No wonder he asked me . . . he was gonna set me up. Just like he did the last time. God, am I stupid—"

Trit said, "If you're going to talk, at least let me get you immunity."

"Depends on who he implicates," Katherine stated.

"Who are you going to implicate, Sean?" Martinez asked.

"Don't answer that!" Trit said. "I'll let him talk. But anything he says can't be entered in court unless we strike a deal—"

"No dice—"

"So you go to trial with Carey as your star witness?" Trit muttered. "Good luck to you."

Martinez said, "Can we just hear the kid out?"

Katherine said, "No, we can't just hear the kid out. Unless we deal, the entire statement can't be entered as evidence."

"So even if that happened, we'd be no worse off," Martinez plowed on. "We'd just go to court with Carey."

"Good point, Kate," Trit said.

*"Katherine!"*

"Deal?" Trit asked.

Katherine threw up her hands.

"I'll take that as an affirmative response."

Webster said, "Tell us about David Garrison, Sean."

"I don't know anything about *David* Garrison. That's what I'm *trying* to tell you."

"He's your girlfriend's brother, isn't he?"

Sean became crimson, didn't answer.

"We're referring to Jeanine Garrison," Martinez said. "Don't insult our intelligence and deny that you know her."

"Of course I know her. She's my tennis partner."

Webster said, "Sean, you've been blabbing 'bout her and you to just about everyone in your class."

"We're just friends."

"That's not what you've been telling people."

The boy was sweating. "Rumors get started. Maybe I went along with them. So what? That doesn't mean—"

"Sean, listen up," Martinez said. "You are seventeen, she is twenty-eight. If you two were in on some nasty thing . . . guess who's gonna wind up the baddie."

"We're not *in* on anything, let alone something nasty!"

Still the boy continued to sweat.

Webster said, "And you expect us to b'lieve that?"

"Why would I lie?"

" 'Cause I reckon you got some kind of misguided notion that by protecting her, you're being noble. Well, you're not being noble. You're just being stupid. Might want to start thinkin' about savin' your own skin."

"He's not stupid," Martinez countered. "He loves her." He turned to the teen. "That's it, isn't it? You do love her, don't you?"

Silence. Sean swiped his eyes. Talked in a hush. "It

wasn't supposed to happen like that. It's just that . . .
David Garrison . . . he was really *bugging* her."

"Who is her?" Martinez asked. "Jeanine Garrison?"

Sean nodded.

"How was he bugging her?"

"Just asking her for money—all the time. Guy was
a hype, shooting up dollars into his veins. Jeanine . . .
like she helped him. But enough was enough, you
know. Me? I just wanted to help."

Martinez commiserated. "Jeanine was so upset.
You just couldn't turn her down."

"Turn her down?" Sean was confused.

"When she asked for your help," Martinez said.

"She never *asked* for my help." Sean was indignant.
"She never asked anything from me."

Webster and Martinez exchanged glances. Webster said, "Sean, there's no sense protecting her—"

"I'm not protecting anyone. It was all *me*. Actually
it was all Mal. *He* was the one—"

"Sean, *you're* the one in trouble," Martinez said.
"You're looking at a long jail sentence . . . or maybe
worse—"

"But I—"

"Sean, don't be an idiot," Webster said. "You can't
mean to say you're going to let Jeanine get off scot-
free—"

"But she didn't *do* anything."

"Sean, listen to me," Martinez said. "Your girlfriend's been two-timing you, making time with Wade
Anthony—"

"No—"

"While you're holed up in jail, about to have your
life flushed down the crapper."

"It doesn't have to be like this," Webster said, "Jeanine's the adult, you're the minor. She's the one responsible—"

"No—"

"Sean, she set you up!"

"No!" Sean shook his head vehemently. "No, *she* didn't do anything except *help* me—"

"Sean—"

"It was Malcolm who set me up." Sean's eyes bulged from their sockets. "Don't you *morons* get it?! It was Malcolm! IT WAS MALCOLM!"

The room was quiet. Trit broke it. "Y'all so anxious to hear him out, why don't you let him get through his story?"

Sean spat out, "You want facts, then listen to me, goddammit! *It . . . was . . . Malcolm!*" Suddenly, the boy slumped, shook his head, and rubbed his eyes. "I'm tired."

Trit said, "Go on, boy. You may never get this chance again. Tell them your story."

"I don't need lessons in talking. Problem is, I talk too *much*! Too much and to the wrong people. I musta been complaining to Mal. Just spouting shit. How hard things were on Jeanine. How much easier things would be on her if he croaked."

"He . . . being David Garrison," Webster said.

Sean nodded.

"Next thing I knew . . . he did croak. I remember thinking . . . what incredibly good luck!" He laughed bitterly. "Next day, Malcolm came over to me . . . asked me to pay up. Twenty-five grand in cash. I asked him what the hell he was *talking* about. He said

'David Garrison.' I almost dropped dead on the spot. I swear to holy Jesus, I never offered him a dime to kill anyone including David Garrison!"

A pause.

"Mal acted totally on his own. Totally. But to hear him talk . . . like I asked him to do it. But I didn't, I swear."

"And he asked you for twenty-five grand," Webster said.

Sean nodded. "Needless to say, I panicked. I didn't have that kind of bread at my fingertips. My dad holds the purse strings real tight. I can get around it, but I need time. I tried to explain that to Malcolm, but he got threatening. And when Mal threatens . . . he doesn't shit around. He gave me three days."

He wiped sweat off his brow.

"I didn't know what to do. So I went to Jeanine. Told her what happened."

Martinez said, "When you told Jeanine about your predicament, how'd she react?"

"She was *furious*! Really pissed! Ready to turn me in! I *deserved* to be turned in! 'Cause it was all my fault!"

The teen was breathing hard.

"*I* was in big trouble. With her, with everything."

Webster said, "Why did you feel you were in trouble if you didn't order the hit?"

"Because I made specific remarks."

"Like what?" Martinez prodded.

"Like how nice it would be if . . . someone stuffed something in his veins. Jeanine said that my joking could be misinterpreted. And since I was . . . connected to Jeanine in a personal way—and David had been bothering her—people might believe that I was actually capable of . . . planning it."

Moisture welled up in his eyes.

"She took pity on me when I was at my lowest. Even though she was real angry, she said she'd help me. Oh, God, when she told me that, I swear I fell down and kissed her feet. She *believed* me. You couldn't possibly realize what that meant."

"I b'lieve I'm getting the picture," Webster said.

Martinez said, "What'd she do for you, Sean?"

"She loaned me money to pay off Malcolm, that's what she did. Loaned me money from her own pocket."

"Twenty-five grand?"

"Actually ten."

"In cash?" Martinez asked.

Sean shook his head. "A bearer bond. Know what that is?"

"Yes," Webster answered. "Bearer bonds haven't been issued in years. Who'd she get the bond from?"

Sean shrugged. "I don't know."

"Jeanine Garrison gave you a bearer bond? And you gave it to Malcolm Carey?"

Sean nodded.

"And what did he say?" Martinez asked. "It wasn't the twenty-five grand he asked for."

"He said he'd accept it—this time. And that I should consider myself lucky."

He stopped talking.

"And?" Martinez asked.

"That was it," Sean said. "Jeanine never mentioned it again. And I never said anything."

"What about the rumors?" Martinez said. "Half the school thinks you popped David Garrison."

"Probably Mal started those. I played along. I was too scared not to. Mal wouldn't like it if the truth came out."

"You were never in David Garrison's apartment?" Webster asked.

"Never!"

"What were you doing with those pictures of Wade Anthony?" Martinez asked.

Sean sighed. "Earlier in the day . . . God, I'm such a *jerk* . . ." He sighed again. "Jeanine and I got into this big fight over Wade. With the tournament . . . she had to spend time with him. All those pictures of them together. I know it's her profession but it pissed me off. His attitude. Like he *owned* her! Ordering her around. Mr. Fucking Roller-Legs! I guess I was complaining about him to Malcolm."

"And?" Martinez encouraged.

"What's to say?" Sean said. "Next thing I know, Mal's got pictures of Wade Anthony and this weird look on his face. *He* brought over those pictures. Not *me*. Then he starts telling me stuff . . . like how easy it would be to pop him. He was just starting to talk about it when the cops busted in—"

"So why did you flush the pictures down the toilet?" Martinez persisted.

"I told you, I panicked. I just grabbed whatever shit I could reach and stuffed it in the toilet."

"Now why don't I b'lieve that?" Webster asked.

Sean said. "Give me a lie detector test, if you don't believe me."

Webster said, "If you're lying, you won't beat the test, Sean."

Sean smiled wryly. "Sir, believe me. It'll be the *easiest* test I've ever passed."

# ❧ 38

*Closing the door* to Decker's office, Marge said, "What is it with today's teenagers? Are all of them psycho?"

Oliver took a chair. "You know what? I believe Sean Amos—"

"He snowed you," Webster said.

"It's Carey who's doing the snowing. Kid's giving off more flakes than a bad case of dandruff."

Marge said, "Scott, we went into the interview charging Amos with a murder one. What was he supposed to say? I did it, yada yada yada?"

"Works in the prison movies—"

"Of course Sean's going to try to shift the blame," Marge went on. "The more he can pin on Carey, the better."

"Scott, you can't seriously believe Carey hit Garrison on his *own*." Webster frowned. "That don't make any sense."

"Carey thought he could squeeze a rich boy like Sean," Oliver said. "Plus he's a flaming psycho who likes hurting people."

Farrell Gaynor scanned through a thirty-page

list of bearer bonds that had recently been called or redeemed. "This is going to take me a long time."

"Why are you even bothering?" Oliver said.

"The Loo says try to verify where the bond came from." Gaynor shrugged. "Have to start somewhere. At least we know it's state of California."

"Yeah, that narrows it to about thirty million—"

"Not quite that much."

Oliver said, "Decker *blew* it when he went with Carey. He should have gone with Sean Amos."

"Scotty, we needed Sean to get to Jeanine," Marge reminded him.

"Yeah, well, his strategy didn't work. We're not any closer to Jeanine Garrison than we were before."

"Not quite true," Martinez said. "If we go with Sean's story, we can hit Jeanine with aiding and abetting—accessory after the fact."

Webster said, "That's another thing I can't buy."

"What?" Martinez asked.

"That Jeanine's sole crime was aiding and abetting. By all accounts that woman is a manipulative bitch. Now you're telling me she's putting her own ass on the line to help some punk kid? C'mon . . . she had to be in on it. Sean is talking from his butt. Amos killed David and he did it for Jeanine."

Decker came into his office, glanced at the clock. One-thirty. "Anyone hungry? We can order in."

Oliver said, "How'd the polygraphs go?"

Decker said, "Elaine Reuter's still talking to Malcolm—"

"It's been over an hour!" Webster complained.

"To Elaine, that's a rush job," Decker said. "She likes to talk to her examinees at least a couple of hours before she does the test. So we'll just have to wait. Who's hungry?"

"Tuna on rye," Marge said.

"Times two," Martinez said. "Actually, give me two tunas. I'm hungry."

"Roast beef," Oliver said.

"Turkey," Webster said.

A pause.

Marge said, "Anything, Farrell?"

"Sounds good," Gaynor answered.

Oliver said, "*What* sounds good, Farrell?"

"Turkey. No mayo. Fruit instead of chips. Trying to watch my fat."

Marge picked up the phone to place the order. "Loo?"

"I'm fine." Decker showed her his brown bag, opened it. A barbecued-beef sandwich with pasta salad. The smell made his stomach growl, but, out of politeness, he waited for the others.

To Decker, Oliver said, "We were just discussing how you dealt with the wrong guy."

"No wrong guy in this case," Decker answered. "They're both psycho."

Oliver stated, "Question is which is the bigger psycho."

Decker said, "No, the question is who's more credible in front of a grand jury. Because Sean's going to tell his story and Carey'll tell his. Both tales have holes bigger than grottoes. And neither hands over Jeanine Garrison."

Martinez said, "Sean's story delivers Jeanine as an accessory after the fact. It's better than nothing."

"It's worse than nothing," Decker corrected. "Say

we try her as an accessory. She gets on the stand, starts chucking up some sob story about not thinking it through because of the incredible stress she's been under since losing her parents, then her brother . . . blah, blah, blah."

Decker made fists.

"Let's say we even win. And she's convicted. Here's a woman without a record. If anything spells probation, this does. Then she goes merrily on her way." He paused. "Then, say six months later, we find out that she was involved in her brother's hit. Say we try to charge her. You know what's going to happen? Her lawyer'll raise hell, claim we can't retry her because of double jeopardy."

Marge said, "Pete, the hit's a new charge. That's not double jeopardy."

"It's still the same case. The law's not so clear-cut. It's like retrying O. J. for breaking and entering—"

"That's a damn good idea!" Oliver said.

Decker said, "All I'm saying is that a judge could easily rule that all the criminal charges against Jeanine should have been made at the onset of the first trial. Before we charge her with anything, I want to make sure she's completely innocent of David Garrison's death."

Martinez said, "Neither one's claiming she ordered the hit, Loo."

Decker frowned. "I know. Problem is, if we drop our deal with Carey, we won't be able to use *anything* he told us about David Garrison's hit. And Sean's confession isn't usable because we haven't struck an official deal with him. Besides, the idea *wasn't* to use Sean to get to Carey. We have plenty of narcotics charges on Carey. The idea was to use Sean to get to Jeanine. And he ain't playing that game."

"Maybe she wasn't involved, Loo," Martinez said.

Decker slumped down into his desk chair. "We're going to have to drop David Garrison until we get better evidence. Just bring the kids up on drug charges."

"We got lots on Carey, but not much happenin' against Sean Amos." Webster held his anger in check. "First-time drug conviction. . . . kid'll probably get probation. Not bad for a cold-blooded murderer—"

"Tom—"

"David Garrison's dead and now no one is gonna take the fall."

Decker scowled. "So what do you suggest, Thomas?"

"Run with Carey."

Gaynor said, "What about the gun recovered at the bust?"

"What about it?" Oliver said.

"I just think it's interesting that it was called in stolen about two months ago—"

Decker interrupted, "Farrell, *when* did this come in?"

"About a half hour ago." Gaynor shrugged. "Sorry. Must have slipped my mind."

Decker held his temper. "Who reported it stolen?"

"Lily Amos."

The room went quiet.

"So it was *Sean's* gun?" Marge said.

"No, it was Lily's gun," Farrell said.

"I knew that boy was evil," Webster gloated. "Now y'all gotta ask yourselves, why would Sean bring a gun to the party *unless* he was planning to do something with it?"

"Meaning?" Oliver probed.

"Meaning Sean was gonna give it to Malcolm to off Wade Anthony. Just like Malcolm said. Of *course* Sean has to claim that he didn't know anything about the pictures of Wade Anthony. Yet the Loo and Marge bust in, Amos has pictures of Anthony, his daily schedule, and a gun."

Martinez said, "We know that Amos was upset at Jeanine a few hours earlier. The Loo saw them arguing."

Webster said, "That argument was the final straw. Amos went berserk. He planned another hit . . . just like Carey said—"

Oliver said, "You're missing a crucial point, Tom. Paraffin test shows that Carey fired the gun."

"So what? He heard police coming, he just picked up whatever weapon was handy and let it rip. Loo, before you came in, I was saying that I just couldn't buy Sean's story. If Sean didn't hire Carey for the hit, why would Carey have gotten involved?"

"Money," Oliver said. "Sean's loaded. Mal was squeezing him."

Decker said, "And if Sean wasn't *hiring* Carey to pop Anthony, what was Sean doing with Anthony's pictures, the daily schedule, and a gun?"

Oliver said, "Maybe Mal was setting up Sean for a second squeeze."

The other detectives groaned.

Webster became frustrated. "You're being a broken record, Scott."

Suddenly, the light went on. Decker slapped his forehead. "Ker-rist! Scott's right!"

"I am?" Oliver grinned. "I mean, of course I'm right." He paused. "Why?"

Someone knocked at the door. Lunch had arrived. After five minutes of sorting out what belonged to whom, Decker spoke as everyone munched. Excitedly he said, "Who reported the gun stolen?"

"Lily Amos," Farrell said, between bites of turkey. "Didn't I just tell you that or is my memory that bad?"

Decker smiled. "It was a rhetorical question, Farrell. Look at this, people. Say Sean wants his mother's gun . . . why would he have to *steal* it?"

Decker dug into his sandwich. Chewed rapidly, then swallowed.

"Makes much more sense for Sean to borrow the weapon, then bring it back unnoticed. Which means—"

Marge broke in, "It means the gun was stolen by someone other than Sean."

"Malcolm Carey!" Oliver said. "Bastard stole the gun from Sean's house."

Decker said, "And that's why *Carey* fired at us. Because at that point, the gun didn't belong to Sean, it belonged to Carey."

Martinez gulped down tepid coffee. "I'm lost. Let's start with the basics. Wade Anthony. Who was planning his hit?"

Decker said, "Malcolm Carey—"

"C'mon, Loo!" Webster was dubious. "Why would Carey give a solitary shit about Wade Anthony?"

"He doesn't give a shit about Anthony, Tom,"

Decker said. "Carey was using him to set up Amos. Just like he did the first time with David Garrison—"

Webster broke in, "Loo, why would Carey take it upon himself to hit Garrison on his own? It just doesn't make sense!"

Decker said, "Malcolm Carey didn't hit Garrison on his *own*. He had a partner—"

"Jeanine!" Marge cried. "Carey was in on David Garrison's hit *with* Jeanine from the beginning!"

"Jackpot!"

Oliver said, "And that was why Jeanine loaned Sean the money. She wasn't helping Amos out. She was furthering the myth of being innocent. Because she had planned it with Carey from the beginning."

Ideas poured into Marge's brain like tumbling waves. "To save her butt, she made it seem as if the idea came from Sean's ramblings! So if the investigation ever turned up David's OD as a murder, she could pin it on Sean."

"And the ten-thousand-dollar bearer bond was the hit price from the beginning," Oliver said. "Instead of paying Malcolm directly, she acted like she was helping out Sean. Keeping him permanently in her debt." He grinned at Webster. "So whaddaya think, Tulane Tom?"

"Gotta admit. The scenario's starting to sound like Jeanine."

Decker said, "Manipulating men, Tom. You said it from the beginning. She loves to manipulate men. Just like with Harlan Manz. From the beginning, I'm sure she set Harlan up. She probably knew that Harlan had been fired from his job at Estelle's, had been bitter over his dismissal. You want to know how I think Estelle's went down?"

Everybody waited.

Decker said, "Jeanine's a primo manipulator. She wants her parents out of the way, but she wants it to look like a random murder. Better than a murder, how about a mass murder using Harlan Manz as a mass murderer? Bet she knew he fit the profile."

"That's absolutely malevolent," Marge said.

"It's absolutely Jeanine," Decker said. "So what does she do? She has an affair with Harlan Manz. We know from talking to Harlan's girlfriend that Harlan fooled around. And we also know from talking to everyone else that Harlan loved money and big shots."

Oliver stated, "Harlan musta thought he died and went to heaven when he met this dream girl."

Decker said, "Schmuck must have been made delirious by his good fortune. Only snag was that he had to keep it quiet. But even that was okay. Because Harlan had a girlfriend and it made it exciting."

Martinez said, "Okay. They have an affair. Then suddenly Harlan turns into a mass murderer?"

Decker said, "Check this out, Bert. Jeanine and Harlan have this affair. This way she can get Harlan to talk. Which is no big accomplishment. We know from our interviews that Harlan loved to talk."

"So they talk," Marge said. "Then what?"

"She gets him to open up about his unfair experience at Estelle's. She works him up. She works him up until people recall Harlan talking about how bitter he was at Estelle's for canning him so unjustly. She works him up until one day, she convinces him to go into the restaurant . . . man, it's all coming down."

Decker paused, gulped down water.

"She convinces him to go to the restaurant and confront the management. She even picks out his clothes. A noticeable *green* jacket. And the day Jeanine chose for him just happened to be a day her parents made reservations at Estelle's. Which I bet wasn't unusual. They probably ate at Estelle's often. Maybe they even had a standing reservation."

"A cold woman," Oliver said.

Decker said, "Meanwhile, Jeanine has contracted an unknown hit man to follow Harlan. She tells the second guy what Harlan's wearing—"

Marge said, "Remember what Tess Wetzel said about that odd man. *He* was wearing a green jacket."

Decker said, "Exactly. Any of you think that was just a coincidence?"

No one spoke.

Decker said, "At the agreed-on moment, Mr. Unknown Hit Man makes his move and starts popping people—"

"So you're saying we have only one shooter?" Marge asked. "So how do you explain the bullet-wound patterns on the Garrisons? The ones that led you to speculate on a second shooter in the first place?"

Decker thought a moment. "Could be the shooter had two guns. He used one to ice Harlan and left it at the scene. The other, he took with him. That's how he could do so much damage so fast. Also, he probably shot from all sides and angles. The shooter knew Harlan was going to be the fall guy. Betcha he popped Manz and the Garrisons early on. The Garrisons he wanted dead for Jeanine. Harlan . . . he wanted him dead and out in the open. To take the blame."

Martinez said, "Deck, I think *someone* would have noticed this real hit man."

"Someone did, Bert," Decker said. "Tess Wetzel noticed a second man. And maybe a few others did as well. But no one was *sure.* Because they were dressed similarly. And once the bullets start flying, you duck, close your eyes, and pray."

Marge said, "So Harlan was a dupe."

Decker said, "Just like Sean Amos. It's Carey who's the real psycho. Leading us to believe that he was in cahoots with Sean. When in reality Carey was collaborating with *Jeanine.* Which is why he struck a deal with us. Because he really did pop David Garrison. So he saved his butt by turning state's witness against Sean, who didn't have anything to do with it. Worked us *perfectly,* the little fuck!"

"You're making logical leaps," Webster said.

"'Course I'm making some leaps," Decker answered. "But I'm also making some sense. You know what we're going to do? Instead of going with Carey's story, we're going to *drop* the murder one charge against him. Try him on the drug charges alone. I'm going to find the nastiest antidrug judge in the court system. Someone who'll lock that bastard up and throw away the key."

"What about Sean?" Webster wanted to know.

"He'll be tried on his drug charges, resisting arrest . . . probably get off light."

"Stinks," Webster said. "Carey's deal gives the kid *seven* years in prison. If David Garrison was a contract hit with Jeanine as the brains behind the operation, Carey should have rolled over and given us Jeanine to save his own butt."

Marge's eyes grew wide. "He didn't do that because he was beholden to Jeanine in a *big* way. As in Estelle's—"

"Carey as Estelle's *hit* man?" Webster shrugged. "Marge, where is the evidence?"

Decker said, "Lily Amos's gun was stolen about two weeks before Estelle's went down. We know we recovered more bullets than can be accounted for by the one gun we recovered. And Carey's weapon was a semi-automatic. Let's go back to Ballistics."

Martinez said, "Something is still bothering me. By all accounts, Jeanine got *along* with her parents. The woman had everything she wanted. Why would she whack her parents?"

Decker said, "From the start, we knew that Jeanine was dependent on Dad's good graces to run her charities. David Garrison said that Daddy was getting tired of Jeanine's tantrums. Maybe she figured out she couldn't manipulate Daddy forever. Maybe Daddy actually stood up and told her *no*."

# ❧ 39

*"Even forgetting about* the admissibility of polygraphs as evidence . . ."

Elaine Reuter scratched a nest of curls, licked her prominent teeth with a snakelike tongue. She had a long face and wide eyes. Today, she wore a zebra-striped shirt under a black suit, reinforcing her equine features.

"Tell you the truth, I wouldn't go to court on either one of these. Too murky."

Decker said, *"Both* of them were inconclusive?"

"Both had what I'd call unusual reactions—not clearly lying but nervous."

"How many questions did you ask?"

"Pertinent questions? Six. Which in this case is a lot. If I *had* to go with one, I'd pick Sean Amos. Talking to him . . . maybe he's redeemable. I think he might be lying, but could be he's very confused. Carey, on the other hand, is a hard case. I think he beat the test."

Decker nodded.

Elaine said, "Don't tell me. You dealt with Carey."

"Yes, I went with Carey. But it doesn't matter because we're not going to charge him with murder."

"You've got him on drugs, haven't you?"

"Yep."

"Then the kid'll serve *some* time." She smiled wanly. "Just probably turn him into a better psycho."

"Probably."

Elaine sighed. "I'm sorry. It's always hard when the big one gets away."

"The big one isn't even in the picture." Decker shrugged. "Damn shame. But life goes on."

The chill of fall tickled Decker's nose as he got out of the unmarked. The air smelled sweet—fresh, cool, and slightly mulchy from fallen flora. Evening mist blanketed his face. Though tired—having slept only three hours in the last two days—he nevertheless felt content. Life was good. He took a final whiff, then checked his watch. He had made it to his front door before six.

The house held the aroma of home cooking and love. The dining-room table had been set for dinner. Included was a place mat for him. That made him smile. He walked into the kitchen, expecting to find his wife. Instead, he found his daughter, his sons, and Joachim Rush sitting around the small kitchen table, playing Scrabble. Rush had brought along a girl. A pint-size thing who looked to be around fourteen. She had long blond hair and hazel eyes. Not a drop of makeup. She was also the first one who graced him with a smile. Decker smiled back.

Cindy stood, nodded, looking very policelike and official. "Hello, sir."

Decker nodded. "Officer Cohen . . ."

Sam looked up. "You need anything, Dad?"

"No, I'm fine. Where's your mom?"

"Out in the barn with Hannah."

The horses. Guilt pricking his skin. It had been a while since Decker had taken time to exercise and feed them. Rina had picked up the slack. He thought about joining her. In a minute. He said, "I thought the game was for four maximum."

"I'm just kibitzing," the girl answered. She introduced herself as Allison Berg.

Joachim said, "Have a seat, sir."

Decker regarded the teen. "You think it's a good idea for you to be here, Joachim?"

"Probably not."

"I invited him," Cindy said. "He was feeling a little antsy after the bust so I took him out for a ride. We wound up here. I hope that's not a problem."

"No, not at all."

"Did everything go okay?" Joachim asked. "I mean with the bust? No one at school could concentrate on anything else today. That's all anyone could talk about. Rumor has it that the haul was tremendous. And that Carey'll be gray before he sees the light of day. Any of that true?"

"It was a good tip," Decker said. "A very good tip and a good bust. But it's not in your best interests to be associated with the police. Let alone at my house. For your own sake."

The boy tried to hide his nervousness. "No one mentioned me, right?"

"No, Joachim. Your name never came up."

The teen looked relieved. Cindy said, "C'mon, Joachim. I'll take you home."

Decker turned to his daughter, "A word with you,

Officer?" They stepped into the dining room. Decker said, "He call you or did you call him?"

"He called me. He was really nervous, Daddy. I was worried he'd do something stupid. Blurt out something. So I suggested we go for a ride to talk it out. To calm him down actually. I figured I owed him that much."

"You did the right thing. Is he okay?"

"Yeah, he seems to be fine now."

"I'll keep a watch on him. Thanks."

"No one mentioned his name?"

"Nah, he wasn't even in the viewfinder, let alone in the picture."

"You look frustrated."

"Tired."

"Maybe tired and frustrated. You didn't get her."

"All things come to those who wait. And if you wait long enough, you die so it doesn't matter anyway."

"Love that optimistic attitude."

The front door opened, Rina came in, Hannah tugging at her arm, giving one of her famous four-year-old lectures. She saw her father and Hannah jumped into his arms. "Daddy! We fed the horses!"

"That's great."

"They ate a lot. Their tummies were reeeeal full."

"Good to have a full tummy."

Rina brushed his lips. "You're home. How wonderful!" She looked at her stepdaughter. "How's the game going?"

"I'm leaving with Joachim."

"Are you coming back for dinner?"

"Not tonight, Rina. But thank you." She went back into the kitchen.

Decker plopped his younger daughter on top of

his shoulders. Hannah said, "We found garbage outside, Daddy."

He turned to Rina. "Is that good or bad?"

"Garbage is packing peanuts. She collects them, then glues them onto paper for her artwork. I wonder if Warhol started this way."

"So it's a good thing to find garbage."

"Very good."

"I found four garbages," Hannah continued.

"Wonderful, Hannah Rosie. I'm very proud of you." Decker paused. "If Cindy came with Joachim . . . who's the girl in our kitchen?"

"Allison Berg. She goes to the yeshiva's high school with the boys—I mean, the girls' section of the boys' school . . . I'm getting this wrong—"

"Rina, I know that the boys and girls are in separate classes." A smile formed on Decker's lips. "Obviously not that separate. Sammy bring her?"

"No, Jacob did."

"*Jacob?*" Decker grinned. "No wonder he was so motivated to move."

"Behave yourself."

"Why? That never got me anywhere."

The kitchen door opened and out came the wordsmiths. Sammy held the car keys. "I'm taking everyone home. Be back in around a half hour."

"No longer, Shmuel," Rina said. "I'm sure your father's hungry."

"I can wait. But not too long." Decker held out his hand to Joachim. "Call me if you need anything."

"Got it."

"Half hour," Rina reiterated. Sammy nodded, then left with his brother, Allison, and Joachim.

Cindy removed the keys from her purse, kissed Hannah's baby-soft thigh. "Couldn't you just eat her—"

"Noooo, don't eat me."

"It's a metaphor, kid." Cindy smiled. "Gotta go . . . oh, Grandma called."

"What did she want?" Decker asked, anxiously.

Cindy chuckled. "The message was for Rina, Daddy. She said she's bringing her own corn, squash, green beans, and pumpkin for Thanksgiving dinner next week. So don't waste your money and buy them."

"That's a direct quote?" Rina said.

"Indeed it is." Cindy blew a kiss to Hannah. The tot touched her fingers to pouty lips and returned the gesture. Waving, Cindy walked out the door.

Decker waited a moment, then said, "We have groceries here. Do you know how much a pumpkin weighs?"

"She probably grew the vegetables in her garden," Rina said. "If it makes her feel good and useful to bring them, I say, more power to her."

"Agreed."

Silence.

Rina said, "I'm sure if anything was serious, she would have told us by now."

"Not true. She could be on her deathbed and say straight-faced that everything was fine."

"Then there's nothing we can do."

Decker nodded, helpless and anxious.

Though upset, Rina spoke in a cheery voice. "Good news. Your brother's wife called this morning. Randy managed to trade shifts so they're all coming out as well. Looks like we'll have a full house next week."

Decker said, "Oh, happy days!"

"They're your relatives!" Rina took off her coat, put it in the closet. "Also, I invited Marge for dinner. She said she'd love to come, but she already promised Scott Oliver that she'd have Thanksgiving with him. So I was kind of stuck. I invited him, too."

"Why don't we just open up a mission and dish out turkey to indigents?"

"It's not a bad idea. Giving a little charity when we have so much."

"Saint Rina."

She whacked him gently. "And while you're feeling so ebullient, I might as well tell you that we've received a counter offer—"

"So fast?"

"He's motivated."

"I'm sure he is. He found a sucker—"

"Peter—"

"Did he come down?"

"He split the difference—"

"It's too much!"

"Peter—"

"All right, just give me the papers and I'll sign the damn thing." He remembered he was holding Hannah. "The darn thing. I'll sign the *darn* thing. How about a video, pumpkin?"

The child's face lit up. "I want to watch *Wonderful World of Bugs*. You watch it with me, Daddy?"

Decker stifled a groan. She'd seen the tape a hundred times, feasting with delight on such gruesome visuals as a hill of ants devouring dead beetles and a Venus flytrap snaring its unsuspecting victim in cold blood. "I'll come watch in a few minutes. First I want to talk to Mommy, okay?"

"Okay."

"Take off her coat, Peter. I don't want her to get overheated."

"Yeah, yeah." Decker set up the machine, placed the child—sans jacket—in front of the boob tube, waited for the ominous theme music to start. As soon as it did, Hannah squealed with joy. Then came the credits with pictures. The child sang out, "There's the beetle. And there's the mill-i-pede. Oh, Daddy, the little praying mantis. He's so *cute*—"

"I'll be right back, sweetie—"

"Look, Daddy, the hissing cockroach!"

"Lovely, Hannah. I'll come watch in a minute." Decker went into the kitchen where Rina was putting the finishing touches on dinner. He said, "That child is strange."

"She likes bugs. You should be delighted she isn't squeamish."

"Thrilled."

Rina regarded her husband. "It didn't go well, did it?"

"On the contrary, the bust went very well. We took a nasty kid off the streets and that's very good."

Rina paused, "And Jeanine?"

Decker shrugged. "God works in mysterious ways. Who am I to judge?"

"So she's a lost cause?"

Decker said, "I have a glimmer of hope. Ballistics

is running a gun we picked up at the bust. I want to see if it matches any of the strays we bagged at Estelle's. I don't expect anything." He paused. "I never expect anything. That way, I'm rarely disappointed."

Slowly, Marge walked into Decker's office. He hung up the phone, offered her a seat and a newspaper. "She's taking it on the road."

"Pardon?"

"To wit: Today's sports section. The wheelchair tournament was so successful, she's taking it on the road with Wade." Decker waited a beat. "The article refers to Wade as her *fiancé*. Think I should send him a card?"

"Not unless it's for sympathy."

Decker laughed softly. "Anyway, you're just the woman I was looking for. You're coming over on Thursday, aren't you?"

"Of course. What can I bring?"

"You're bringing Scott. I think that's enough—"

"Pete, what could I do—"

"Nah, I'm just teasing you. Bring some flowers." Decker looked her in the eye. "Before you come, let's get one thing straight. My mother's going to be there—"

"Really?" Marge grinned. "This should be very interesting—"

"And my brother," Decker said. "You or Scotty breathe a word of anything that has to do with my youth, your jobs are on the line."

Marge laughed, then grew serious. Tossed the paper on his desk.

"What?" Decker asked.

She said, "Not the kind of news you were hoping for before a holiday, but . . . Ballistics called. They couldn't find anything—"

Decker hit his desk. "They couldn't have tested everything! Not *that* fast."

"No, they just picked out a couple of random samples—"

"A *couple* of random samples—"

"Pete—"

"A *couple*? As in *two*?"

"Maybe a few more than that—"

"Marge, we recovered over a hundred bullets."

She sighed. "Look, Scott and I worked our butts off. Pressured them to move for us especially because of the holiday week. This was the best we could do."

Decker counted to ten. "You did great. I couldn't have done any better."

"Pete, we can press it. But I don't know how much good it'll do. You know how slowly the wheels turn over there."

Decker nodded. The state crime labs were in sorry shape—backlogged and understaffed. Innocent people languished in jail, hardcase criminals were prematurely released because the labs didn't have the manpower to process the evidence fast enough for court-date trials. A case like Estelle's—two months old with an established perpetrator—was very low priority.

Decker said, "We've got time. We can wait for them to finish the job."

"Good, 'cause it's likely to take months, maybe years."

Decker cursed under his breath. "Maybe we should consider a private lab."

"Believe it or not, I checked into it. It's really expensive. I just don't have that kind of money lying around."

Decker thought of his newly purchased shack lying on a small plot of forest grounds. Unless he got it together, it was going to remain a shack. "Neither do I."

"Time to move on." Marge shrugged. "We tried our best. Nothing else we can do."

"We can wait for a miracle."

Marge chuckled, "Sure. Let's wait for a miracle. Won't cost me money, I can't get pregnant from it, and most important, it won't put any fat on my hips."

# ❧ 40

*Fixed in front* of the TV—the Macy's Thanksgiving Day Parade—Hannah was captivated by a dinosaur float that breathed out dry-ice smoke. She kept trying to convince everyone around that the dinosaur wasn't real. But there was too much commotion in the room, and her tiny voice was blighted by adult drone.

Rina kissed her forehead.

"He's not real," Hannah said.

"No, he's not real."

"He's pretend."

"Yes, honey."

"Not real."

Rina smiled, rubbed her temples. Lots of people. Peter's parents, Randy, his wife, Lurene, and their three school-aged children. Plus Clark—Randy's seventeen-year-old son from his first marriage. Clark, Sam and Jacob, were slouched across the living-room furniture, tossing a football back and forth. Lurene was out in the orchard with her kids, picking oranges.

Lyle Decker walked into the dining room, studying a blueprint as he stood in front of the TV. His burly body completely obscured Hannah's view of her beloved dinosaur. She shrieked out, "I can't see, I can't see."

Rina gently moved her father-in-law away from the screen. "Why don't you sit outside on the patio, Dad?"

"Where?" he yelled out.

"Come." Rina held his arm, led him out the side door into the backyard. A bricked patio held a round umbrella table and six plastic chairs. "Have a seat here. It's quiet and comfortable. You want some more coffee?"

"Coffee?"

"Yes, coffee. I've just brewed a fresh pot—"

"I'll take a cup of coffee."

"Great." Rina started to walk away.

Lyle said, "Where's Peter?"

"He's in the barn with Randy—"

"Where?"

"Over there in the barn, Dad. You want me to get him for you?"

"When are we going to the house?"

"Do you mean the new house?"

"Yeah. The new house." Lyle held up the blueprint. "This house."

"I think Peter was planning on taking you there in about a half hour."

"Before the game then?"

"Yes, before the game. I know you like the game."

Lyle laughed heartily. "What's Thanksgiving without turkey and the game?"

"Not much," Rina smiled. Such a sweet, sweet man, with twinkly blue eyes, a round, red face and thin, silver hair. He announced, "I found the sewer line."

It took a moment for Rina to switch gears. "Oh. That's great. Is the bathroom going to be a problem?"

"Nah!" Again the laughter. "We should be able to knock it out in no time."

Rina's smile was genuine. "I'll get you the coffee."

"I'd *love* a cup of coffee."

"Right away." She came into the kitchen through the back door. Ida Decker was basting an eighteen-pound stuffed torn turkey with seasoned broth. Pete's mother was tall and bony, her knobby hands made even more gnarled by persistent, long-standing arthritis. Short gray hair framed a noble face which was long and aristocratic. High cheekbones, wide-set, midnight blue eyes. A very handsome woman. She held her mouth tight, lips pressed together. Lips that rarely expressed emotion, let alone love. But lips that never gossiped and never complained.

Rina asked, "How's it looking, Mom?"

"It'll pass muster."

"Dad wants another cup of coffee—"

"He's already had three."

"It's decaf."

"The heart's not the problem. It's the stomach. Too much acid."

Rina said, "I'll make him herbal tea if you're concerned."

"He hates tea," Ida snorted, waved her hand in the air. "Oh, give him the coffee. It *is* a holiday. You want to check the pies in the other oven for me, Rina? They're no good if they're overcooked. Like eating rubber."

Rina opened the door to the twin side of her double oven. "They look perfect! The crust is golden, the filling has set but is still moist." She took one out. "A-one—"

"They may look perfect but I don't know how they'll taste. I usually make my pies with evaporated milk."

"I'm sure they'll be fine—"

"Never made pies with Mocha Mix before."

"I'm sure these will be the best ever."

"Well, we'll see."

Rina took the pies out of the oven, then poured a cup of coffee. "I'll just take this out to Dad."

Ida let out another small snort and started noodling with the candied yams. Rina returned outside. At the moment, Peter and Randy were standing over their father's shoulders as Lyle pointed out details in the blueprint, lecturing about structural beams. Ginger had fallen asleep under the table. Since both Randy and Peter were adopted, they held no physical resemblance to each other except for their stature. Peter was the taller of the duo, but topping six two, Randy was no tiny toon. The man was barrel-chested with short legs and long arms. He had short black hair, a wide forehead, and a ruddy complexion. Big brown eyes that sparkled. A coarse black mustache sat over his upper lip.

Lyle had moved on to floor joists.

Rina set down the coffee cup.

Randy said, "That looks good."

"I'll get you a cup."

"I'll get it," Decker said.

Randy smiled. "She got you trained, bro?"

Decker shot him a hard look, then slipped his arm around his wife's shoulders. Whispered, "Let's walk the *long* way."

Rina nodded enthusiastically. Randy shouted out, "Cream and sugar, Peter."

"No prob." With Ginger on his heels, Decker and his wife returned to the house via the side door, into the dining room. Ida had perched Hannah on her lap, both of them entranced by the floats. Ginger sniffed Hannah, then Ida. The old woman gave him a gentle tap on her nose.

"Down."

To Decker's surprise, the dog obeyed. "Never works for me."

"That's because he don't take you seriously." Ida looked away from the TV, announced, "Poor Hannah. Just sitting here. She wasn't getting a lick of attention."

Rina nodded. "Thanks for helping out."

Hannah said, "I like the birdies, Grandma. They're flying high in the sky."

Ida's instant smile was very real but very brief. She kissed her granddaughter's cheek. "Wouldn't you just love to go fly with them, Hannie? Just go over the sun and visit the moon and stars?"

Hannah pondered the statement. "Could Mommy go, too?"

Ida bit back a smile. "'Course Mommy could come."

Rina said, "You have some dreams, Mom?"

Ida scowled, "Just trying to amuse my granddaughter. Might want to baste the turkey. And glaze it, too. You know how to glaze it with a little sugar syrup and orange juice?"

"Sure." Rina went into the kitchen. Decker made his move. He said, "How you doing, Mom? You all right?"

"Of course I'm all right." Ida answered. "Why shouldn't I be all right?"

"So you're feeling fine?"

"Stop repeating yourself!"

Hannah said, "Look at that doggie balloon, Grandma."

"Now I like that one. What kind of dog is that, Peter?"

"Looks like a spaniel of some sort."

"Don't look like any dog I've ever seen."

"Artistic license."

Ida snorted. Decker used that as his exit line, joined his wife in the kitchen. He leaned against the counter. "*How* many days are they staying?"

Rina looked up from the oven, closed the door, and stood. "Think of us as Norman Rockwell with an edge."

Decker looked at the ceiling. "Is she giving you a hard time?"

"No, she's just angry that she can't use evaporated milk for her pies."

"I'm sor—"

"I'm teasing, Peter." Rina paused. "Actually, she's doing a bang-up job in the kitchen. She moves well for seventy-five."

Decker sighed. "I see her taking pills. She tell you what that's all about?"

Rina shook her head. "I'm watching her, Peter. Making sure she's not overdoing it. And I think she's smarter about it than she lets on. Sitting down with Hannah. She knows how to pace herself."

"So you think something's wrong?"

"Nothing obvious. Whatever it is, she's not going

to tell us if we push. And she seems happy to be here . . . thrilled with Hannah. And I'm the first to admit that the feeling is mutual. Hannah loves her."

From the dining room, Randy shouted, "Where's the coffee?"

Ida told him to pipe down.

Decker rolled his eyes, brought in the coffee cup, and slapped his brother's gut. "What am I? Your friggin' maid?"

Randy broke into laughter.

"Hush up, the lot of you," Ida said. "Can't you see the child is trying to watch."

They piled into the living room. Decker said, "Take it outside, boys!"

Instead, Sammy hurled a fast one to Randy, his *kippah* nearly flying off his head. Randy shot it back to Decker, who caught it easily. Decker said, "What are you *doing*?"

Randy relieved him of the ball, smacked Decker back. "Loosen up." He lobbed it to Jacob.

The doorbell rang.

Marge and Oliver. She was carrying a huge bouquet of fall-colored mums. "We're a little early."

Decker looked at his watch. More like two hours early. "Hey, glad you could make it. We're not doing much."

Jacob threw the ball to Oliver, who buzzed it to Clark, the boy's long blond bangs hanging over his eyes. The teen threw it back to Sammy.

Decker said, "Guys, take it *outside*!"

"C'mon," Randy said. "Let's get a game going. We'll choose up sides." He offered his hand to Oliver. "Randy Decker."

"Scott Oliver."

"You look like one of us."

"Got the look, huh?"

"Got the look. Let me guess. GTA?"

"No, Homicide."

"Ah, one of my brother's dicks—"

Oliver broke into laughter. "Never knew he had more than one."

Randy guffawed out loud. Decker said, "Glad you're having fun."

Sam lobbed the ball back to Clark, who threw a bullet to his father. It missed Peter's head by an inch. Decker said, *Outside! Now!*"

Randy smiled. "You in, Peter?"

"Yeah, yeah, in a minute. Just get out of here. And take the dog."

Randy whistled to Ginger. The setter came in a flash.

Marge handed the flowers to Decker, said, "I'm in."

Randy said, "You?"

Oliver said, "She's not my wife, she's my partner."

"Ah, sorry." Randy held out his hand. "Randy Decker."

"Yeah, the Narc in Miami. Marge Dunn—"

"So *you're* the famous Marge? Nice to meet you." Randy shook her hand vigorously. "You play forward, I can play defense. Are you coming, Dad?"

"I thought we were going to the house." Lyle was disappointed.

"In about a half hour, Dad," Decker said.

"Let's go outside, Dad," Randy said. "You'll be on my team. You can help me with defense—"

"Randy!" Decker scolded. "He's seventy-seven—"

"I'll take care of it. Don't worry. Are you coming or not?"

Decker showed him an armful of flowers. "I got to put these in a vase."

Randy patted his brother's butt. "I didn't know you were so *inclined*."

Decker was about to swear but realized his father was in the room. "I'll be there in a minute."

When they had all left, Decker dropped onto the couch. "Blessed *silence!*"

His solitude was short-lived. The front door opened.

"Cindy!" Decker exclaimed.

"Hi there." Cindy looked at the mums. "How sweet. For me?"

Decker said, "They're actually from Marge—"

"I'm kidding, Daddy." Cindy paused, noticing her father's off-kilter expression. "You look shell-shocked."

Decker didn't answer.

Cindy relieved her father of the flora. She said, "Maybe I should put those in a vase for you."

"That would be great." Decker blinked several times. "It's all coming back to me."

"What?" Cindy asked.

"Why I moved out of state." Decker focused his eyes on his daughter. "I thought you were with your mom today."

"They're going to a friend's at six for the dinner. I told her I'd be back before then."

"Did she know you were coming here?"

"I think so. But she was smart enough not to ask."

"Good for Jan." Suddenly, Decker embraced his daughter, then moved away.

"What was that for?" Cindy said, smiling.

"For being you. For helping me out like you did."

Cindy looked away. "Sorry I couldn't do more—"

"You did plenty. We got a great bust."

"What's happening with Carey?"

"Ten to twenty-five. He'll be eligible for parole in four and a half years—"

"That's outrageous!" Cindy shrieked.

Decker shrugged. "It's not a slap on the wrist. I've had worse outcomes."

"Considering what he probably did, it's a horrid miscarriage of justice."

"We can't prosecute on a 'probably.' After a couple of months on the street, you'll learn that quickly enough." Decker swallowed hard. "I'm very *proud* of you. You're a wonderful daughter, a fine human being, and you'll make a great cop—"

"Oh, God, don't *start*." Cindy's eyes started to water.

Decker laughed, "You gotta control that leaky tap of yours."

"I know, I know." Cindy wiped her eyes. "It's terrible."

"No, it's not terrible." Decker kissed his daughter's cheek. "But it's not a desirable asset for a cop."

She showed him the flowers. "I'll just go put these in water."

"While you're there, say hello to Grandma."

"Grandma's *here*?"

"In the flesh. Along with Randy, Lurene, and your cousins. They're out playing football. Why don't you join them?"

"Think I'll pass. Rather grump with Grandma."

Decker laughed and so did Cindy. She stood on her toes, kissed her father. "I love you."

"I love you, too."

Gently, she hit him over the head with the flowers, then headed for the kitchen. Once again, Decker was alone. He took a deep breath in, then let it out slowly.

Repeated the inhalation . . . the exhala—

The damn doorbell!

He swung open the door, eyes growing in circumference as he regarded the visitor. Then he gave him a bear hug but not too hard. Because the man was as thin as a piece of hay, his sport coat hanging on his body like a zoot suit. His hair had been braided tightly, his beard neatly combed and smelling like pine needles.

Abel broke the embrace, leaned against his cane. "Don't you look like a million bucks."

"Green and wrinkled," Decker answered. "I don't believe . . . to what do I owe this unexpected surprise? Are you trying to mooch a holiday meal or something?"

"More like the or something."

Decker continued to look at him. "What's wrong? Are you in trouble?"

Abel smiled. "Not this time. Actually, I've been working, found a temporary job."

"Really? Doing what?"

"Know that big wheelchair tennis tournament that went down 'bout two weeks ago?"

Decker tried to keep his face flat. "Of course. It was for the victims of the Estelle's massacre."

"Yeah, that was some horrific thing, wasn't it?"

"Horrific is a good adjective, yes." Decker paused. "How'd you get involved with the tournament?"

Abel hit his false leg. "Through the network. I heard they were hiring gimps. Sounded like it was an easy way to pick up some spare change. Lots of food, too. The woman . . . Jeanine Garrison . . . man, she catered one party after another. 'Course, we peons weren't invited to the festivities. But there was always plenty of leftover grub. Her beau, Wade Anthony, he brought us the leavings the next day."

"Considerate of him."

"Yeah. If it had been up to her, she would have pitched it in the garbage. She is one interesting lady."

"Yes, she is."

"And beautiful, too."

"Yes."

Abel stroked his beard. "Actually, she's kinda the reason why I'm here, doc."

A long, long pause.

"Oh?" Decker said.

Abel shifted his weight on his cane. Decker hit his forehead. "Where are my manners? Come in. Sit down."

"I'm all right. Let me just get this off my chest . . . 'bout this Jeanine. You know when you're doing manual labor, no one pays you too much mind. Certain people think that when you work with your hands, it means you don't have a brain. They talk freely . . . like you're not there. So you pick up a thing or two especially when people fight. . . ."

Another pause.

"Go on," Decker urged.

"This woman, Jeanine Garrison. You know Jeanine t'all?"

"I've met her."

"Wade Anthony is her beau now. But before that . . . I mean to tell you that this gal has all sorts of admirers. Big admirers, little admirers, old ones and *young* ones, too. Specifically a kid named Malcolm Carey. You know the name?"

Decker stared at Abel's face. It revealed nothing. With great effort, he kept his voice even. "Yes, I know the name."

Abel nodded. "He'd come around to see her—on the sly."

"Interesting. Why on the sly?"

"Probably Jeanine wanted it that way. Even so . . . us termites . . . we'd hear things . . . see things. Like a stolen kiss. He was mighty fond of the lady."

Abel paused.

"Fond is too weak a word. He was smitten. She, on the other hand, was nervous when he was around. Told him it was dangerous to talk to her. Still, whenever Mal would come sneaking in, Jeanine would talk to him."

"Know what they talked about?" Decker asked.

"Don't know what they said when they talked in low voices. But oftentimes things got heated. Ended up with her saying something like: 'It'll work out, but it takes time. You've got to have patience.' Clandestine talk. You'd think they were making a drug deal."

Again, Abel shifted his weight. A million thoughts flooded Decker's brain. Though tense and nervous, he refrained from barraging Abel with questions.

His old friend's style was slow and casual. Best to keep it that way. Decker said, "Sure you don't want to sit?"

"No, I'm fine, thanks. You really look good."

"You look too thin. We've got to feed you."

"In a minute. Got a little more to tell you."

"Sure."

Abel cleared his throat. "I read in the paper that Malcolm Carey was arrested in a big drug bust."

"Yep."

"Your case?" Abel asked.

"Yes. That's why I know the name."

"Ah . . ." Abel paused. "Thing is . . . I felt kinda sorry for the kid. 'Cause it sounded to me like he was taking the fall for someone."

"Taking the fall?"

"All this talk about him needing patience. Then the next thing the kid knows, he's bagged. I was wondering just how did the police find out about that drug party?"

"A tip," Decker said.

"By whom?"

"It wasn't Jeanine."

"Sure about that?"

"Yes."

"So you know who tipped you?"

"I know who tipped Narc, yes."

Abel paused, tapped his only foot. "And you're sure they received just the *one* tip?"

Heat coursed through Decker's body.

Just the *one* tip.

The tip had come through Narcotics. Niels never identified the sex of the caller.

Why . . . *why* would Joachim have called *Narcotics* when he had been given *Decker*'s number, had been given *Oliver*'s number, had been given *Marge*'s number?

In fact, Joachim *did* call Marge.

*Kid's thorough,* she had said.

It was clear as a bell. Joachim didn't call Narc. There had been two phone calls made. Two phone calls, two tips. One had been from Joachim to Marge.

And Jeanine had tipped Narcotics.

Using Malcolm Carey as an ally, Jeanine had set up both Harlan Manz to take the fall for Estelle's and Sean Amos to take the fall for David Garrison. Then—in the end—she had set up Malcolm himself, tipping Narc to the dope party.

Unbelievable. Incredible. It defied logic.

It was evil.

It was Jeanine.

He wiped his mouth with his fingers, rubbed his neck.

"Thinkin' 'bout something, Pete?" Abel asked.

"An interesting theory."

Abel nodded. "Thing is, Pete. Even though the kid's a punk, I kinda felt sorry for him. You know how I feel sorry for the underdog."

"You got a kind heart, Abel."

"See, I really think he was set up—"

"You heard someone make a phone call maybe?"

"Well, maybe if you look up the phone records of a certain public phone booth I'm gonna tell you about, you might find a call that went into Narc."

"Interesting."

Abel rocked on his feet. "Actually, that's not the

only reason I'm here. See, I just come back from jail, Pete. Paid the kid a visit—"

"*What*—"

"Kid didn't want to see me till I told the jailer that I had a message for him from Jeanine."

"Did you?"

"Of sorts. But not the kind of message he wanted to hear. See, I told Mal my theory, Pete. Told him how I thought Jeanine set him up. The boy wasn't pleased. Told me to stick it where the sun don't shine—"

"Sounds like Malcolm."

"Yeah, I was about to leave. Then I delivered the kid my *real* message from Jeanine—a photograph from Tuesday's paper of Jeanine and Wade, announcing their engagement."

Abel laughed.

"Kid went absolutely apeshit. My opinion is that Jeanine made the boy some promises. Promises that she didn't keep. Promises that she never had any intention of keeping. And that's why she set him up."

"What kind of promises, Abel?"

"Romantic promises *if* he agreed to do certain things."

"*What* certain things?"

Abel shrugged. "To be patient and wait. If he'd do his time nice and quiet, then she'd wait for him. And he agreed to it. What can I say? Sometimes a man does strange things for a beautiful woman. Especially if that man is a teenage boy with a constant boner who thinks he's in love. He just might go through all sorts of shit."

Abel cleared his throat.

"But once the bubble's been burst, and it's clear

the boy ain't gonna live happily ever after . . . that's another story. I showed Mal the article and the boy's demeanor changed considerably. He started screaming that he was framed, started asking for a lawyer, just spouting off all kinds of things—"

"*What* kind of things?"

"Talking about Jeanine's brother, David, for one thing. How she popped him with a needle. Talking about the murders at Estelle's—saying very different things from the official story. I told him . . . I told him, 'Mal, my friend, it looks like you been had. Might as well grow some donkey ears and a tail and bray 'cause you've just been made into an ass.' "

Decker's heart sank. "Why'd you tell him *that*?"

"Because it was the truth."

No one spoke.

"Boy was real upset," Abel said. "Man, I told him not to get mad. I told him to get *even*. Then I thought of you. Mentioned your name. Son of a gun, he said you were responsible for the bust. You were the reason he was in the clink in the first place—"

"Shit—"

"Wait a minute. Just hold on. I told him you weren't the reason, I told him *Jeanine* was the reason. I told him you had clout with the DA . . . which wasn't hard for him to believe, being as you sent him to jail. I suggested he talk to you . . . about David Garrison . . . about Estelle's.

Silence.

Decker took a breath, let it out. "Is he willing?"

"Yeah, he's willing. Says he's got some interesting names for you. Names and dates and letters: Things like notes from Jeanine to Harlan Manz. Apparently, Malcolm was in Manz's apartment right after the murders at Estelle's, cleared the place of some interesting mementos. Notes from Jeanine. Also some audiotapes. Stuff he hid, just in case. Tapes where she says stuff you'd be interested in."

Decker could feel his body float. "When would he like to speak with me?"

"I b'lieve right now."

"*Now?*"

"Boy is fighting mad at the moment, Pete. Don't think it would be wise for him to cool off—"

"I'll get my jacket." Decker tried to keep his thoughts coherent. "I've got some of my detectives on the case here at the house—"

"Don't think it would be wise to overwhelm the boy, Pete. Let's make it the two of us. We can reminisce about old days on the ride over."

"Fine. Just let me find Ri—" Decker stopped talking. Rina was a few feet away, her head down, blushing scarlet.

Decker said, "How long have you been standing there?"

"Long enough to hear."

Decker blew out air. "You remember Abel?"

"Of course." Rina held out her hand to him. "So, you two are on your way to County?"

Decker nodded.

"For how long?"

"Whatever it takes, Rina. I can't let this opportunity—"

"Of course."

Decker ran his hand through his hair. "I can't tell Oliver and Marge about this. Not just yet. Make excuses for me. Tell them . . . God, I can't use work as an excuse—"

"You can use me, doc," Abel said. "They know I'm a needle in your rear. Tell them I needed your help."

"Good idea," Rina said.

Decker patted Abel's shoulder. "You're a good friend, Abe."

"Likewise, I'm sure."

Rina said, "I'll keep the turkey warm."

"You already do that every night." Decker smiled, but it was wistful. "I'm never around when you need me."

"Nonsense. Besides I don't need you now. Go."

"You're crying. I'm so sorry—"

"No, no, no!" Rina wiped her eyes. "I'm not crying. I was peeling onions." She looked at Abel. "Of course you'll stay for dinner afterward. Whenever it is. Even if it's two in the morning. And don't say no. I'm very persistent."

"I figured as much. I'd love dinner, Mrs. Decker."

"It's Rina."

Decker slipped on his jacket, made sure he had his official identification and his gun. "Let's move it."

Abel held the door open for him. Before he left, he turned around, winked at Rina.

She winked back, dammed back tears. One day Peter would figure it out. By then, it would all be past. She watched them peel rubber, zoom off in Peter's Porsche. Closing the door, she went back into the kitchen to baste the turkey.

# 🦢 41

*And it came* to pass at midnight.

A line from the Passover Seder. Decker didn't know why it had flashed into consciousness since the holiday was still months away. Guess it had something to do with the magic of the witching hour: the first ticks of a new day so promising with hope. It had been a long night, replete with frantic activity and never-ending paperwork. Maybe there would even be a payoff.

He brought the Volare to a stop at a red light. A deserted intersection. He looked around, charged through the light. From the backseat, Oliver chuckled.

Decker said, "Hell with it. I'm tired. Just let some punk uniform *try* to stop me."

"The man is on a mission." Marge sat shotgun, nervously sipped cold coffee from a paper cup. "You lost out on a great meal, Pete. Never seen so much variety. Rina outdid herself."

"Rina and Mom are a deadly combination."

Oliver grinned. "Mom's got a bit of a 'tude, don't she?"

"Watch your mouth."

"Hey, I behaved myself." He turned to Marge for support. "Didn't I behave?"

"You were a very good boy."

Decker felt his stomach growl. "So I'll have left-overs. Sometimes that's better. The flavors are blended." Anxiously, he tapped the wheel of the car. "Just want to finish up and call it a night."

Marge slapped the warrant against her knee. "I can't believe we're actually *doing* this."

"It's long overdue," Decker said.

"More than overdue, Deck," Oliver stated. "It's *weird*! Abel popping up . . . like pulling a rabbit from a hat."

"*Deus ex machina*." Decker licked his lips. "Providence. What else could it be? Abel hasn't worked even a *part*-time job in years."

Oliver said, "Okay. I can see him working this job, doing something for the tournament. After all, your friend's a gimp—"

"An amputee," Decker corrected.

"A lame-o." Oliver was undeterred. "Okay. So he worked the tournament. I still don't understand *why* he took an interest in a bit player like Malcolm Carey."

"Lord only knows," Decker said. "Abel always had an eye for the bizarre."

But his own explanation didn't sit well. Something was off. *Way* off! But he couldn't concentrate on that now. More important things to do.

They rode for a few moments in smothering silence. The minutes before an arrest were always tense. Time elongated, time contracted. Everyone on edge, overly focused. The blackness of night seemed bright and shiny, reflective roadway surfaces slick with mist.

Marge spoke in a tight voice. "You should have let Scott and me handle Malcolm, Pete. That way, you could have eaten with your family."

"Carey asked for me specifically. I didn't want to take the chance—"

"I know how particular perps can be," Marge cut him off. "But you didn't have to lie."

Decker knew she was hurt by the exclusion. He should have taken both Marge and Scott into his confidence. But everything had been so rushed. He tried to keep his voice even. "I was thinking expedience. I brought you both in as soon as I could."

"I know," Marge said. "I'm just sulking." A sigh. "I would have *loved* to have been there."

"At least you had a good meal."

"A fantastic meal," Oliver expounded. "You know your brother's a real funny guy. Not at all a stiff."

*Not like you* was the implication. Decker laughed, too exhausted to be insulted. "Glad you found a soul mate."

"He does remind me of me. Kinda a fuckup. I got the feeling you've pulled him out of some rough spots."

"What can I say? He's my bro."

Oliver said, "You got Randy, you got me, you got Marge, you got Abel. You just love the strays, don'tcha, rabbi?"

"I beg your pardon," Marge said, stiffly.

Decker smiled. The chitchat eased the gripping tension.

A beat. Then Marge said, "Unbelievable that Jeanine thought she could work around Malcolm."

"With him in the hole, she had at *least* four-plus years breathing room."

"But she had to figure that Carey would find out about the engagement," Marge persisted.

"Jails keep you isolated. Malcolm was completely dependent on Jeanine for outside news."

"They get newspapers," Oliver said.

"Obviously Carey didn't read the social section because Abel's revelation came as a total shock. He was still under the delusion that she intended to wait for him. Because that's what she told him: Behave yourself and I'll wait."

Marge said, "Carey could have learned about the engagement from Sean Amos."

"Amos wouldn't dare to go *near* Carey. Kid's been handed an undeserved reprieve. Even *he's* not stupid enough to spit in Lady Luck's eye." Decker smoothed his mustache. "Jeanine was Carey's eyes to the outside world. As long as she strung him along, he remained quiet."

"Idiot that he is," Oliver said.

"Idiot that he *was*," Decker said. "He thought he was in love."

"How'd he get involved with Jeanine in the first place?" Oliver asked. "Through Amos or Greenvale?"

"Both actually," Decker said. "Carey happened to be at Greenvale one day when Jeanine and Sean were playing tennis together. Sean introduced them. Mal was smitten. Or in his words . . . 'Fuck, I had the hots for her.' Talked at great length about the boner she gave him."

Oliver smiled. "He's still a kid."

"A kid but a lethal one."

A pause.

Marge said, "Who approached Mal to do Estelle's? Sean or Jeanine?"

"Sean had nothing to do with Estelle's or Garrison. He was just a dumb dupe."

"Like Manz?"

"Yep." Decker tried to relax his shoulders. "According to Carey, Jeanine approached him to shoot up the restaurant. Now his word isn't worth a damn. But he does have tapes to back him up."

Oliver said, "I haven't heard them yet. You have Jeanine soliciting Carey to shoot up Estelle's?"

"No such luck. But Carey's tapes have them talking about the shootings. Lots of details. We'll go over them at great length in the morning."

Another drawn silence. This time Decker broke it.

"Carey told me that Jeanine had been thinking about popping her parents for a long time. When they met, she was working on Harlan, trying to get him irate enough to go in and blast the place. Of course, she was failing miserably. Harlan was a fuck-up, but no killer. It was Carey's idea to use Harlan as a dupe. Jeanine got him mad enough to charge into Estelle's and confront the management . . . specifically the manager who fired him months earlier. Mal followed on Harlan's heels, went inside and just *sprayed* the place, leaving a dead Manz to take the blame."

A pause. Marge squeezed her empty coffee cup. "Jeanine and Mal. What a pair."

Decker said, "Two really . . . *evil* people who found

each other. It's true that Estelle's was Jeanine's idea. But Carey jumped at the opportunity. I think he liked shooting people. You'll note that even though he wanted Jeanine, he demanded payment for the job. Carey *wanted* to be a hit man . . . talked about how being a ninja was a time-honored, noble profession. Incredible how far we've fallen as a society."

"But shooting up Estelle's was *Jeanine*'s idea," Marge said.

"Yes. I guess it just took her a while to find an acceptable cast of characters. The woman was right about one thing. She was one hell of an organizer."

Marge asked, "Did Jeanine ever state *why* she wanted to kill her parents?"

"Money, Dunn! Why else?" Oliver cleared his throat. "Carey probably did it for money too. What'd you say she gave him? Something like thirty grand in bearer bonds."

"Thirty-five." Decker cleared his throat. "Carey liked the money. Matter of fact, I think popping David Garrison was also Malcolm's call and he did it for money. Of course, he really liked Jeanine and wanted to impress her. The one thing Carey never factored into the equation was Jeanine's genuine affection for Wade Anthony. Since Anthony was a paraplegic, Carey didn't view him as a romantic threat. But later, Carey began to suspect things. Especially since Sean kept complaining about the two of them. Even so, Carey couldn't seriously believe that Jeanine would marry a guy stuck in a wheelchair."

Oliver said, "At some point, Mal must have felt Anthony's threat. We did find all those pictures of

Wade and his daily schedule at the bust. Looks like he was planning a hit to me."

"I can believe it. Kid was stricken with bloodlust."

"And he'd probably try to pin it on Sean," Marge added. "Just like he did with David Garrison."

"Makes sense."

Decker felt himself clutching the wheel and relaxed his fingers.

"I guess Jeanine figured she could string Mal along until he lost interest in her. But when Wade came into the picture, she accelerated her plans. She knew Mal would drop a dime if she bailed out on him so soon. So she got rid of him. Making the call to Narc to get him busted."

Oliver shook his head. "Carey's a dumbshit. By going state's witness on Estelle's, he ain't going to lessen his own jail time."

"Not by a minute."

"It'll probably screw up his parole, make him serve an even longer sentence."

"No doubt."

Marge said, "At least this way he can't be prosecuted for Estelle's."

"Dunn, without Carey turning state's witness and his tapes, the state *has* no case. All he did was create a mess for himself."

"Teenagers are impulsive," Marge said. "They don't think things through."

"C'mon. Had to be more to it."

Decker said, "You never craved revenge?"

"Not if it screwed me blue."

"A sane man," Marge said.

Decker said, "Lucky for us that Carey wasn't so

sane. And like Marge said, lucky that he was impulsive. Because at that point, more than anything, Carey craved *revenge*. And you know what, Scott? When he spoke about the big get-even with her, I can tell you that old Mal and I were of one mind."

The condo was set atop undulating hillside that peered out into city lights, and looked down into deep sweeps of lush canyons. The air was wet and sweet-scented; a gentle breeze rustled through the brush. A lovely setting to plan a mass murder.

Instinctively, Decker felt for his gun. Never could tell what was on the other side of the door. But he didn't anticipate trouble. He nodded to the others; they walked up to the building. A twenty-four-hour doorman sat at a desk behind locked glass doors. He was heavyset and moved with effort. His face was moon-shaped and registered surprise when confronted by the badges of the midnight posse. Slowly, he unlocked the doors, let them cross the threshold. He was wary but cooperative.

"Should I ring Ms. Garrison?"

"No," Decker said. "But I want you to come up with us."

"All right."

"Unlock her door if necessary."

Pink permeated the doorman's face. "I don't know if I can do that."

Oliver said, "Surely you don't want us to break it down."

"All the noise," Marge added. "Plus it's not an easy thing to do."

The doorman looked over his shoulder as if trying

to spot a hidden ally. "Well, all right. I guess . . ." He nodded.

Decker said, "Can you tell me if Ms. Garrison has any visitors at the moment?"

"Just Mr. Anthony."

Decker pushed the elevator button. "Let's go."

The ride up to the penthouse was stone silent. The elevator stopped. They got out. Decker took a deep breath, balled his hands into fists. The rap on Jeanine's door was rapid and loud.

Waiting.

Nothing.

Decker tried again. Firmer. Louder.

Shuffling noises. Stomping noises. Seconds later, Garrison's voice asking who it was. She spoke in an angry tone.

Decker said, "Police, Ms. Garrison! Open up now!"

"Of all the *nerve*!" The door swung open. Jeanine dressed in black sweats, a rosy face damp with perspiration. Beads of moisture were resting above her upper lip, tendrils of blond hair cascading across her cheeks and down her shoulders.

Obvious what she had been doing.

A male voice emanated from the other room, asked what was going on. Her livid face glaring upward. "Just *who* the hell do you think you are?"

Decker said, "Jeanine Holly Garrison, you are under arrest for the murder of—"

Immediately the door flew at Decker's face. He blocked it with his shoulder, shoved it back open. She was waiting for him, her arm raised high above her shoulder, a furious open palm arcing downward to smack his face. He caught her wrist in midair and set it firmly behind her back. Brought the other wrist down and around and cuffed her hands together.

Once restrained, Jeanine melted. She burst into unrestrained sobs, water exploding from her eyes.

*At last!* Decker thought. *Genuine tears! Camus would have been proud.*

Jeanine wailed out, "But you have no *right*!"

Decker said, "Ms. Garrison, this is America. Everyone has rights. Now let me tell you some of yours."

Available now in hardcover from

WM
WILLIAM MORROW

the next book in

# FAYE KELLERMAN's

thrilling Decker/Lazarus series

gun games

*It was bad* news walking through the door.

They were coming his way: five of them—three guys, two girls—all of them looking older than him by a couple of years but probably still in high school. The guys had some muscle, but none of them was steroidal, meaning he could take any of them one-on-one. Collectively, he didn't stand a chance. Besides, Gabe wasn't spoiling for a fight. Last time that happened, he messed up his hand—temporarily. He'd been lucky. Maybe he'd be lucky again. If not, he had to be smart.

He pushed his glasses up on his nose and kept his eyes on the book until the group was on top of him. Even then, he didn't look up. Nothing was going to happen to him inside a Starbucks . . . staring at the page in front of him, his mind going a mile per sec.

"You're sitting in my seat," one of the guys said.

His dad had always emphasized that if he were about to be jumped, it was best to take on the leader. Because once the leader was gone, the others fell like dominoes. Gabe counted to five before he looked up. The guy who spoke was the biggest of the three.

"Excuse me?" Gabe said.

"I said you're sitting in my seat." And as if to emphasize the point, he pulled back his jacket, giving Gabe a five-second peek at the gun stuck into his waistband—positively one of the worst places to keep an unharnessed weapon. There were only two people in the world that Gabe would take crap from and he wasn't looking at either one of them. To acquiesce would be a mistake. On the other hand, to confront would also be a mistake. Luckily, the dude gave him an out.

Gabe held up an index finger. "Do you mind?" Slowly and carefully, he pulled back the guy's jacket with his finger and stared at the gun. "Beretta 92FS with some kind of a custom grip." A pause. "Sweet." He let the jacket drop. "You know the company just came out with an advanced model—a 96A or something like that. Same thing as the 92 series except it has a higher magazine capacity."

Gabe stood up. Nose to nose, he was a couple of inches taller than the gunslinger, but the height differential wasn't something he was about to flaunt. He took a half step back, giving them both some personal space.

"I like the plinkers . . . like the 87 Cheetah .22LR. First of all, it's got great reliability. Second, it's one of those ambidextrous pieces. I'm right-handed, but I got a real strong left. You know how it is. You never know which hand it's gonna be convenient to use."

They were locked in a staring contest, Gabe's focus on the dude with the piece. As far as he was concerned, the other four didn't exist. Then, with a sudden, fluid motion, Gabe stepped aside and held out his hand, magnanimously offering the dude his seat. "Be my guest."

A few seconds ticked by, each waiting for the other to blink.

Finally, the guy said to Gabe, "Have a seat."

"After you."

The two of them eyed each other, then they both sat down at the same time with the dude taking up the leather chair that Gabe had formerly occupied. He kept his eyes on the guy's face, never letting up for a moment. Dude was around five ten, one eighty, broad chest, strong arms. Brown hair past his ears, blue eyes, strong chin. Under his leather jacket, he had on a gray T-shirt and wore black, tight-fitting jeans. He was a good-looking guy and probably had a posse of admirers.

Dude said, "Where'd you learn about guns?"

Gabe shrugged. "My dad."

"What does he do?"

"My father?" At this, Gabe broke into a slow grin. "Uh . . . actually, he's a pimp." The expected pause. "He owns whorehouses in Nevada."

The dude stared at him with newfound respect. "Cool."

"It sounds a lot cooler than it is," Gabe said. "My dad's a nasty guy—a real mean motherfucker. He also owns about a zillion guns and knows how to use every single one of them. I get along with him because I don't cross him. Plus, we don't live together anymore."

"You live with your mom?"

"Nah, she's in India somewhere. She took off with her lover and dumped me into the care of complete strangers—"

"Are you shittin' me?"

"I *wish* I was shittin' you." Gabe laughed. "Last year was a total nightmare." He rubbed his hands together. "But it worked out okay. I like where I am. My foster dad is a police lieutenant. You'd expect him to be the hard-ass, but compared to my own dad, the man is a saint." He looked at his watch. It was almost six in the evening and night was inches away. "I gotta go." He stood up and so did Dude.

"What's your name?" Dude asked.

"Chris," Gabe lied. "And you?"

"Dylan." They fist-bumped. "What school do you go to?"

"Homeschooled," Gabe said. "Almost done, thank God. Hey, nice to meet you, Dylan. Maybe I'll catch you on the shooting range."

He turned his back to the group and slowly swaggered away. It took all his energy not to glance back.

Once he was out the door, he ran like hell.

Rina was arranging roses when the boy came in, flushed and panting. She said, "Are you all right?"

"Just out of shape." Gabe tried to steady his breathing. He attempted to give his temporary mother a smile, but it probably didn't come out too sincere. He could tell that Rina was scrutinizing him, her blue eyes concentrated on his face. She was wearing a pink sweater that matched the flowers. His mind was desperately trying to figure out small talk. "Those are pretty. From the garden?"

"Trader Joe's. The roses in the garden won't start blooming for another couple of months." She regarded her charge, his emerald eyes flitting behind his glasses. Something was off. "Why were you running?"

"Trying to be healthy," Gabe told her. "I really need to do something about improving my stamina."

"I'd say anyone who can practice for six hours a day has a great deal of stamina."

"Tell that to my beating heart."

"Sit down. I'll get you something to drink."

"I can do it." Gabe disappeared into the kitchen. When he came back, he was holding a bottle of water. Rina was still giving him funny looks. To distract her, he picked up the paper from the dining room table. The front page showed a picture of a boy, the caption stating that fifteen-year-old Gregory Hesse had committed suicide by a single gunshot to the head. He had a round face and big round eyes and looked much younger than fifteen. Gabe started reading the article in earnest.

"Sad, isn't it." Rina was looking over his shoulder. "You think to yourself, what on earth could have been so bad that this poor kid was willing to end it all?"

There were lots of reasons for despair. Last year he had gone through all of them. "Sometimes life is hard."

Rina took the paper from him and gave him her serious eye-to-eye contact. "You looked upset when you came in."

"I'm fine." He managed a smile. "Really."

"What happened? Did you hear from your dad or something?"

"No, we're cool." When Rina gave him a skeptical look, he said, "Honestly. I haven't spoken to him since we came back from Paris. We texted a couple of times. He asked me how I was doing and I told him I was fine. We're on good terms. I think he likes me a lot better now that my mom is out of the picture."

He took a swig of water and averted his eyes.

"Did I tell you my mom IMed about a week ago?"

"No . . . you didn't."

"Must have slipped my mind."

"Uh-huh—"

"Really. It was no big deal. I almost didn't answer her because I didn't recognize the screen name she was using."

"Is she okay?"

"Seems to be." A shrug. "She asked me how I was." Behind his glasses, his eyes were gazing at a distant place. "I told her I was fine and not to worry . . . that everything was cool. Then I signed off." He shrugged again. "I didn't feel like making chitchat. Tell you the truth, I'd rather she not contact me. Is that terrible?"

"No, it's understandable." Rina sighed. "It'll take a lot of bridge building before you get some trust—"

"That's not gonna happen. It's not that I have anything against her. I wish her well. I just don't want to talk to her."

"Fair enough. But try to keep an open mind. When she contacts you again, maybe give her a few more seconds of your time. Not for her sake, but for yours."

"*If* she contacts me again."

"She will, Gabriel. You know that."

"I don't know anything. I'm sure she's busy with the baby and all."

"One child isn't a substitute for another—"

"Thanks for the pep talk, Rina, but I really don't care. I barely think about her." But of course, he did all the time. "The baby needs her way more than I do." He smiled and patted her head. "Besides, I've got a pretty good substitute right here."

"Your mom is still your mom. And one day, you'll see that. But thank you very much for the nice words."

Gabe returned his eyes to the newspaper article. "Wow, the boy was local."

"Yes, he was."

"Do you know the family?"

"No."

"So like . . . does the lieutenant investigate cases like this?"

"Only if the coroner has questions about whether it was a suicide."

"How can the coroner tell?"

"I really don't know. You can ask Peter when he gets home."

"When's he coming home?"

"Sometime between now and dawn. Do you want to go out to the deli for dinner?"

Gabe's eyes lit up. "Can I drive?"

"Yes, you can drive. While we're there, let's pick up a sandwich and take it to the Loo. If I don't bring him food, he doesn't eat."

Gabe put down the paper. "Can I shower first? I'm a little sweaty."

"Of course."

Gabe could tell that Rina was still evaluating him. Unlike his father, he wasn't an adroit liar. He said, "You worry too much. I'm fine."

"I believe you." Rina mussed his hair, damp with perspiration. "Go shower. It's almost seven and I'm starving."

"You bet." Gabe smiled to himself. He had just used one of the Loo's favorite expressions. He had been with the Deckers for almost a year and certain things just filtered in. He became aware of hunger pangs. It had just taken time for his stomach to calm down for his brain to get the message that he hadn't eaten since breakfast and that he was famished.

It's not that he had a nervous gut. But guns did strange things to his digestive system.

Completely unlike his dad.

Chris Donatti never met a firearm he didn't like.

**New York Times** Bestselling Author

# FAYE KELLERMAN

## FALSE PROPHET
978-0-06-199933-8

When Lilah Brecht is beaten, robbed, and raped in her own home, L.A.P.D. Detective Peter Decker finds it hard to put too much credence into the victim's claims that she has psychic powers that enable her to see the future. But when Lilah's dark visions turn frighteningly real, Decker's world is severely rocked.

## THE BURNT HOUSE
978-0-06-122736-3

A small commuter plane crashes into an apartment building. Among the dead inside the plane's charred wreckage are the unidentified bodies of four extra travelers. And there's no sign of an airline employee whose name was on the passengers list.

## THE MERCEDES COFFIN
978-0-06-122737-0

Lieutenant Peter Decker resents having to commit valuable manpower to a cold case, but when the retired detective who originally investigated the murder case commits suicide, Decker realizes something evil has returned.

## BLINDMAN'S BLUFF
978-0-06-170241-9

Peter Decker is summoned to investigate the brutal murders of a billionaire philanthropist, his wife, and four employees. At the same time a chance meeting puts Decker's wife, Rina Lazarus, directly into the path of the relentless killers.

Visit www.AuthorTracker.com for exclusive information on your favorite HarperCollins authors.

Available wherever books are sold or please call 1-800-331-3761 to order.

FK1 0411

**New York Times**
**Bestselling Author**

# FAYE KELLERMAN

**SACRED AND PROFANE**
978-0-06-199925-3

**MILK AND HONEY**
978-0-06-199926-0

**SANCTUARY**
978-0-06-199935-2

**JUSTICE**
978-0-06-199936-9

**PRAYERS FOR THE DEAD**
978-0-06-208787-4

**SERPENT'S TOOTH**
978-0-06-208788-1

**DAY OF ATONEMENT**
978-0-06-199927-7

**THE RITUAL BATH**
978-0-06-199924-6

**JUPITER'S BONES**
978-0-06-208790-4

**STALKER**
978-0-06-208817-8

**THE FORGOTTEN**
978-0-380-73084-1

**MOON MUSIC**
978-0-380-72626-4

**THE QUALITY OF MERCY**
978-0-380-73269-2

**GRIEVOUS SIN**
978-0-06-199934-5

Visit www.AuthorTracker.com for exclusive
information on your favorite HarperCollins authors.

FK2 1211

Available wherever books are sold or please call 1-800-331-3761 to order.